Sergio Franzese – Felicitas Kraemer
Fringes of Religious Experience

PROCESS THOUGHT

Edited by

Nicholas Rescher • Johanna Seibt • Michel Weber

Advisory Board

Mark Bickhard • Jaime Nubiola • Roberto Poli

Volume 12

Sergio Franzese
Felicitas Kraemer

Fringes of Religious Experience

Cross-perspectives on William James's
The Varieties of Religious Experience

∀

ontos
verlag

Frankfurt I Paris I Ebikon I Lancaster I New Brunswick

Bibliographic information published by Deutsche Nationalbibliothek
The Deutsche Nastionalbibliothek lists this publication in the Deutsche Nationalbibliographie;
detailed bibliographic data is available in the Internet at http://dnb.ddb.de

North and South America by
Transaction Books
Rutgers University
Piscataway, NJ 08854-8042
trans@transactionpub.com

United Kingdom, Eire, Iceland, Turkey, Malta, Portugal by
Gazelle Books Services Limited
White Cross Mills
Hightown
LANCASTER, LA1 4XS
sales@gazellebooks.co.uk

Livraison pour la France et la Belgique:
Librairie Philosophique J.Vrin
6, place de la Sorbonne ; F-75005 PARIS
Tel. +33 (0)1 43 54 03 47 ; Fax +33 (0)1 43 54 48 18
www.vrin.fr

©2007 ontos verlag
P.O. Box 15 41, D-63133 Heusenstamm
www.ontosverlag.com

ISBN 13: 978-3-938793-57-2
2007

Printed on acid-free paper
ISO-Norm 970-6
FSC-certified (Forest Stewardship Council)
This hardcover binding meets the International Library standard

Printed in Germany
by buch bücher **dd ag**

SUMMARY

Foreword

The original core of this book has to be tracked back to the International Centenary Conference in celebration of William James's Gifford Lectures 1901/1902 that took place at the University of Edinburgh in July 2002. The central topic of that conference was, as it often happens in such cases, an analysis of James's *The Varieties of Religious Experience* and a consequent attempt to evaluate, as it were, what was alive and what was dead of that important work a century from its publication.

As a matter of fact the conference was characterized by a clearly split frontline. On one hand, the American and in general the Anglo-Saxon participants locked on the religious question, which not seldom took theological and fideistic shades. At that time, special historical and political reasons pushed in that direction and spurred the quest for an affirmation of religious and cultural identity. Thus, around the dominant question whether William James did actually believe in God or not, crowded all the other issues concerning the value of religion, the truth of religious knowledge or belief; the possibility of a dialogue between different religions and many others of the same kind that after five years is impossible to remember in detail.

On the other hand, the continental European participants, as well as the Asian and the Middle-Eastern, appeared more interested in the clarification of certain technical aspects of James's theory and in the possibility to connect it with similar aspects in other authors' philosophy. Some of them, according to a deeply rooted historical tradition tried to highlight the reception of James's ideas in the cultural context of their own countries.

Briefly, an almost impossible dialogue.

As a consequence of such a split, and for several other reasons hard to remember after so long time, the proceedings of that conference, such was the decision, had to be published in two separate groups.

Several hindrances and problems of different kind delayed the publication of this second group of papers. In the meantime some of the original participants published their papers elsewhere and some new contributors joined in, whose interest and perspective, however, were quite akin with the general attitude of the original group. Accordingly it is more than fair to say that, as a whole, such later additions have enriched more than changed or distorted the original mood of that important event.

This short premise seems useful to give account of the general character of this book and of its neat division in two sections one with more theoretical character and the other displaying a more definite historical bend. It is also useful in order to explain the specific character of the single articles which altogether were intended to outline a sort of cultural fringe of James's text in order to evaluate its cultural vitality rather than disentangle unfathomable metaphysical problems.

If any need be there to single out a common thread running across so different contributions and perspectives, such a thread, with only few exceptions, should possibly be found in the problem of subjectivity as the major issue stemming out of James's account of religious experience. As far as for James religious experience turns out to be a fully individual and subjective experience, it becomes almost necessary to inquire about the *status* of the subject who enjoys such an experience. Such an inquiry concerns essentially two aspects: the consciousness of the subject—its structure and activity—the religious experience itself as it is experienced—its content and meaning.

Such a focus on the problem of subjectivity, in the twofold perspective we have just stressed, far from being whimsical or farfetched, matches the very problematic core of James's text, in which just a new account of subjectivity and experience are coming out. It is enough to remember that the *Varieties* is the major document of James's energetic turn, which leads James to account for the "self" as "centre of energy" and in turn to approach Myers' theory of subliminal self as the "sea of energy", in which the individual self is rooted in and from which it draws a "surplus of energy". Such an energetic reassessment of subject and experience, and religious experience in particular, necessarily calls for a further analysis of what "consciousness" and "experience" could possibly mean for James in that context, also in view of the oncoming development of James's gnoseology through the doctrine of radical empiricism.

In this perspective, Michel Weber's paper on the problem of the embodiment of consciousness and the transmarginal fields of experience, nicely sets the frame within which the other contributions will cross casting their own light on the multifaceted problem of subjectivity.

In the light of cognitive psychology and neurosciences, Harald Atmanspacher and Wolfgang Fach insightfully analyze the states of dissolution of the ego, typical of extreme religious and mystical experiences, through the notion of *acategorial* states of consciousness. A neater ethical perspective is endorsed by Craig Eisendrath, Ilaria Possenti and Ramón del Castillo. Eisendrath evaluates James's notion of God and religious commitment with reference to Whitehead's process metaphysics and his notion of moral responsibility of the universe; Possenti starting with the notion of plasticity of the self focuses on the process of transformation of the self as presented in James's account of religious conversion in order to outline a notion of education as self-(trans)formation; whereas Del Castillo zeroes on the contradiction involved in the narcissistic attitude at the bottom of Emerson's and James's religious individualism.

An open door to religious pluralism and dialogue is offered by Majeda Omar through her assimilation of James's notion of conversion and Kuhn's paradigmatic revolution. Religion and science are not dogmatic truth but models of understanding of the world liable of comparison, confrontation and change. More radically the present writer put in question the very possibility to talk about any sort of religious and/or theological truth coming from James's account of religious experience. Religious experience is a subjective different look onto the world and not the experience of something outside the world.

In the historical section Jaime Nubiola and Izaskun Martínez, Mathias Girel, and Natalyia Nikolova offer three different cases of reception of James's thought in European culture. Nubiola and Martinez show the influence of James's works on Spanish philosophy and in particular on Miguel de Unamuno with special reference to Unamuno's reading of the Varieties and his use of James's account of the type of the saint in Unamuno's analysis of Don Quixote. A well documented and detailed account of French reception of James is provided by Girel who canvasses a topical moment of James's philosophical development such as his relation with Renouvier and the *Critique Philosophique*. In her short survey, Nikolova sketches the story of the reception of James and pragmatism in the Bulgarian culture in XX century, made difficult by ideological and philosophical misunderstanding.

The aim of an introduction is not to tell the reader what he or she has to think nor to replace the full reading but only to ease the reader into the special occasion every book is in itself, insofar it is possibly true that the best introduction is the shortest one. A final remark is due though.

It seems noteworthy to the present writer, who also attended the presentation of the original papers at the Conference in 2002, that despite the time intervening and the due revision they underwent before publication, the papers still display all their original power and novelty, and provide some unmatched insights into James's thought or some substantial fresh information on James's cultural influence. This seems the best evidence of the high quality these works originally had and have kept in time. (*S.F.*)

James's Mystical Body in the Light of the Transmarginal Field of Consciousness

Michel Weber[*]

This paper discusses James's understanding of body in the context of his study of the "varieties of religious experience". In other words, our title does not refer primarily to James's body of mystical works but concentrates on the issue of the status of embodiment in *The Varieties of Religious Experiences*.[1] It will appear promptly in this context that the concept of the body has to be treated together with the question of the field-like nature of consciousness.

The argument proceeds in five stages. First, we explicate how body and consciousness are intertwined in the "normal" state of consciousness; second, we develop the concept of the spectrum of consciousness; third, the correlated concept of spectrum of bodies is introduced; fourth, the transmarginal field of consciousness and its subliminal door are invoked in order to bridge the apparent gap between the two spectra; fifth we conclude with some speculations on the scale of natural states of vigilance and its ins and outs.

1. Consciousness-zero

Unsurprisingly, James's mystical body is first and foremost his *own* body. It is indeed from ones own embodied existence, as it is lived in everyday conscious life, that we have to start any inquiries whatsoever. This is taught by sheer common-sense and critically settled by radical empiricism. Accordingly, three steps pace our progression: first, we propose a heuristically useful definition of the "normal" state of consciousness and a first overview of its characteristics; second, overlapping sets of beings and the nucleus/fringe distinction makes sophisticate this preliminary sketch; third, a synthesis, insisting on the concept of selection, is proposed.

---

[*] Directeur du Centre de philosphie pratique "Chromatiques Whiteheadiennes"
[1] W. James, *The Varieties of Religious Experience. A Study in Human Nature*. Penguin Books, NewYork, 1985. [1902] (Hereafter VRE)

1.1. Heuristic Definition

What is the lived body pictured by James? The most forthright answer is perhaps: it is not a body that one *has*, but a body that one *is*. However, although we are actually living in every fibre of our bodies, we are almost never consciously aware of this. Consciousness is "at all times primarily a *selecting agency*": a matter of choosing, emphasizing, accentuating, suppressing afferent and efferent data, mainly through attention and deliberation (See *Principles of Psychology* I, 139 and 284; this point is made particularly striking when one debates hypnosis).[2] Furthermore, although mental experiences are all physically correlated—if not produced—, our body cannot be properly understood by scientific materialism alone. These two complementary conceptual stretches impose a double direction on James' writings: towards the ideal of a full understanding of the unconscious derivation of mentality from physicality; and towards an organic reform of dualistic materialism. These two stretches converge in an seemingly paradoxical expression: *pluralistic monism*.

It is well-known that James was relieved of the "automaton-theory" only by the reading (started, according to the material gathered by R. B. Perry, in 1868) of Charles Renouvier (1815–1903). Renouvier's emphasis on liberty and his powerful pragmatic pluralism (of Kantian and Comtian origin) reformed James's physiological psychology so much that he could see a door opening in the gloomy night of his manic-depression.[3] PP's chapters IX and X are especially helpful to circumscribe the intertwining of body and consciousness and thereby to show why we need to go beyond the simplistic dualisms of the body/mind and conscious/unconscious schemes of thought. Let us define the so-called "normal state of consciousness" in the following way: normal consciousness emerges in an embodied standpoint through the rational treatment of sense-perceptive data. "Consciousness-zero", as we will call it to avoid the derogatoriness of the label "normal", has thus four main characteristics. First, it is *emergent and holistic*: the resulting whole differs from the simple concatenation of its parts; it cannot be reduced to the product of the algorithmic treatment of data by a computer-like device. Second, consciousness-zero is strictly correlated to a given *embodied standpoint*: it does

---

[2] W. James, *The Principles of Psychology*, Dover Publications New York, 1950 [1890]. (Hereafter PP)
[3] James refers to C. Renouvier, *Essais de Critique Générale*, Librairie Armand Colin, Paris, 1851-1864; of special relevance is also "Les arguments philosophiques pour et contre le libre arbitre", *Critique philosophique*, 12ième année, nn° 22, 23, 24, 26, 30, pp. 337-349, 353-362, 369-381, 401-412 and 49-59.

not occur independently of some mundane organic anchorage that, by its very existence, discloses a peculiar perspective (and lever) on its environment.

"The knower is not simply a mirror floating with no foothold anywhere, and passively reflecting an order that he comes upon and finds simply existing. The knower is an actor, and coefficient of the truth on one side, while on the other he registers the truth which he helps to create."[4]

Third, this environment is known through *sense-perception*, which means two complementary (however paradoxical) facts: on the one hand, the "external" world is known through the body; on the other hand, this body itself is mostly bracketed by the process. Sense-perception is, by definition, exteroception and the existence of some environmental horizon is essential to it: consciousness-zero does not occur in a vacuum, the embodied standpoint always belongs to a given ontological region made of sentient and insentient beings alike, to say it with the old-fashioned contrast. Fourth, *reason* and its linguistic vector are responsible for the most often discussed dimensions of consciousness: the stream of thought is made of discriminative and synthetic judgments allowing adaptive action.

Living acts of perception—and action—are what ultimately matter for James, all the more so, since "there is always a *plus*, a *thisness*, which feeling alone can answer for." (VRE, 455) The subtlety of nature flies beyond every science, i.e., beyond every attempts of rationalization. Let us not deprive ourselves of the following beautiful passage:

"Philosophy lives in words, but truth and fact well up into our lives in ways that exceed verbal formulation. There is in the living act of perception always something that glimmers and twinkles and will not be caught, and for which reflection comes too late. No one knows this as well as the philosopher. He must fire his volley of new vocables out of his conceptual shotgun, for his profession condemns him to this industry, but he secretly knows the hollowness and irrelevancy. His formulas are like stereoscopic or kinetoscopic photographs seen outside the instrument; they lack the depth, the motion, the vitality. In the religious sphere, in particular, the belief that formulas are true can never wholly take the place of personal experience. (VRE, 456-457)[5]

---

[4] W. James, "Spencer's Definition of Mind as Correspondance", quoted by H. Putnam, *Pragmatism. An Open Question*, Blackwell, Oxford UK & Cambridge USA, 1995, p. 17.
[5] "There are so many geometries, so many logics, so many physical and chemical hypotheses, so many classifications, each one of them good for so much and yet not good

Having said this, James, quoting John Caird and John Henry Newman, promptly acknowledges that, however, such a religious feeling is "private and dumb, and unable to give an account of itself", it is the task of the philosopher to "redeem religion from unwholesome privacy, and to give public status and universal right of way to its deliverances" (VRE, 432). In conclusion, philosophy's task is thus to use reason in order to *point at* what cannot be properly accounted for in order to circumscribe its legitimate territory and thereby rescue religious experience from its primitive (collective) tendencies.

1.2. Fringed Overlapping Sets

This first overview has to be sophisticated in two steps. First, it is expedient to acknowledge with James (PP I, 292 ff) that consciousness-zero dwells at the centre of overlapping sets of beings—in the widest sense of the word (the introduction below of the concept of field will improve the coherence of this sketch). The *Principles* proposes the following onto-psychological sets: the pure Ego, the spiritual Self, the social Self, and the material Self. In the VRE, he claims:

"A conscious field *plus* its object as felt or thought of *plus* an attitude towards the object *plus* the sense of a self to whom the attitude belongs—such a concrete bit of personal experience may be a small bit, but it is a solid bit as long as it lasts; not hollow, not a mere abstract element of experience, such as the "object" is when taken all alone. It is a *full* fact, even though it be an insignificant fact; it is of the *kind* to which all realities whatsoever must belong; the motor currents of the world run through the like of it; it is on the line connecting real events with real events. That unsharable feeling which each one of us has of the pinch of his individual destiny as he privately feels it rolling out on fortune's wheel may be disparaged for its egotism, may be sneered at as unscientific, but it is the one thing that fills up the measure of our concrete actuality, and any would-be existent that should lack such a feeling, or its

---

for everything, that the notion that even the truest formula may be a human device and not a literal transcript has dawned upon us. We hear scientific laws now treated as "conceptual shorthand," true so far as they are useful but no farther. Our mind has become tolerant of symbol instead of reproduction, of approximation instead of exactness, of plasticity instead of rigor." (MT, p. 58)

analogue, would be a piece of reality only half made up. (VRE, 499)[6]

What matters here—beyond the egotic mystery—is the perspectival cross-construction that occurs at the intersections of these sets: all these (more or less abstract) entities are created by the standpoint and are creating the standpoint. Relativity works both ways without compromising the ontological weight of the actors. Remember that consciousness is an emergent *selective function*. A given embodied standpoint is the processual result of various micro- and macro- processes. Now these processes are susceptible of various definitions, especially since their rates of change are variable: although the rule is the flow, one can distinguish the *transitive* parts and the—comparatively restful and stable—*substantive* parts.

Second, everyday experience, and especially its refinement through introspection, teach us that that overlapping set is actually clearly prehended but rationalized only partially. There is a "clearly" perceived nucleus surrounded, as it were, with "dimly" perceived fringes. The former is fully rationalized (or possibly so) while the later remains "primitive and unreflexive" (VRE, 431). The "chromatic fringe", "penumbra" or "halo" of relations (or "felt affinity and discord") which we obscurely feel surrounding us at every moment is "a vital ingredient of the mind's object"[7]: not yet distinctly in focus, it could become so, to a certain extent at least. James speaks:

"The sense of our meaning is an entirely peculiar element of the thought. It is one of those evanescent and 'transitive' facts of mind which introspection cannot turn round upon, and isolate and hold up for examination, as an entomologist passes round an insect on a pin. In the (somewhat clumsy) terminology I have used, it pertains to the 'fringe' of the subjective state, and is a "feeling of tendency." (PP I, 472)

A remarkable exemplification of that contrast between nucleus and fringes

---

[6] An interesting recent exemplification of this debate can be found in A.R. Damasio, *The Feeling of Consciousness*, Harcourt Brace Jovanovich, Inc., New York, 1999. Damasio models consciousness as a "three layered edifice" featuring increasingly more abstract self images. The first layer is the "proto-self" (shared with animals and reptiles); it comprises precise, orderly sensory and motor maps of the body surface onto central neural structures. The second layer is the "core consciousness" (shared with most animals); it comprises the sense of the body in space, and is supported by activity of the inferior parietal cortices and the hippocampus. The third layer is the "extended consciousness" (unique to humans); it comprises improvements of one's self image with autobiographical memories.

[7] See PP I, p. 82 and especially PP I, pp. 258-271.

11

can be found in the complementarity at work between, on the one hand, reason and exteroception and, on the other hand, the primitiveness of proprioception and interoception. Exteroception (the five senses directed toward the "outside") provides a more or less clear-cut picture of our surroundings, thereby carving consciousness; while interoception (internal sensitivity) and proprioception (messages of position and movement allowing, with the help of the internal ear's semi-circular canals, a spatialisation of the body) belong more to the unconscious experience of the body-*in*-the-World.

1.3. Synthesis

Consciousness-zero thus could be sketched in the following manner: at the cross-roads of a (outer) world in continuous evolution and of a given individual seat of adaptive (if not creative) action, one can find a rational-perceptive (hence perspectival) process, emerging out of two functional loops, and worthy of the name "consciousness". The core retroactive loop consists in the information of reason by perception and in the formation of perception by reason. The peripheral (but by no means subsidiary) loop consists in the impact the action of the considered embodied standpoint has on its pluralistic environment and in the necessary influence this will have on the given conscious being-in-process itself. It goes without saying that both loops are actually *multitrack* processes. In any case, isolation and abstraction are consciousness-zero key-features.

The "Ur-concept" which supports these two intricate feedback loops is indeed the one we have already seen at work with the nucleus/fringe contrast: *selection*. To be an embodied standpoint means indeed two things. On the one hand, the contingencies of spatio-temporal existence define, *de facto*, a certain *perspective* on mundane processes: one is directly influenced by, and can directly influence only, contiguous events (the questions of parapsychological influences and of technical appendages is bracketed here). On the other hand, thoughts (reason) are carved by feelings (percepts) while the mind adds a second selection on the data provided by the senses (themselves receptive only to some messages—this being the first selection).

The latent Kantianism of these conceptions is to be considered from the perspective of James's processual pragmatism and in particular from its roots in evolutionary epistemology—roots that can be traced back to Herbert Spencer, who in his *Principles of Psychology* (published in 1855, four years before Darwin's *Origin of Species*) argues for the now classical "biological theory of knowledge"[8] based on a dazzling foundational claim: the structure of human intellect is "*a priori* for an individual" but "*a posteriori* for the whole species". Kant is sanctified on a new empirical basis with a fairly simple core argument: the original function of knowledge is purely utilitarian because our mental apparatus is the product of the struggle for life, i.e., of our continual adjustment to the sector of reality important for survival purposes. Since our cognitive functions are of empirical origin, they can have only limited applicability. *In illo tempore* there was not—but now is there—an unchanging *a priori* structure of human intelligence. It goes without saying that here utilitarianism means limited but *real* applicability. Some form of necessity seals the relativity of our categories.

This quick overview of the basic features of James' depiction of consciousness-zero could not be fair unless we stressed the emotional tone that comes with all experiences. The important point is that emotions owe "their pungent quality" to the bodily sensations which they involve; reason and emotion are not natural antagonists.[9] Concept, percept and affect necessarily unfold together.

2. Spectrum of Consciousness

James's account of what we call the *spectrum of consciousness* can be presented in three conceptual waves. We will start with the *Principles*, the *locus classicus*, progressively moving on to the VRE. Our aim is not to devise a strict hierarchy of states but to suggest the continuity existing between the

---

[8] On the development of "evolutionary epistemology", see e.g. D.T. Campbell's "Evolutionary Epistemology" (in P.A.Schlipp (ed.), *The Philosophy of Karl Popper*, La Salle, Illinois, The Open Court Publishing Company, The Library of Living Philosophers, XIV, 1974, pp. 413-451).

[9] "The *fons et origo* of all reality, whether from the absolute or the practical point of view, is thus subjective, is ourselves. As bare logical thinkers, without emotional reaction, we give reality to whatever objects we think of, for they are really phenomena, or objects of our pausing thought, if nothing more. But, as thinkers with emotional reaction, to give what seems to be a still higher degree of reality to whatever things we select and emphasize and turn to *with a will*. These are our living realities; and not only these, but all the other things which are intimately connected with these." (PP II, pp. 296-7 sq.) See PP II, Chapters XXIV and XXI; J.M. Barbalet's "William James' Theory of Emotions. Filling in the Picture" (*Journal for the Theory of Social Behaviour* 29, 3, 1999, pp. 251-266); R. de Sousa's *The Rationality of Emotion* (Cambridge (Mass.), The Massachusetts Institute of Technology Press, 1987), and Damasio's work above referred to.

(necessarily ill-defined) consciousness-zero state and the mystical states focused on in VRE. First, states of thoughts and feelings are sketched; secondly, different breaches in consciousness-zero are discussed; finally, altered states are introduced.

2.1. States of Thoughts and Feelings

In the *Principles* James argues very early for a critical use of the introspective method of observation (*passim*, see esp. PP I, 185)[10] and remarks that consciousness should be understood pluralistically—"*every one agrees that we discover states of consciousness*" (*Ibidem*, James's emphasis)—, not only in the sense that there are as many consciousnesses as there are individual standpoints, but in the sense that each embodied consciousness is transitive, within an everlasting stream, *and* polymorphic. More precisely, by "states of consciousness", the quoted passage indiscriminately refers to states of thoughts and states of feelings (See PP I, 185-186 and 224). As we have seen supra, the two are intermingled and, *within each personal consciousness* (whose idiosyncrasy and endurance are a major ontological puzzles for James), thought is always changing. This is another form of the old philosophical problem: how can change be possible in a *cosmos*, i.e., a stable universe?—or, conversely, how can stability be (locally) possible in a *chaos*, i.e., a world in perpetual flux? Only few protagonists of that chronic epistemo-ontological debate have vaguely understood that some type of *chaosmos* is needed, but those who maintained it steadily (the paradox being of course quite spicy) are rare.

Anyway, it is the purpose of PP's famous chapter IX to systematise the question. Thinking of some sort always goes on, together with a correspondent bodily sensation. The interpretation of this general rule is however susceptible of important variations: on the one hand, in case of the irruption of genuine novelty, the strict correlation is broken; on the other hand, physical and physiological data can be treated to a significant extent by the experimental method, while more subjective ones belong to the introspective realm. To take but a few examples:

---

[10] Compare "Why has optics neglected the open road to truth, and wasted centuries in disputing about theories of color-composition which two minutes of introspection would have settled forever?" (PP I, p. 157) with "The attempt at introspective analysis in these cases is in fact like seizing a spinning top to catch its motion, or trying to turn up the gas quickly enough to see how the darkness looks." (PP I, p. 244)

"The eye's sensibility to light is at its maximum when the eye is first exposed, and blunts itself with surprising rapidity. A long night's sleep will make it see things twice as brightly on wakening, as simple rest by closure will make it see them later in the day. We feel things differently according as we are sleepy or awake, hungry or full, fresh or tired; differently at night and in the morning, differently in summer and in winter, and above all things differently in childhood, manhood, and old age. Yet we never doubt that our feelings reveal the same world, with the same sensible qualities and the same sensible things occupying it. The difference of the sensibility is shown best by the difference of our emotion about the things from one age to another, or when we are in different organic moods. What was bright and exciting becomes weary, flat, and unprofitable. The bird's song is tedious, the breeze is mournful, the sky is sad. (PP I, 232)

Obiter scriptum, there is a very good concept to name that interdependence of thoughts, sensations, subjective moods and objective state of affairs: *Stimmung*. No doubt it was in James's own fringes when writing these lines: someone as fully aware as James of the German (as well as the French) cultural atmosphere could not miss its relevance.

2.2. Breaches in Consciousness-zero

This first glance at the palette of experienced states of consciousness-zero inevitably leads to cast some doubts on any serious attempts to *define* (to freeze) the so-called normal or "immediate" state of consciousness. This relativistic slant will get stronger as we explore more remote shades of the phenomenology of consciousness. Let us continue with three progressive points emphasizing the continuity of the shades of consciousness.

Differences in rates of change have already been evoked (remember the substantive/transitive concepts introduced supra); their significant impact on the emotional tone of the experience should be kept in mind.

Breaks—or sudden contrasts—in quality or content are remarkable as one can pass very promptly, for instance after the arrival of bad news, from joy to sorrow, from a cheerful landscape to a dull one (See PP I, 232 quoted above). However, that transition (like between the thought of one object and the thought of another one) "is no more a break in the thought than a joint in a bamboo is a break in the wood. It is a part of the consciousness as much as the joint is a part of the bamboo." (PP I, 240)

There remains the possibility of a *real* discontinuity of consciousness (PP I, 199 ff.) James considers first the case of pure and simple interruptions or *objective* time-gaps. Distinguishing felt gaps (like sleep) and unfelt gaps (e.g., epilepsy, fainting, anæsthetics and hypnosis), he acknowledges that—since the question is the possibility of a *complete unconsciousness*—no rigorous objective answer is available (PP I, 238). Since mental and physical processes are correlated, James' point is (again: independently of his parapsychological and mystical inquiries) that while the organism is alive some form of consciousness must occur; when it dies, the question of immortality (see his Ingersoll Lecture of 1898) and of panpsychism (see infra) arise. Exactly, limit-phenomena like fainting, coma or epilepsy suggest two evidences: on the one hand, it is still the same personal thread that is woven unremittingly; on the other, it is getting difficult, in these cases, to use coherently the functors of consciousness-zero to estimate their characteristics. The basic problem comes from three main lacks or misconstructions (from the strict perspective of consciousness-zero): **(i)** lack of adequate exteroception of the world in process and of one's own embodiment (interoceptive and proprioceptive losses); **(ii)** bias in the perspectival cross-construction of the overlapping sets; and **(iii)** lack of clear prehension and fruitive rationalization of the sets. The plasticity of the concept of consciousness remains but some conceptual vulcanisation is required. This is the object of the next section.

2.3. Altered States

To underline it once more: the concept of *altered state* does not bring any discontinuity in the spectrum but merely enlarges it: it simply happens that, at one point, the state of consciousness debated is so different from consciousness-zero that it is expedient to use another tag. Here again we propose a three-layered unfoldment.

The question of sleep was already introduced in our discussion of PP I, 232 and 238. In sleep (our argument don't necessitate yet the discrimination and gearing of its well documented phases), the exteroceptive slowing down slackens off the existence of the external world and of our pragmatic potentialities (i.e., our potentialities for action). Hence, it is no surprise that reason-at-large is free to unfold modes of thought that are otherwise silenced. The feedback loop of the exteroceptive input and the pragmatic output is partly replaced by the loop of the interoceptive and proprioceptive input and the imaginative output. James remarks:

"Problems unsolved when we go to bed are found solved in the morning when we wake. Somnambulists do rational things. We awaken punctually at an hour predetermined overnight, etc. Unconscious thinking, volition, time-registration, etc., must have presided over these acts." (PP I, 166)

Phenomena like anæsthesia, hypnosis, somnambulism and hysteria could be—to some extent at least—interpreted in continuity with sleep *per se*. We will specify this in section V.

Purposeful and unintentional intoxications alike—especially of the hallucinogenic type—reform the entire perspectival set that constructs consciousness-zero. James' pragmatic struggle to reach an "ontological intuition, lying beyond the power of words to tell of"[11] is well-known. As VRE reminds us, the philosopher considered that he never really succeeded himself. Henri Michaux (1899–1984)[12], who gave himself the opportunity to systematically discover the addictive modes of crystallisation of subjectivity and their typical melancholy, shows straightforwardly how far any drug modifies your supports or footholds ["appuis"] in two ways: the resting of consciousness-zero on sense-perception is shifted; and the resting of the senses on the world itself transformed. However, even when the *miserable* miracle becomes an *horrifying* miracle, one gets resourced by a contact with the Ultimate. Whereas Michaux is primarily a Continental figure who, like Antonin Artaud, has attracted the attention of philosophers such as Bachelard, Blanchot, Deleuze and Merleau-Ponty, Aldous Huxley is a more well-known figure in the Anglo-Saxon cultural sphere. His *Doors of Perception* (1954)[13] belongs to the lineage of these Gnostic adventurers who are filling up their grail with mescaline. Bridge between William Blake's *Marriage of Heaven and Hell*

---

[11] W. James, "Review of *The Anaesthetic Revelation and the Gist of Philosophy*", *The Atlantic Monthly*, November 1874, Volume 33, No. 205, pp. 627-628.

[12] H. Michaux, *L'Infini turbulent*. Édition revue et augmentée, Paris, Éditions du Mercure de France, 1964; *Connaissance par les gouffres*. Nouvelle édition revue et corrigée, Paris, Gallimard, 1967; *Misérable miracle. La mescaline avec quarante-huit dessins et documents manuscrits originaux de l'auteur*. Nouvelle édition revue et augmentée, Paris, NRF Gallimard, 1972. Interestingly enough, he distinguishes *accelerating* and *decelerating* substances.

[13] A.L. Huxley, *The Doors of Perception* [Chatto & Windus Ltd, London, 1954] and *Heaven and Hell* [Chatto & Windus Ltd, London, 1956]. With a Foreword by J. G. Ballard and a Biographical Introduction by D. Bradshaw, London, Flamingo, Modern Classic, 1994.

(1885)[14] and Alan Watts' *Joyous Cosmology* (1962)[15], he offers well-tempered speculations that cannot be found in William Burroughs, Timothy Francis Leary or Charles T. Tart—and that are far more open (if not eclectic) than Carl Gustav Jung's or Stanislav Grof's. Unlike *Brave New World*, the *Doors* does not refer directly to VRE (or any other of James' works)—but it argues with C. D. Broad and Bergson for a claim defended by James (and Frederic W. H. Myers) as well: "the function of the brain and nervous system is to protect us from being overwhelmed and confused by this mass of largely useless and irrelevant knowledge, by shutting out most of what we should otherwise perceive or remember at any moment, and leaving only that very small and special selection which is likely to be practically useful."[16]

Time is ripe now to focus on the mystical and on the VRE itself. James makes it clear that he will address only "first-hand and original forms of [religious] experience"—i.e. (by definition) absolutely authoritative *individual* religiousness—, factually putting into brackets (by definition) *collective* religion *qua* "second-hand religious life".[17] His lectures intended to cast as much light as possible on all forms of religiousness by proposing a heuristic grid respectful of all guises of the mystical. Of course, James—although he was obviously sincerely willing to explore the culturally most remote phenomena— never went very far from his own Christian and familial legacy (Emersonian and Swedenborgian). That question cannot be treated in any depth here; it is enough to remember his pragmatic *modus operandi*:

"Our spiritual judgment, I said, our opinion of the significance and value of a human event or condition, must be decided on empirical grounds exclusively. If the fruits for life of the state of conversion are good, we ought to idealize and venerate it, even though it be a piece of natural psychology; if not, we ought to

---

[14] W. Blake, *The Mariage of Heaven and Hell*, Edmonton, Middlesex - London, W. Muir - B. Quaritch, 1885

[15] A.W. Watts, *The Joyous Cosmology. Adventures in the Chemistry of Consciousness*, New York, Pantheon Books, 1962

[16] On the cross-influences of James and Bergson, see the precious inquiries of M. Capek: "The Reappearance of the Self in the Last Philosophy of William James", *The Philosophical Review* 62, 1953, pp. 526-544; "La signification actuelle de la philosophie de James", *Revue de Métaphysique et de Morale*, 67è année, 1962, pp. 291-321; and "La pensée de Bergson en Amérique", *Revue internationale de philosophie* 31, 1977, pp. 329-350.

[17] VRE, pp. 6-7; "first-hand and original forms of experience" (VRE, p. 201); "first-hand individual experience" (VRE, p. 335); "genuine first-hand religious experience" (VRE, p. 337; See 6, 30, 95). The abbreviations used are listed in the Bibliography.

make short work with it, no matter what supernatural being may have infused it." (VRE, 237)

If one approaches the mystical states from the perspective of their good consequential (or practical) fruits for life[18], the impact or strain on consciousness-zero becomes visible and the scientific narrow-mindedness in the field evident:

"To the medical mind these ecstasies signify nothing but suggested and imitated hypnoid states, on an intellectual basis of superstition, and a corporeal one of degeneration and hysteria. Undoubtedly these pathological conditions have existed in many and possibly in all the cases, but that fact tells us nothing about the value for knowledge of the consciousness which they induce. To pass a spiritual judgment upon these states, we must not content ourselves with superficial medical talk, but inquire into their fruits for life." (VRE, 413)

Of the different definitions of religion *qua* religiousness proposed throughout the VRE, the one featured by the conclusion is probably the most potent:

"There is a certain uniform deliverance in which religions all appear to meet. It consists of two parts:—1. An uneasiness; and 2. Its solution. 1. The uneasiness, reduced to its simplest terms, is a sense that there is *something wrong about us* as we naturally stand. 2. The solution is a sense that *we are saved from the wrongness* by making proper connection with the higher powers." (VRE, 508; See VRE, 128)[19]

In other words, first-hand religious experience is—consciously or not (!)—

---

[18] See also VRE, pp. 15 and 259. Maritain apparently agrees: "J'entendrai en général par "expérience mystique" une expérience fruitive de l'absolu." (J. Maritain, "L'expérience mystique naturelle et le vide", in *Quatre essais sur l'esprit dans sa condition charnelle*, Paris, Desclée De Brouwer, Bibliothèque française de philosophie. Série 3, 1939, 129-177; p. 132.)

[19] Compare with Bergson: "À nos yeux, l'aboutissement du mysticisme est une prise de contact, et par conséquent une coïncidence partielle, avec l'effort créateur que manifeste la vie. Cet effort est de Dieu, si ce n'est pas Dieu lui-même. Le grand mystique serait une individualité qui franchirait les limites assignées à l'espèce par sa matérialité, qui continuerait et prolongerait ainsi l'action divine." (H. Bergson, *Les Deux Sources de la Morale et de la Religion* [1932], Paris, Presses Universitaires de France, Bibliothèque de Philosophie Contemporaine, 1969, p. 233=Œuvres, p. 1162)

universally sought because of the deep enigmatic unsatisfaction dwelling in each of us... in consciousness-zero: James insists on its moral dimension of "feeling inwardly vile and wrong" (VRE, 170)—if not on the ideas of sin and evil themselves—, but it remains essential to keep the door wide open to all forms of wrong "bone-feeling". As he himself claims:

"If we admit that evil is an essential part of our being and the key to the interpretation of our life, we load ourselves down with a difficulty that has always proved burdensome in philosophies of religion." (VRE, 131)

Moral action itself might be paralysed by such a standpoint. The concept of evil could nevertheless be salvaged if it names that broad idea of mal-adjustment, i.e., of a "wrong correspondence of one's life with the environment" (one speaks then of "sins"); but it could not if it names something more radical, like "a wrongness or vice in his essential nature", i.e. "Sin" (See VRE, 134). The reason of that contrast lies in the evidence that the former is curable (in principle at least) upon the natural plane, while the later embodies "something ineradicably ingrained in our natural subjectivity, and never to be removed by any superficial piecemeal operations" (ib.). (Besides, the dogmatic attitude characteristic of second hand religious experience is not primordial for the VRE.)

The message delivered by James is very strong: yes, there is a genuine "incompleteness or wrongness" (VRE, 209) in our perspectival standpoint, a sense of alienation and distance, a (Gnostic?) feeling of being "thrown" in a foreign world—but there is a solution available and it lies within the reach of most (if not each) of us. It is a matter of "proper connection", of establishing contact with "higher powers", expression that should be taken to mean not only establishing personal relation of contact with "higher beings" that are contiguous with the mesocosmic entities of consciousness-zero, but also triggering higher levels of consciousness within (as it were) the given individual.

"Let me then propose, as an hypothesis, that whatever it may be on its *farther* side, the "more" with which in religious experience we feel ourselves connected is on its *hither* side the subconscious continuation of our conscious life. Starting thus with a recognized psychological fact as our basis, we seem to preserve a contact with "science" which the ordinary theologian lacks. At the same time the theologian's contention that the religious man is moved by an external power is vindicated, for it is one of the peculiarities of invasions from the subconscious region to take on objective appearances, and to suggest to the Subject an external control. In the religious life the control is felt as "higher"; but since on our hypothesis it is primarily the higher faculties of our own hidden mind which are controlling, the sense of union with the power beyond us is a sense of something, not merely apparently, but literally true." (VRE, 512-513)

That contact with the "absolute realities" (VRE, 503) can be a contact with the "Parent-Soul, and an influx of life, love, virtue, health, and happiness from the Inexhaustible Fountain" (VRE, 118 quoting Henry Wood) or a "personal relation of contact with the mysterious power of which it feels the presence" (VRE, 464), but James is looking for a formulation compatible with an impersonal intercourse with the unnamed Absolute—a more basic feature that can be provided by the concept of a spectrum of consciousness and that will get clarified in the next section with the concept of transmarginal field. In sum,

"When stage 2 (the stage of solution or salvation) arrives, the man identifies his real being with the germinal higher part of himself; and does so in the following way. He becomes conscious that this higher part is conterminous and continuous with a *more* of the same quality, which is operative in the universe outside of him, and which he can keep in working touch with, and in a fashion get on board of and save himself when all his lower being has gone to pieces in the wreck." (VRE, 508; See VRE, 128)

We feel the need, in other words, for nothing less than a full *cosmic reconciliation*. It appears that to become reconciled with oneself is the same as—or requires—to become reconciled with others and with our entire environment. Please notice that the philosopher speaks of a *conterminous and continuous* "higher part" that obviously explodes the dualism pervading consciousness-zero and occasions a "cosmic emotion" inevitably taking the form of "enthusiasm and freedom" (VRE, 79). In conclusion: since the cure lies in the *connection*, it is definitively clear that the problem lay in the *insulation*— the ultimate metaphysical puzzle haunting already the *Principles* (PP I, 226, See 237-8). The point James is making is thus the urgency of the promotion of a change of consciousness, of a shift from a mal-adjustment to a well-adjustment to a world in the making. But what does the breaking of the absolute insulation, of the *irreducible* pluralism exactly involve? Before envisaging this question, we need to specify the concept of spectrum of bodies.

21

3. Spectrum of Bodies

So far we have displayed, hopefully forcefully, the different layers of meaning of the concept of consciousness-zero and argued that, especially in the light of mystical phenomenology, that concept demands a spectral contextualization. Consciousness-zero belongs to a continuum of consciousness that is stretched between "higher" states—mystical arousal—and "lower" states—sleep... Now, the activation of the cosmic reconciliation sketched in the previous section requires an ontological counterpart that is very often named "panpsychism". In James' own words, there has to be *only one primal stuff*—without this ground, it is plain that reconciliation will only remain wishful thinking. Three steps are expedient: the question of the gearing of subjectivity and objectivity is first introduced to allow the discussion of, on the one hand, the panpsychist solution and of, on the other, its refined version that is "pure experience".

3.1. The Gearing of Subjectivity and Objectivity

An interesting way of introducing the debate is to ask about the possibility (and nature) of the organic causation of a religious state of mind. According to James, when classical materialism claims that a pure and simple mechanistic explanation of mysticism can—and should—be provided, mysticism's very essence is emasculated. This does not mean, however, that mysticism *per se* should be abandoned (this would be illogical and arbitrary) or that it should be explained from above (this would be speculative cowardliness): it means instead that we need a reformed naturalism to do justice to "inwardly superior" states of mind. VRE, 13 ff. speaks of a simple-minded, dogmatic and arbitrary "medical materialism".

The idea, that we are about to unfold, of a transmarginal field of consciousness is not simply the ontological consequence, within the realm of subjectivity, of Myers's doctrine of subliminal energies: the "up-rushes", into the ordinary consciousness, of "energies originating in the subliminal parts of the mind" (VRE, 234; See 478 ff.) have to receive an *objective* status in order to explicate the link existing between emotion and energy and to allow the cosmic reconciliation all humans are dying for (no pun intended). Please already notice that what matters for James is the *meaning* of the concept:

"If the word "subliminal" is offensive to any of you, as smelling too much of psychical research or other aberrations, call it by any other name you please, to distinguish it from the level of full sunlit consciousness. Call this latter the A-region of personality, if you care to, and call the other the B-region. The B-region, then, is obviously the larger part of each of us, for it is the abode of everything that is latent and the reservoir of everything that passes unrecorded or unobserved. It contains, for example, such things as all our momentarily inactive memories, and it harbors the springs of all our obscurely motivated passions, impulses, likes, dislikes, and prejudices. Our intuitions, hypotheses, fancies, superstitions, persuasions, convictions, and in general all our non-rational operations, come from it." (VRE, 483)

If all phenomena have a subjective *and* an objective side, the "wider world" (VRE, 523) is an experiential web made of living connections that are prehensive (and sometimes reflexive) knots. But would that reformed naturalism be worthy of the name "panpsychism"?[20] Before proposing an answer, we need to flesh out the meaning and significance of the concept of panpsychism itself. Like most philosophical concepts, it has been used in numbers of ways and carries nowadays a wealth of meaning that does not help clarifying the debate.

3.2. Panpsychism

The question that the concept of panpsychism seeks to answer is indeed properly ontological: what can be predicated of *all* actualities? For the sake of the present short discussion, it will suffice to examine the two main sources of difficulties. On the one hand, the prefix "pan" can either refer to the Whole (See the concept of World-Soul) or to all parts (See the concept of hylozoism). A complementary—Leibnizian—version of that basic contrast is the one between aggregates and individuals.[21] Please notice that this first partition makes no pretence of exhausting the set of possibilities (*tertium datur*); moreover it points at the necessity of the specification of the relation(s) existing

---

[20] See our "Whitehead's Reading of James and Its Context", in *Streams of William James*, Volume 4, Issue 1, Spring 2002, pp. 18-22 and Volume 5, Issue 3, Fall 2003, pp. 26-31.
[21] This difference is stressed by Griffin, e.g., in D.R. Griffin (ed.), *Founders of Constructive Postmodern Philosophy. Peirce, James, Bergson, Whitehead, and Hartshorne*, New York, State University of New York Press, *SUNY Series in Constructive Postmodern Thought*, 1993, p. 35n17. In other words, it is our contention that the meaning and significance of Whiteheadian panexperientialism is foreshadowed in the *Essays in Radical Empiricism*.

between the parts and the whole. On the other hand, the root word "psychism" works at various *stages* or *levels* that can be heuristically identified and hierarchized in the following way. First, it stands for *psyche* itself and, in conjunction with the prefix "pan" leads irresistibly in the direction of animism. Second, it stands for *subjectivity*, i.e., for consciousness-zero or at least for an awareness of some sort: self-experience is its key-word. Third, it stands for some *mental activity*, which means capacity of abstraction, of valuation, together with some freedom (or spontaneity, depending on how you define your variables). Fourth, it stands for *pure experience*, in the sense that everything that "is" either experiences or is experienced.

Quid of the nature and extent of James's panpsychism from the perspective of our heuristic abstractive progression (psychism/subjectivity/mentality/experience)? At the very least, it is doubtful that his entire philosophical development belongs to the same panpsychic level. We claim that the above abstractive progression is indeed at work in James, who first (already in the *Principles*) embraced a rather non technical (or gut) panpsychism—in 1909, he is still speaking of "mother-sea" or "common reservoir of consciousness"[22]— and later (especially in the *Essays in Radical Empiricism*)[23] spelled the (dry) basics of a panexperientialist framework.[24] The quest for higher generalities and the striping of immediate (sometimes naive) experience of its "obvious" and "subjective" features are the two faces of the same coin. At any rate, these various conceptual stops do make sense from the perspective of the "infinite number of degrees of consciousness, following the degrees of complication and aggregation of the primordial mind-dust" (PP I, 149).

3.3. Pure Experience

To resume our argument: the panexperientialism required by the Jamesean

---

[22] W. James, "Confidences of a 'Psychical Researcher' [1909], in *Essays in Psychical Research*. F.H. Burkhardt, gen. ed.; F. Bowers, text. ed.; I.K. Skrupskelis, ass. ed., Cambridge (Mass.), Harvard University Press, 1986, pp. 361-375.
[23] W. James, *Essays in Radical Empiricism* [Posthumously published by Ralph Barton Perry], New York, Longmans, Green, and Co., 1912. (Hereafter ERE)
[24] Griffin proposed the concept of "panexperientialism" in 1977 to name Whitehead's attitude: See D.R. Griffin, "Whitehead's Philosophy and Some General Notions of Physics and Biology", in J. B. Cobb, Jr. & D.R. Griffin (eds.), *Mind in Nature. Essays on the Interface of Science and Philosophy*, Washington D. C., University Press of America, 1977. For a more recent discussion, see D.R. Griffin (ed.), *Founders of Constructive Postmodern Philosophy.* op. cit.

lure towards full-fledged reconciliation can be found in the polysemial concept of "pure experience" worked out by the *Essays in Radical Empiricism*. Wrestling with the status of the marrow of experience, James coins the concept in order to name what cannot bear names, or better: in order to *point to* what remains of the order of bare factuality, i.e., of pre-predication. Out of the intricacy of the various meanings he confers on the concept, three dimensions can be isolated for the sake of analysis, and articulated for the sake of synthesis. On the one hand, pure experience is the "subjective"—or inner—immediate flux onto-logically (not temporally) preceding the institution of differences between subject and object. It is appropriate to hyphenate "onto-logical" in order to underline that the primacy belongs to the primordial structure of the Whole itself, as understood from a certain logical outlook. On the other hand, pure experience is the "objective"—or outer—primal stuff that embodies the thickness acknowledged in practice by everyone. Realism is not a vain word for James. From a unitive—or in-between—perspective, the concept puts the ineffable union between subjective and objective mundane features in the hot seat, thereby opening the speculative horizon in the direction of a ladder of levels of consciousness.

Every feature of the World is either an "experiencing" or an "experienced". Pure experience names the radical eventfulness (i.e. the asubstantialism) of the inner and outer worlds, as well as their unison. Experience is what actually holds the world together: not only are relations *experienced*, but they are themselves *experience*. Since everything is experience, there is no more dichotomy between, on the one hand, a substance that is experiencing and unextended and, on the other, a substance that is unexperiencing and extended (remember Descartes' bicameral substantialism). Radical empiricism is first and foremost a radical constructivism.[25]

Precisely, it is not coincidental that, out of the four characteristics of mystical experience (VRE, 380 ff.) proposes, three are directly interpretable in terms of pure experience: ineffability, noetic quality and transciency. Hence the idea that passivity (the fourth characteristics) is only a matter of relativity.

4. Transmarginal Field of Consciousness

The first step required by a radical empiricism is to accept all possible states

---

[25] See our "The Polysemiality of the Concept of *Pure Experience*", *Streams of William James*, Volume 1, Issue 2, Fall 1999, pp. 4-6 and "James' Contiguism of *Pure Experience*", *Streams of William James*, Volume 1, Issue 3, Winter 1999, pp. 19-22.

of consciousness as a matter of fact and as a resource of utmost importance for a meaningful life—and thus for speculative philosophy; the second step James makes is to acknowledge that "some states of mind are inwardly superior to others, and reveal to us more truth" (VRE, 14); the third one is to provide the pragmatically soundest theorisation possible of this incipient scale—James, because of his temperament, is here more shy. This section first contextualizes the genesis of the concept of transmarginal field of consciousness; then it sketches James' use; and finally it provides an exemplification with the practice of hypnosis. The goal is to display the modalities of the conjunction of the spectral consciousness with the panexperientialistic world it requires and sustains.

4.1. Historical-Speculative Context

The broad context that welcomed James speculations can be polarised with the help of the two major scientific revolutions of his time: Charles Darwin's *Origin of Species by Means of Natural Selection* (1859) and James Clerk Maxwell's *Treatise on Electricity and Magnetism* (1873). No doubt James's own background made him more sensitive to the former, but both really pervaded the entire cultural atmosphere of the second half of the XIXth century. The discussion of evolutionism was actually on the scientific agenda since Jean-Baptiste de Monet de Lamarck and Herbert Spencer (Alfred Russel Wallace and Ernst Haeckel renewing later the debate); it shouldn't obliterate the major advances operated, on the one hand, by Claude Bernard, whose *Introduction à l'étude de la médecine expérimentale* (1865) had a huge ideological impact in terms of the naturalisation and socialisation of life (i.e., the reinforcement of the ancient analogies between organism and society); and on the other hand by Louis Pasteur with his famous *Mémoire sur la fermentation lactique* (1857).

The narrow context of James's VRE speculations on the concept of spectral consciousness consists primarily in the works of Frederic W. H. Myers, who creatively renewed the intuitions of Franz Anton Mesmer with the idea of **(i)** a transmarginal field of consciousness inspired by the recent advances in electromagnetism (VRE, 511)[26] and **(ii)** of the subliminal door. According to

---

[26] F.W.H. Myers, *The Subliminal Consciousness*. With an Introduction by James Webb [Selections reprinted from Proceedings of the English Society for Psychical Research, 6, 1889-1895], New York, Arno Press. A New York Times Company, 1976. James refers especially to his essay on the *Subliminal Consciousness* (1892).

"The expression "field of consciousness" has but recently come into vogue in the psychology books. Until quite lately the unit of mental life which figured most was the single "idea," supposed to be a definitely outlined thing. But at present psychologists are tending, first, to admit that the actual unit is more probably the total mental state, the entire wave of consciousness or field of objects present to the thought at any time; and, second, to see that it is impossible to outline this wave, this field, with any definiteness." (VRE, 231; See 231-5 and PP I, 256, 495; II, 151)

4.2. James's Concept of "Subliminal Door"

The meaning James attempts to convey could be set out in the following way. The total mental state consists in the intermingling of two waves or fields (hence the appropriateness of the metaphor of the interference patterns): on the one hand, the entire wave of consciousness-zero and its temporal fluctuations; and, on the other hand, the entire wave of subliminal (unconscious, subconscious, underground, extramarginal, ultramarginal) consciousness and its temporal fluctuations.

Now, although in its essence the total field-like mental state is continuous with its environment, in everyday consciousness-zero, it is fragmented in two main parts: the focal (internal) mental field is consciously prehended with its external—"physical"—correlate, the "field of nature" (VRE, 518). Moreover, in the same way mentality ("the soul") is a succession of overlapping "fields of consciousness" (VRE, 195), the concrete, in its many-layered processual complexity, is in constant change. From the perspective of the necessity of reconciling these two abstractions, consciousness could be seen as a multidimensional interferential pattern *creating* a centre of energy.

The main tool we have to analyse the fluctuations of consciousness-zero consists in the differentiation of the nucleus and the fringes; it is complemented by the estimate of the width of the given state: a wide state is enjoyable and rich in its epistemic potentialities, while a narrow state is akin to a mere spark endowed with emotion (VRE, 231). The main tool at our disposal to speculate about the subliminal wave consists in the incursions of subliminal energies in the liminal realm. These bursts of energies are typically made responsible by James for the sudden conversions that are reported every so often. If filtration is strong, no irruption is easy (VRE, 242 speaks of a "hard rind of a margin");

otherwise the individual is likely to be sensitive to all inframarginal fluctuations.

The concept of the "subliminal door" appears thus to be a useful abstraction to understand the complex intercourse that the interference of the fields involved in consciousness-zero thematizes. It is especially helpful to discuss the nature and characteristics of spirituality. The concept of the "door" (or "doorway") to the subliminal (See VRE, 242-243, 270, 418, 484, 513 and 524) instruments the idea that "spirituality is chiefly subconscious" (VRE, 100) while allowing James to critically promote his monistic-pantheistic-optimistic (briefly: panexperientialistic) insights[27]:

"Just as our primary wide-awake consciousness throws open our senses to the touch of things material so it is logically conceivable that *if there be* higher spiritual agencies that can directly touch us, the psychological condition of their doing so *might be* our possession of a subconscious region which alone should yield access to them. The hubbub of the waking life might close a door which in the dreamy Subliminal might remain ajar or open. [...] If there be higher powers able to impress us, they may get access to us only through the subliminal door. (See below, p. 506 ff.)" (VRE, 242-3)

The correspondence between the spectrum of consciousness and the spectrum of bodies is plain: the two intermingled continua are nothing but abstractions from the one primal stuff of experience. Again: "If the grace of God miraculously operates, it probably operates through the subliminal door" (VRE, 270; See 389). These "incursions" from beyond the subliminal or transmarginal (VRE, 426, 478, 483, 511, 513) of "higher spiritual agencies" (VRE, 242, See 515) testify for the "decidedly pantheistic" higher nature of human beings:

"The spiritual in man appears in the mind-cure philosophy as partly conscious, but chiefly subconscious; and through the subconscious part of it we are already one with the Divine without any miracle of grace, or abrupt creation of a new inner man." (VRE, 100)

---

[27]"But even this presumption from the unanimity of mystics is far from being strong. In characterizing mystic states an pantheistic, optimistic, etc., I am afraid I over-simplified the truth. I did so for expository reasons, and to keep the closer to the classic mystical tradition. The classic religious mysticism, it now must be confessed, is only a "privileged case"." (VRE, pp. 424-425)

Naturalistic pantheism does not need to argue for a second birth in the case of sudden conversions: they are made possible by the simple possession of the "active subliminal self" (VRE, 240)—whence a more coherent worldview, pregnant with beautiful pragmatic consequences

"The theistic explanation is by divine grace, which creates a new nature within one the moment the old nature is sincerely given up. The pantheistic explanation (which is that of most mind-curers) is by the merging of the narrower private self into the wider or greater self, the spirit of the universe (which is your own "subconscious" self), the moment the isolating barriers of mistrust and anxiety are removed." (VRE, 111)

The question of evil bounces back here; we have already evoked VRE, 131-134: the reader is referred to the VRE itself for further contextualization.

4.3. Hypnosis

Hypnosis ranks, with hysteria and dreams, among the main clues that put psychologists on the path of the extra-marginal. Whereas the PP, because of its topic, refers mostly to Alfred Binet and Pierre Janet[28], the VRE, again because of its focus, mainly refers to Myers, while "the wonderful explorations" of Binet, Janet, but also of Étienne Azam, Hippolyte Bernheim, Josef Breuer, Jean Martin Charcot, Richard von Kraft-Ebbing, Auguste Liébeault, Rufus Osgood Mason, Morton Prince, Théodule Ribot, and of course Sigmund Freud are selectively mentioned.[29] In order to refresh James' own endeavours in the field of hypnosis (see especially PP II, ch. XXVII), we propose to use François Roustang's recent powerful speculations, inspired in part by Léon Chertok and Milton H. Erickson.[30] The goal of this section remains to display the correlation that exists between the ladder of states of consciousness and the hierarchy of beings.

Chertok proposes a few provisional definitions of the hypnotic state

---

[28] A. Binet, *La psychologie du raisonnement. Recherches expérimentales par l'hypnotisme*, Paris, Éditions Alcan, Bibliothèque de philosophie contemporaine, 1886; P. Janet, *L'automatisme psychologique*, Paris, Éditions Alcan, 1889.

[29] See VRE, pp. 115, 125, 233-5, 240-241, 269-270, 401, 413, 484, 501, 516.

[30] See especially F. Roustang's *Qu'est-ce que l'hypnose ?* (Paris, Éditions de Minuit, 1994).

stemming from the old—but still actual—concept of *animal magnetism*[31] and insisting on the affective core of the hypnotic trance; it is a natural potentiality that manifests itself already in the relation of attachment to the mother; it is the matrix, the crucible in which all subsequent relations will come within the scope; its essence is very archaic, pre-linguistic, pre-sexual.[32]

Keeping this in mind, let us first sketch the induction of the hypnotic state (or "trance" as it is called by James). For the sake of the present argument, we can bypass the distinction between self-hypnosis and hypnosis *suggested* on a willing and co-operative subject by a clinician. The basic conditions for entering hypnosis are fairly simple: it is just a matter of fixation of ones own attention. As one concentrates on a single stimulus by gradually bracketing most of the other afferent stimuli, attention becomes more and more invasive and the waking state gets dramatically transformed: sense-perception is now nuclear, while action becomes cataleptic and reason drifts from its judgmental concern to get closer to affects. Discussing the related topic that is *attention*, a major mystic of the XXth century—Simone Weil—puts it this way: "attention consists in the suspension of one's thought, in letting it available, empty and penetrable by the object; it consists in keeping in oneself the proximity of thought and of the various acquired knowledge that one is usually forced to use, but at a lower level and without contact with it".[33]

---

[31] The concept, of course present in PP, has been recently reboosted by B. Cyrulnik (See, e.g., his *L'ensorcellement du monde*, Paris, Éditions Odile Jacob, 1997).

[32] "On peut seulement affirmer que c'est au niveau de l'affect, c'est-à-dire de la réalité la plus évidente, puisqu'elle est de l'ordre du vécu, et la plus difficile à comprendre. [...] C'est un quatrième état de l'organisme, actuellement non objectivable (à l'inverse des trois autres : veille, sommeil, rêve : une sorte de potentialité naturelle, de dispositif inné prenant ses racines jusque dans l'hypnose animale, caractérisé par des traits qui renvoient apparemment aux relations pré-langagières d'attachement de l'enfant et se produisant dans des situations où l'individu est perturbé dans ses rapports avec l'environnement. L'hypnose garde sa spécificité par rapport à la suggestion, bien que celle-ci, sous quelque forme qu'elle se manifeste, soit nécessaire à la production de celle-là. La suggestion nous apparaît ainsi comme la relation primaire, fondamentale entre deux êtres, la matrice, le creuset dans lequel viendront s'inscrire toutes les relations ultérieures. Nous dirons encore qu'elle est une entité psycho-socio-biologique indissociable, agissant à un niveau inconscient très archaïque, pré-langagier, pré-sexuel, et médiatisant l'influence affective que tout individu exerce sur un autre." (L. Chertock, *L'Hypnose. Théorie, pratique et technique*. Préface de H. Ey. Édition remaniée et augmentée [1959], Paris, Éditions Payot, Petite Bibliothèque, 1989, pp. 260-261

[33] "L'attention consiste à suspendre sa pensée, à la laisser disponible, vide et pénétrable à l'objet, à maintenir en soi-même la proximité de la pensée, mais à un niveau inférieur et

What about the characteristics of this gradual relaxation or sleepiness? Hypnotic wakefulness features indeed, as its etymology suggests, "many affinities" (PP II, 599) with ordinary sleep: muscular relaxation and redistributed brain activity (patterns that remind us of paradoxical sleep as disclosed in EEG and EMG), anæsthesia and/or hyperæsthesia (although not genuinely sensorial), amnesia (while hypermnesia is possible), perceptive distortions (including hallucinations), increased suggestibility (besides post-hypnotic—i.e., deferred—suggestions) and the possibility of role-enactment and of alteration of the personality.

But it features as well remarkable differences (that James would claim are only of degree) with ordinary sleep; to outline them coherently, it is essential to go through the four (non-necessary) steps to full hypnotic actualisation. First, the *induction* of the hypnotic state occurs through perceptive fixedness; fascination starts where ordinary perception stops. Second, the hypnotic state installs *indetermination*: all customary differences can be abolished, paving the way for confusion, blindness, loss of reference point and possibly feeling of helplessness. Third, the positive side of the dispersed attitude of the attention (PP II, 599) is the opening of the *possible*: resting on this indeterminate waiting, spring dissociations, withdrawal and hallucinations; and with them the possibility of transforming one's appraisal of life. Everything can be reframed: percepts can be put in a wider context by reverie, absence, or imagination. Fourth, the hypnotic trance displays itself as enhanced vigilance, mobilised power, energy ready to implement action, i.e., to shape the world. All the acquired knowledge is gathered, actively taken in, and one has them at one's disposal. This explains why the hypnotherapist suggests only what is possible for the patient, s/he reveals the power the patient has on its own becoming.

Roustang concludes: "to understand something of paradoxical wakefulness, we have to do violence to ourselves and—at a great expense—invent in our culture a new cosmology and a new anthropology".[34] All the consequences of the contiguum of the states of consciousness and of the levels of beings, i.e., of bodies, have to be thought. This is exactly what panexperientialism provides: one single onto-psychical field that allows, as it were, only unwillingly, the bifurcation of subject and object. Since there is one organising and differentiating power endowed by many centre of forces, the mesocosmic

---

sans contact avec elle, les diverses connaissances acquises qu'on est forcé d'utiliser." (S. Weil, *Attente de Dieu*, Paris, La Colombe, Éditions du vieux colombier, 1957, pp. 76-77.)

[34] "Pour comprendre quelque chose de la veille paradoxale, il faut nous faire violence et inventer dans notre culture, à grands frais, une nouvelle cosmologie et une nouvelle anthropologie." (*Qu'est-ce que l'hypnose ?*, op. cit., pp. 98-99)

perception of an object by a subject ceases to be mysterious: in pure experience, subject and object, subject and subject, grow together and reciprocally (com)prehend themselves.[35] Each experience has both a physical and a mental dimension that can be pulled apart only in abstraction. The concreteness of experience, in other words, goes beyond the limited perspectives of "physicality" and "mentality". After many others, Deleuze has suggested the metaphor of the *fold* to intuit how such a bimodal ontology is possible; James provides us with a concept.

5. Conclusion

The VRE hopes to free religious experience from obscurantists and dualists alike. It is looking for the fundamental unity of all experiences and, beyond, for the unity of the organic Whole itself. Now, if consciousness-zero is "continuous with a wider self" (VRE, 515), and if, moreover, the entire wave of consciousness leads us to consider the world as one unit of absolute fact (VRE, 131), medico-materialistic reductionism has to go. However, if spirituality cannot be stretched to fit the Procustean materialistic bed, for all that we don't have to renounce a healthy naturalism. Embodied consciousness is simply not to be conceived with the usual dualistic categories: experience—and, startlingly, mystical experiences—evidently ask for an organic framework respectful of the unity of all feelings.

We have basically seen (i) that consciousness-zero *makes* sense—properly speaking—only from the perspective of the continuum in which it is inscribed; (ii) that, conversely, the embodied standpoint necessarily belongs to a continuum of standpoints; and (iii) that the concepts of transmarginal field and of subliminal door are the keys to the required reformed ontology. Pluralistic monism is one of the names James uses for that purpose. Three further points deserve to be underlined in conclusion: the overall importance of feeling in James' work; the general aspect of the scale of natural states of vigilance

---

[35] "Grâce à cette puissance qui organise et différencie, représentée par l'anticipation, toute une série de faux problèmes tombent d'eux-mêmes. Il n'y a plus à se demander comment un sujet peut percevoir un objet, puisque l'un et l'autre grandissent ensemble et s'appréhendent dans une action réciproque, ni comment un humain peut en comprendre un autre, puisqu'ils n'existent dès l'origine que par cette compréhension, ni comment peuvent se tisser entre eux des interrelations: l'identification et le lien affectif n'ont dû être inventés que par la supposition erronée que les individus d'abord confondus, ont été ensuite séparés." (*Qu'est-ce que l'hypnose ?*, op. cit., p. 87)

required by his argument; the typology of philosophies that could be deduced from his discussion.

5.1. Feeling

"Only what we partly know already inspires us to desire to know more" says *The Briefer Course*: ones own living existence is the sole starting point for any inquiry whatsoever. This basic pragmatist principle is reflected in VRE's willingness to deal only with first-hand religious experiences as they impact on consciousness-zero. James argues:

"In short, you suspect that I am planning to defend feeling at the expense of reason, to rehabilitate the primitive and unreflective, and to dissuade you from the hope of any Theology worthy of the name. To a certain extent I have to admit that you guess rightly. I do believe that feeling is the deeper source of religion, and that philosophic and theological formulas are secondary products, like translations of a text into another tongue. But all such statements are misleading from their brevity." (VRE, 431)

Interestingly enough, just like for Chertok (and for Bradley and Whitehead of course…), feeling is the key-word of James' individualistic approach.

"Individuality is founded in feeling; and the recesses of feeling, the darker, blinder strata of character, are the only places in the world in which we catch real fact in the making, and directly perceive how events happen, and how work is actually done. Compared with this world of living individualized feelings, the world of generalized objects which the intellect contemplates is without solidity or life." (VRE, 501-502)

Living acts of perception *constitute* the field of consciousness and, thereby, the cosmic experiential web. The whole universe is everywhere feeling, alive— if not conscious.

5.2. Scale of Natural states of vigilance

Finally, we can now position the main states of consciousness encountered during our argument on a, necessarily arbitrary, scale of awareness complementary of the mystical ladder proposed in VRE, 382 ff. At the lowest level of awareness of oneself and of the environment we find NREM sleep— the blissful total obliteration evoked in the *Phaedo*. One step higher there is paradoxical sleep, that owes its name to the fact that the subject in REM sleep is both hard to arouse (apart from jerky movements, the muscles are completely relaxed) and near consciousness-zero (from the perspective of his/her brain activity). Roustang, influenced by Jouvet and Stern,[36] sees in this state a preparation for action. Higher we find all forms of limited wakefulness like somnolescence, drowsiness and day-dreaming. Right in the middle of the scale (by hypothesis) lies the pivotal consciousness-zero and its correlated rationalized mesocosm. Higher dwell the so-called "altered states". The hypnotic trance, according to Roustang, who refers himself to Chertok and Rausky,[37] is worthy of the concept of "paradoxical—or generalized— wakefulness". It is intermediary between consciousness-zero and the "noetic but ineffable" mystical states because the subtle dialectic between individuation and cosmization perfectly exemplified in mysticism is announced in hypnosis: through focalisation, i.e. sensorial purgation, one reaches totalization.

Awakening *per se*—or total liberation—necessitates indeed two apparently paradoxical features: individuation *and* cosmization. James shows that (I) religion is what the individuals do with their own solitariness insofar as (II) they apprehend themselves as standing in relation to whatever is considered divine. At the apex of the growth process, individuation leads to cosmization and cosmization to individuation. Enstasis leads to extasis, immanence to transcendence, the *Odyssey* is an *Exodus*. One returns from the solitude of individuation into the consciousness of unity with all that is. With that regard, it is of the highest importance to understand—as Arendt does—that solitude is not strictly speaking commensurable with loneliness. The former is the seat of awakening or contemplation ("theoria"); the latter occurs when the borderline individual is deserted by, and feels deprived of, human company and even of the possible company of him/herself.[38] If one wishes to dare a topological metaphor, the Möbius' band suggests how stretching consciousness towards its

---

[36] D.N. Stern, *The Interpersonal World of the Infant. A View from Psychoanalysis and Developmental Psychology*, New York, Basic Book, 1985; M. Jouvet, *Le sommeil et le rêve*, Paris, Éditions Odile Jacob, 1992.

[37] F. Rausky, "Le quatrième état organique : réflexions théoriques et cliniques sur une hypothèse chertokienne", in I. Stengers (sous la direction de), *Importance de l'hypnose [À la mémoire de Léon Chertok]*, Paris, Édition des Laboratoires Delagrange / Institut Synthelabo, Les Empêcheurs de penser en rond, 1993.

[38] H. Arendt, *The Life of the Mind*. One-volume edition, San Diego, New York, London, Harcourt Brace Jovanovich, Inc., 1978.

pure immanence can suddenly induce its dissolvent toppling into the Whole. This is furthermore pointed at by the fact that limited and paradoxical wakefulness live together: there are constant "symbiotic" fluctuations of consciousness-zero between these two close states.

That scale of awareness must correspond to a scale of (sets of) beings—better: events—such as the ones Whitehead's *Process and Reality* has systematically layouted. This complementary scale can only be alluded to here. A thorough examination would show that such a scale is not only a matter of grade (intensity) of events but of complexity of structural craddle. Please carefully notice however that we do not argue for a mere parallelism of the mental and physical spectra—and hence for the existence of a "mystical body" parallel to mystical consciousness. These two scales are not even, properly speaking, complementary: each abstractly displays, from the perspective of the categories that have proven their pragmatic (mesocosmic) worth, one facet of experience taken in its entirety. In other words, the "mystical body" is body and mind, weaved (fusioned) together by their ontological commonness (explicited here with the help of the panexperientialistic hypothesis), and stretched towards higher levels of experience (exactly by virtue of the continuity of levels that is reflected by the two ladders).

5.3. Typology of Philosophies

One could claim that the entire history of philosophy (even Medieval philosophy and, at least to *some* extent, analytic philosophy) is made of "spiritual exercises"[39] aiming at transforming our very existence by an empowering therapy of the soul. Abstract theories and scholarly exegesis matter only if they can inspire a concrete—existential—impact. Either philosophy has an holistic transfigurative virtue, or it is only another of the doxastic lures of our times. Philosophy *qua* hygiology has—has to have—a bright future. No doubt James's works belong here.

This bold claim can be contrasted with a simple criterion: what is the exact status confered, explicitly or not, on consciousness-zero by a given philosopher? Three rough philosophical temperaments could be thereby revealed: some thinkers are exclusively focused on consciousness-zero; some are accepting the possibility (or even the existence) of altered states but don't intend to speculate about these "fringes"; some give a spin to their argument in

---

[39] P. Hadot, *Exercices spirituels et philosophie antique*. 2e éd. rev. et augm. [1981], Paris, Études augustiniennes, 1987.

35

order, not only to explicitly acknowledge the altered states, but to *lure* the reader towards a cosmic consciousness and to actualize its transfigurative virtues. In order that, as Bergson famously concludes, the essential function of the Universe—a machinery to create gods—be achieved.[40] This is why some ancient thoughts like Plotinus' are not only still relevant to our lives but remain as fascinating as James'. "If beauty is not a gateway out of the net we were taken in at our birth, it will no long be beauty."[41]

Reason classes, defines, interprets facts—all conceptual processes that are selective and approximating: the immediate Givenness of the event-in-the-making cannot be fully grasped by regional ontologies. But these are *vital* approximations: James makes it plain that he argues for a monistic pantheism on non-mystical grounds and that he thereby takes an existential risk.[42] It is from that perspective that the puzzling factual correlation of the concepts of God and of immortality in some his writings has to be understood (See VRE524 and 510). Solely the spiritually saturated philosopher *understands* that one has to go beyond the ego-construct and *lives* accordingly. No moral holidays are allowed.

To *live* is *to be religious* (VRE, 500), and yet, the exploration of the transmarginal field has hardly been seriously undertaken (VRE, 511): James diagnosis is still valid for most of the Western philosophical legacy. The

---

[40] "[…] pour que s'accomplisse, jusque sur notre planète réfractaire, la fonction essentielle de l'univers, qui est une machine à fabriquer des dieux." Henri Bergson, *Les Deux Sources de la Morale et de la Religion*.

[41] W.B. Yeats, *The Celtic Twilight. Myth, Fantasy and Folklore* [Texts of 1892 & 1902; First published in 1893], Bridport, Dorset, Prism Press, 1990, p. 55. Compare with VRE, p. 362.

[42] "Those of us who are not personally favored with such specific revelations must stand outside of them altogether and, for the present at least, decide that, since they corroborate incompatible theological doctrines, they neutralize one another and leave no fixed results. If we follow any one of them, or if we follow philosophical theory and embrace monistic pantheism on non-mystical grounds, we do so in the exercise of our individual freedom, and build out our religion in the way most congruous with our personal susceptibilities. Among these susceptibilities intellectual ones play a decisive part. Although the religious question is primarily a question of life, of living or not living in the higher union which opens itself to us as a gift, yet the spiritual excitement in which the gift appears a real one will often fail to be aroused in an individual until certain particular intellectual beliefs or ideas which, as we say, come home to him, are touched. These ideas will thus be essential to that individual's religion;—which is as much as to say that over-beliefs in various directions are absolutely indispensable, and that we should treat them with tenderness and tolerance so long as they are not intolerant themselves. As I have elsewhere written, the most interesting and valuable things about a man are usually his over-beliefs." (VRE, pp. 514-515; See 379)

remaining question might be: how far is this true of the non-Western traditions that have been—until quite recently—traditionally repudiated?

Acategoriality as Mental Instability. A Dynamical Systems Approach to James's Account of Mental Activity.

Harald Atmanspacher* and Wolfgang Fach

1. Introduction

The scientific investigation of mental processes began in the 19th century with the development of the field of psychology, with the work of Fechner, Helmholtz, Wundt and others. Psychological research was mainly carried out in the spirit of an "external perspective", also called "third person perspective". But unlike contemporary practice, the so-called "first person perspective" (introspection) was also regarded as an admissible approach, e.g. by James or Titchener. It was particularly elaborated especially within philosophical phenomenology, e.g. by Bergson, Whitehead, Husserl, and later on by Heidegger or Merleau-Ponty.

The study of mental processes changed significantly in the 1940s, when von Neumann, Turing, and Wiener began to examine the epistemological foundations of the natural sciences. This was done in the spirit of then highly popular positivistic approaches with their rigorous criteria regarding formal description and empirical verification. As far as these epistemological questions are related to the capabilities and limits of cognitive systems, the idea developed quickly that these systems process information in a computer-like way. Chomsky, Minsky, and Simon are seen as protagonists of this idea, which today is subsumed under the term cognitivism and can be regarded as a precursor of contemporary, highly diversified cognitive sciences.

The conception that cognitive systems are responsible for the internal processing of information representing external reality has been criticized as too simple in many respects.[1] First, the relation between internal mental representations and elements of an external reality is not at all unidirectional, but bidirectional. In addition to the realistic (sensualistic, bottom-up) component of this relation, there is a constructivistic (top-down) component,

---

[1] See F. Varela, *Kognitionswissenschaft – Kognitionstechnik*, Suhrkamp, Frankfurt. 1990.

39

which can be massively influential in particular situations.[2] Second, it is difficult to cover more than purely syntactic aspects of information processing using the computer metaphor alone. Aspects of meaning and its conversion into action require more involved approaches, if it is not assumed that semantics follows from syntax "automatically", as it were.[3]

Cognitivism has become a strong direction for the investigation of cognitive processes, but there were and are alternative views. Already at the end of the 19th century, James pointed out that, in addition to mental representations ("substantive states") themselves, transient states between them ("transitive states") are crucial. The two kinds of states differ in their different pace of change:

"When the rate [of change of a subjective state] is slow we are aware of the object of our thought in a comparatively restful and stable way. When rapid, we are aware of a passage, a relation, a transition *from* it, or *between* it and something else. ... *Let us call the resting-places the 'substantive parts', and the places of flight the 'transitive parts', of the stream of thought.* It then appears that the main end of our thinking is at all times the attainment of some other subjective part than the one from which we have just been dislodged. And we may say that the main use of the transitive parts is to lead from one substantive conclusion to another."[4]

Although current cognitive science hardly considers transient states, several authors revitalized the antinomy of "substantive parts" and "transitive parts" and related it to James' terms of the "nucleus" and the "fringe" of a mental state. states play a crucial role in meditation techniques and spiritual conceptions, especially in Eastern cultures.[5] In addition, transient states could achieve paramount significance for the investigation of so-called altered (anomalous) states of consciousness. [6] Moreover, it is evident that each transition between two mental representations requires a process passing through transient states that are located in between. Jean Gebser, a Swiss philosopher whose work emphasized the development of structures of consciousness, suggested the term "acategoriality" to characterize such

[2] See H. Emrich, *Psychiatrische Anthropologie*, Pfeiffer, München. 1990.
[3] See H. Atmanspacher, *Die Vernunft der Metis*, Metzler, Stuttgart, 1993.
[4] W. James, *Principles of Psychology*, Vol. 1, Dover, New York, 1950, p. 243
[5] See B.A. Wallace, *The Bridge of Quiescence*. Open Court, Chicago, 1998.
[6] See E. Taylor, *William James on Exceptional Mental States*. University of Massachusetts Press, Amherst. 1998.

transitive states. In his own words:

"Every categorial system is an idealized ordering schema by which actual phenomena are fixed and absolutized; as such it is a three-dimensional framework with a static and spatial character. Such categorial systems are able to deal with the world only within a three-dimensional and conceptual world-view. We shall have to be accustomed to recognizing acategorical elements ... Wherever we are able to perceive acategorial effectualities as such and not as categorial fixities, the world will become transparent."[7]

This programmatic quote makes clear that Gebser's concept of *acategoriality* aims at a description of states of consciousness beyond usual categorial representations. Unfortunately, an integration of Gebser's description of acategorial states into the relevant sciences is not trivial at all. His description is conceived rather heuristic and often too abstract to be easily translated into scientific terminology. The present contribution tries to enable such a translation and to relate it to results of modern cognitive and neurosciences. The conceptual framework is adopted from the theory of dynamical systems, whose influence on models of cognitive processes has considerably increased within the last 20years.[8] The stability (resp. instability) of dynamical systems is the key concept utilizedin this framework. Our central argument is that instabilities in mental systems possess a number of characteristic features which are related to Gebsers' acategorial states.

In order to make this relation more explicit, it will be briefly reviewed how stability properties are treated in dynamical systems. The corresponding formalism will then be used to describe ("metaphorically") the stability or instability of mental states. The merits of such a description—especially with respect to a precise terminology and a classification of different mental states— will be demonstrated. Subsequently, experimental results deriving from psychological and neurophysiological studies concerning unstable aspects of perception will be presented. Finally, phenomenological aspects of acategorial and unstable states will be discussed.

---

[7] J. Gebser, *The Ever-Present Origin*, Ohio Univesity Press, Athens, Ohio, 1986, p. 285-286.
[8] See W.J. Freeman, *Societies of Brains*, Lawrence Erlbaum, Hillsdale, 1995; J.S. Nicolis J.S., *Chaotic Information Processing*, World Scientific, Singapore, 1991.

41

2. Stability properties of dynamical systems

For the purpose of this contribution it is sufficient to discuss the stability of dynamical systems evolving continously as a function of time $t \in$ R. A particularly simple class of such systems can be described by ordinary differential equations of first order:

$$dx/dt = F(x(t); \eta) \qquad (1)$$

Here, $x = (x_1, ..., x_n)$ is the state of the system, represented by the observables $x_1, ..., x_n$, which, at the same time, are the axes of the n-dimensional state space. The matrix F contains the (generally nonlinear) coupling between the observables. The trajectory of the state of the system in the state space is described by the function t → $x(t)$, and η is a control parameter, which can be used to control of the behavior of the system externally.

The stability of the system (1) concerning small perturbations or fluctuations dx with respect to a reference state x_r can be analyzed by a so-called stability analysis. The relevant literature offers detailed explanation about how to proceed.[9] The result of the stability analysis are numerical values Λ_i ($i = 1, ...,$ n), indicating to which extent fluctuations vary as a function of time t:

$$dx_i(t) = \Lambda_i \, dx_i (0) \qquad (2)$$

It should be pointed out that the values of Λ_i in general depend on the reference state x_r, thus differing along a trajectory $x(t)$. Fluctuations are damped, if $\Lambda_i < 1$; they are amplified, if $\Lambda_i > 1$; for $\Lambda = 1$ they remain unchanged. In order to extend the local statement of a stability analysis, one can consider the temporal mean value of Λ_i, leading to the so-called Ljapunov exponents:

$$\lambda_i = \lim_{T \to \infty} \int_0^T \log |\Lambda_i(t)| dt. \qquad (3)$$

---

[9] See J. Guckenheimer and P. Holmes P., *Nonlinear Oscillations, Dynamical Systems, and Bifurcations of Vector Fields*, Springer, Berlin, 1983; R.W. Leven, B.-P. Koch, , and B. Pompe, *Chaos in dissipativen Systemen*, Akademie, Berlin,1994.

The Ljapunov exponents describe the average change of fluctuations along the trajectory x(t) according to

$$dx_i(t) \approx dx_i(0) \exp \lambda_i t. \qquad (4)$$

Positive values of λ thus indicate an exponential growth of fluctuations, whereas negative values indicate that they are damped exponentially. The sum of all Ljapunov exponents is smaller than zero for dissipative systems and equal to zero for conservative systems. In the dissipative case there exists a subspace of the state space, onto which the trajectory of the system is restricted (after an initial "transient" phase). This subspace is called the attractor of the system. Another subspace, which is constituted by all those (initial) states asymptotically evolving into the attractor, is called the basin of attraction. For a given attractor, the Ljapunov exponents are independent of the initial conditions. Moreover, they are invariant with respect to continuous transformations of the observables representing the axes of the state space.

In the simplest case, an attractor is a point in state space ("fixed point"), such that all λ_i are negative. If there is no other attractor in the state space, the entire (admissible) state space is the corresponding basin of attraction. Particularly interesting (and complicated) are situations in which the sum of all λ_i is negative, yet individual λ_i are positive. In this case one speaks of strange attractors or chaotic attractors. The behavior of a corresponding system is "chaotic", although it obeys deterministic equations of the form (1).

The stability of attractors can be studied *qualitatively* using a method also introduced by Ljapunov (see Alligood et al. 1996, Chap. 7.6). In order to do so, a function $V = V(\mathbf{x}) > 0$ or $V(\mathbf{x}) = 0$ is considered in a neighborhood G of a reference state $\mathbf{x_r}$, where $V = 0$ for $x = \mathbf{x_r}$. The temporal derivative of V, dV/dt, describes the temporal change of V along the trajectory $\mathbf{x}(t)$ in G. It is obtained from:

$$\frac{dV}{dt} = \sum_j \frac{\partial V}{\partial x_j} \frac{\partial x_j}{\partial t} = \mathbf{F} \nabla V \qquad (5)$$

Intuitively, the significance of V is that of a potential, whose extremal properties in G determine the stability of a state.

1. A state $\mathbf{x_r}$ is stable, if $dV/dt = 0$ or $dV/dt < 0$ in G. In this case, V is called a Ljapunov function.

(a) A state x_r is asymptotically stable if $dV/dt < 0$ in G (except at x_r itself).

(b) A state x_r is marginally stable if $dV/dt = 0$ everywhere in G.

2. A state x_r is unstable, if $dV/dt > 0$ in G.

In the simplest case of a fixed point attractor in one dimension, Fig. 1a illustrates case 1a for a quadratic potential $V(x) = \alpha x^2$, $\alpha > 0$, which is concave in the neighborhood of x_r ($\nabla^2 V > 0$). The solution x_r at the minimum of V is an asymptotically stable fixed point with one negative Ljapunov exponent, whose value corresponds to ∇V, the gradient of V. In case 1b, the gradient of the potential vanishes ($\nabla V = 0$), and each solution for this potential is marginally stable (Fig. 1b). This corresponds to a Ljapunov exponent which vanishes as well.

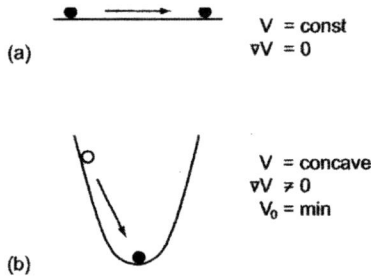

(a)   V = const
       ∇V = 0

(b)   V = concave
       ∇V ≠ 0
       V_0 = min

Fig. 1: Kinds of stability of a state: (a) marginal stability for a constant potential V with gradient $\nabla V = 0$; (b) asymptotic stability at a critical point V_o of a concave potential with a non-vanishing gradient $\nabla V \neq 0$.

A combination of case 2 with case 1a is illustrated in Fig. 2. In the neighborhood of x_r, at the local maximum, V is convex ($\nabla^2 V < 0$), whereas V is concave around the potential minima. The solution at the local maximum is therefore unstable. If the system is in such a state, it will spontaneously relax into one of the two asymptotically stable minima. During this relaxation, the potential difference ΔV will be converted into the motion of the state. The regions left and right of the local maximum are basins of attraction for two coexisting attractors. (For potentials with more than one independent variable, V_1 is usually a saddle rather than a local maximum.)

44

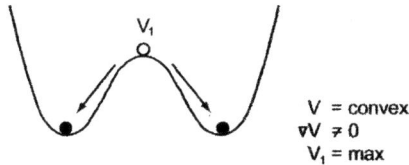

$V = $ convex
$\nabla V \neq 0$
$V_1 = $ max

Fig. 2: States in the neighborhood of a critical point V_1 of a locally convex potential are unstable and relax into adjacent potential minima.

3. Stability properties of mental states

In recent years there has been a steady trend to describe the behavior of neural networks resp. cognitive systems in terms of nonlinear dynamical systems.[10] Applications extend as far as into psychological therapies.[11] Freeman (1979) was the first to introduce corresponding approaches in neurophysiology, and only a little later Nicolis proposed a related description of cognitive processes.[12]

The central idea (cf. Nicolis 1991) is that internal mental representations, the basic "objects" of a cognitive system, play the role of "attractors" for neurally encoded external stimuli.[13] The relation between the description of cognitive systems and the formal theory of dynamical systems can basically be characterized by three points:

---

[10] K. Kaneko and I. Tsuda, *Complex Systems: Chaos and Beyond*, Springer, Berlin, 2000; H. Haken and M. Stadler (eds.), *Synergetics of Cognition, Springer*, Berlin, 1990.

[11] K. Grawe, *Psychologische Therapie*, Hogrefe, Göttingen, 1998, pp. 453–526; F. Caspar, "Ätiologie und Therapie psychischer St¨orungen aus der Sicht eines integrativen Modells", *Lehrbuch der Psychotherapie und psychosomatischen Medizin*. (Edited by S. Ahrens and W. Schneider), Schattauer, Stuttgart, 2002, pp. 569–580.

[12] For more recent accounts see Beer R.D., "Dynamical approaches to cognitive science". *Trends in Cognitive Sciences* 4, 91–99; Fell J., "Identifying neural correlates of consciousness: The state space approach". *Consciousness and Cognition* 13, 709–729; Tsuda I. (2001): "Toward an interpretation of dynamic neural activity in terms of chaotic dynamical systems". *Behavioral and Brain Sciences* 24, 793–847; van Gelder T.(1998): "The dynamical hypothesis in cognitive science". *Behavioral and Brain Sciences* 21, 615–661.

[13] Nicolis, cit.

45

1. The cognitive system, which is materially realized by a neural network, is treated as a dynamical system S.

2. Mental representations within the cognitive system are treated as co-existing attractors of S with particular stability properties.

3. Neurally encoded stimuli within the cognitive system are treated as initial conditions of S, whose temporal evolution leads to an attractor.

In this scenario, the creation and/or evolution of mental representations remains unconsidered so far. Moreover, the state space in which the dynamics evolves, often remains undefined or is not even addressed. Eventually, it should be mentioned that mental and material states and properties, resp., of a system need not be identical a priori. Therefore, many approaches are based on assumed but poorly understood correlations between the two.

Cognitive processes which are represented by the mapping of a stimulus onto a mental representation can be illustrated by the motion of a state in a potential. The form of the potential then characterizes the stability properties which the possible states of the considered system can have. The states themselves and their associated observables can be conceived in two basically different ways. One can consider both states of "consciousness", or of the mental/cognitive system, and states of the material/neural system correlated with them.

The subsequent discussion focuses on the former option, so that the notion of "state" refers to a state ϕ of the mental system (which can be conscious or unconscious). The state space remains unspecified insofar as no (canonical) formalization of mental observables is available so far. Furthermore, the exact form of the dynamics of states ϕ remains unspecified insofar as no corresponding equations of motion are known. And, finally, the significance of the potential V, which is often (e.g., in physics) related to the concept of energy, remains undefined. To what extent mental systems can have "mental energy" is an unresolved matter.[14] Given these limitations, the following deliberations should be understood as a formal framework which has to be both specified and concretized.

---

[14] For an historical perspective, see Y. Elkana, *The Discovery of the Conservation of Energy*, Harvard UP, Cambridge (Mass), 1974. See also Y. Elkana, "Helmholtz's Kraft: eine Betrachtung über fließende Begriffe". In *Anthropologie der Erkenntnis*, Suhrkamp, Frankfurt, 1986, S. 125–157, and Y. Elkana, "Die Entlehnung des Energiebegriffs" in *Freudschen Psychoanalyse*, im gleichen Band, S. 376–397.

3.1. Mental representations and stable categorial states

It is mandatory to distinguish potentials V and states ϕ if one wants to utilize the theory of dynamical systems for the description of mental systems. A state ϕ can be anywhere on a potential (hyper-)surface. Stability is a property of a state ϕ on a potential surface, not a property of a potential V. This means that mental representations regarded as attractors or potentials provide boundary conditions for the motion of a mental state $\phi(t)$ as a function of time. If a mental state is located in the minimum of a potential (i.e. on an attractor), the corresponding mental representation is "activated" or "actualized". In psychological terms, "one thinks something", "has a picture of something", or one feels or anticipates something. If the mental state is located in a particular mental representation, it is (asymptotically) stable with respect to perurbations (compare Fig. 1a).

The measure of stabilitiy can be quantified, e.g., by Ljapunov exponents. Representations with shallow potential minima stabilize mental states less than those with deep potential minima. Accordingly, less or more effort is necessary for a mental state to "leave" a particular representation. If this happens, the corresponding mental representation may be considered as "deactivated" or "potentialized".

However, not only states can be temporally modified, $\phi = \phi(t)$, but also the potential surface $V = V(t)$ can evolve. Not only can the dynamics of a state activate or deactivate an already existing mental representation, but new representations can be generated or existing ones can be altered as well. New representations are created when the mental system generates new potentials; old representations are changed when the corresponding potentials are deformed. Interesting parallels to this differentiation, which will be discussed later on in more detail, can be found in psychological applications of process philosophy, in particular according to Whitehead (Brown 2000).[15]

It should be pointed out again that the illustration in Fig. 1a refers to an especially simple special case, a caricature as it were. It is to be expected that mental representations are not limited to fixed point attractors or limit cycles (periodic processes), but in general correspond to chaotic attractors. Asymptotically stable states according to Fig. 1a are those states which Gebser called categorial. Their stability indicates what he denoted as a fixation of a static world of concepts. Gebser's categorial states correspond to James' stable, substantive states.

---

[15] See J.W. Brown, *Mind and Nature*, Whurr, London, 2000.

The case of marginal stabilty of ϕ illustrated in Fig. 1b characterizes the limiting case in which V vanishes or is constant anywhere in the neighborhood of a state ϕ. This case can be psychologically interpreted as an "unbounded" state which "goes without thinking", a kind of content-free state referring to nothing. In this respect one can speak of a non-categorial state. Smallest perturbations, which are neither damped nor amplified, will cause ϕ to move.

The process of a deactivation of a mental representation means that the state $\phi(t)$ has to be changed to such an extent that it leaves not only the attractor but also the basin of attraction of V, and moves towards another attractor where it finally arrives. A corresponding dynamics of ϕ necessarily exceeds the conceptual repertoire of mental representations, stable categories and substantive states.

3.2. Mental instabilities and acategorial states

Insofar as mental representations are asymptotically stable, a transition between them is possible only via an unstable intermediate state. Fig. 2 illustrates this situation. To effect the transition, $\phi(t)$ has to overcome the potential barrier ΔV. (As an alternative one could think of quantum mechanical processes, so-called tunneling processes, whose realization in the brain is discussed controversially, however.) The stronger the stability of the involved representations, the smaller is the probability of a spontaneous transition. A particularly illustrative and frequently studied class of processes with such transitions is the perception of bi-or multistable stimuli (see e.g. Kruse and Stadler 1995).[16]

Moreover, the attribution of meaning is a crucial issue requiring changes of the state ϕ. So-called "aha-experiences" in particular are obviously related to changes between representations or with the emergence of novel representations (Atmanspacher 1992).[17]

---

[16] See P. Kruse and M. Stadler (eds.), *Ambiguity in Mind and Nature,* Springer, Berlin, 1995.
[17] H. Atmanspacher, "Categoreal and acategoreal representation of knowledge", *Cognitive Systems* 3,1992, pp. 259–288.

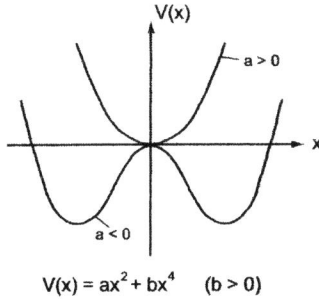

$$V(x) = ax^2 + bx^4 \quad (b > 0)$$

Fig. 3: Deformation of a potential $(a > 0)$, whose minimum becomes a local maximum $(a < 0)$ with two new minima evolving in addition. A state in the new potential relaxes from the formerly stable solution at $x = 0$ into one of the two new stable solutions. Since only one of the two symmetric solutions can be chosen, this is called a symmetry breaking.

This does not only require a change of ϕ, but also a change of the potential surface V. For instance, it can be expected that the depth of existing potential minima increases in learning processes. This would mean that with increasing α in a potential $V = \alpha x^2$ the stability of a state increases. If α goes to zero, the gradient of the potential goes to zero, too, and the limiting case of marginal stability is obtained.

Another possibility consists in the differentiation of existing representations, where a potential with a minimum is deformed in such a way that two minima are generated. Such a kind of symmetry breaking can be described by changing the parameter α from positive to negative values in a potential $V = \alpha x^2 + \beta x^4$ $(\beta > 0)$, where the case $\alpha > 0$ is qualitatively similar to the quadratic one-minimum potential (Fig. 3). Conversely, one could think of the integration of representations by changing α from a given negative value until it becomes positive.

In James' terminology, the process leading from one to another "substantive" state corresponds to a temporal sequence of "transitive" states. The unstable point at V_1 in Fig. 2 is a "transitive" state distinguished by a local maximum of V. James writes:

"Now it is very difficult, introspectively, to see the transitive parts as what they really are. If they are but flights to a conclusion, stopping them to look at them before the conclusion is reached is really annihilating them. Whilst if we wait till the conclusion be reached, it so exceeds them in vigor and stability that it quite eclipses and swallows them up in its glare. Let anyone try to cut a thought across in the middle and get a look at its section, and he will see how difficult the introspective observation of the transitive acts is. ... The results of this introspective difficulty are baleful. If to hold fast and observe the transitive parts of thought's stream be so hard, then the great blunder to which all schools are liable must be the failure to register them, and the undue emphasizing of the more substantive parts of the stream."[18]

Gebser addresses transitive states at a local maximum of V with his concept of acategoriality and emphasizes their temporal, dynamical aspect (Gebser 1986, p. 308):

"Something with a temporal character cannot be spatially fixed. It cannot be fixed or prescribed in any form, and if we attempt to do so we change it by measurement into a spatial quantity and rob it of its true character. This is a clear indication that the qualities of time which are today pressing toward awareness cannot be expressed in mere categorial systems."[19]

These mentioned "unfixable temporal qualities" can – in a more prosaic way – be related to the evasive, transient behavior of complex systems around instabilities. This situation is not governed by the equations of motion describing the system on its attractor. As a consequence, the trajectory of a system in the vicinity of instabilities cannot be predicted by its equations of motion.

4. Experimental material

Distinguishing mental representations (in V) and mental states ϕ from each other offers the possibility to treat both, V and ϕ, and their dynamics, V(t)and ϕ(t), separate from each other. Of course, this does not imply that V and ϕ are ultimately independent from each other; however, their differentiation allows us to explicitly describe potential interdependencies of V and ϕ. In the following sections we will outline some paradigmatic results whose interpretation is based on the motion of a mental state ϕ in different potentials

---

[19] J. Gebser, cit., p. 308.

V. We disregard the problem how a coupling of ϕ (t)with *V*(t) could be implemented.

4.1. Psychological results: Binocular depth inversion

For several decades, Emrich and coworkers have been studying perceptive illusions which can be modeled using the approach discussed above.[20] Emrich's original idea was to demonstrate that, in addition to a "sensualistic" (bottom-up) and a "constructivistic" (top-down) component in the process of perception, a so-called censor has to be considered as a third element. This censor defines the interplay between the other two components and hereby moderates the "illusory extent" of a perceptive act.[21]

As an experimental paradigm for corresponding results the method of binocular depth inversion was applied, which generates a particular variant of a visual perceptive illusion. Objects whose plausibility differs depending on different orientations, e.g. ordinary masks versus inverted masks, are shown to subjects. Properly illuminated, inverted masks (nose backward) are not recognized appropriately by normal subjects, but they are interpreted as ordinary masks (nose forward). The corresponding effect of illusion is an example for censoring as mentioned above. Since hollow masks usually do not occur in everyday life, the mental system tends to ignore any evidence that the masks appear not as ordinary masks, and maps the stimulus onto the representation of an ordinary mask.

Additional interesting observations have been made by Leweke and others. They reported that the censor is weakened if subjects are under the influence of psychoactive cannabinoids,[22] so that hollow masks indeed are recognized as what they are. A related study with schizophrenic patients provided similar results. It seems that schizophrenia implies a malfunction of the censoring activity which facilitates the identification of the inverted masks.[23]

---

[20] See H. Emrich, cit.
[21] H.M. Emrich, "A three-component-system hypothesis of psychosis. Impairment of binocular depth inversion as an indicator of a functional disequilibrium". *British Journal of Psychiatry* 155, 1989, S37–S39.
[22] F.M. Leweke, U. Schneider, M. Radwan, E. Schmidt, and H.M. Emrich, "Different effects of nabilone and cannabidiol on binocular depth inversion in man", *Pharmacology Biochemistry and Behavior* 66, 2000, pp. 175–181.
[23] U. Schneider, M. Borsutzky, J. Seifert, F.M. Leweke, T.J. Huber, J.D. Rollnik, and H.M. Emrich, "Reduced binocular depth inversion in schizophrenic patients", *Schizophrenia Research* 53, 2002, pp. 101–108.

Within the approach proposed here, the censor can be easily understood by the stability properties of the mental states which are involved in the contributing mental representations. Obviously, both the influence of cannabinoids and specific processes in schizophrenia seem to imply that the potential differences distinguishing existing categories (mental representations) decrease. Thus, the basin of attraction of the implausible (inverted mask) representation is increased. Small alterations due to the switch of the stimulus from ordinary mask to inverted mask are no longer damped out within the plausible (ordinary mask) representation, but can lead to a switch of the representation.

In this way, the censor component is naturally integrated into the picture and, at the same time, acquires direct explanatory potential. The censor is strong, if the involved potentials are deep and the corresponding states are stable; which can happen as a result of learning or habituation processes. By contrast, the censor is weak, if the potentials are flat and the corresponding states tend to be marginally stable, e.g. at the beginning of a learning process or with blurring memory. (The interesting link to memory structures resp. processes becomes apparent here, but will not be further elaborated here.)

[24]Within this interpretational framework for the censor function, the change of V is primarily considered and determines the dynamics of mental states ϕ. At the physiological level, such a change should be accompanied by a change of the connectivities in the neural assemblies involved, thus implying that categories become hardly distinguishable from each other or almost disappear, respectively. In the experiments described, this is caused by exogeneous influences (cannabinoids) and long-time endogeneous (disease-induced) influences, resp.

4.2. Physiological results: Perception of bistable stimuli

A situation in which the dynamics of ϕ operates on a time scale different from the depth inversion paradigm is the perception of bistable stimuli. Here, the dynamics $\phi(t)$ is coupled to a fast dynamics $V(t)$. Moreover, $\phi(t)$ is influenced by fluctuations which can be significant, especially around instabilities, for the behavior of the system.

---

[24] An interesting link to memory structures (resp. processes) can be found here, but it cannot be developed in this article.

A standard example for a bistable stimulus is the Necker cube. Compared to other stimuli with higher complexity, its semantic content is essentially limited to 3-D interpretation. This has the advantage that the cognitive processes during the perception of the Necker cube can be considered as fairly basic. The two perspectives, under which the Necker cube can be perceived, constitute two mental representations, thus two potential minima V. The state ϕ evolves spontaneously from one potential minimum into the other after a few seconds (Borsellino et al. 1972).[25]

In James' terminology, this situation corresponds to two substantive states, between which the transitive domain is located. The Necker cube example shows illustratively that the difficulty of an introspective perception of this transitive domain is due to the fact that transiency is tied to instability. Intuitively, one would assume that the unstable situation must somehow be stabilized to be introspectively accessible, or any introspective access must refer to a completely different mode, e.g. some dynamical instead of structural aspect of "representation". This, however, is speculation so far.

Less speculative is the question for a neural correlate of the perceptual reversal. Two types of correlates that have often been reported are 40Hz (γ-band) oscillations in the EEG as well as the often observed P300 component, a positivity at around 300 msec, in event related potentials. Both correlates, however, are not specific for the reversal process itself, but rather accompany many mental processes requiring attention.

Recently, an early negativity at about 250msec was found as a highly specific correlate for the reversal process for ambiguous stimuli using a modified experimental setup.[26] The evidence of this result was supported by the fact that another negativity at about 200msec was observed for the switch between two different, externally presented non-ambiguous perspectives of the Necker cube. The time difference of 50msec indicates that exogeneously induced reversals are processed faster than endogeneous reversal, which (e.g., due to endogeneous 3-D interpretation) requires additional top-down mechanisms.

Such endogeneous, "constructivistic" components of perception complement the naive-realistic ("sensualistic") idea that perception (only) refers to exogeneously occuring events. The discussed results show that differences

---

[25] A. Borsellino, A. de Marco, A. Alazetta, S. Rinesi, and R. Bartolini, "Reversal time distribution in the perception of visual ambiguous stimuli", *Kybernetik* 10, 1972, pp. 139–144.

[26] J. Kornmeier, M. Bach, and H. Atmanspacher, "Correlates of perceptive instabilities in event-related potentials", *International Journal of Bifurcation and Chaos*, 2003.

between the perception of endogeneous and exogeneously induced reversals concerning almost the same stimulus can be empirically demonstrated. Although both "constructivistic" and "realistic" elements play a role in both variants, their relative contribution differs: the processing of ambiguous, bistable stimuli requires more top-down processing than the processing of successive non-ambiguous stimuli.

5. On the phenomenology of acategorial mental states

5.1. Non-categorial and acategorial states

As an alternative to asymptotically stable representations and corresponding categorial states, the criterion of stability provides two additional options. One of them is the limiting case of a flat potential V with vanishing gradient, where no stable categories exist and mental states are marginally stable. This means that states ϕ are displaced by arbitrarily small perturbations or fluctuations. Asymptotically stable behavior as required for a reliable representation of categories does not occur in this situation—states ϕ are *non-categorial*.

The second option refers to the unstable regions between asymptotically stable representations. Such a situation presupposes the existence of categories. However, the state ϕ of the mental system does not actualize one of these categories but something "in between" them. If the state ϕ is located in the neighbourhood of an instability, it will move towards one of the neighbouring minima under the influence of the corresponding potential valley.

Following Gebser's conception, a mental state in the (close) neighborhood of an instability of V is called *acategorial*. In James' terminology one would speak of "fringe consciousness", if a non-dynamic, structural conception is preferred. From a dynamical point of view, states in the neighbourhood of instabilities are "transitive" states. Without external influence, they move spontaneously into "substantive" states in stable categories. The duration of this motion is determined by the stability properties of these categories.

An essential difference between non-categorial and acategorial states consists in their fundamentally different location within V. Interpreting different values of V in a wide sense and provisional with respect to an adequate definition as a kind of "psychic energy" (e.g. as an attentional effort), acategorial states are always "energetically excited" and they "relax spontaneously" if this not explicitly prevented. By contrast, non-categorial states are "energetically neutral" insofar as marginal stability offers no "energy differences" in the neighborhood of any considered state. What could prevent the evasiveness of acategorial states due to their spontaneous relaxation? First, there is the option to balance the relaxation dynamics $\phi(t)$ with an externally controlled dynamics $V(t)$, thus permanently readjusting the potential V with respect to the motion of the state ϕ. At the neuronal level this would mean that the connectivity matrix of the neuronal assemblies defining V would have to be adapted to the dynamics of ϕ with an extremely fine tuning. Such a strategy could be understood analogous to the balancing acts of an "equilibrium artist", in terms of a kind of "mental acrobatics".

Under particular circumstances, a second possibility is to stabilize locally unstable parts of a neuronal assembly by their global coupling. Atmanspacher and Wiedenmann proposed this idea which has recently been worked out concretely by Atmanspacher and Scheingraber.[27] Its essence is that stabilization in this setting operates inherently and without any need for external control.

Non-categorial and acategorial states have in common that neither of them actualizes representations in a traditional sense. It is unclear which cognitive content can be perceived if these states can be sustained long enough to enable the emergence of a phenomenally experienced perception. It is likely that this cannot happen in an ordinary state of consciousness but requires the training of special degrees of awareness.

Methods for a systematic generation of corresponding altered states of awareness play a central role in the spiritual traditions of Eastern cultures. An outstanding example is the Buddhist Satipatthana-Sutta, lectures on the "foundations of mindfulness", dating back to the first[28] century BC. They present detailed instructions for the perception of increasingly subtle objects of phenomenal experience. Starting with the perception of the body and its autonomous functions (e.g. respiration), progressive training expands awareness to emotional states and mental processes including those constituting the perceiving subject. This demands that the awareness does not adhere to any object of perception. In other words, such awareness does not refer to stable

---

[27] H. Atmanspacher and G. Wiedenmann, "Some basic problems with complex systems", *Large Scale Systems: Theory and Applications*. (Edited by N.T. Koussoulas and P. Groumpos), Elsevier, Amsterdam, 1999, pp. 1059–1066; H. Atmanspacher and H. Scheingraber H., "Inherent global stabilization of unstable local behavior in coupled map lattices". (*Submitted* 2003)

[28] Nyanaponika, *Geistestraining durch Achtsamkeit*, Beyerlein & Steinschulte, Stammbach. 2000, see also P. Gäng, *Was ist Buddhismus?*, Campus, Frankfurt, 1996.

categorial states:

"The practice of pure attention will bring it forcibly home that change is always with us; that even in a minute fraction of time the frequency of occurring changes is beyond our ken. Probably for the first time it will strike us in what kind of world we are actually living, namely its exclusively dynamical nature, within which static notions can only be meaningful for practical orientation or scientific and philosophical ordering schemes."[29]

The similarity of this quotation with Gebser's characterization of acategoriality (cf. Sec. 1) is striking. Due to the significant conceptual differences between non-categorial and acategorial states, important differences in their phenomenal perception are to be expected. This is reflected by a heuristic model developed in a clinical-therapeutic context by Petzold.[30] Starting from the ordinary receptive and reflexive awareness in the (categorial) wake state, altered processes of consciousness are described in two directions, either with a decreasing or an increasing reflexivity of the associated cognitive operations. Petzold proposes a spectrum of consciousness, extending from an "areflexive" consciousness (quasi noncategorial "unconscious" in the terminology of this contribution) over increasingly reflexive categorial states up to acategorial hyper-and transreflexive states. These different states are accompanied by different qualities of experience in tinge, lucidity, intensity and range.

A regression, which can be induced by body therapies,[31] can lead to a decreasing role of reflexive thinking and to associative, increasingly pictorial experiences with growing involvement of emotions and autonomous physiological functions. In the limiting case of areflexive unconsciousness, a bodily centering is achieved without a representation of the subject separated from its physiological functions. This process corresponds to a temporary regression of the functions of the mental system which develops an ego-representation with increasing category formation and conceptual thinking only during its ontogenetic evolution. The "subsidence" into the bodily, which is connected with the gradual loss of the eccentric observer distance, is connected with experiential qualities such as "dark", "deep", "diffuse" for the individual

---

[29] Nyanaponika, cit., p. 34.
[30] H.G. Petzold, Integrative *Therapie. Schriften zu Theorie, Methodik und Praxis* Bd. II/1, Junfermann, Paderborn, 1993, pp. 248–270.
[31] Cfr. H.G. Petzold, *Integrative Bewegungs-und Leibtherapie. Schriften zu Theorie, Methodik und Praxis* Bd. I/1, Junfermann, Paderborn. 1996, pp. 104–110)

concerned. Petzold distinguishes such a non-categorial "experience of unity", from states of "hyperreflexive lucid consciousness" in which usually drawn distinctions are lifted without obfuscated consciousness or lost categorial differentiation:

"Here, centricity and excentricity do not fall apart, subject-object distinctions are overcome—an *integral consciousness*, which nevertheless does not abandon complexity or level differences."[32]

States of lucid consciousness occur together with creative activity and contemplative practice, but also spontaneously in other situations. They are associated with creative inspiration, existential insight, and experiences of wholeness or religious content. They can lead as far as to the limits of a trans-reflexive "nothing-consciousness", to experiences of void as they are addressed in Eastern spiritual traditions. States of lucid consciousness are comparatively rare and of short duration, hence unstable. They are described as "bright", "clear", "high" and are distinguished by a strong experience of evidence. The characteristics of lucid consciousness suggest an acategorial scenario which must not be confused with the non-categoriality of unconscious states:

"As far as hyperreflexive lucid consciousness is concerned, two possible misunderstandings must be dispelled: identifying lucid consciousness (or nothing-consciousness) with the *unconscious* [...] as well as relating lucid consciousness to an interior orientation. [...] It is precisely lucid consciousness, as an immersion into the milieu of the body and, thus, into the lifeworld, which lifts the opposition of inside and outside. As the Buddhist teachers do not get tired to indicate, lucid consciousness in the sense of *mindfulness* is intended, not drifting away into trance-like depths."[33]

5.2 The category of the first person singular

The category of the first person singular, the "I" or "ego", can be regarded as one of the most basic mental representations. Although it is not given a priori, it seems that its generation and development over time is something like an anthropological constant – even if the very complex manifestations of an ego are everything else than uniform. Among the extensive body of literature

---

[32] H.G. Petzold 1993, cit., p. 261.
[33] Ivi, p. 260–261)

on this topic we refer to Metzinger (2003),[34] who speaks of a self-model in this context.

The stability properties of the ego category are crucial for the continuous maintenance of the perception of one's own identity. In this context, the distinction between two different modes is essential, in which deviations from a stable ego are possible. Both the destabilization of the category, hence a flattening of the potential V, and the dynamics of the mental state ϕ out of a (more or less) stable category can lead to such deviations.

The varieties of altered states of consciousness constitute rich material which can be used to illustrate this distinction empirically. A flattening of the potential would correspond to a regression into ontogenetically earlier levels of the categorial differentiation and integration of mental representations. Therefore, it leads inevitably to a diminished stability of the ego representation – in the limiting case as far as to the borders of non-categoriality.

However, a destabilization of the ego category can also be triggered by dissociative processes. Dissociation can be regarded as a concept generalizing different variants within the wide range between loosening the context among categories and, ultimately, their dissolution. Different[35] from regression, where levels of differentiation and integration are both diminished, differentiated partial categories of the mental system are conserved in dissociation. Due to impaired integration efforts, they only loose their context by becoming decoupled from more complex categories to which they originally belong. The dissociation of different ego categories in multiple personality disorders can therefore be understood as the disintegration of an originally stable ego category as a whole into partial categories which are stable and between which transitions of the mental state f are possible. As a result, different ego categories can emerge, which are not necessarily linked to each other consciously.

Following the results by Schneider and others[36], it can be assumed that schizophrenic symptoms fall into the same class of destabilized potentials and are conditioned by the loss of integrative functions. From the point of view of the dissociation model, schizophrenia is the most extreme form of pathological dissociation. In limiting cases, the category of the ego can become entirely fragmented. Metzinger describes a number of further kinds of ego impairments

---

[34] T. Metzinger, *Being No One*, MIT Press, Cambridge, (Mass.), 2003.
[35] C. Scharfetter, *Dissoziation, Split, Fragmentation*, Huber, Bern. 1999, p. 52.
[36] U. Schneider and oths. cit.

such as neglects, anosognosia and obsessions, up to mystical experiences. [37]
With particular regard to mystical experiences, the concept of acategorial states as a conceptual alternative to non-categorial scenarios such as regression, schizophrenia and depersonalization is an interesting option. Descriptions of mystical experiences show a phenomenology which, if taken together, differs from the mentioned psychic disorders. Stace elaborated some elementary features based on sources of most different mystical traditions:

1. No separated physical and mental objects are represented; rather, a "pure",
"void", or "unified" conscious state emerges.
2. Spatial and temporal localization are lifted.
3. The experience has real and objective character.
4. It is accompanied by an intense emotion of peace, joy, bliss, and blessedness.
5. It is experienced as contact with something "sacred", "divine" or "absolute".
6. Fundamental opposites appear as unified, the laws of logic as abolished, and
normal intellectual functions as replaced by a "higher" mode.
7. The experience cannot be communicated in conventional language. [38]

Ego alterations corresponding to acategorial mental states are assumed not to lead to a dissolution of the ego category. This category is maintained, but the state of consciousness itself is no longer located within the category. One can imagine this as a kind of "in between" state, at the border of the ego, or between ego and non-ego, as it were. (In case of multiple personality disorders, this is conceivable as a transition state between different ego categories.)

How could an acategorial state outside (or at the border) of an existing ego category be experienced? With regard to this question, there is a long tradition in Eastern philosophies, in particular in the discipline of mindfulness meditation: [39]

---

[37] See Scharfetter, cit.; T. Metzinger, "Ich-Störungen als pathologische Formen mentaler Selbstmodellierung". In: *Neuropsychiatrische Phänomene und das Leib-Seele-Problem.* Edited by G. Northoff, Schöning, Paderborn, 1993, pp. 169–191; T. Metzinger 2003, cit.
[38] Cfr. W.T. Stace, *Mysticism and Philosophy*, Lippincott, Philadelphia, 1960 and D.M. Wulff, "Mystical experience", *Varieties of Anomalous Experience.* (Edited by E. Cardena, S.J. Lynn and S.C. Krippner), American Psychological Association, Washington D.C., 2000, pp. 397–440.
[39] Nyanaponika, cit., p. 72.

"The three contemplations of feeling, state of mind and mental objects dealing with the mental part of man converge, as does the contemplation of the body, in the central concept of the Buddha, the concept of egolessness (anatta). Its essence is that the entire reality until its most sublime manifestations is void of eternal ego and inertial substance. The whole discourse on the "foundations of mindfulness" may be regarded as a comprehensive instruction for the realization of the liberating truth of egolessness, which will bring about not only a deep and thorough understanding of that truth but also its visible demonstration through an experience achievable by exercise."

Classic Zen anecdotes point out how acategorial experiences can be hampered by being attached to the category of the ego:[40]

A monk: Where is the Tao?
Kuan: Directly before us.
The monk: Why don't I see it?
Kuan: You cannot see it because of your egotism.
The monk: If I cannot see it because of my egotism,
is Your Reverence able to see it?
Kuan: As long as there is an "I" and a "You",
this makes the situation difficult and no Tao can be seen.
The monk: Can it be seen, when there is neither "I" nor "You"?
Kuan: When there is neither "I" nor "You",
who should be able to see it here?

A particularly important element of meditation in the practice of Zen Buddhism is the use of koans. They are rationally unsolvable problems and questions which the meditating subject has to deal with until his or her ego becomes abandoned. Suzuki comments this:

"The koan is neither a riddle nor a joke. It pursues a very serious goal, namely arousing doubt, which it carries to extremes. ... All rivers surely reach the ocean somewhere, but the koan stands in the way like an iron wall and resists even the most intense intellectual efforts ... We waver, we doubt, we get anxious and excited since we do not know how to break through this apparently insurmountable obstacle ... This attack of our deepest essence against the koan opens, unexpectedly, hitherto unknown realms of the mind. From an

---

[40] According to M. Kluge, *Augenblicke der Stille*, Heyne, München., 1986, p. 27.

intellectual point of view this means transgressing the boundary of logical dualism, but at the same time it is a rebirth [...]"[41]

Suzuki compares the acategorial border experience of the so-called "satori" with a renascence. This is metaphorically related to the Buddhist notion of the "Great Death", meaning "to die for ordinary life, a death putting an end to the analyzing mind and liberating us from the idea of an ego." This idea is not entirely foreign to occidental literature as well. For instance, Musil uses a very similar figure of thinking when he writes:

"To die is just a consequence of our way to live. We live from one thought to another. For our thoughts and affects do not flow quietly as a stream, but they "occur to us", they fall into us like stones. If you observe yourself accurately, you feel that the soul does not change its colors gradually but thoughts jump out of it like numbers out of a black hole. Now you have a thought or an affect, and suddenly another one stands there as if it jumped out of nothing. If you are attentive you can even sense the instant between two thoughts, in which everything is black. This instant, once recognized, is nothing else than death for us."[42]

Autobiographical reports on the experience of a drastically relativized ego category, which does not fit standard psychopathological patterns, have been published by Roberts and Segal.[43] Possibly more familiar and common experiences are the "flow-experiences" studied by Csikszentmihalyi.[44] Human beings at the limits of their capacities in physical, artistic or other competences report the incidental experience of being completely absorbed in their activities. This "fusion" of agents with their activity shows acategorial characteristics. Challenging activities of this kind are unlikely to proceed automatically resp. without the controlling functions of an ego category. The other side,

"[...] paradoxically, is a feeling which seems to make the sense of control irrelevant. Many people we interviewed, especially those who most enjoy

---

[41] D.T. Suzuki, *Die grosse Befreiung*, Scherz, München. 1980, pp. 150–151.
[42] R. Musil, *Die Verwirrungen des Zöglings Törleß*, Suhrkamp, Frankfurt, 2002, pp. 171–172.
[43] B. Roberts, *The Experience of No-Self*. Shambala, Boston, 1982; S. Segal, *Collision with the Infinite*. Blue Dove, San Diego, 1998.
[44] M. Czikszentmihalyi, "Beyond Boredom and Anxiety", Jossey-Bass, San Francisco, 1975.

whatever they are doing, mentioned that at the height of their involvement with the activity they lose a sense of themselves as a separate entity, and feel harmony and even a merging of identity with the environment. In some ways, this finding ought not to be unexpected. The great Eastern traditions of physical and "spiritual" control, for instance, are clearly built around this same paradox."[45]

Studying such experiences, it is important to distinguish between the dissolution of the ego, thus the loss of the corresponding category, from the lifted bondage to a still existing ego category in the sense of acategoriality. The first case may be related to a change of a potential V to the effect that its gradient vanishes, while the second case can be related to a dynamics of a mental state ϕ which is conceivable independently of a change of V . Gebser formulates this difference as the difference between the loss of the ego and freedom from the ego (Gebser 1986, p. 532):

"Only the overcoming of the "I", the concomitant overcoming of egolessness and egotism, places us in the sphere of ego-freedom ... Ego-freedom means freedom from the "I"; it is not a loss or a denial of the "I", not an ego-cide but an overcoming of ego. Ego-consciousness was the characteristic of the mental consciousness structure; freedom from the "I" is the characteristic of the integral consciousness structure."[46]

One of the occidental pioneers of the idea of a relativized ego was Jung. He uses the notion of the "self" to refer to situations beyond the ordinary category of the ego and comprising largely unconscious realms. According to Jung, there are connections of the ego-complex and corresponding ordinary states of consciousness with a substantially larger realm, from which the ego is regarded to emerge.[47] Such connections offer the possibility of extreme expansions of the world view, which are neither categorially restricted nor strictly delimited from the world of external objects (Holm 2001, chap. 4.5, 6.5).[48] The category of the ego appears, projectively as it were, as a personified manifestation of the self. In this picture, the relation of self and ego is context-dependent: while the ego is included in the self from the perspective of the self, the self is

---

[45] Ivi, p. 194)

[46] J. Gebser, cit., p. 532. NOTE #7

[47] See the definitions in C.G. Jung, *Gesammelte Werke* Band 6, Walter, Olten. 1995, §730, §§ 814–816.

[48] A. Holm, *Selbstmodell und Ich-Begriff*, Studie am IGPP, Freiburg, 2001, chapp. 4.5, 6.5.

62

antinomically opposed to the ego from the perspective of the ego. The relativization of the category of the first person singular has recently achieved much consideration as a central topic in transpersonal psychology and psychotherapy.[49], In this respect Wilber has pointed out frequent misunderstandings based on the so-called "pre/trans-fallacy", confusing different modes of consciousness which clearly refer to pre- or non-categorial experiences on the one hand and trans-or acategorial experiences on the other.[50]

5.3 Acategorial elements of creative processes

The formation of an ego-complex can be understood as a tedious process which—if all possible modifications of an ego representation over time are taken into account—is of lifelong duration. The event at which an individual experiences itself as an ego for the first time should be understood as an instantaneous and ephemeral "aha"-experience, in which a category is formed. However, such experiences are not restricted to the development of an ego. They are a basic feature of any creative activity providing any kind of insight. A comprehensive review of different aspects of and approaches to this field of research is due to Knoblich and Öllinger (2006).

Based on a wealth of biographical material on creative thinking, mainly in mathematics and physics, Hadamard suggests four stages, each of which is inevitable for genuinely creative work.[51] He calls these stages *preparation, incubation, illumination,* and *verification.* The first and the last of them mainly function at the level of conscious, analytical thinking. The second and the third stages, however, strongly involve unconscious processes as the core of actual insight. Here is a compact characterization of Hadamard's scheme with some additional comments.

1. Preparation: As emphasized by Poincaré, no creative insight can "happen except after some days of voluntary effort which has appeared absolutely fruitless."[52] Intense conscious work on a problem, sometimes even for years (as

---

[49] See C. Tart, *Transpersonale Psychologie*, Walter, Düsseldorf. 1991.
[50] K. Wilber, *Eye to Eye: the Quest for the New Paradigm*, Anchor Books, Garden City, 1983.
[51] J. Hadamard, *The Psychology of Invention in the Mathematical Field*, Dover, New York, 1954.
[52] H. Poincaré, "Mathematical creation". *The Foundations of Science*, Science Press, New York, 1913, p. 387. Reprinted in J. Hadamard, cit., pp. 12 ff.

Gauss reported in a letter to Olbers), precedes the final solution. Frustrating efforts without success characterize this stage.[53]

2. Incubation: At some point the problem is removed from conscious focus, intentionally or by distraction, but the preceding conscious work "has set going the unconscious machine". Unconscious elements "rose in crowds; I felt them collide",[54] and "this combinatory play seems to be the essential feature in creative thought."[55]

3. Illumination: When "the mentioned associative play is sufficiently established",[56] "pairs [of unconscious elements] interlocked, so to speak, making a stable combination."[57] A particular configuration of unconscious elements stabilizes and, thereby, becomes conscious. This is the crucial moment in which an insight reveals itself. Often this happens holistically, not successively unfolded in time.

4. Verification: Finally, this insight has to be reconstructed in a logical way, i.e. by a succession of rational arguments which can be communicated. "Conventional words or signs have to be sought for laboriously only in a secondary stage."[58]

A particular difficulty of the last stage has to do with the fact that typically insight does not present itself by way of successive steps, but as a holistic impression. Logical steps of a mathematical proof or the succession of tones ultimately constituting a musical composition are results of a temporal sequentialization of such a holistic impression. A good example is the following letter by Mozart:

"When I feel well and in good humor, or when I am taking a drive or walking after a good meal, or in the night when I cannot sleep, thoughts crowd into my mind as easily as you could wish. Whence and how do they come? I do not know and I have nothing to do with it. Those which please me, I keep in my head and hum them; at least others have told me that I do so. Once I have my theme, another melody comes, linking itself to the first one, in accordance with the needs of the composition as a whole: the counterpoint, the part of each

---

[53] As reported by Gauss in a letter to Olbers, see C.F. Gauss, "Brief an H.W. Olbers". Published in *Revue des questions scientifiques*, October 1886, p. 575. Reprinted in J. Hadamard, cit., p. 15.

[54] Poincaré, cit.

[55] A. Einstein (1905?): "Appendix II" in J. Hadamard cit.

[56] Ibidem

[57] Poincaré, cit.

[58] Einstein, cit.

instrument, and all these melodic fragments at last produce the entire work. Then my soul is on fire with inspiration, if however nothing occurs to distract my attention. The work grows; I keep expanding it, conceiving it more and more clearly until I have the entire composition finished in my head though it may be long. Then my mind seizes it as a glance of my eye, a beautiful picture, or a handsome youth. It does not come to me successively, with its various parts worked out in detail, as they will be later on, but it is in its entirety that my imagination lets me hear it."[59]

Max Frisch describes the same phenomenon quite differently:

"Time? It would be just a magic tool unfolding and making visible our essence by disentangling life, the omnipresence of all possibilities, into successive stages; only therefore it seems like a transformation to us, and therefore it urges us to assume that time, the successive, is not essential but apparent, an ancillary tool, an unwinding that indicates in succession what actually is enfolded, a simultaneity which we cannot perceive as such as we cannot perceive the colors of light when its rays are not refracted and spectrally decomposed. Our consciousness is the refracting prism decomposing our life into a succession of stages, and dreaming is that other lens which focuses it back into its original whole; dream and poetry, which tries to comply with it in this sense."[60]

Simonton has developed a fairly detailed "chance-configuration model" for the second and third stages above, in which the central issue is stability.[61] The permutating unconscious elements during incubation are not (asymptotically) stable, but float freely, coming and going by chance until a particular one among these configurations has stability properties implying its transition into a conscious categorial representation. In an evolutionary formulation of creative processes, stability provides a selection criterion among many chance possibilities.

In Simonton's model, creative processes are explicitly related to a transition from unconscious to conscious domains of the psyche. The formation of a novel category, experienced as yielding insight, can be characterized by a

[59] F. Paulhan, *Psychologie de l'Invention*. Alcan, Paris. 1901, quoted in J. Hadamard, cit., p. 16.
[60] M. Frisch, *Tagebuch 1946–1949*, Suhrkamp, Frankfurt, 1997, p. 15.
[61] D.K. Simonton, *Scientific Genius: A Psychology of Science*, Cambridge University Press, Cambridge, 1988.

deformation of the potential landscape leading to a novel minimum of V (and, maybe, changing the vicinity of this minimum decisively). Thus, the aspect of novelty which is an essential criterion for creativity, is settled at the level of conscious processing. It is inevitable for a concrete "aha"-experience that the mental state f is not yet located within the newly forming category, but moves into it simultaneously with the process of category formation.

The question of why and how particular configurations are distinguished by their stability is left unanswered in Simonton's approach. In this respect, some speculative ideas concerning the role of the unconscious, formulated by Pauli and inspired by Jungian depth psychology, are of interest. Similar to other so-called dual-aspect approaches, Pauli and Jung proposed the idea of psychophysical correspondences ("synchronicities") between psychological and physical subdomains of an underlying hypothetical background reality:

"A cosmic order detracted from our voluntary influence must be postulated which governs both external material objects *and* inner images. *The ordering factors must be considered beyond the distinction of physical and psychic* – as Plato's 'ideas' share the character of a 'notion' with that of a 'natural force'. I am very much in favor of calling these 'ordering factors' 'archetypes'; but then it would be inadmissible to *define* them as contents of the *psyche*. Instead, the inner images are *psychic* manifestations of the archetypes, which, however, also would have to create, produce, cause *everything* in the material world that happens according to the laws of nature. The laws of the material world would thus refer to the *physical manifestations of the archetypes*." [62]

In Jung's depth psychology, the elements of the psychophysically neutral background reality are denoted as archetypes, which "coordinate" (in an unknown manner) correspondences between mental and material states. Similar conceptions can be found in the hisotry of philosophy (e.g. Spinoza or Leibniz), and Fechner argued explicitly in the same way during the pioneering days of psychology[63] Among physicists of the 20th century, related ideas were taken up by Pauli, Wigner, Bohm and, more recently, d'Espagnat and Primas with different terminologies.[64] In their conceptions, mental and material domains acquire clearly epistemic significance, whereas the basic "objective order" is

---

[62] W. Pauli, "Brief an M. Fierz vom 7. Januar 1948", *Wolfgang Paulis wissenschaftlicher Briefwechsel*, Band III (Edited by K. von Meyenn), Springer, Berlin, 1993, pp. 496 ff.
[63] See M. Pauen, *Grundprobleme der Philosophie des Geistes*. Fischer, Frankfurt, 2001.
[64] See H. Atmanspacher, "Mind and matter as asymptotically disjoint, inequivalent representations with broken time-reversal symmetry". *BioSystems* 68, 2003, pp. 19–30.

considered as ontic relative to its decomposition into mind and matter. In such a framework, the origin of the stability properties addressed above must then be conceived at the level of the objective, psychophysically neutral order. Stable configurations would manifest themselves in the selection of particular correspondences out of many possible ones. Since any archetypal order is empirically inaccessible per definition, these correspondences are the only option to obtain indications for the psychophysically neutral domain of archetypes. Examples of serendipity, described by Simonton (1988) and resembling features of Jungian synchronicity, are interesting candidates fitting into this picture.

At this point it becomes clear that Jung's conception of an ego which is relativized by an archetypal self is not comprehensible without explicitly taking into account the psychophysical problem. If the relativization of the ego is to be successful, the connection to the psychophysically neutral domain of the archetypal self must be developed at least so far as to realize that the distinction of the psychical and the physical is not a priori given. It is evident that this can have enormous consequences for the worldview and the lifeworld of an individual.

6 Summary

This contribution discusses a formal and conceptual framework to describe the dynamics of mental states in terms of their stability properties. Mental states are understood as states of the mental system which evolve in a state space characterized by a generalized potential surface. Its local minima correspond to mental representations or categories, resp. They are actualized if they are occupied by asymptotically stable *categorial* states.

Since there is always a local maximum between two potential minima, transitions between stable categorial states must pass through instabilities. The behavior of the mental system in the vicinity of instabilities is a topic which – with historical exceptions such as William James – was and is notoriously neglected in the relevant literature. Jean Gebser proposed the concept of *acategorial* states in this context. A state is acategorial if it is located between possible categorial states, i.e. between mental representations.

Recent results in cognitive neuroscience can be elegantly and compactly described using the concepts of instability and acategoriality. For instance, censored perceptions, leading to illusions in particular situations, can be understood in terms of the stability of the involved categories. Another example is the perception of multistable stimuli, intrinsically containing the switch from one existing category to another.

Using acategorial states to analyze introspective reports of unusual mental experiences is particularly promising. A rich repertoire in this direction are alterations in the representation of the first person singular, the category of the ego, which only partially fit ordinary patterns of psychopathology. The difference between a mental state within an almost dissolved ego-category and a mental state located outside of an existing ego-category is conceptually similar to the difference between a weakly stable categorial state and an acategorial state. Particular processes accompanying particular stages of creative activity can be addressed in the same framework.[65]

---

[65] **A slightly different version of this article has already been published in the *Journal of Mind and Behaviour*, 26 (2005), pp. 181-206.**

The Unifying Moment: Toward a Theory of Complexity. Whitehead on Universe's Responsibility and the Role of God

Craig Eisendrath (PhD)*

1. The Responsibility of the World for Its Own Order and Novelty.

What impresses one with the philosophy of Alfred North Whitehead is his vision of an active universe structuring itself, rather than being determined. Although, as we will see, his break with traditional determinism, and the ideas which support it, is not clean, Whitehead nevertheless helped point philosophy in a new direction.

In doing this, Whitehead drew on a number of source. One was the field theory of Clerk Maxwell. Maxwell had established in 1873 that the Newtonian idea of simple location, of objects which are "self-sufficient," or which have the limited parameters of their spatial and temporal outlines, simply does not describe the physical world. Rather, Maxwell stated, objects are the *loci* of their electro-magnetic and gravitational fields, and integrate their entire universes in their location. Thus, new inputs into the object's field produce novelty in the resulting integrated object.

Another important influence was William James's description of the integration of the conscious field, a notion further refined by the American psychologist, Harry Stack Sullivan. In this mode of thinking, a threatening bear which we perceive in the woods is at the center of a conscious field which includes the bear's surroundings, particularly highlighting our routes of escape. The idea of an integrated conscious field is clearly opposed to Locke's isolated objects or Hume's separate sensations.[1]

---

* Temple University Philadelphia (USA).

[1] For the relation of William James to Whitehead, and a general explanation of their thought, see Craig R. Eisendrath, *The Unifying Moment: The Psychological Philosophy of William James and Alfred North Whitehead* (Cambridge, MA.: Harvard University Press, 1971), reissued by toExcel, 1999. For James's psychology, see, in particular, his *The Principles of Psychology*, 2 vols. (New York: Henry Holt and Col, 1890), and his *Essays in Radical Empiricism* (New York: Longmans, Green and Co., 1912). James anticipated a number of developments in cognitive psychology which would not become current until the 1960s. See Ulric Neisser, *Cognitive Psychology* (New York: Appleton-Century-Crofts, 1967). For a relation of Whitehead and James to more modern developments in physics and

In drawing on these sources, Whitehead creates a sense of an active universe which effects its own integrations. He begins by using organisms, rather than things, or inert matter, as his basic unit, a notion suggested both by Aristotle, Locke, and by William James. Whitehead attempts to build the physical and mental worlds out of his understanding that each such element of the world experiences itself. This is as true for the simplest element, such as an electron, as for the most complex, a human being. By ascribing experience to all being, Whitehead breaks down the metaphysical wall between the physical and biological worlds.

For Whitehead, the Platonic description of experience, with its ideas like red and round — what the philosophers call *qualia*, is inadequate because they are the conceptual form which feelings take, and are thus an abstraction. The description of experience using *qualia* is also inadequate because it ignores the *integration* of the sensations or objects into larger wholes, a notion, as we have seen, based on field physics and on William James' depiction of the conscious field.

For Whitehead, unlike Plato, Locke or Hume, perception is not just a mental activity, but a physical one, what Whitehead calls a "prehension," a notion which connects his and William James's psychology with physical field theory. For example, for Whitehead, a proposition is embedded in an "environment" out of which it comes, and to which it initially relates. Like objects, it does not exist by itself. "All men are created equal" had an *original* environment, the experience of Thomas Jefferson in the eighteenth century, to which it initially referred, however later its reference might be extended, say, to social relations in the twentieth or twenty-first centuries. It relates to this entire environment, rather than existing as a self-sufficient statement.

Perception ultimately rests on our absorbing energy, for example, photons, from another source. Expressed in field theory, that source becomes part of our physical field. In this sense, a stone which we see or prehend is both part of our field, and therefor is part of us. The percept is then not *just* a "representation" of the object, as Descartes maintained. The mind is not, for Whitehead, as it was for Descartes, a substance—a soul —which requires nothing but itself in order to exist, and which can then simply entertain itself with its own Platonic ideas, such as round and red. Rather, the mind consists of its physical constituencies, including neurons, blood, and, at an even more basic physical level, its field's electromagnetic and gravitational forces, which sometimes includes the prehended stone. In this way, Whitehead attacks the discontinuity

biology, see my *At War With Time: The Wisdom of Western Thought from the Sages to a New Activism for our Time* (New York: Helios Press, 2003).

between mind and body, and between the mental and physical worlds.

But perception, for Whitehead, is not direct, as it is for Locke and Hume. We do not directly perceive ideas like "round" or "red." Rather, the perceiver's body will transform the original energetic stimuli into high-level perceptions, which Locke and Hume called "simple ideas." For Whitehead, such ideas are, then, abstractions and cannot adequately describe our full experience. Integration of the physical energetic particles constituting the active brain is reflected in our capacity to relate disparate elements into wholes, or to unite the world aesthetically.[2]

Whitehead sees the same processes involved in creating purpose as in perception. He believes that what produces the body's purpose or subjective aim, to the extent it is centrally controlled, is a qualitative adjustment of the Platonic ideas of the impulses contributed by the cells, as mediated and re-enacted by the nerves and the brain, and of the Platonic ideas of the impulses generated by the integrating brain without *direct* relation to the rest of the body. The mixture of perception and purpose, as these are centralized, is the organism's "presiding personality." This transformation of energy into mentality and purpose is a core notion in Whitehead's thought.

Here novelty does not require an additional outside force, which, as we will see, Whitehead himself sometimes argues. Rather by the integration of the physical elements, a new object is produced, which has both a physical and mental aspect. In this way, novelty is created naturally by the world.

Whitehead holds that what distinguishes living things from the inert world is this working of purpose or direction. Whitehead writes, "In the case of an animal, the mental states enter into the plan of the total organism and thus modify the plans of the successive subordinate organisms until the smallest organisms, such as electrons, are reached."[3]

An example is thirst. There is a physical feeling, and there is a conceptual form which the physical feeling takes. This form is an urge toward the future realization of a fact, the drinking of water, a change which, in this case, will stimulate the complex of cells, called the organism, to seek water, and will

---

[2] Whitehead also asserts plainly, as did Locke, that we feel influence, or, technically, a vectorial, or directional, reference to an outside cause, for example, a blow on the head, which sends us reeling, or a candle flame which burns our hand. We should note that such direct evidence of causation contradicts Hume, and also questions Kant's need to designate causation as a category of the mind. However, Whitehead would also say that due to the complexity of the human brain, the neurons probably mimic causality, rather than directly experience it, as lower organisms may do.

[3] A.N. Whitehead, *Science and the Modern World* (London: Cambridge University Press, 1925), p. 111.

eventually involve the absorption of new elements into the organism's constitution.

Whitehead is also concerned with how organisms respond to external stimuli with a certain originality. He explains this by saying that as the external stimuli or data come in, they are objective; when they are integrated into the organism, they are private and subjective. They can then prompt the organism to some new response. The capacity for novelty is a function of the organism's capacity for integration into complexity. Novelty is here the integration of the novelties of the physical field, or the neural field.

A living organism may passively perceive data, for example, the organism's realization of a "green tree out there." Whitehead would call such a realization a "positive prehension." But negative prehensions, that is, experiences which are *instigated by* but not *realized directly* in the data, are ways he believes the world advances into novelty.

For Whitehead, human consciousness generally involves negative prehensions which can be translated as propositions. Consciousness always includes some realization that looks beyond the body's immediate delivery. Even a statement like "This ball is red," carries the idea that the ball might be some other color, a notion, incidentally, which Freud also advances. Other propositions, such as "This ball is not red," or "This ball might be blue," or "I'd like to be a doctor," more clearly show the relation between consciousness as mere awareness and consciousness as the vehicle of purpose, or what Whitehead calls the "subjective aim." Again, Whitehead shows his profound debt to philosophers like William James and John Dewey who speak of the purposefulness of conscious integration, which James sums up in his work, *Pragmatism*.[4]

For Whitehead, this integration of objects is built into the very nature of the world, and acts as a guiding principle. Whitehead's explanation of the creation of novelty applies not only to appetites, intentions, and behavior, but also to the formation and evolution of organisms. Whitehead explains that a new subjective form arises to guide the composition of the organism's felt Platonic ideas as they readjust to new inputs from the environment. Such inputs might be a high-speed particle altering a genetic molecule, or a new element in the organism's chemical environment. This would be Whitehead's explanation of how pleiotropic adjustment occurs, in which the total organism reconfigures itself in response to small genetic changes.

Today, scientists are increasingly using complex computer models to

---

[4] W. James *Pragmatism* (London, Bombay, and Calcutta: Longmans, Green and Co, 1907); see also James's *The Principles of Psychology*.

represent mental or organic processes. The models show how adjustments at the informational or symbolic level predict and direct adjustments or reconfigurations at the material or energetic level. If one substitutes the more modern idea of "information" for Whitehead's Platonic ideas, and then attempts to determine how information adjusts in the organism to organize organic processes, as in the quenching of thirst, or to configure the organism, as in pleiotropy, Whitehead's thought has a quite contemporary ring.[5]

Whitehead also suggests that the adjustments in the organism which organize organic process are essentially aesthetic. (This aesthetic valuation of symbolic adjustment is what mathematicians, he tells us, frequently refer to as "beautiful" proofs.)[6] He explains the world's advance into novel complexity as aesthetic, writing that "the teleology of the world is directed to the production of Beauty."[7] Whitehead here suggests that there is some genuine analogy between the integration of a mathematical system, the readjustment of a biochemical balance as in the quenching of thirst, the way an organism creates a new composition as a result of slight alterations of the genes (pleiotropy), and the way an artist alters an entire painting to adjust to changes of color or shape in a small section, or creates the art work itself from paint and canvas.

Art, which, in Whitehead's phrase, is "deficiently real," projects the full realization of concrete fact in the physical world, just as a diagram or blueprint of a building anticipates its construction. Whitehead says, "It requires Art to evoke into consciousness the finite perfections which lie ready for human achievement."[8] This advances not only the organic roots of art, but also its prophetic role in the world's historic progress. Whitehead suggests that standards of beauty may not be merely cultural, but also reflect their relation to organic integration and complexity, an idea which lifts artistic standards out of total cultural relativism.

---

[5] For a complex discussion of these ideas, see Stuart A. Kauffman, *The Origins of Order: Self-Organization and Selection in Evolution* (New York and Oxford: Oxford University Press, 1933); Ilya Prigogine, *The End of Certainty: Time, Chaos, and the New Laws of Nature* (New York, Toronto, Sydney, and Singapore: The Free Press, 1997); and Gerald M. Edelman's trilogy *Neural Darwinism: The Theory of Neuronal Group Selection* (New York: Basic Books, 1987), *Topology: An Introduction to Molecular Embryology* (New York: Basic Books, 1988), and *The Remembered Present: A Biological Theory of Consciousness* (New York: Basic Books, 1989).

[6] See Alfred North Whitehead, *Modes of Thought* (New York: Macmillan Co., 1938).

[7] A.N. Whitehead, *Adventures of Ideas* (New York: Macmillan Col, 1933), p. 341. This notion also emerges in the last works of Sigmund Freud with his concept of the integrating work of Eros.

[8] A.N. Whitehead, *Adventures of Ideas*, pp. 346 and 271.

Finally, Whitehead holds that organisms create not only their own internal organization and consequent forms, but also their regular modes of interaction, which are called the natural laws. In both these ways, the world advances into novelty. That this is done spontaneously throughout the universe, what Whitehead calls the "creative advance," is Whitehead's supreme insight. The origin of creativity and order is implicit in the very nature of the world. Whitehead takes this idea partly from William James, partly from biology, and partly from his own work in physics, in which objects create their own ordered fields, which reflect their constituents' interaction. Objects thus do not follow God's laws, as Newton said they did; rather, Whitehead believes, they create them. In physics, this notion seems an enormously useful corrective to Newtonian determinism. In biology, by emphasizing the way in which an organism achieves integration in itself and with its larger environment, Whitehead points to what may be the weakness of present-day Darwinian theory.[9]

When Whitehead surveys the world, he finds evidence everywhere for the creative advance, that is, the growth of complexity or "intensity of experience." This is, Whitehead believes, the world's indisputable progress as it transforms chaotic nature into all its complex forms and laws. The progress toward complexity is apparent at every level, from quantum particles, through molecular structures, to biological organisms and human beings. There is no doubt that complexity is growing on this planet, if not throughout the reaches of the universe. Four billion years ago there was no life here at all; today there are highly complex organic forms. Whitehead attempts to explain this phenomenon through a philosophy based not on traditional ideas of creation or even Platonic notions of a permanent ideal order, but on self-generated process.

2. The Role of God, or the Second Explanation.

However, at times, Whitehead seems to believe that this explanation of the creation of organic forms or systems does not suffice. In this "second explanation," Whitehead believes he must go beyond the data and their interrelations to find an ultimate source for the world's novelty. In this "second explanation," he says that purpose, or the subjective aim, instead of emerging from an integration of feeling, and more basically from the integration of its physical constituents, guides the organism from the outset. For Whitehead, this

---

[9] For a full-scale attack on these weaknesses, see Stuart A. Kauffman, *The Origins of Order*.

guidance comes prefigured from the "primordial nature of God," which contains all possible combinations of ideas. God's "judgment" is his supplying the emerging subjective aim which is particularly relevant to that organism. Whitehead writes, "Thus an originality in the temporal world is conditioned, though not determined, by an initial subjective aim supplied by the ground of all order and of all originality."[10]

In raising this second mode of explanation, Whitehead reverts to notions of order which lie at the base of Western thought from Plato to Hegel, and to the monotheistic religion of his youth. Whitehead, like many modern philosophers, as the American philosopher Joseph Margolis points out,[11] here seems simply unwilling to carry through on the primary thrust of his ideas.

In many ways, Whitehead's "primordial nature of God" looks very much like Plato's God. It also resembles the single, unified, and absolute mathematics which began to dissolve in the nineteenth century, and which Whitehead and Bertrand Russell attempted to save through their *Principia Mathematica,* completed in 1910. Subsequent developments have made this unity even less persuasive.

If the unification of ideas is highly questionable in mathematics, the unification of all ideas in the world is even more so. What is the relation between $2 + 2 = 4$ and Jefferson's idea that all men are created equal, although both are ideas? Assumed coexistence or membership in the class of God's mind does not imply a necessary relation. Our idea of integration is based on structure and limit, precisely what seems missing here. As the notion of God expands to include any possible relation, or the inclusion of any entity, it loses any semblance to this ideal. William James writes, as if anticipating Whitehead's thought, "Yet if . . . we assume God to have thought in advance of every *possible* flight of human fancy in these directions, his mind becomes too much like a Hindoo idol with three heads, eight arms and six breasts, too much made up of superfoetation and redundancy for us to wish to copy it . . ."[12]

For Whitehead, in his second mode of explanation, God's nature forms the basis for all potentiality in the world, as it does for Kant and Hegel. Whitehead asks: How can novelty enter the world if it is not already somewhere? As here Whitehead seems to be denying the possibility of novelty altogether, he must find its source in the mind of God. It is God who supplies the plan or set of

---

[10] A.N. Whitehead *Process and Reality* (New York: Macmillan Co., 1929), p. 164.
[11] J. Margolis, *The Flux of History and the Flux of Science* (Berkeley, CA, Los Angeles, and London: University of California Press, 1993).
[12] Jottings of 1903-1904, quoted in Ralph Barton Perry, *The Thought and Character of William James*, 2 vols. (Boston and Toronto: Little, Brown and Co., 1935), Vol. II, p. 384.

eternal ideas which persuades each organism to achieve what complexity or organic beauty it is capable of, and which guides the organism toward novelty. Each "judgment" of God is relevant particularly to that organism and represents a particular selection from the infinite interrelation of ideas which constitutes God's nature. Accordingly, in Whitehead's second mode of explanation, "proximate relevance" of eternal objects, as a guide to an organism in the process of becoming, "means relevance as in the primordial mind of God."[13]

At first blush, this is not how evolution proceeds, at least as Darwin explains it. Rather than a purposeful operation involving the total organism, the evolution of individuals and eventually of species proceeds by random variation of genetic material, which then produces a phenotype that is supported by the environment—that is, when the organism survives and multiplies. Purposefulness seems curiously absent, and would seem closer to what Aristotle would call accident, or randomness.

But the rearrangement of the total organism following relatively minor genetic changes, or pleiotropy, suggests a drive for order which is not accidental, but which may not be inconsistent with Darwinian evolution. Equally, the organism's choice of organic development following regular mathematical forms suggests that more than accident is involved, and that the drive for integration seems built into the system of the universe.

What does not seem evident, however, is any *central direction* for the universe as a whole. The sheer proliferation of forms belies any such central vision. How many different tries there have been in the biological world, how many false starts; as the biologist Stephen Jay Gould points out, whole genera have perished irrevocably in the Paleozoic past.[14]

Even in Whitehead's time, one could walk through a biological museum, with its glass cases of fossils and preserved species, from mollusks to mammals, and sense the energy and fecundity of the biological world, but also its seeming lack of unified direction. Is it meaningful, as Whitehead suggests, to think that this variety achieves unification in the mind of God?

By invoking God as the initiator of organic compositions, and the world's aesthetic unifier, Whitehead thereby re-establishes determinism, a problem faced by philosophers from Plato to Hegel. In Whitehead's "second explanation," God is immanent in the world, guiding each organism. Although Whitehead says there is freedom, this mechanism for limiting it seems enormously powerful.

---

[13] *Process and Reality*, pp. 315 and 73.

[14] See S. J. Gould, *Wonderful Life: the Burgess Shale and the Nature of History* (New York: W.W. Norton, 1989).

As God is necessarily ubiquitous, God, of course, would also be responsible for results which are clearly destructive, or Whitehead would be forced to parcel out good results to God and bad results to other agencies. The first position would sully Whitehead's notion of God; the second would make attributing results to God dependent on Whitehead's moral or aesthetic judgments. Whitehead must here deal with the problem raised by Hume, of arguing from an imperfect creation to a perfect Creator.

How does Whitehead deal with the related problem of evil? It is not reassuring. He writes: "The revolts of destructive evil, purely self-regarding, are dismissed into their triviality of merely individual facts; and yet the good they did achieve in individual joy, in individual sorrow, in the introduction of needed contrasts, is yet saved by its relation to the completed whole."[15] If one thinks of evils such as the Holocaust or Rwanda, this becomes patently wishful thinking, although Whitehead is right, for example, that stealing may be satisfying for the thief, however destructive it is for the victim. Yet to say, as Whitehead seems to be doing here, that premature death, suffering, or genocide are somehow "saved" by being absorbed into God's nature, is to argue them away.

Such salvation occurs, Whitehead says, because the world, as a completed fact, is God's "consequent nature," a concept close to Hegel's. In this sense, God is the entire world, which constitutes an ultimate theory of immanence. Not only is God *in* everything, but everything *is* God. In this sense, the world is a holy place. Every effort is part of a divine effort, and nothing is lost or wasted. Here the distinction between God and the world dissolves, as do Whitehead's arguments for God's separate role. It then does not matter whether one sees the world's complexity as the work of God, or of the world itself. For if the world is God, or is infused with God through and through, if it is holy and charged with divine energy, the problems for thought created by the Hebraic God who is metaphysically separate from the universe, or the distant God of Isaac Newton, do not arise.

Here we are tempted to conceive of a very different nature of God, one suggested by gnostic thought,[16] the writings of Meister Eckhart or Jacob Böhme, at times, suggested by Kant and Hegel, and stated outright by the American philosopher, Ralph Waldo Emerson, a friend, incidentally, of William James' father. This is the notion of an immanent God, who is present in all creation, and is there as a well of creative energy to be tapped by the

---

[15] *Process and Reality*, p. 532.
[16] See, for example, Elaine Pagels, *The Gnostic Gospels* (New York: Random House, Inc., 1979).

organic world and the religiously adept. It is also a concept found in Eastern thought with the ideas of the Self or Brahmin.

Whitehead's ultimate argument for God's persuasive work in the world, like Plato's, is the intuition which artists know as art, and moralists know as right, and workmen know as effective, and statesmen know as just, and organisms know, or feel, as healthy. All men seek the Good, Plato tells us, and all men choose it, if they know what it is, for when they find it, it is supposedly persuasive. But not all effects in the world are benign; this persuasion does not always work. However, the world's general growth toward complexity, and the role of ideas and art in history and culture, would argue that a drive toward complexity is perhaps in the nature of things. Whether this drive comes from God or from the universe remains open in Whitehead's thought, and continues to haunt modern religion and philosophy.

While denying a sectarian religious purpose, Whitehead's "second explanation" seems generally to be concerned with reformulating the Judeo-Christian tradition in the light of the modern world so it can continue to deliver its principal object—an abiding sense of permanence in the midst of the world's flux and evolution. While concerned with process, Whitehead here posits an eternal, unified set of ideas; a God who unifies these ideas and guides each occasion; a God who sanctions every aesthetic and moral act in God's nature; and the permanent deposit of all effort in God as well.

3. The Legacy of Whitehead.

Despite these problems, Whitehead, particularly in his "first explanation," provides a wealth of suggestion as to how the universe moves toward complexity and beauty, and thereby provides a physical-psychological model which looks surprisingly contemporary and useful in reconfiguring thought. While his "second explanation" reinstalls God as the ultimate cause of the process, it is also possible to see in Whitehead's philosophy, in his "first explanation," how the universe itself takes responsibility for its own advance. Whether or not the universe is holy; whether it is useful to speak of the universe as divine, or its drive toward complexity and beauty as God's, seems less important than Whitehead's overall vision in which intelligence, embedded in all beings, drives the universe forward to whatever perfections it is capable of achieving.

His awe before the universe is indeed like Plato's or Kant's. Lucien Price recorded Whitehead saying, "Here we are with our finite being and physical senses in the presence of a universe whose possibilities are infinite, and even though we may not apprehend them, those infinite possibilities are actualities."[17]

It is this sense of wonder which filled the scientists of the twentieth century, and provided for many of them, and for those who read their work, the spiritual equivalent of an earlier religion. It is this legacy which we inherent today in 2004, and which, drawing upon new findings in physics and biology, only vaguely discerned by Whitehead, can form the basis of a new integration of thought.

---

[17] *Dialogues of Alfred North Whitehead*, as recorded by L. Price (Boston: Little, Brown and Col, 1954), p. 11.

Education and Conversion. The Plasticity of the Self

*Ilaria Possenti**

As Richard Sennett argues in his *The Corrosion of Character*,[1] the word *flexibility* stands for the capacity of a tree to resist, as well as its capacity to return to the former situation (that is, both the deformation and the restoration of the form). From an ideal point of view, the human behaviour should have the same features: the capacity to adapt itself to the changing events without breaking.

The late nineteenth century observation of William James on the plasticity of the self, that is on its possibilities of transformation, presents a remarkable similarity with the issue raised by Sennett. In fact, James observed that "all our life, so far as it has definite form, is but a mass of habits—practical, emotional, and intellectual"—and that "so far as we are thus mere bundles of habit, we are stereotyped creatures",[2] qualified by a certain *rigidity*. At the same time he underlined that our habits represent a second nature, that is the way in which we reunify and build up ourselves thanks to our fundamental plasticity. As for Sennett, to be plastic meant to him, in James's words, "the possession of a structure weak enough to yield to an influence, but strong enough not to yield all at once."[3]

1. Plasticity

In the fourth chapter of the *Principles of Psychology*, dealing with habit, James starts off saying that "when we look at the living creatures from an outward point of view, one of the first things that strike us is that they are bundles of habits."[4] In the case of the living matter, in general, talking about

---

* Adjoint Professor of Social Pedagogy at the Dept. of Philosophy, Università di Pisa (Italy)
[1] R. Sennett, *The Corrosion of Character*, W.W. Norton & Co. 2000.
[2] W. James, *Talks to Teachers on Psychology and to Students on Some of Life's Ideals* (1899), Harvard Univ. Pr., Cambridge (Mass.), 1983, [hereafter TT], p 96.
[3] W. James, *Principles of Psychology* (1890), Dover Publ. Inc., New York, 1980 [hereafter PP], p. 105.
[4] PP I, p. 104. Here, I took advantage of some significant remarks on the distinction in human beings between instinct, as "habits to which there is an innate tendency", and habit

81

habits means to bring to a very complex level a fundamental feature of the matter: its plasticity, that is, the possibility of a change of habits in action and reaction, without implying the definitive disintegration of the matter ("as when a bar of iron becomes magnetic or crystalline through the action of certain outward causes, or India-rubber becomes friable, or plaster 'sets'"[5]).

A similar change is usually gradual and slow: old habits resist to transformation, and it is precisely this phenomenon of resistance that preserves the matter from disintegration. If a matter is plastic, old habits allow it to undergo some kind of influence, but they preserve it from a structural collapse. Thanks to this kind of process, after a phase of oscillation, the matter can reach new conditions of stability, founded on a new set of habits: "each relatively stable phase of equilibrium in such a structure is marked by what we call a new set of habits."[6]

Now, as James points out, the nervous tissues present a very extraordinary degree of plasticity: "so that we may without hesitation lay down as our first proposition the following, that *the phenomena of habit in living beings are due to the plasticity of the organic materials of which their bodies are composed*"[7]. As we may observe, for James, as for John Stuart Mill, the forming of habits in the living beings coincides with the forming of character: therefore the plasticity of the nervous system represents the biological basis on which stands the plasticity of the self.[8]

Human beings, as plastic creatures of habits, have a double chance: they have to find their balance, namely, their specific way of adaptation to the surrounding environment, through the formation of a specific character, namely, of a specific set of habits; yet, in some circumstances they have also to face situations of crisis, incertitude, change, questioning non functional habits and substituting them with a new set of habits.

In this work of adaptation and reconstruction of habits, a prominent role is played by the habits of attention. The conscious experience of the living beings is plunged in a perfect chaos of sensations, perceptions and stimuli of every

---

in a strict sense as "[habits] due to education" and their plasticity in S. Franzese, *L'uomo indeterminato. Saggio su William James*, D'Anselmi, Roma, 2000, p. 56 sgg.

[5] PP I, p. 105

[6] Ibidem.

[7] Ibidem.

[8] See PP I, p. 125. Contemporary neurosciences are now developing scientific research on neuroplasticity (intended as the lifelong ability of the brain to reorganize neural pathways based on new experiences, learning and memory), beginning from Donald Hebb's neuropsychological theory. See D.O. Hebb, *The Organization of Behavior*, John Wiley and Sons, New York 1949.

kind: it cannot completely cover the world, so it has to determine its field. The condition to gain awareness of the world is that of learning to choose some objects of attention among the infinite number of objects, letting some of them to fade out gradually towards the margin of the field of consciousness while leaving out the most of the others. This work of selection is the task of attention, which selects its objects on the basis of practical, ethical and esthetical criteria and ends.[9] Thus, consciousness, intended by James as a function rather than as a substance, consists in a permanent selective activity, engaged in a continuous process of filtering and organising the stream of experiences. Such a process begets the construction of real habits of thinking, which gradually contribute to the construction of one's own character and, in turn, one's own view of the world:

"Next, in a world of objects thus individualized by our mind's selective industry, what is called our 'experience' is almost entirely determined by our habits of attention. A thing may be present to a man a hundred times, but if he persistently fails to notice it, it cannot be said to enter into his experience. [...] Let four men make a tour in Europe. One will bring home only picturesque impressions -- costumes and colors, parks and views and works of architecture, pictures and statues. To another all this will be non-existent; and distances and prices, populations and drainage-arrangements, door- and window-fastenings, and other useful statistics will take their place. A third will give a rich account of the theatres, restaurants, and public halls, and naught besides; whilst the fourth will perhaps have been so wrapped in his own subjective broodings as to be able to tell little more than a few names of places through which he passed. Each has selected, out of the same mass of presented objects, those which suited his private interest and has made his experience thereby."[10]

The habits of attention represent the usual, and in a certain way internalized, modalities with which we make our esthetical, practical and ethical choices.

---

[9] James makes a distinction between different varieties of attention. The attention (depending on a sensorial or intellectual stimulus) can be immediate or derivated. The immediate attention (addressed to x as interesting for itself) is always non-voluntary: for example if in the crowd I suddenly recognize the voice of a friend, in the act of turning myself the will is not implied. Instead the derivated attention (addressed to x as interesting due to y) can be non-voluntary or voluntary: in fact the will is implied if we have some idea, even if faint and indefinite, of the fact that the attention effort addressed to x can be useful for y. The voluntary attention is always a contrasted will, with strong opposition by our habits of attention and by our traditional interests. See PP, I, p. 416 ff.
[10] PP I, pp. 286-287. See also PP II, pp. 344-345.

In James's perspective, however, this seems to raise at least two problems: first, the construction of a primary stabilizing character; second, the need for an effort of voluntary attention in order to transform the character, that is, to acquire a set of new stabilizing attitudes for the self.

As for the first problem we need only to remember that for James a fundamental feature of the stream of consciousness is its *personal character*. This means that we are always dealing with thoughts and feelings which are thought or felt by some particular individual. However, the personal character of the stream of consciousness does not exclude the idea of a manifoldness of the self at all: unity is the result of a process of unification of such multiplicity of our conscious experiences, and it can be constructed by stabilizing the several selves around a paramount character. That is why James says that the consciousness *tends* to the personal form:

"[...] the thoughts which psychology studies do continually tend to appear as parts of personal selves. I say 'tend to appear' rather than 'appear,' on account of those facts of sub-conscious personality, automatic writing, etc., of which we studied a few in the last chapter. The buried feelings and thoughts proved now to exist in hysterical anæsthetics, in recipients of post-hypnotic suggestion, etc., themselves are parts of *secondary personal selves.*"[11]

Here we find an implicit reference to Janet's studies on hysteria.[12] As we know, James considered the study of hysterical multiple personalities a fundamental achievement in psychology, for the secondary selves, however rudimentary, are "still organized selves with a memory, habits, and sense of their own identity."[13] In this prospect we can affirm that there are no impersonal thoughts but rather lightning thoughts which elude the synthesis of the primary self and create secondary selves with their own characters.

As for the second problem, it is noteworthy that James relates selection and

---

11 PP I, p. 227.

12 See PP I, p. 202-213. P. Janet (1859-1947) successor of Jean-Martin Charcot at the Salpetrière Hospital in Paris, the top European school of psychiatry at the time, where famous studies on hysteria which deeply influenced the thought of Sigmund Freud were conducted. He stressed psychological factors in hypnosis and contributed to the modern concept of mental and emotional disorders involving anxiety, phobias, and other abnormal behaviour. He introduced the words dissociation and subconscious into psychological terminology and attributed hysteria and hypnotic susceptibility to inherited dispositions toward imbalances in psychic energy and psychic tension. Janet's most popular work is *L'automatisme psychologique*, Félix Alcan, Paris, 1889.

13 PP I, p. 229.

choice in our everyday life to the habits of attention (i.e. to the steadiest of *character*) rather than to voluntary attention. Will, however, intervenes in order to explain the possibility of a change of habits, namely, of the transformation of the character. That is how it is presented both in the *Principles* and in the *Talks to Teachers*, where the psychological and philosophical reflection turns to the problem of education. In the *Varieties of Religious Experience*, however, when it comes to the issue of conversion, James's argument takes quite a different direction. Accordingly, the two questions, respectively the problems of education and conversion, need to be dealt with separately.[14]

2. Education

At first, in the *Talks to Teachers* James stresses how above all education consist in the construction of habits, insofar as habits help to choose. James's target is the indecisive person, that is, "the nerveless sentimentalist and dreamer, who spends his life in a weltering sea of sensibility and emotion."[15] The indecisive man does not know how to choose because he has not built a character, that is, a personal set of habits, and to that extent suffers of a sort of inability to will or act.

That is why the *Talks*, as well as the *Principles*, present a pretty stern pedagogical ideal focusing on the worth of habit. In fact, habit minimizes the voluntary attention involved in everyday actions, and by that allows to save energies for the unexpected events which require a special focus of attention or an effort of the will. Education, then, is intended as determining the character as an organized set of habits of reaction able to opposes resistance, when exposed to possible changes, and to avoid the collapse of the structure of the personality. Thus, in a famous passage of the *Talks*, James accounts for the task of education:

"To quote my earlier book [*The Principles of Psychology*] directly, the great thing in all education is to *make our nervous system our ally instead of our enemy*. It is to fund and capitalize our acquisitions, and live at ease upon the interest of the fund. *For this we must make automatic and habitual, as early as possible, as many useful actions as we can*, and as carefully guard against the growing into ways that are likely to be disadvantageous. The more of the

---

[14] W. James, *The Varieties of Religious Experience* (1902), The Modern Library, New York, 1994 [hereafter VRE].
[15] PP I, p. 125.

85

details of our daily life we can hand over to the effortless custody of automatism, the more our higher powers of mind will be set free for their own proper work. There is no more miserable human being than one in whom nothing is habitual but indecision, and for whom the lighting of every cigar, the drinking of every cup, the time of rising and going to bed every day, and the beginning of every bit of work are subjects of express volitional deliberation."[16]

James took from Alexander Bain[17] some precepts on "moral habits" which have to be followed with great involvement and decision, resisting to opposite temptations and catching each useful occasion to practice them. James adds a fifth precept, the rule of the "effort of attention", following which we may always do something like this:

"[...] keep the faculty of the effort alive in you by a little gratuitous exercise every day. That is, by systematically ascetic or heroic in little unnecessary points, do every day or two something for no other reason that you would rather not do it, so that when the hour of dire need draws nigh, it may find you not unnerved and untrained to stand the test."[18]

The *Principles* does not ignore the pedagogic problem subtended to a vision of the educative process based on the construction of habits; if it is thus defined, education can lead to a certain rigidity of the character. However in these pages the habit assumes a particular ethical value, because it is a conservative agent of the interior and social order.

"Habit is thus the enormous fly-wheel of society, its most precious conservative agent. It alone is what keeps us all within the bounds of ordinance [...]. It dooms us all to fight out the battle of life upon the lines of nurture or our early choice, and to make the best of a pursuit that disagrees, because there is no other for which we are fitted, and it is too late to begin again [...]. Already at the age of twenty-five you see the professional mannerism settling down on the young commercial traveller, on the young doctor, on the young minister, on the young counseller-at-law. You see the little lines of cleavage running through the character, the tricks of thought, the prejudices, the ways of the "shop", in a word, from which the man can by-and-by no more escape than his coat-sleeve can suddenly fall into a new set of folds. On the whole, it is best

---

16 TT, p. 28. See also PP I, p. 122.
17 See A. Bain, *The Emotions and the Will*, Longmans, Green and Co., London 1865.
18 PP I, p. 125.

he should not escape. It is well for the world that in most of us, by the age of thirty, the character has set like plaster, and will never soften again"[19].

Here the whole educative question seems to turn out into the problem of the construction of a strong character able to resist to any kind of crisis. The well educated individual will stand like a tower when everything rocks around him: "Could the young but realize how soon they will become mere walking bundles of habits, they would give more heed to their conduct while in the plastic state."[20]

James's position seems more problematic when he turns his attention to education. In the *Talks to Teachers,* education essentially means "training pupils to behaviour", taking behaviour, not in the sense of his manners, but in the sense of every possible sort of fit reaction on the circumstances into which he may find himself[21]. In other words, education is *"the organization of acquired habits of conduct and tendencies to behaviour"*[22], so that for any situation the pupils will cope the most appropriate attitude. What we accomplish through education is a personal conception of how to name and classify any state of affairs:

"An 'uneducated' person—James says—is one who is nonplussed by all but the most habitual situations. On the contrary, one who is educated is able practically to extricate himself, by means of the examples with which his memory is stored and of the abstract conceptions which he has acquired, from circumstances in which he never was placed before."[23]

Although James apparently does not draw all the conclusions of this definition of the nature of education, it seems clear enough that here the view changes: the training of will, particularly the construction of the habit of an effort of the will, here does not seem to have the purpose of forming a completely strong character anymore. Rather, education as formation of the will should enable the individual to re-enact a formative process: if once one has been able to construct his/her habits through a voluntary effort of attention, by keeping such an ability of effort he/she should probably be able to construct new habits in a situation of crisis. Consequently, it is not by chance that James

---

[19] PP I, p. 121.
[20] PP I, p. 127.
[21] TT, p. 26.
[22] TT, p. 27.
[23] TT, p. 32.

includes a voluntary dimension in the process of religious conversion, viewed as self-formative psychological experience leading to a true transformation of the self.

3. Conversion

Lesson VIII of *Varieties,* named *The divided self and the process of its unification,* is an interesting premise to the ninth and tenth lessons dedicated to the religious conversion. James considers the possibility of a "second birth", as it happens in conversion experiences, as an opportunity open to specific kind of people and, in a certain sense, as an exceptional opportunity in the life of individuals.[24]

"The psychological basis of the twice-born character seems to be a certain discordancy or heterogeneity in the native temperament of the subject, an incompletely unified moral and intellectual constitution"; if a certain incoherence appears as an amiable weakness, "a stronger degree of heterogeneity may make havoc of the subject's life. There are persons whose existence is little more than a series of zig-zags, as now one tendency and now another gets the upper hand."[25]

James is not talking of the usual character perturbation: in one of his examples, when President Roosevelt goes fishing, he does not turn into another person, he does not change his character; the habitual centre of his personal energy, made of his aims, interests and habits, does not change[26]. Otherwise, opening to the possibility of conversion means researching a new centre around which reunify and stabilize our own self. James considers religious conversion as a particular case of a general psychological process: "to find religion is only one out of many ways of reaching unity"[27].

According to James's account of the stream of consciousness, what is

---

[24] We would like to highlight, en passant, that before the advent of the post-modern societies, the plasticity of the self was not celebrated as a psychological basis for continuous personality changes and wandering existential journeys. On this subject, see Z. Bauman, *Education: under, for and in spite of postmodernity,* in Z. Bauman, *The Individualized Society,* Polity Press, Cambridge 2001.

[25] VRE, pp. 164-66.

[26] VRE, pp. 190-93.

[27] VRE, p. 172.

traditionally called soul is just a sequence of fields of consciousness, organized in a *focus* and a *fringe*[28]. During the unwinding of the stream of consciousness, as James observes in *Varieties*, some of the themes of the marginal conscience can obviously move, for different reasons, inside the focal area; what normally does not destabilize the character. Yet, if a subject appearing into the marginal conscience can shake the whole organization of the "self", a process of conversion may start. Even if habits put up resistance, the new subject can finally win and trigger off a complex transformation of the character[29]. In James' opinion, will plays its own role in these processes: more precisely, in the so said "volitional type" of conversion, "the regenerative change is usually gradual, and consists in the building up, piece by piece, of a new set of moral and spiritual habits"[30].

Once more, as for education, James considers the habit of the voluntary effort of attention fundamental. Once the soul has been shaken by a sign, it is necessary to protect the desired object, together with the self we want to become, from contradictory ideas. In one of the tales quoted by James, for example, the protagonist affirms: "After this distinct revelation had stood for some little time before my mind, the question seemed to be put, 'Will you accept it now, to-day?' I replied, 'Yes; I will accept it to-day, or I will die in the attempt!'". After that, as James stresses, "[he] went into the woods, where he describes his struggles"[31].

The subject matter of "The Will to Believe",[32] one of the most controversial of James' work, has its origins in the philosophical problem of the perception of reality and in the close connection between will and belief stated in chapter XXI of the *Principles*: to believe in something means to acquiesce, as it were,

---

[28] See VRE, p. 226 ff. See also PP, Chapter IX ("The Stream of Thought"); *Psychology. Briefer Course* (1892), Harvard University Press, Cambridge-Mass. and London, 1984, Chapter XI ("The Stream of Consciousness"); *On Some Omissions of Introspective Psychology*, "Mind", January 1884 (republished in W. James, *Essays in Psychology*, Harvard University Press, Cambridge-Mass. And London 1983, pp. 142-167). On the subject of the field of consciousness and the fringe, see C. Lloyd Morgan, *An Introduction to Comparative Psychology* (1894), Walter Scott Publishing, London 1903; A. Gurwitsch, *Théorie du champ de la conscience*, Nauwelaerts, Louvain 1957; B. Mangan, *Sensation's Ghost. The Non-Sensory "Fringe" of Consciousness*, "Psyche", 7 (18), October 2001.
[29] VRE, pp. 193-94.
[30] VRE, p. 202.
[31] VRE, p. 204.
[32] W. James *The Will to Believe*, New World, June 1896. Republished in *The Will to Believe and Other Essays in Popular Philosophy* (1897), Harvard Univ. Pr., Cambridge (Mass.), 1979.

89

that is, to accept it as existing, to hold that it has "reality". So belief means what in the psychology of volition is defined as *consent*[33].

After all—James states—the distinction between real and unreal, together with the whole psychology of belief, non-belief and doubt, "is based on the fact that we can think differently the same and we can choose which way of thinking to adhere to and which to disregard."[34]

As a matter of fact, to the extent the will to believe can be related to voluntary attention, such a statement raises quite a momentous theoretical problem. In fact since attention depends for the most upon previously built in habits of attention, to believe or not to believe can never be purely a matter of "will".

This ambivalence of the *belief,* as an active as well as passive attitude, is clearly reflecting in the issue of education. In fact, in the *Talks to Teachers* James challenges the sense of a self stiffened by its own habits of attention (and so in its own beliefs): habits make sense because its automatism save energy and attention for taking care of new and more stimulating tasks. Thus, if we take account of James's pedagogical doctrine, effort appears like sort of a paradoxical habit, for it works like a habit opposing one's own habits, an heroic availability which should constantly mature at the margin of conscious life, in order to be activated in case of necessity. In other words, taking the theory of the plasticity of the self, James has to draw the field of consciousness as a field in which focus and fringe are or should be in tension: the focal conscience activities are guided by habits of attention, while the marginal conscience offers occasions and possibilities of resistance to the habit.

Then this complex vision of the role of will in the transformation of the self seems to become deeper in the reflection on religious conversion. After the "volitive type" conversion, James talks about the "self-surrender type", where the principal factor is the renunciation of the effort of will. James says clearly that here we are facing the involuntary and unconscious way in which mental results may get accomplished:

"Of the volitional type of conversion it would be easy to give examples, but they are as a rule less interesting than those of the self-surrender type, in which the subconscious effects are more abundant and often startling. I will therefore

---

[33] See PP II, pp. 283-287 and James's distinction between the object coming into consciousness "as simply thought of [vorgestellt]" and the object coming "as admitted [anerkannt]" (PP II, p. 286). James quotes on this subject F. Brentano, *Psychologie vom empirischen Standpunhkt* (1874), Felix Meiner Verlag, Hamburg 1973.
[34] PP II, p. 290.

hurry to the latter, the more so because the difference between the two types is after all not radical. Even in the most voluntarily built-up sort of regeneration there are passages of partial self-surrender interposed; and in the great majority of all cases, when the will has done its uttermost towards bringing one close to the complete unification aspired after, it seems that the very last step must be left to other forces and performed without the help of its activity. In other words, self-surrender becomes then indispensable. "The personal will" says Dr. Starbuck, "must be given up. In many cases relief persistently refuses to come until the person ceases to resist, or to make an effort in the direction he desires to go."[35]

Here it seems rather important to mention the notion of a psychic region of subconscious experience, completely outside the field of consciousness. Ordinary psychology, observes James, thinks that focus or marginal conscience, as well as attentive or casual one, is inside the field and what is left out is absolutely non-existent. To this regard the author makes reference to the notion of the "subliminal consciousness" expressed by Frederic W. H. Myers in 1886:

"[…] one's ordinary fields of consciousness are liable to incursions from it of which the subject does not guess the source, and which, therefore, take for him the form of unaccountable impulses to act, or inhibitions of action, of obsessive ideas, or even of hallucinations of sight or hearing. The impulses may take the direction of automatic speech or writing, the meaning of which the subject himself may not understand even while he utters it; and generalizing this phenomenon, Mr. Myers has given the name of automatism, sensory or motor, emotional or intellectual, to this whole sphere of effects due to 'uprushes' into the ordinary consciousness of energies originating in the subliminal parts of the mind."[36]

In other words, the difference between gradual conversion (voluntary) and sudden conversion (involuntary), lays in the fact that for the latter we don't

---

[35] VRE, pp. 203-05.
[36] VRE, p. 229. See also W. James, *Frederic Myers's Services to Psychology*, in "Proceedings of the Society for Psychological Research", XVIII, 1901. Although very far from the strict Freudian account of unconscious, Myers's subliminal consciousness can be placed among its theoretical antecedents. See F. W. H. Myers, *The Subliminal Consciousness*, in "Proceedings of the Society for Psychical Research", VIII, 1892. See also F. W. H. Myers, *Human Personality and Its Survival of Bodily Death* (2 vols.), Longmans Green and William, London 1903.

need to invoke a more incisive intervention of the divine, but rather conclude that sudden conversion is connected with the possession of an active subliminal self, where experiences which, in special circumstances, could emerge at a conscious level mature[37]. Thus, it seems that in such cases the most relevant activity occurs in the marginal conscience, which is conceived as an area with extremely blurred and unfathomable borders, as a sort of grey area between conscious and subconscious region. Such a faint border, as it were, allows for the passage of subconscious experiences towards the centre of the field of consciousness, creating forms of sudden conversion. On the contrary, when the borders are more resistant, "conversion must be gradual if it occur, and must resemble any simple growth into new habits"[38].

4. Conclusion

The reflection on religious conversion, as it now clearly appears, enhances that inner dialectic of consciousness (will and belief, habits of attention and voluntary attention, focus and margin) which we may connect to the essential plasticity of the self. Introducing the notion of subconscious, particularly inspired by the first studies on hypnosis and to be intended in a pre-freudian sense (as the region of those psychic contents which are not assigned to the field of the conscience), James refers to the fact that the tension between focal conscience and marginal conscience is not entirely delivered to our higher powers of mind: the transformations of the self go beyond the possibility of a conscious control of the individual who is undertaking a work of formation or of self-formation. As James himself observes in the pages of the *Varieties*, "the 'will to believe' cannot be stretched as far as that"[39].

The formative and self-formative work develops at the periphery of the conscience. It is a constant tension between centripetal and centrifugal forces in the elaboration of the stimuli showing at the window of our attention. The transformations of the self are mainly to be played at the boundary of the marginal conscience.

---

[37] See VRE, p. 235.
[38] VRE, p. 237.
[39] VRE, p. 208.

The Glass Prison. Emerson, James and the Religion of the Individual

Ramón del Castillo *

1. A Religion of Their Climate

Emerson's influence on James's religious individualism is neither simple nor free from contradictions, particularly in view of the close relation between religion and morality in some of James's writings. Both Emerson's creed and James's pragmatic gospel did strive to achieve some kind of heretical individualism as an alternative to that rapacious individualism which in their own days was allied with an increasing mass culture and leveling democracy. Emerson's and James's "divine self" is radically opposed to selfish individualism, although it is essentially *egotistic*. Of course, James's "pragmatization" of Emerson meant, among other things, that he did really tone down Emerson's glorification of solitude (or that he urbanized his private garden—if you prefer a more poetic tone). But things are not that easy, since James still shows a particular dependence on Emersonian tropes.

In both Emerson and James, social criticism did not spring merely out of opposition against possessive individualism, but of a defense of moral egotism grounded on a conception of a *deeper* self able to resist to social assimilation and false illusions. Such a conception, however, commits the individualist hero, as he/she tries to refuse false commitments, to a too anxiogenic obligation: to be completely loyal to him/her-self, and, to be loyal to the exclusive small circle of other selves that could recognize *each other* as unique and sovereign.

Needless to say that VRE contains a very Jamesian reading of Emerson. There are systems of beliefs, James asserts, which one could call religious and which, however, do not positively assume the existence of a God. "We must interpret the term 'divine' very broadly, as denoting any object that it is god*like,* whether it be a concrete deity or not."[1] From a pragmatic point of view, a "godless" devotion can be considered "religious", if that which

---

*Professor of Contemporary Philosophy and Cultural Studies at UNED, Madrid (Spain)
[1] *The Varieties of Religious Experience* Longmans & Green, New York 1902 [Penguin Books, 1982] (Hereafter VRE), p. 34. All the references to other works by James are to *The Writing of William James. A Comprehensive Edition.* McDermott, J. J. (ed.), The University of Chicago Press, 1977 (Hereafter "WJ").

individuals consider divine bears concrete consequences to their lives. Indeed, since the object of the transcendentalist cult, neither a deity *in concreto* nor a superhuman person, but rather an immanent divinity, Emerson assumed God as an abstract Ideality identified as the moral force of the universe (VRE, 32). Such is the Emersonian religion, in James's own words:

"[T]he universe has a divine soul, which soul is moral, being also the soul within the soul of man. But whether this soul of the universe be a mere quality like the eye's brilliancy or the skin's softness, or whether it be a self-conscious life like the eye's seeing or the skin's feeling, is a decision that never unmistakably appears in Emerson's ages... Whatever it is, though, it is active. As much as if it were a God we can trust it to protect all ideal interests and keep the world balance straight."[2]

Of course, for James the inner and intimate experiences which underlie such expressions of faith on moral energies were quite worth to be called "religious" experiences. After all, Emerson himself had already offered a pragmatic *substitute* of religion in his famous 1838 "Divinity School Address", and it is natural that James evoked it just after having offered his over-individualistic definition or religion (VRE, 31). The essence of religion, Emerson proclaimed, is the intuition or perception of a certain universal "power", hidden deep inside the soul of the individual. From the point of view of practical religion, it is not really relevant whether Emerson speaks of one Will, Mind of Divinity, Spirit, Oversoul or universal Law, or the metaphysical attributes of such an over-principle, but its practical effect in the moral life of individuals. As James will claim later, what is important about what individuals consider as divine is that it determines positively their fears and hopes, their doubts and expectations and operates as the primal energy for their moral life (VRE, 447). The sentiment of reverence and delight in the presence of certain moral laws awakens in the individual "a sentiment which we call the religious sentiment, and which makes our highest happiness. Wonderful is its power to charm and to command." The essence of religion—Emerson claims, much before James— is this *moral* "divine and deifying" sentiment, such an "insight of the perfection of the laws of the soul".[3] Then, although Emerson's idea of the divine is too vague, it

---

[2] VRE, p. 33.
[3] Emerson "Divinity School Address", *Essays and Poems,* Library of America, 1996, (Hereafter EEP), p. 76. Passages from Emerson's Address quoted by James himself are in VRE, pp. 32-33.

works as a support for a practical individual morality. It was just the kind of religious attitude displayed by many of those people inclined to reject the old Calvinist moral.[4] The Emersonian God is a God that dwells so deep inside one's own being that it can be pragmatically identified with the best part of oneself, namely, the worthy, archetypal and more authentic self.[5] Accordingly, in the emersonian religion the individual is one with the divine *only* when he or she is at distance from society.[6] In *solitude* only, personal consciousness and inner life are possessed by the sense of an unseen power that *exceeds* and inhabits the self at once; a power *immense* enough to be *divine* but *inner* enough to be just *me*. As James himself observed in his 1903 "Address at the Emerson Centenary in Concord":

"If the individual open thus directly into the Absolute, it follows that there is something in each and all of us, even the lowliest, that ought not to consent to borrowing traditions and living at second hand... Emerson writes: "As long as any man exists there is some need for him; let him fight for his own". This faith that in a life at first hand there is something sacred is perhaps the most characteristic note in Emerson's writings [...] the present man is the aboriginal reality. The Institution is derivative, and the past man is irrelevant and obliterate for present issues. [...] The commonest person's act if genuinely actuated, can lay hold eternity." (WJ, 583, 585).

---

[4] Consider the pragmatic core of some Emerson's *dicta* which, to be sure, James could use in favor of his own reading: "So is it with us, now sceptical, or without unity, because immersed in forms and effects all seeming to be of equal yet hostile value, and now religious, whilst in the reception of spiritual law. Bear with these distractions, with this coetaneous growth of the parts: they will one day be members, and obey one will. On that one will, on that secret cause, they nail our attention and hope. *Life is hereby melted into an expectation or a religion.* Underneath the inharmonious and trivial particulars, is a musical perfection, the ideal journeying always with us, the heaven without rent or seam ("Experience", EEP, p. 484) "It is for us to believe in the rule, not in the exception. The noble are thus known from the ignoble. So in accepting the leading of the sentiments, *it is not what we believe concerning the immortality of the soul, or the like, but the universal impulse to believe,* that is the material circumstance, and is the principal fact in the history of the globe". ("Experience", EEP, p. 486) [ours italics].

[5] "That is always best which gives me to myself. The sublime is excited in me by the great stoical doctrine: Obey thyself. That which shows God in me, fortifies me. That which shows God out of me, makes me a wart and a wen" ("Divinity School Address", EEP, p. 81).

[6] "It is simpler to be self-dependent. The height, the deity of man is, to be self-sustained, to need no gift, no foreign force. Society is good when it does not violate me; but best when it is likest to solitude" ("The Transcendentalist", EEP, p. 195).

Accordingly, the Emersonian hero feels free to believe *as if* he or she were living a fresh relation with the universe, free from traditions, past, history, but also from conventions, customs, churches, institutions and family. There is, Emerson states, a way to experience who or what you are before you enter in this world, before the society imposes you a name and compels you to use its own language. Pragmatically, individuals can feel free if they think that their true individuality depends on hidden forces outside the social world, or, in Emerson's terms, that they possess a secret *intuition* previous to any *tuition*. For Emerson, all assertions of the self in the instituted language are destructive of individuality, since, as he declares in "The Poet", "Language is fossil poetry". Consequently, "Self-reliance", or self-trust, depends on a strange kind of insight which cannot be received second hand.

"Who is the Trustee? What is the aboriginal Self, on which a universal reliance may be grounded? [...] The inquiry leads us to that source, at once the essence of genius, of virtue, and of life, which we call Spontaneity or Instinct. We denote this primary wisdom as Intuition, whilst all later teachings are tuitions."[7]

"Nature", we all know, was the name that Emerson applied to this enormous surplus which inhabits the deeper self. "Nature" was for him not a challenge to men's power of domination or a vast stock to be domesticated and exploited, but rather a force that would appeal directly to individuals without the mediation of cultural or social determinations.[8] The religion of the individual would be, in fact, a creed of the infinity, namely, the absence of measure, of the individuals in their solitude: "If there is anything grand and daring in human

---

[7] "Self-Reliance", EEP, p. 269.

[8] Emersonian wisdom, as Harold Bloom claims, is not "faith" in the old Christian sense. Acquaintance with what is godlike in the deepest self implies trust, loyalty, or fidelity, and certain experiences of the numinous. The numinous has the effect to change the personal consciousness; but, at the same time, it is more fictive and egotistic than Christian faith (something like a *necessary* illusion). It is, if you like, a kind of love, but as Bloom says, is neither *ágape*, nor *philía* nor *cháritas*. It is rather a "love of power". Which power? The power of usurpation. But, usurpation of what? Of "a place, a stance, a fullness, an illusion of identification or possession, something we can call our own or even ourselves". Bloom, Harold: *Agon, Towards a Theory of Revisionism*, Oxford, Oxford University Press, p. 17; Bloom, by the way, opposes the "Will to power" with this "power to will", or power of appropriation. See also Bloom's references to Emerson in his *The American Religion. The Emergence of the Post-Christian Nation*, Simon & Schuster, New York, 1992.

thought or virtue—Emerson said in "The Transcendentalist"—any reliance on the vast, the unknown; any presentiment; any extravagance of faith, the spiritualist adopts it as most in nature".[9] Emerson sometimes gave this measureless the name of *whim*, rather than the less provocative and more civic name of "freedom".[10] A passage of "The Transcendentalist" in which he interprets in his own way Jacobi's atheism illustrates very well the main point: the lawgiver self demands something godlike, since that self refuses all measure of right and wrong except the determinations of the private spirit, which means that "it pardons faults according to the letter and exerts the sovereign right which the majesty of his being confers on him; he sets the seal of his divine nature to the grace he accords [...] every one must do after his kind, be he asp or angel, and these must".[11] The Puritan haunted by the obsession with pitfalls and sin, one could say, is replaced by a "man of native force" who absolves to himself and accepts cheerfully that surplus or excess which nurtures moral propensities. Morality, for the better or the worse, depends on impulses that resist any external authority and force the self to reject any measure in his own trustworthiness.

"An attitude might be called *religious*", James will repeat in *Varieties,* "though no touch were left in it of sacrifice or submission, no tendency to flexion, no bowing of the head" (VRE, 77). However, if religious impulses represent an absolute expansion of the subject's range and sphere of power, an "added dimension of emotion, an enthusiastic temper of espousal, in regions where morality strictly so called can at best but how its head and acquiesce..." (VRE, 48) Could such an individualistic creed really be a religion of peace? If the only basis for discrimination between right and wrong is found in the fact that some acts tend to expand and strengthen the deepest self, could not the Emersonian believer consume the world and other selves into its own fantasy of self-consummation? Since the extemporaneous divine-like self creates his own law as if it were a god, what could stop its own expansion except another god-like self?

---

[9] "The Trascendentalist", EP, p. 197.

[10] According to his own *motto*: "I shun father and mother and wife and brother, when my genius calls me. I would write on the lintels of the door-post, *Whim.* I hope it is somewhat better than whim at last, but we cannot spend the day in explanation" ("Self-Reliance", EP, p. 262)

[11] Among Jacobi's examples I would highlight Pilades's lies and deceits when he supplants Orestes, which surely Emerson would take as an example of *philia* over and above the law of the polis. True moral laws, as given by lawgivers—Emerson also claim in "Divinity School Address" (*op. cit.*, p. 76) — refuse to be adequately written on paper or spoken by the tongue.

Let's turn, then, to the supposedly well-tempered James. Is Emerson's religious individualism (or religion of the individual) too strenuous and violent for the mediating and reconciling spirit of James's own gospel? I would answer in the negative, and the best reason is James's insistence in the *Varieties* that the essence of the religion is essentially *egotistic*. On the one hand, we have the cheerful welcoming of religion and its substitutes as a means of liberating repressive impulses. Like love, wrath, hope, ambition, jealousy, like every other instinctive eagerness and impulse, James states, religion adds to life an *enchantment* that is not rationally or logically deducible from anything else. "This enchantment, coming as a gift when it does come, —a gift of our organism, the physiologist will tell us, a gift of God's grace, the theologians say—, is either there or not there for us" (VRE, 47-48).[12] James transpose Emersonian *whim*, into psychological terms, as it were, as the action of some subconscious experience. In Frederick Myers's terms –James observes— it would be a dimension of experience which can never manifest itself completely, a hidden power of expression in abeyance or reserve, sometimes associated with things as insignificant as imperfect memories, silly jingles, inhibitions, or "dissolutive" phenomena (as Myers called them), but also— James adds— "with many performances of *genius*" (VRE, 512). In the work of geniuses, Emerson already said, "we recognize our own rejected thoughts and they come back to us with a certain alienated majesty".[13] To some extent, then, James preserved the Emersonian jargon giving it a new expression in terms of subliminal consciousness.

On the other hand, however, no matter how much James tempered the Emersonian doctrine of the lawgiver, the representative man or the genius, the core of his own psychology of religion is as ethically provocative as Emerson's own doctrine. James was very clear about this point: "The pivot round which the religious life revolves is the interest of the individual in his private personal destiny. Religion, in short, is a monumental chapter in the history of human egotism" (VRE, 491). The forces, impulses or energies in which crude savages or cultivated persons believe, today as much as in any previous age, agree with each other *only* in recognizing *personal demands* —James adds—. But if religious-like sentiments satisfy personal needs, then the personal need to be oneself acquires something of a religious crusade:

"That unshareable feeling which each one of us has of the pinch of his individual destiny as he privately feels it rolling out on fortune's wheel may be

---

[12] On James's idea of "genius" see VRE, pp. 6 ff., 16, and 335.
[13] "Self Reliance", EEP, p. 259.

disparaged for its egotism [...] but it is the one thing that fills up the measure of our concrete actuality, and any would-be existent that should lack such a feeling, or its analogue, would be a piece of reality only half made up [...] The axis of the reality runs solely through the egotistic places [...] The recesses of feeling, the darker, blinder strata of character are the only places in the world in which we catch real fact in the making, and directly perceive how events happen, and how work is actually done."[14]

One would say that this is another version of Emerson's original creed in its core. The provocation, however, is still there, since James's religion of the individual (or individualistic view of religion) does lead to an unavoidable polytheism which he describes as the highest expression of freedom, but also as the source of an eternal fighting between gods:

"If an Emerson were forced to be a Wesley, or a Moody forced to be a Whitman, the total human consciousness of the divine would suffer. The divine can mean no single quality, it must mean a group of qualities, by being champions of which in alternation, different men may all find worthy missions [...] So a "god of battles" must be allowed to be the god for one kind of person, a god of peace and heaven and home, the god for another [...] we live in partial systems, and that parts are not interchangeable in the spiritual life (VRE, 487)."[15]

Struggle and danger, then, are essential to a religion of the individual. Even if James sometimes insinuates some desirable harmony or balance achieved in the long run, some ideal unity between elementary moral forces, he maintains that *prima facie* there is no definitive compromise between them. It is true that

---

[14] VRE, pp. 501-502; 499-500.

[15] Compare this passage with James's polytheism in the last chapter of *Pragmatism*. Reading the former text, one should highlight that for James there is no essential difference between crude savages and cultured individuals, since both are believers in gods as allies of personal needs, the value of the divine only lying in its face value, in its realization as a present and actual good. No matter which kind of ideality God has embodied in the past, pragmatic religion only retains the *actuality* of God as a power beyond, with which one may come into *beneficent* contact. Santayana, in fact, considered in his *Poetry and Religion* (1900) that American faith in the *actuality* of ideals or in the continuousness of the ideal and the real, as a new *barbarism*, Emerson and Whitman being the American prophets of it, although one should add James himself to the list (See R. B. Perry's comments on Santayana's idea of American barbarism in "James as reformer", *The Thought and Character of William James*, Nashville, Vanderbilt University Press, 1996, pp. 250-251).

"the course of history is nothing but the story of men's struggles [...] to find the more and more inclusive order"[16], but a more inclusive order of ideals, however, is not at all the same as an unifying whole which can include all parts. As James also says, there are possibly as many elementary moral forces as there are *physical* forces, and the various ideals, spirits, gods, demons (or whatever name individuals give to certain powers towards which they adopt a solicit observance, respect, devotion or love) have *no* common character "apart from the fact that they are ideals. No single abstract principle can be so used to yield"[17]

In consequence, when in a famous passage James claims that what characterizes religious experience is the feeling of a union of our extra-marginal self with a wider and greater self through which invigorating or saving experiences come (VRE, 515), James sounds as individualistic as Emerson was. The *only* thing that religious experience proves is the existence of a larger power which is friendly to *each* individual:

"All the facts require is that the power should be both other and larger than our conscious selves. Anything larger will do, if only it be large enough to trust for the next step [...] it might conceivably even be only a large and more godlike self, of which the present self would then be but the mutilated expression, and the universe might conceivably be a collection of such selves, of different degrees of inclusiveness, with no absolute unity realized in it at all. Thus would a sort of polytheism return upon... a polytheism which, by the way, has always been the real religion of common people and it is so still to-day [...] If there be different gods, each caring for his part, some portion of some of us might not be covered with divine protection, and our religious consolation would thus fail to be complete...[there can be] portions of the universe that may irretrievably lost. Common sense [...] can suffer the notion of this world being partly saved and partly lost. The ordinary moralistic state of mind makes the salvation of the world conditional upon the success with which each unit does its part."[18]

The wider self, maybe as the Emersonian Over-soul, then, is no all-inclusive ideal, or universal monistic principle at all. The higher self is an operative force in the universe, which *each* individual "can keep in working touch with" (VRE, 508). Despite the fact that James invoked from time to time monistic entities as

---

[16] "The Moral Philosopher and the More Life", WJ, p. 623.

[17] *Ibid.*, p. 621.

[18] VRE, p. 525.

"Mother Earth", "Nature", or the "Mother-sea of Consciousness", the primal language of his moral vision is radically individualistic and pluralistic. *Prima facie* divine forces form a multifarious jungle, and many of them exclude each other. On the one hand, religious quality of the moral life makes the individual merge into a larger communal life, but on the other hand that same quality also express es the most *un*shareable strata of a divine-like self in its solitude, and therefore they also constitute *repulsive* forces. The sacred element which exists deep inside each self can be similar from one person to the next, but to be really sacred it must be essentially unique, unapproachable, and it must incarnates a strenuous resistance against any obligation *external* to the self. Was not Emerson ambiguous enough when he defined Self-Reliance?

"To believe that what is true for you in your private heart is true for all men, —that is genius—. Speak your latent conviction, and it shall be the universal sense; for the inmost in due time becomes the outmost, and our first thought is rendered back to us by the trumpets of the Last Judgment."[19]

2. Seers and Friends

We need then to go back to the thorny question: What kind of sociability can provide a religion of the sacred self? "Self-reliance" and the "will to believe" do not strike us as social attitudes. If they do, then they stand for a polemic sense of "social" since they further partial loyalties. One could say that the individualistic standpoint offers only a negative view of socialization, since it entitles each individual to feel right against the opinion of the majority. Emerson remarked that the representative man can influence society, but only indirectly. The charismatic seers can inspire or illuminate other individuals in their own quests, but as Emerson clearly claims in "Experience", individuals' effective influence will always depend on contingent casualties and some gratuitous spontaneity between them:

"Life is a series of surprises, and would not be worth taking or keeping, if it were not [...] All good conversation, manners, and action, come from a

---

[19] "Self-Reliance", EEP, p. 259. Again, in Bloom's radical version of Emerson's creed: if you don't believe in your own conviction, if your are not loyal to it, then don't bother anyone else with it, but if you do, then don't care whether anyone else agrees with it or not. If it is strong enough, then they will come round to it anyway, and you should just shrug when in the end they tell you that it is a right conviction. Bloom, *Agon*, pp. 19-20.

spontaneity which forgets usages, and makes the moment great. Nature hates calculators; her methods are saltatory and impulsive. Man lives by pulses [...] We thrive by casualties. Our chief experiences have been casual. The most attractive class of people are those who are powerful obliquely, and not by the direct stroke: men of genius, but not yet accredited: one gets the cheer of their light, without paying too great a tax [...] In the thought of genius there is always a surprise; and the moral sentiment is well called "the newness", for it is never other; as new to the oldest intelligence as to the young child, – "the kingdom that cometh without observation". In like manner, for practical success, there must not be too much design. A man will not be observed in doing that which he can do best. There is a certain magic about his properest action, which stupefies your powers of observation, so that though it is done before you, you wits not of it. The art of life has a pudency, and will not be exposed."[20]

I think James would mostly agree with this, since for him some "heretical sort of innovation" (VRE, 334) represented the main source of a true morality, a morality faced with a pale democracy which cover up its predatory impulses with soft and polite manners.[21] However, social criticism led by extemporaneous moral leaders has a very problematic face. The fact that some individuals engage each other in face to face dialogue and discussion, the fact that they cultivate friendship or fellowship, hinges on some *previous* affinities between them. Affinity is not created as effect of mutual understanding, but it is rather what makes possible any further understanding.[22] In the end, individuals can connect with each other because they are able (more or less

---

[20] "Experience", EEP, p. 483.

[21] In this point, James seems to follow Emerson almost literally. Compare these two inflammatory diatribes, the first by Emerson, the second one by James: "In this our talking America, we are ruined by our good nature and listening on all sides. This compliance takes away the power of being greatly useful" (*Ibid*, EEP, p. 490) "...Mediocrity, church sociable and teacher's conventions, are taking the place of the old height and depths and romantic chiaroscuro [...] Even now, in our country, correctness, fairness and compromise for every small advantage are crowding out all other qualities. The higher heroisms and the old rare flavors are passing out of life. [...] It looks indeed... as if the romantic idealist with their pessimism about civilization were, after all, quite right" (James, "What Makes a Life Significant", WJ, pp. 648-650).

[22] "By oldest right, by the divine affinity of virtue with itself, I find them, or rather not I, but the Deity in me and in them derides and cancels the thick walls of individual character, relation, age, sex, circumstance, at which he usually connives, and now makes many one" ("Friendship", EEP, p. 343).

unconsciously) to recognize beyond the social appearances a exemplification of authenticity. James himself described the essence of Emerson's creed:

"For Emerson the individual fact and moment were indeed suffused with absolute radiance, but is was upon a condition that saved the situation —they must be worthy specimens— sincere, authentic, archetypal; they must made connection with what he calls the Moral Sentiment, they must in some way act as a symbolic mouthpieces of the Universe's meaning. To know just which thing does act in this way, and which thing fails to make the true connection, is the secret (somewhat incommunicable, it must be confessed) of seership, and doubtless we must not expect of the seer too rigorous a consistency. Emerson himself was a real seer. He could perceive the full squalor of the individual fact, but he could also see the transfiguration."[23]

But how did James himself appropriate and transform this ideal of non-calculated and spontaneous affinity between unique individuals? Despite the fact that James endorsed a democratic creed, his own moral gospel did not imply a leveling of differences. As Ralph Barton Perry noted, James *never* believed that one individual was as good as another, or that all causes were equally commendable. On the contrary

"[...] his politics was governed by the principle of discrimination. The educated man was the man who knew how to criticize, and it was his role in politics to offset to the best of his power both the self-seeking of the ambitious and the blind passion of the crowd [...] He allied himself with a minority whose function it was to apply critical reflection to public affairs, and whose destiny it was to remain a minority. [...] In domestic politics he would be bound by no party allegiance, but would use his vote to tip the scales in favor of rationality and righteousness".[24]

But once again, what idea of democracy does a visionary company embrace? What kind of social good does a minority of insiders provide? Neither Emerson nor James were escapist or antisocial; they both sought a kind of public commitment. The Emersonian prophet and the Jamesian moralist conceive themselves as individuals that enrich society, although at the same time they do not trust in far-reaching, wide or extensive social organization

---

[23] "Address at the Emerson Centenary in Concord", WJ, 586.
[24] Perry, *op. cit.*, pp. 238, 239. See the connection between what Perry calls "principle of discrimination" and James's criticism of "political correctness" in footnote 21.

103

(even less on society as "State", "organization"... or similar things). That is because the key is *friendship*, a curious ideal of sociability according to which one can cherish secretly deep anti-social sentiments while identifying some groups of individuals with the ultimate source of cultivated democracy.[25] Far from hindering the connection with the others, then, individualism rather stimulates it: by encouraging skepticism towards larger society, it redirects the individuals towards concrete *experiences* of love, friendship, sympathy, comradeship... In other words: distrust of abstract institutions and large modes of social organization make desires of direct recognition flourish. Democracy is not an institutional and historical way of government, but an ideal collection of associations with different degrees of inclusiveness, yet with no absolute unity realized in it at all; a multitude of strangers whose background, values or ideals could diverge radically and who do not share loyalty to the same creed except, perhaps, to the very creed of individualism.[26] No doubt, one could say of James

---

[25] "Certain persons have a enormous capacity for friendship and for taking delight in others people's lives; and such persons knows more of truth than if their hearts were not so big" in "What Makes a Life significant", WJ, p. 646). It is noteworthy that James does not mean that friendship could provide us *all* the truth, but only that without friendship we surely miss a good deal of truth.

[26] "Temperance and non-resistance societies [...] movements of abolitionists and of socialists; in Sabbath and Bible Conventions [...] even the insect world was to be defended". "New England Reformers", EEP, p. 591). But compare with the next passage from "The Transcendentalist" (EEP, p. 203): "What you call your fundamental institutions, your great and holy causes, seem to them [the transcendentalists] great abuses, and, when nearly seen, paltry matters. Each 'Cause', as it is called —say Abolition, Temperance, say Calvinism, or Unitarianism —becomes speedily a little shop, where the article, let it have been at first never so subtle and ethereal, is now made up into portable and convenient cakes, and retailed in small quantities to suit purchasers". Elisabeth Peadboy, for example, described Brook Farm as "a few individuals, who, unknown to each other, under different disciplines of life, reacting from different social evil", nonetheless aim to be "wholly true to their natures as men and women" which sounded Emersonian enough. Emerson, however, did *decline* to join Brook Farm (quoted by Rosenblum, N., "Romanticism", *A Companion to American Thought*, Oxford, Blackwell, 1995, p. 603). Emerson ambivalence was magisterially grasped by James's words although to some extent one could also apply them to James himself. "He might easily have found himself saying of some present-day agitator against our Philippine conquest what he said of this o that reformer of his own time. He might have called him, as a private person, a tedious bore and canter. But he would infallibly have added what he then added: «it is strange and horrible to say this, for I feel that under him and his partiality and exclusiveness is the earth and the sea, and all that in them is, and the axis round which the Universe resolves passes through his body where he stands»". James, W. "Address at the Emerson Centenary", WJ, p. 586). The American scholar, then, does not exclude anything by himself (since he tries to sustain in the sublime

what is sometimes said of Emerson, that is: what he opposed to mass democracy was not a better social organization, but rather a "dazzle of personalities seeing in society the spectacle of diversity that other Romantics saw in Nature".[27]

Of course, James's detachment from large politics and institutions does not contradict his firm belief in the *moral* utility of groups articulated around utopian over-beliefs rather than in abstract ethical principles. But it also expresses his more hidden conviction that democracy requires the moral leadership of representative men. Morality is ultimately committed to moral character, which includes intuitions and practice, imagination and action at once. Hopes and illusions, ideals and ends must be realized in a concrete and effective way, what does not mean in a way expedient for established social purposes. On the contrary, the social realm could represent the dissolution of authentic morality in the abstract sea of social conventions. For James, practical morality means *concrete* human commitments opposed to *abstract* ways of social relationship.

The fact is that James still thought of the utility of the individualist hero in romantic terms: natural gifts, unbounded impulses and unconscious powers in some individuals let them be in contact with *residual* moral forces, unruly sensibilities and ways of being which evade the tyranny of majorities. "Divinity lies all about us, and culture is too narrow-minded to even suspect the fact".[28] What does exactly "divinity" mean as opposed to "culture"?

"In God's eyes the differences of social position, of intellect, of culture, of cleanliness, of dress, which different men exhibit, and all the other rarities and exception on which they so fantastically pin their pride, must be so small as practically quite to vanish; and all that should remain is the common fact that here we are, a countless multitude of vessels of life, each of us pent in to peculiar difficulties, with which we must severally struggle by using whatever of fortitude and goodness we can summon up. The exercise of courage, patience and kindness must be the significant portion of the whole business, and the distinctions of position can only be a manner of diversifying the phenomenal surface upon which these underground virtues may manifest their effects. At this rate, the deepest human life is everywhere, is eternal. And, if any human attributes exist only in particular individuals, they must belong to

---

realm of radical pluralism, where a one-sidedness means a lose), but ironically he praises enthusiastically exclusion and one-sidedness *by others*.
[27] Nancy Rosenblum, "Romanticism", *op. cit.*, p. 602.
[28] "What Makes a Life Significant", WJ, pp. 648-650.

the mere trapping and decoration of the surface-show."[29]

What individuals have in common, then, is that they all can be denied or alienated from their full humanity, "humanity" meaning not any substantive principle or essence except the common uniqueness of each individual as an individual, a doctrine that truly signaled a commonness that leveled differences between individuals (*every* individual is sacred, *all* individuals are equally divine), but also condemned them to recognize each other as equals only on their mutual perception of their sacred uniqueness, the quest for social justice becoming a spiritual rather than political enterprise, personal rather than collective; a question, indeed, of acquaintance between individuals of their sacred individuality, rather than a question of group self-consciousness; a claim of recognition rather than one of re-organization.

Just because the post-romantic individualist drearily fears the "mass man", just because he identifies the public world with conformity and homogenization of personality, self-assertion acquired the quality of an act of *salvation*, or at least it became a surrogate or substitute of it. Society, as we have suggested above, is only an aggregate of intimate transactions between selves isolated in their private dreams. To deal with others as others, one has to reveal something about oneself (a revelation can only be answered with another) which in some sense also means to betray or deceive oneself. Communication, then, is conceived basically as a revelation of the truest personality and human relationships are seen as dead when the others do not serve us as a resource of our self-knowledge. Social grouping, plain political one-sidedness, is too little refined in comparison with the authenticity of the individualist who oscillates between ardour and piety, rebellion and charity, and who does not confuse patronizing tolerance of individual differences with the perennial *agon* of distinct gods and goods. Moral regeneration is accomplished by the efforts of men and women imbued with personal faith, and not by a mode of association which could subordinate the godlike essence in each individual to any external and transitory political authority.

The irony of that view is that in order to be truly a moral individualist one cannot trust too much on his/her own powers of discernment. Moral authenticity requires, to be sure, a bit of a self-dramatizing character (a public display of one's own uncertainties) which does not exclude a bit of anxiety. One should admit that Emerson was much more sceptical about recognition between selves than any other prophet of individualism, including James. Emerson was relatively clear about his scepticism. Friendship can be taken, on

---

[29] WJ, p. 650.

its good side, as a force that intensifies *sociability* in the sense of *face-to-face* relations, rather than in the sense of large social associations. Friendship can be the ground of contingent companies of individuals, of small circles of individuals, but it cannot serve as the glue of a large community:

"I please my imagination more with a circle of godlike men and women variously related to each other, and between whom subsists a lofty intelligence. But I find [the] law of *one to one* peremptory for conversation, which is the practice and consummation of friendship. Do not mix waters too much. The best mix [is] as ill as good and bad."[30]

As he also says, as each electrical state induces the opposite, the individual looks for friends for the sake of getting a larger self-acquaintance or solitude which, in turn, could exalt his social relation with others. "The instinct of affection revives the hope of union with our mates, and the returning sense of insulation recalls us from the chase".[31] This sounds well, and it seems that some kind of balance could rule, but things are quite different, as Emerson's suggests in ones of his more ambivalent digressions on friendship:

"Friendship, like the immortality of the soul, is too good to be believed […] In the golden hour of friendship, we are surprised with shades of suspicion and unbelief […] In strictness, the soul does not respect men as it respects itself. In strict science all persons underlie the same condition of an infinite remoteness."[32]

"We seek our friend not sacredly, but with an adulterate passion which would appropriate him to ourselves […] Almost all people descend to meet. All association must be a compromise, and, what is worst, the very flower and aroma of the flower of each of the beautiful natures disappears as they approach each other. What a perpetual disappointment is actual society, even of the virtuous and gifted! […] Our faculties do not play us true, and both parties are relieved by solitude."[33]

"Friendship requires that rare mean betwixt likeness and unlikeness, that piques each with the presence of power and of consent in the other party. Let

---

[30] "Friendship", EEP, p. 351.
[31] *Ivi*, p. 345.
[32] *Ivi*, pp. 343-344.
[33] *Ivi*, p. 345.

me be alone to the end of the world, rather than that my friend should overstep, by a word or a look, his real sympathy. I am equally balked by antagonism and by compliance. Let him not cease an instant to be himself. The only joy I have in his being mine, is that the *not mine* is *mine*. I hate, where I looked for a manly furtherance, or at least a manly resistance, to find a mush of concession. Better be a nettle in the side of your friend than his echo. The condition which high friendship demands is ability to do without it. That high office requires great and sublime parts. There must be very two, before there can be very one. Let it be an alliance of two large, formidable natures, mutually beheld, mutually feared, before yet they recognize the deep identity which beneath these disparities unites them."[34]

Consequently, even the very *one to one* law seems condemned to turn out a motive of deep discomfort. Even if friendship is reduced to a society of two individuals, individuals seem invariably and finally invaded by an anxious *suspicion* about their own interest in others and about the sincerity of others about them. Emerson's thoughts contain many examples of this skepticism, especially when he insists again in the *illusory* character of realities or the infinite *distance* between the self and the others. As he annotated in his journals, the individual is essentially insular and cannot be touched; every individual being an infinitely repellent unit. As he also crudely declared in "Experience", our relations to each other are essentially oblique and casual. Like physical particles, individuals can spin around each other, but if they get close in extreme, they inevitably are repelled.

"Was it Boscovich who found out that bodies never come in contact? Well, souls never touch their objects. An innavigable sea washes with silent waves between us and the things we aim at and converse with. Life will be imaged, but cannot be divided nor doubled. Any invasion of its unity would be chaos. The soul is not twin-born, but the only begotten, and though revealing itself as child in time, child in appearance, is of a fatal and universal power, admitting no co-life. Every day, every act betrays the ill-concealed deity. We believe in ourselves, as we do not believe in others. We permit all things to ourselves, and that which we call sin in others, is experiment for us."[35]

"It is a main lesson of wisdom to know your own from another's. I have learned that I cannot dispose of other people's facts; but I possess such a key to

---

[34] *Ivi*, p. 350.
[35] "Experience", EEP, p. 473.

my own, as persuades me against all their denials, that they also have a key to theirs. A sympathetic person is placed in the dilemma of a swimmer among drówning men, who all catch at him, and if he give so much as a leg or a finger, they will drown him."[36]

The price that the deeper self pays for its regression to the aboriginal stance is clear: perennial dissatisfaction. Cheerful egotism spills out in a negative Sublime, since the positively enigmatic nature of the core self falls into a dark abyss. On the one hand, the will to believe or self-reliance should drive us to our own comfortable climate, whereas the cost of regression makes it almost unbearable. Antithetic forces, antagonist feelings, between enthusiasm and panic, hope and horror…love and fear, are the mark of moral authenticity which seems to cause ironic waste rather than mere nihilistic destruction.[37]

Emerson has a gloomy but lucid awareness of world's iniquity, of the irremediable coexistence of good and bad within the true self, and of our "ape and angel" double nature—as he likes to say—which includes a sort of tragic quality. Such a quality James assumed far more than any other of Emerson's successors, since he also gave voice to a characteristic sorrow, or apathetic melancholia, a vague discontent, namely, that French *ennui* "for which Anglo-Saxons have no name"—as Emerson writes in his *Diaries*— and which for the most other prophets of individualistic religion such as Whitman lack.[38] Emerson's idea of absorption, inability to feel, sensation of inner emptiness, disinterestedness and cool detachment is not incidental to the individualist Gospel. Definitely, the religion of the individual is not a doctrine of calm and

---

[36] *Ivi*, p. 490.

[37] Emerson and James preached the cheerful liberation of the self, it is true, but as Marcus Cunliffe observes, they were aware of what Calvinist ministers meant by 'pitfalls': falls into the pit of damnation, James dwells "*more* than Emerson upon the perils of the everyday". See Cunliffe's comparison between Emerson's evocation of horror in "Fate" from *The Conduct of life* and James's terrible final lines of "The Sick Soul" in VRE (Cunliffe, M., *The Literature of the United States*, London, Penguin, 1986, pp. 124-125).

[38] Emersonian religion, James suggests, lies between two extremes: light irony and heavy gravity. On the one hand, Emersonian joviality is far from smart chaffing. It does not mean looking upon the world as a farce even when it becomes dramatic and tragic. It could include an ennobling and sincere sadness, even melancholy but always excluding peevishness, petulance, anger or exasperation of European post-romantics. Emerson's mood, James noted, excluded that peevishness, petulance, anger or exasperation which James attributes to the mood of a Schopenhauer, of a Nietzsche or of a Carlyle whose sallies remind him nothing but the "sick shriekings of dying rates" (VRE, p. 38). However, James should have considered Nietzsche's own judgement in 1872 about Emerson in *The Twilight of the Idols*:

easy happiness, but rather of restlessness and distress for an anxious self questing for authenticity.[39] Self-trust is the ground of truth, the native force of love, the heart of companionship, the base of morality, but also the source of permanent suspect about our own powers, about the truth of our love for others and the sincerity of others' interest on us. We need to trust on the native genius in ourselves and in others, but temperament sinks us in mere repetition. We will to believe that there is impulse, courage, ingenuity in ourselves and in our friends, but it seems that we all are prisoners of a permanent illusion.

"Temperament also enters fully into the system of illusions, and shuts us in a prison of glass which we cannot see. There is an optical illusion about every person we meet. In truth, they are all creatures of given temperament, which will appear in a given character, whose boundaries they will never pass: but we look at them, they seem alive, and we presume there is impulse in them. In the moment it seems impulse; in the year, in the lifetime, it turns out to be a certain uniform tune which the revolving barrel of the music-box must play [...] temperament is a power which no man willingly hears any one praise but himself [...] Temperament puts all divinity to rout."[40]

And a few pages later:

"Our friends early appear to us as representatives of certain ideas, which they never pass or exceed. They stand on the brink of the ocean of thought and power, but they never take the single step that would bring them there [...] There is no adaptation or universal applicability in men, but each has his special talent, and the mastery of successful men consists in adroitly keeping themselves where and when that turn shall be oftenest to be practised. We do what we must, and call it by the best names we can, and would fain have the praise of having intended the result which ensues. I cannot recall any form of man who is not superfluous sometimes. But is not this pitiful? Life is not worth the taking, to do tricks in."[41]

---

[39] "We cannot say too little of our constitutional necessity of seeing things under private aspects, or saturated with our humors. And yet is the God the native of these bleak rocks. That need makes in morals the capital virtue of self-trust. We must hold hard to this poverty, however scandalous, and by more vigorous self-recoveries, after the sallies of action, possess our axis more firmly. The life of truth is cold, and so far mournful; but it is not the slave of tears, constrictions, and perturbations" ("Experience", EEP, p. 490).

[40] Ivi, p. 474.

[41] Ivi, p. 477.

Emerson's individualism, then, was not free from an ironical and even distrustful moral stance. What, then, could James add to this peculiar vision of society as almost a company of strangers?

3. Blindness and Insight

We should now consider what I would call James' own version of the dilemma between self-affirmation and recognition. Emerson spoke of a glass prison, but did not James talk about a certain blindness in human beings? Emerson insisted in the constitutional necessity of seeing things under private aspects, or saturated with our temperaments. Yet, did not also James insist in the constitutive limits of our moral perception? For the first, James knows pretty well what Emerson always hid behind the surface. Far from merely exalting him as a pious and edifying thinker, even less as prophet of optimism Emerson's conviction that Divinity is everywhere—in his 1903 "Address at the Emerson Centenary", James wrote:

"[...] may make easily make of one an optimistic of the sentimental type that refuses to speak ill of anything. Emerson's drastic perception of differences kept him at the opposite pole from this weakness. After you have seen men a few times, he could say, you find most of them as alike as their barns and as pantries, and son as musty and as dreary. Never was such a fastidious lover of significance and distinction, and never an eye so keen for their discovery. His optimism had nothing in common with that indiscriminate hurrahing for the Universe with which Walt Whitman has made us familiar."[42]

Maybe Emerson did incarnate what James attributes here to him, but one would say that, in spite of his optimistic and Whitmanesque moments, James himself also incarnated some moderate version of Emersonian skepticism.[43] Many followers of James are likely to stress the positive side of "On a Certain Blindness in Human Beings", that is, the moment in which we get an opener and broader vision of things. But it is really difficult to ignore the side of the story in which he considers seriously the roots of our *constitutive* narrowness of

---

[42] "Address at Emerson Centenary", WJ, pp. 585-586.
[43] James appealed to Whitman's optimism trying vainly to balance this more drastic and discriminative kind of individualism. But Whitman is not a solution, but another symptom of the same illness. See my "James, Whitman y la religión americana", en Martín, F. and Salas, J. (eds.), *Aproximaciones a William James*, Madrid, Biblioteca Nueva, 2005.

perception.

"We are practical beings, each of us with limited functions and duties to perform. Each is bound to feel intensely the importance of his own duties and the significance of the situations that call these fort. However, this feeling is in each of us a vital secret, for sympathy with which we vainly look to others. The others are too absorbed in their own vital secrets to take an interest in ours [...] We are but finite, and each of us has some single specialized vocation of his own. It seems as if energy in the service of its particular duties might be got only by hardening the heart towards everything unlike them. Our deadness toward all but one particular kind of joy would thus be the price we inevitably have to pay for being practical creatures."[44]

Each of us is bound to feel intensely the importance of our own duties and ideals, the primal impulse, beyond good and evil, then, is egotism; morality rising as an ambivalent fighting between the will to assert ourselves and the need to open to others. Even when acquiescing in other's dreams or ideals is achieved, the individual must at once assert his uncompromising inwardness, his inevitable devotion to its own divinity. And since the point of departure for moral life are individuals in their own private prison-house, relationships with others can only be conceived in contradictory terms, as if the same opportunities that lead us out of the cold prison could also destroy our most valuable inwardness. For James, careless individualism, as opposed to possessive individualism, does not depend on a suspension of self-assertion, but rather on self-interest or egoism. Only a "gleam of insight" can reveal both the illusions that our practical being creates in us and bring us into a larger life beyond us:

"[...] it seems almost as if it were necessary to become worthless as a practical being, if one is to hope to attain any breadth of insight into the impersonal world of worths as such, to have any perception of life's meaning on a large objective scale. Only your mystic, your dreamer, or your insolvent tramp or loafer, can afford so sympathetic an occupation, an occupation which will change the usual standards of human value in the twinkling of an eye, giving to foolishness a place ahead of power, and laying low in a minute the distinctions which it takes a hard-working conventional man a lifetime to build up. You may be a prophet, at this rate; but you cannot be a worldly success [...] Only in some pitiful dreamer, some philosopher, poet, or romancer, or when the

---

[44] "On a Certain Blindness in Human Beings", WJ, pp. 629, 634.

common practical man becomes a lover, does the hard externality give way, and a gleam of insight into the ejective world, as Clifford called it, the vast world of inner life beyond us, so different from that outer seeming, illuminate our mind. Then the whole scheme of our customary values gets confounded, then our self is riven and its narrow interests fly to pieces, then a new centre and a new perspective must be found."[45]

Moral sense, then, depends on sudden raptures, lighting flashes or insights, inspirations of a quasi-mystic or poetic quality. In order to avoid blindness to others we need what James associates with an intuition between the religious and the aesthetic, namely, a perception of the hidden meaning of human life without which any articulated moral doctrine would be empty. In James's view, however, too many things seem to depend on the *intensity* of that emotion, an intensity that operates as a trusted guide to rightness and goodness, but that cannot be measured, since its own *gratuitousness* is what ultimately preserves it from the immediate practical interest...[46]

"The answer of appreciation, of sentiment, is always a more or a less, a balance of sympathy, insight and good will. But it is an answer, all the same, a real conclusion. And, in the course of getting it, it seems to me that our eyes have been opened to many important things...your imagination is extended. You divine the world about you matter for a little more humility on your own part, and tolerance, reverence, and love for other; and you gain a certain inner joyfulness at the increased importance of our common life. Such joyfulness is a religious inspiration and an element of spiritual health, and worth more than the large amounts of that sort of technical and accurate information which we professors are supposed to be able to impart."[47]

Thus, only by means of this intuition rather than by any moral tuition, the self grasps other's life in all its intensity. Morality stands on mysterious insight which lies between poetry and religion, a gratuitous power (a *gift of birth* James

---

[45] *Ibid.,* WJ, pp. 637, 634.
[46] "In the glowing hour of excitement... all incomprehensibilities are solved, and what was so enigmatical from without becomes transparently obvious" (VRE, p. 325). Compare with VRE, p. 283: "Can there in general be a level of emotion so unifying, so obliterate of differences between man and man, that even enmity may come to be an irrelevant circumstance and fail to inhibit the friendlier interests aroused? If positive well-wishing could attain so supreme a degree of excitement those who were swayed by it might well seem superhuman beings. Their life would be morally discrete from the life of other men".
[47] "What Makes a Life Significant", WJ, p. 658.

says in VRE, 325), which can be illustrated by means of the archetypal figures of the unpractical poet, the converted, the saint and the mystic, or by a mix of all such things (think again of Whitman). Moral judgments presuppose a self-surrender transportation into other's world similar to religious experience; a careless stance in which the will to assert ourselves is temporarily suspended; a collapse or break down of a personal point of view, an abolition of egotistic impulses and propensities, an abrupt change of the personal center of energy, which somehow subconsciously allow us to perceive what it was always at one's doorstep. The transition from anxiety, tenseness (and even from pressing self-responsibility) to…. peace, sensibility, equanimity and receptivity is…

"[…] the most wonderful of all shiftings of inner equilibrium… an the chief wonder of it is that is so often comes about, not by doing, but by simply relaxing and throwing the burden down. This abandonment of self-responsibility seems to be the fundamental act in specifically religious, as distinguished from moral practice. It antedates theologies and is independent of philosophies."[48]

However, James's moral vision tries to reconcile both impulses, passivity and activity.[49] Avoiding blindness to other human beings requires some kind of *abandonment* of the self, but also the positive effort to actualize intuitions into moral action. Something more tan intuitions are required if the seer seeks moral authority, something more is necessary in order to be a "morally exceptional individual": pluck and will –James claims—[50]. Insights do really change the real world only by means of action. According to James, moral authenticity must include unusual revelation and common action ("the sterner stuff of manly virtue"[51]), that is, illumination and practice, intuition and tuition, inspiration and skill. What ultimately makes a romantic pragmatist of James is his tendency to conceive the highest moral life as unexpected performances of spirit which join both imagination and action:

"In point of act, there are no absolute evils, and there no non-moral goods: at the highest ethical life […] consist at all time in the breaking of rules which have grown too narrow for the actual case. There is but one unconditional commandment, which is that we seek incessantly, with fear and trembling, so

---

[48] VRE, p. 289
[49] "What Makes a Life Significant", WJ, p. 658.
[50] *Ibidem.*
[51] *Ivi*, p. 657.

114

to vote and to act as to bring about the very largest total universe of good which we can see."[52]

But the will to realize good, however, cannot be identified with the exacerbated interest to increase control. And that is because the transformation of insight into practical power paradoxically requires a good deal of relaxation or "not to care".

"Neither are pluck and will, dogged endurance and insensibility to danger enough, when taken alone. There must be some sort of fusion, some chemical combination among these principles, for a life objectively and thoroughly significant to result."[53]

A combination that, ideally, would lie just beyond the usual opposition between thinking and acting, knowing and feeling. So, in James's own schema, morality also seems to depend on incidental chemical combination between selves isolated in their own private infinitude. In short: the "will to perceive", to use Felicitas Kraemer's suggestive expression, is less than a conscious volitional exertion but much more than a mere passive revelation or quiescent ecstasy.[54] It lies mysteriously somewhere between force and prudence, since "force destroys enemies [...] and prudence keeps what we already have in safety" (VRE, 358). The will to perceive can turn strangers into friends and restore others into their own sacred individuality, but is not at our complete disposal. That effect escapes, by definition, from voluntary decision, from any calculation, from self-responsibility and consciousness.[55]

---

[52] "The Moral Philosopher and the Moral Life", WJ, p. 626.
[53] "What Makes a Life Significant", WJ, p. 626.
[54] See Kraemer, F. "The Athlete's Surrender. The role of activity and passivity for James's conception of the real in 'Varieties'", in *Streams of William James*, vol. 5, issue 2, summer 2003. I think that Kraemer's conclusion could reinforce the idea that the religion of the individual merges the *letting-go* and the *controlled waste of action*, the relaxation similar to religious experiences and the careful expenditure of energy similar to the athletes' practice which strength reserves. In romantic terms, the *letting-go* would correspond to the uncontrolled and unconscious forces that invade the poet, meanwhile the *active* side would rather coincide with the heroic and martial temper of the soldier. Kraemer concludes rightly that the *saint* it would be who reconciles both sides, but Could we find a more secular and modernist equivalent of the saint? See also in the same volume of *Streams of William James* Sergio Franzese's remarkable comments on the idea of sainthood: "James versus Nietzsche: Energy and Ascetism in James" (pp. 10-12).
[55] The nobler thing taste better, and that is all we can say—James explains in "The Moral Philosopher and the Moral Life", WJ, p. 613—"Experience of consequences may truly

"The occasion and the experience, then, are nothing. It all depends on the capacity of the soul to be grasped, to have its life-currents absorbed by what if given. "Crossing a bare common", says Emerson, "in snow puddles, at twilight, under a clouded sky, without having in my thoughts any occurrence of special good fortune, I have enjoyed a perfect exhilaration. I am glad to be brink of fear."[56]

Carelessness, then, is allied with *strenuous* mood which, in turn, is the enemy of what in the "Moral Philosopher and the Moral Life" James calls the *easy-going* temper, since the latter shrinks from present ill, whereas the former is indifferent to present ill, if only the higher ideal be attained.[57] Moral eagerness, then, also requires a religious-like attitude as a mean to obtain

---

teach us what things are *wicked*, but what have consequences to do with what is *mean* and *vulgar?*" There is a sense of justice which escapes from any presumptions of utility and all the prepossessions of habit (*Ivi*, p. 612) and which it cannot be explained in terms of a pleasure to be gained and a pain to be avoided. "The feeling of inward dignity of pace, serenity, veracity and simplicity and the essential vulgarity of querulousness and egoistic fussiness are quite inexplicable except by an innate preference for its own pure sake" (*Ivi*, p. 613). Purely inward forces and certain feelings present themselves far less in the guise of effects of past experience than as probable causes of future experience or factors to which exterior conditions must band. Feeling, James came to say, is good and the supremely divine of human gifts. Live more the tumultuous blunderer whose life is an alternation of rapturous excitement, and horrible repentance and longing for the ruined good than the orderly man who never does ill or makes a mistake or has regret. See also James's curious analogy with remember "forgotten names" (with a brief reference to Emerson himself) in VRE, p. 205.

[56] "On a Certain Blindness in Human Beings", WJ, pp. 634, 637. Experience in this passage means just the opposite of James's own idea of it as transition, novelty, change, and challenge. James would perfectly agree with Emerson, the, when the later distinguished between a *mysticism* which fixes and freezes symbols, and a poetic attitude which maintains them fluxional, conveying and ambivalent. It is the difference, Emerson also said in "The Poet", between the *conveyance* of the poet and the *homestead* of the mystic (between ferries and farms, horses and houses.

[57] Compare James's view with Emerson's in "Experience" (EP, p. 478): "The whole frame of things preaches indifference. Do not craze yourself with thinking, but go about your business anywhere. Life is not intellectual or critical, but sturdy. Its chief good is for well-mixed people who can enjoy what they find, without question. [...] We live amid surfaces, and the true art of life is to skate well on them. Under the oldest mouldiest conventions, a man of native force prospers just as well as in the newest world, and that by skill of handling and treatment. He can take hold anywhere. Life itself is a mixture of power and form, and will not bear the least excess of either".

energy, or as pretext for living hard—James says—and getting out of the game of existence its keenest possibilities of zest. The postulation of godless or any subrogate divine-like force beyond finite wills, any divinity or any *ersatz* of God to which we ought ultimately respond, "serves only to let loose in us the strenuous mood" or as a challenge to put our whole character and personal aptitude for moral life on trial. Religion, then, not only represent a self-surrender, but also the kind of energy morality needs to be more than mere delights or empty or easy-going conventions.

"Every sort of energy and endurance, of courage and capacity for handling life's evils, is set free in those who have religious faith. For this reason the strenuous type of character will on the battle-field of human history always outwear the easy-going type, and religion will drive irreligion to the wall".[58]

Since the strenuous type does not exclude a bit of self-surrender, it is understandable that James describes the moral insight as a rapture by which we gain perception of the very zealous energy contained in lives lived by others. By perceiving others in their otherness (by seeing their inward glow, and their causes as real and warm to him or her as is mine to me, and with some equal justification) we gain—he says—a certain inner joyfulness at the increased importance of our common life. But what such a *community* consist of? In the very strenuousness which pulsates within the most ordinary of the human lives. James's examples present workers in skyscrapers or subway tunnels, firemen and farmers, civic volunteers and salvation armies or, in general, *moral* equivalents to heroic soldiers and legendary battlefields. The element that gives the external world all its expressive and picturesque character is always the *impetus of strength, the intensity and danger*.[59] If individuals are able to modify their moral perception it is either because they do perceive a life of struggle where they didn't expect to find it, or, on the contrary, because they discover that there is no epic (no potentiality of *danger* of *death* in sight—James say—)

---

[58] *Ibid*, WJ, p. 628. Strenuousness, then, is the mark of a religious-like temper, for the better and for the *worst*, since the same zeal which inspires an enchantment of the world could also turn into impious religious wars: "Our so called 'Civilization' as is now organized and admiringly believed in, form the more genuine religion of our time [...] Certainly the unhesitating and unreasoning way in which we feel that we must inflict our civilization upon 'lower' races, by means of Hotchkiss guns, etc. Reminds one of nothing so much as the early spirit of Islam spreading its religion by the sword" (VRE, p. 77)

[59] "What Makes a Life Significant", WJ, p. 648. Curiously, James adds that American imperialism is not the kind of heroism of which he is thinking but rather the contrary, a sort of dead ideal.

where it seemed to exists.

Thus, it is the pragmatic seer who can *see* how some human beings are alienated of their common humanity, a common humanity which ultimately consist in that a good live, a life truly lived is a life in which each individual lives his or her life as if it were his or her own conquest, as something where conflict, and struggle has a sense or, if you want, as something of which Shakespeare could had written a piece, or Victor Hugo a novel.[60]

4. Individualism as Narcissism

As we see, Emerson and James showed how disowning socially ready-made identities allow individuals to see our selfhood as transition, movement self-sustained, fighting with no place to rest. The real self, or in Richard Poirier's words, the "soul", would be a performing act, a function

"[...] and yet no determination is made as to when the function occurs or from where it emanates [...] soul appears or occurs only as something we feel compelled to live or to move toward *as if* it were there, it is like James's "will to believe", it hints at Steven's "supreme fiction"... for Emerson the soul always wait us."[61]

The individual, then, lives removed or displaced forever from a firm or transparent self-identity. An individual is as infinitely distant from himself or herself, from a fixed selfhood, as he or she is separated from the others. It is less important who you *are* or what you *possess* (as it could be for a run-of-the-mill individualism), than what you will be able to discover as far as *experience* goes. However, the *drive* to seek the core-self is still there, and very powerful too. It is *as if* it was waiting for us, and its fictitious nature does not make it somewhat less *demanding*. Since the individual disallows any consolatory ready-made identity, s/he is necessarily *compelled* to sustain him or herself in its own performative self. According to the individualistic Gospel, the self and the world are plastic and mold each other all along the run of experience, but by this same reason the individual's experience can never be consummated.

---

[60] If the books on ethics want to touch the moral life, must ally "with a literature which is confessedly tentative and suggestive rather than dogmatic —I mean with novels and dramas of the deeper sort, with sermons, with books on statecraft and philanthropy and social and economical reform". "The Moral Philosopher and the Moral Life", WJ, pp. 626-627.

[61] Poirier, R., *Poetry & Pragmatism*, Cambridge, Harvard University Press, 1992, p. 24.

Individualism abandons firm identity but this is not costless, and the price is an anxious and endless call for an always more intense and fresh experience, with which very often *nobody* can keep pace.

The despairing self, feared to be determined to be what it is, feels compelled to refashion its being *ex nihilo* in the image of its arbitrary desire, conjuring itself up at every moment. But the sincerity of this reshaping does conceal its potential nihilism. If the self can dissolve its own substance into nothing, then its very assertiveness is at one with its nothingness; it will find itself cheerfully reinforced but also cancelled, always enriched but permanently disappointed; as demonstrated by Emerson's shrill oscillation between self-assertion and vacuity:

"Our moods do not believe each other... What I write, whilst I write it, seems the most natural thing in the world, but yesterday I saw a dreary vacuity in this direction in which now I see so much. And a month hence, I doubt not, I shall wonder who he was that wrote so many continuous pages. Alas for this infirm faith; this will not be strenuous, this vast ebb of a vast flow! I am God in nature, I am a weed by the wall."[62]

Maybe, as Emerson said, a true friend always must remain unapproachable, since her or his relative opacity is the very certificate of a true encounter between two authentic personalities (solidarity, in the end, is not sympathetic acceptance of what is different, but a sort of humility which arises from a consciousness of the very *limits* of sympathy). Or in other words: the innermost significance of individuals lays in all their incomprehensible diversity. Yet, there is also a point in which opacity becomes a cause of calmness, as if any encounter represented a challenge to the powers of discernment and attraction of the particular individual. Self-reliance and will to believe requires a desirable isolation; yet, it is this very isolation which makes the individual to feel permanently insecure and threatened. It is this solitude that preserves the inner self from "the mass" but also that invades self with an existential disdain that makes it to call the attention of others:

"[...] it is a sign of our times, conspicuous to the coarsest observer, that many intelligent and religious persons withdraw themselves from the common

---

[62] Quoted by Joel Porter in his perceptive "Emerson: Experiments in Creation" *American Literature. The New Pelican Guide to English Literature*, vol. 9, 1988). Cooper also contrasts Emerson's both claims: the "I have seat my heart on honesty" and the "I'm always insincere, as always knowing there are other moods".

labors and competitions of the market and the caucus, and betake themselves to a certain solitary and critical way of living, from which no solid fruit has yet appeared to justify their separation. They hold themselves aloof: they feel the disproportion between their faculties and the work offered them, and they prefer to ramble in the country and perish of ennui, to the degradation of such charities and such ambitions as the city can propose to them."[63]

Apparently contradicting his own apologia of whim, Emerson also says of the individualist that

"[...] retirement does not proceed from any whim on the part of these separators [...] this part is chosen both from temperament and from principle; with some unwillingness, too, and as a choice of the less of two evils; for these persons are not by nature melancholy, sour, and unsocial, —they are not stockish or brute, — but joyous; susceptible, affectionate; *they have even more than others a great wish to be loved.* Like the young Mozart, they are rather ready to cry ten times a day, "But are you sure you love me?" Nay, if they tell you their whole thought, they will own that love seems to them the last and highest gift of nature; that there are persons that in their hearts daily thank for existing, — persons whose faces are perhaps unknown to them, but whose fame and spirit have penetrated their solitude, —and for whose sake they wish to exist."[64]

Who you are, in consequence, is a fact that relies on who you chose to be and who you don't. Any relationship with somebody, no matter how ordinary (just to have a walk or to obtain a receipt, getting help to repair the drainpipe or satisfying your libidinal drive), will be a decisive event that will tell you *who* you really are. Discovering oneself, in other words, depends on who is able to provoke in you the occasion or opportunity to express better your true self. Egotism includes an irrepressible urge to consider the world in general, and human relations in particular, as if the world and the others were a mirror of the self.

That way, the Emersonian *motto* in "Experience", "to fill the hour, that is happiness; to fill the hour, and leave no crevice for a repentance or an approval" acquires an uncomfortable meaning if one thinks of it as a rule of sociability. The deification of friendship and love as a "here and now", as something which has no measure of value but what it brings with itself, turned

---

[63] "The Transcendentalist", EP, p. 199.
[64] *Ibid*, EP, p. 200, [ours italics].

out to be a peculiar kind of fetishism which actually could block a real social inquiry, no matter if Emerson and James conceived of it as the primal force of sociability. The self is so eager for direct and unmediated experiences with the others; the self feels so compelled to identify with the other without mediations or any image of a group except the counter-image which other selves can provide; the self is so intensely concerned with the instant that.... in the end becomes unable to engage a too large community. Thus human relations are fated to provoke a peculiar kind of distress or apathy. The explicit utterances of the apathetic post-romantic self can be "I'm not able to feel enough" or "I should feel more intensely", whereas the latent content is "the others do not stimulate me" and "the world is not interesting enough to me". As James once said, "an irremediable flatness is coming over the world" which not only meant that mediocrity was dominating America, but also that the new American Scholar was also suffering from a particular kind of disenchantment peculiar to modern times. In broader terms, there is sort of an obsessive dimension in the American Scholar's ethics: otherness is at once *intimidating* and *attractive*. There is always discrepancy between the glamorous and secretive subjectivity and the bland appearance or representation to others as citizen of the public world. For the self to define itself through the others is to find *and* lose simultaneously, oscillating between pleasure and hate, seduction and terror. In Kierkegaard's words, one could say that "friendship" is an "antipathetic sympathy".

"It does not attempt another's work, nor adopt another's facts. It is a main lesson of wisdom to know your own from another's. I have learned that I cannot dispose of other people's facts; but I possess such a key to my own, as persuades me against all their denials, that they also have a key to theirs. A sympathetic person is placed in the dilemma of a swimmer among drowning men, who all catch at him, and if he give so much as a leg or a finger, they will drown him."[65]

On the other hand, since the individualist tries to engage in human relations as if each encounter were the last and highest opportunity of *mutual salvation or redemption*, a mere disappointment can be felt as a symptom of the intrinsic iniquity hidden in each individual. The religion of the individual glorified by Emerson and inherited by James reveals that egotism does not only concern admiration or love to oneself, but also a peculiar kind of disdain toward

---

[65] "Experience", EP , p. 490.

oneself.[66] As Emerson declared: "To every creature Nature adds *a little violence of direction in its proper path*" ("Nature", EP, 549), which, needless to say, does not exclude certain violence onto oneself. So it is, at least, as I read the next ambiguous passage:

"To behold the beauty of another character, which inspires a new interest in our own; to behold the beauty lodged in a human being, with such vivacity of apprehension, that I am instantly forced home to inquire if I am not deformity itself: to behold in another the expression of a love so high that it assures itself, —assures itself also to me against every possible casualty except my unworthiness; —these are degrees on the scale of human happiness, to which they have ascended; and it is a fidelity to this sentiment which has made common association distasteful to them. They wish a just and even fellowship, or none."[67]

My conclusion is that, "narcissism" does not mean mere self-love but rather a certain distressed way of feeling. The difference that Richard Sennett, Christopher Lasch and others remarked between an American romantic Adam and an indolent and afflicted narcissistic individual; between a strenuous subjectivity compelled to transform an open universe and a skeptical sensibility disenchanted with a too trivial society, is less sharp that one can image.[68] In Emerson and James—and this is my final suggestion— the religion of the individual embraces both sides of an essentially divided self.*

---

[66] On this characteristic Jamesian distress see R. Del Castillo, "Portrait of an Anxiety: Santayana on James", en *Under Whatever Sky. Contemporary Readings of George Santayana,* Flamm, M. & Skowronski, C. (eds.), Cambridge Scholars Publishing, Newcastle, England, 2007. See also my: "Una serena desesperación: la ética individualista de William James", *Diánoia,* Vol. LI, n° 57, FCE-UNAM, México, noviembre, 2006, pp. 65-78.

[67] "The Transcendentalist", EP, 200.

[68] See R. Sennett "Narcissism and modern culture", "Destructive Gemeinschaft" or "What Tocqueville Feared" (1977-1980), or the *Culture of Narcissism* (1979) by Lasch. Works coordinated by R. Bellah as *Habits of the Heart. Individualism and Commitment in American Life* (1985) and *The Good Society* (1992) have also influenced in my view. For this paper I have also considered a more recent work by Ray Pahl related with the topic of friendship and sociability in USA: *On Friendship* (Polity Press, 200)

* I thank Antonio Gómez, Felicitas Kraemer, Sonu Shamdasani, Juan Vicente Mayoral, and Stanton McManus for their comments on draft versions of this paper. Randall Albright and Richard Rorty also made opportune suggestions. Thanks to Sergio Franzese's laborious and precise corrections the text was substantially improved.

Science as a Religious Experience: The James-Kuhn Perspective

Majeda Omar (Phd)[*]

1. Paradigm and Theory Choice

Kuhn's seminal ideas which first appeared in his book *The Structure of Scientific Revolutions*,[1] caused lasting radical changes in the way we view the history and nature of science. At the time, these ideas seemed to be without precedence and that Kuhn was the first to propose them. Gradually, however, it became obvious that similar ideas were already implicit in previous philosophies, such as Poincaré's conventionalism and in James's pragmatism. In this paper, we shall focus on the relationship between Kuhn's early philosophy of science and James's pragmatism.

In his account of science, Kuhn holds that the development of science is not purely cumulative.[2] Rather, it is marked by a successive periods of "cumulative normal science" separated by non-cumulative revolutions. "Normal science" depends on some set of received beliefs and tools of research, which he collectively calls a "paradigm", and marks out what the acceptable research problems are and what the acceptable solutions to these problems must look like. A scientific problem in one paradigm may not have an easy and obvious solution in another paradigm. Accordingly, a viable solution in one paradigm can turn out unacceptable in another. It is the case that when a problem cannot receive a solution that satisfies all the adherents to a certain paradigm in the long run, then the anomaly becomes a paradigmatic failure and a paradigmatic crisis may be claimed. Consequently, a new paradigm may develop with reference to which the anomalies of the old paradigm can be resolved when stated in the language of the new paradigm. These anomalies are also seen as crucial evidence against the validity of the old paradigm. Kuhn defines the transition from one paradigm to another as 'scientific revolution'. It is a specific condition in order to recognize a real scientific revolution that the old and the new paradigms show such a structural difference that the relation between them cannot be seen simply as one of extension or refinement. Kuhn defines this

---

[*] Assistant Professor of Contemporary Western Philosophy at the Dept. of Philosophy, University of Jordan, Amman (Jordan).
[1] T.S. Kuhn, *The Structure of Scientific Revolutions*, Univ. of Chicago Pr. 1996 [1962]
[2] Ivi, *p.* 2.

relation as *incommensurability*.[3] The transition from one paradigm to the next is

"[...] far from a cumulative process, one achieved by an articulation or extension of the old paradigm. Rather it is a reconstruction of the field from new fundamentals, a reconstruction that changes some of the field's most elementary theoretical generalizations as well as many of its paradigm methods and applications."[4]

Furthermore, Kuhn writes:

"[...] if new theories are called forth to resolve anomalies in the relation of an existing theory to nature, then the successful new theory must somewhere permit predictions that are different from those derived from its predecessor. That difference could not occur if the two were logically compatible."[5]

According to Kuhn, a scientific revolution is a "relatively sudden and unstructured event" like a "*gestalt* switch", as it can be historically accounted for through scientists' descriptions of the event as "'the scales falling from the eyes', or of the 'lighting flash' that 'inundates' a previously obscure puzzle, enabling its components to be seen in a new way that for the first time permits its solution."[6] Such a phenomenon, Kuhn argues, is not an accidental occurrence but a necessary characteristic of revolutions. The argument runs so that although severe anomalies may initiate a crisis, previous guidelines are already in place; rejecting these guidelines would simply mean rejecting science itself. During the crisis stage large portions of experience, both anomalous and congruent, are collected, but the transformation of these into a new, coherent theory happens "in a flash of intuition".[7]

In explaining what causes a group to abandon one tradition of normal research, Kuhn describes the transfer of reliance from one normal research tradition to a new paradigm as a conversion experience. These conversions, he writes, "will occur a few at a time until, after the last holdouts have died, the whole profession will again be practicing under a single, but now a different,

---

[3] *Ivi*, p. 150.
[4] *Ivi*, pp. 84-85.
[5] *Ivi*, p. 97.
[6] *Ivi*, p. 122.
[7] *Ivi*, p. 150.

paradigm."[8]

Hence, although each particular scientist may experience his or her conversion as a *"gestalt* switch", for the scientific community as a whole the transition from one paradigm to another may be a long-term process. Thus, when Kuhn says that group conversions "like the gestalt switch, it must occur all at once (though not necessarily in an instant) or not at all",[9] the statement must be taken to mean that there are no intermediate positions to rest upon in between old and new paradigm. Each scientist adopts either of the two competing paradigms but cannot gradually slide from the one to the other,[10] for the two positions are incommensurable.

Kuhn's notion of incommensurability covers three different aspects of the relation between the pre- and post-revolutionary normal science traditions: First, incommensurability covers a change in the set of scientific problems and in the way in which scientific problems are attacked: "the proponents of competing paradigms will often disagree about the list of problems that any candidate for paradigm must resolve. Their standards or their definitions of science are not the same."[11] Second, incommensurability covers conceptual change: "within the new paradigm, old terms, concepts, and experiments fall into new relationships one with the other."[12] Third, incommensurability begets a change of world for the scientists: "the proponents of competing paradigms practice their trades in different worlds."[13]

These aspects of incommensurability have important consequences for the communication between proponents of competing normal science traditions and for the choice between them. Recognising different problems and adopting different standards and concepts, scientists may "talk through each other when debating the relative merits of their respective paradigms."[14] But if they do not agree on the list of problems that must be solved or on what constitutes an acceptable solution, there can be no point-to-point comparison between the competing theories, that is, there can be no comparison "by some process like counting the number of problems solved by each."[15] Instead, "[w]hen

---

[8] *Ivi,* p. 152.
[9] *Ivi,* p.150.
[10] *Ivi,* p. 152.
[11] *Ivi,* p.148.
[12] *Ivi,* p. 149.
[13] *Ivi,* p. 150.
[14] *Ivi,* p. 109.
[15] *Ivi,* p. 148.

paradigms enter, as they must, into a debate about paradigm choice, their role is necessarily circular. Each group uses its own paradigm to argue in that paradigm's defense."[16] On this view, theory choice is a conversion that cannot be "forced by logic and neutral experience."[17] Kuhn emphasises that although theory choice cannot be justified by evidence, this "is not to say that no arguments are relevant or that scientists cannot be persuaded to change their minds"[18] According to Kuhn, such arguments are, first of all, about whether the new theory can solve the problems that have led the old theory to a crisis, and whether the new theory displays a quantitative precision strikingly better than its older competitor,[19] and whether the new theory predicts phenomena that the old one was not able to.[20] These arguments "are ordinarily the most significant and persuasive",[21] but apart from such arguments based on the comparative ability in solving problems, aesthetic arguments may work as well. Hence, scientists may also reject an old theory in favour of a new theory that seem 'neater', 'more suitable', or 'simpler'.[22]

As we said above, Kuhn argues that "when paradigms change, the world itself changes with them".[23] Accordingly, Kuhn also speaks of the proponents of competing paradigms as practicing their trades "in different worlds",[24] questioning thereby traditional realism. By the same token, rejecting the view that succeeding theories in turn provide closer approximations to nature, Kuhn had to dismiss the correspondence theory of truth. These views often led to Kuhn being accused of relativism and irrationalism. The correspondence theory of truth, questioned by Kuhn, claims that a proposition is true if and only if it corresponds to reality. However, Kuhn argues, that "truth" can only be 'lexicon-dependent'. He writes:

"evaluation of a statement's truth values is, in short, an activity that can be conducted only with a lexicon already in place, and its outcome depends upon that lexicon."[25]

---

[16] *Ivi*, p. 94.
[17] *Ivi*, p. 150.
[18] *Ivi*, p. 152.
[19] *Ivi*, p. 153.
[20] *Ivi*, p. 154.
[21] *Ivi*, p. 155.
[22] *Ivi*, p. 155.
[23] *Ivi*, p. 111.
[24] *Ivi*, p. 121.
[25] T.S. Kuhn, *The Road Since Structure,* Univ. of Chicago Pr., 2000, p. 77. For further details, see G. *Bird'* Thomas Kuhn, *Princeton University Press, 2000, p. 68.*

A lexicon, in short, is a paradigm-dependent method for interpreting the terms of the theory. This should not be taken, however, as if the same proposition could receive different truth values when embedded in different lexicons. "The point is not that laws true in one world may be false in another but that they may be ineffable, unavailable for conceptual or observational scrutiny. It is effability, not truth, that my view relativizes to worlds and practices."[26]
The fundamental requirement for a theory of truth, according to Kuhn, is its ability to introduce minimal laws of logic, in particular, the law of non-contradiction.[27] Hence, on Kuhn's view, truth should not be seen as an ingredient of reality but merely as a criterion of acceptance or rejection of a statement or of a theory with reference to a given evidence.

Although rejecting the view that science was progressively approaching the "truth", Kuhn maintained, however, that there are shared and justifiable standards that scientific communities use when choosing between theories. According to Kuhn, however, these standards can be used only to decide relatively which among two or more theories is better: "Judgements of this sort are necessarily comparative: which of two bodies of knowledge-the original or the proposed alternative-is *better* for doing whatever it is that scientists do."[28]

Kuhn's view of theory choice was met with perplexity and alarm by several critics who dismissed it as "irrational, a matter for mob psychology",[29] for it suggests that the choice between rival theories can only be made arbitrarily. In fact, Kuhn never attempted to argue for irrationalism. Although arguing from history that in actual scientific practice theory choice does not seem to be forced by logic and neutral experience, Kuhn did not merely want to offer a descriptive account, but a prescriptive account explaining why the development of science requires a decision process that permits scientists to disagree.[30] To understand Kuhn's account of theory choice it is important to note that the principal agents of science are the scientific communities and not the individual scientist. Kuhn repeatedly emphasised that

[26] *Ivi*, p. 249.
[27] *Ivi*, p.99.
[28] *Ivi*, p. 96.
[29] I. *Lakatos & A. Musgrave (eds.)*, Criticism and the Growth of Knowledge, *Cambridge (Mass), Cambridge University Press, 1970, p. 178.*
[30] *T.S.Kuhn*, The Essential Tension: Selected Studies in Scientific Tradition and Change, *The University of Chicago Press, 1977*, p. 332.

"[...] our concern will not be with the arguments that in fact convert one or another individual, but rather with the sort of community decision, that what passes for proof, verification, or falsification in the sciences has not occurred until an entire community has been converted or reformed about a new paradigm"[31]

The reason for this viewpoint is to be found in Kuhn's phase model of scientific development and the functional role played by individuals and communities in this development. On Kuhn's phase model, a new theory competing with the previously accepted theory is developed in response to severe anomalies that have made the reigning theory seem untenable. But when anomalies are severe and when the reigning theory seems untenable are matters of judgement. It was Kuhn's claim that a lack of unanimity is essential to the progress of science. On the other hand, divergence among scientists about which theories to pursue tend to come to an end. In the course of time, usually a new consensus concerning theory choice will be reached within the group of scientists. A process of theory choice which includes both the dissolution of the previous consensus and the emergence of a new consensus in the scientific community requires an intricate relation between individual and sociological aspects of theory choice.

To explain the possibility of consensus to first dissolve and then emerge again, Kuhn pointed out that a scientific community holds a list of values which all its members share. Among others, these values include accuracy, consistency, scope, simplicity, and fruitfulness.[32] These values "provide the shared basis for theory choice. ... Individually, the criteria are imprecise: individuals may legitimately differ about their application to concrete cases."[33] For example, a value like simplicity is not defined in any precise way, but may be interpreted differently by different scientists. Further, the individual values may "conflict with one another".[34] For example, the most accurate and the simplest of a set of competing theories need not be the same. Hence, "[w]hen scientists must choose between competing theories, two men fully committed to the same list of criteria for choice may nevertheless reach different

---

[31] T.S. *Kuhn, "Notes on Lakatos", in* In Memory of Rudolph Carnap. *Boston Studies in the Philosophy of Science, VIII: 1971, pp. 137-146. R. C. Buck & R. S. Cohen (eds): PSA 1970., p. 145.*
[32] *T.S.Kuhn,* The Essential Tension, *cit., p. 321.*
[33] *Ivi,* p. 322.
[34] *Ivi,* p. 322.

conclusions."[35] On this view, when an anomaly emerges the different ways in which individual members of the scientific community employ the shared values may result in different judgements of the anomaly and different attitudes towards the various alternative theories that are developed in response to the anomaly.

The dissent continues until all the members of the scientific community, on the basis of their individual interpretations and evaluations of the shared values, converge on to a single theory. Hence, on this view, "it is the community of specialists rather than its individual members that makes the effective decision."[36]

2. Paradigm, Science and Religion

Let us now discuss the philosophical implications of Kuhn's ideas in connection with James's views concerning science, truth, rationality and their applications in religion.

James's philosophy was greatly influenced by the sciences that emerged at the middle of the nineteenth-century: non-Eucleadian geometries, non-classical logics and the theory of evolution. He argued for variants of his philosophical position from within a scientific model. Hence, it can legitimately be hold that to gain a clear grasp of James's views on science is crucial for any attempt to understand his philosophical views; this having exercised such an influence on shaping his philosophy. Among his views on science, we concentrate on the following: 1) The status of scientific laws. 2) The multiplicity of scientific formulas and criteria of choice.

2.1. Scientific Laws are not Exact Transcripts of Facts

James argued that the implications of his conception of the way we arrive at the formulation of scientific laws suggest that these laws cannot be mere copies of facts. Thus, it is neither impossible nor unthinkable that the same phenomenon can be accounted for by more than one law. James tells us that this view has been arrived at by the radical changes that occurred in science after the half of 19th century. Prior to that, he argues, scientific truths were

---

[35] *Ivi,* p. 324.
[36] *The Structure of Scientific Revolutions,* cit., p. 200.

supposed to be "[...] exact and exclusive duplicates of pre-human archetypes buried in the structure of things, to which the spark of divinity hidden in our intellect enables us to penetrate."[37]

Before 1850, science expressed "truths that were exact copies of a definite code of non-human realities."[38] But after 1850, there emerged several alternative models of geometry, of logics, of scientific hypotheses, each of which is 'good for so much and yet not good for everything'. Thus, the conception of a theory or a law that is a literal transcript of reality seemed to James to be somewhat impossible to maintain. Consequently, our conception of scientific truths had to be more flexible and so should it be, James tells us, in the case of other types of truth, e. g., religious truths.

In fact, James argued that there is a multiplicity of viewpoints from which the world can be seen and no one viewpoint can be deemed to be the truest one.[39] If, in this argument, we replace 'viewpoint' with 'paradigm', we obtain a familiar Kuhnian conception. As has been said earlier, Kuhn argued for the existence of different competing paradigms, each of which offers its own view of the world.

2.2. Multiplicity of Scientific Frameworks and Criteria of Choice

James argued that our dealings with physical phenomena may produce a number of frameworks all of which explain phenomena equally and also are consistent with 'facts'.[40] If the choice should be made between a number of like competing frameworks, on what grounds can the choice be made? James gives the following in answer.

"The suspicion is in the air nowadays that the superiority of one of our formulas to another may not consist so much in its literal 'objectivity,' as in subjective qualities like its usefulness, its 'elegance' or its congruity with our residual beliefs."[41]

---

[37] W. James, The Meaning of Truth: A Sequel to 'Pragmatism', Harvard University Press, Cambridge (Mass), 1975 [1909] (Hereafter MT), p. 40.
[38] Ibidem.
[39] W. James, The Will to Believe and Other Essays in Popular Philosophy, Harvard Univ. Pr., Cambridge (Mass), 1979 [1897] (Hereafter WB), p. 66.
[40] Ivi, p. 66.
[41] W: James, MT, p. 41.

Also in *The Will to Believe,* James makes a similar point. He says:

"of two conceptions equally fit to satisfy the logical demand, that one which awakens the active impulses, or satisfies other æsthetic demands better than the other, will be accounted the more rational conception, and will deservedly prevail."[42]

The applicability of a description does not preclude the 'simultaneous' applicability of another entirely different description to the same empirical phenomena. The procedure of selecting between competing descriptions, where the method of reduction is not available, is based on subjective criteria such as those of simplicity and elegance.[43]

In *Pragmatism,* James distinguishes between three different ways of approaching the concept of reality; the common-sense, the scientific and the philosophical.[44] He expresses his discontent with the view that takes sense reality as the only reality that we know. James argues that sense reality is just too narrow to encompass other realities which he considers as existing. In *The Meaning of Truth,* while defending himself against the charge of subjectivism, James distinguishes between different kinds of ontologies:

"Cognitively we...live under a sort of rule of three: as our private concepts represent the sense-objects to which they lead us, these being public realities independent of the individual, so these sense-realities may, in turn, represent realities of a hypersensible order, electrons, mind-stuff, God, or what not, existing independently of all human thinkers. The notion of such final realities, knowledge of which would be absolute truth, is an outgrowth of our cognitive experience."[45]

James holds that hypersensible realities, which includes theoretical terms such as electron, are the kind of realities that exist independently of all human knowledge. How, then, can we know realities characterised as such? We can never attain a sure knowledge of them. This does not mean, however, that we can never have any knowledge of them of any kind whatsoever. When we think of them, we think of less equal mental replacements that are characterised by

---

[42] W. James, WB, p. 66.
[43] W. James, *Pragmatism: A New Name for Some Old Ways of Thinking,* Harvard Univ. Pr., Cambridge (Mass), 1975 [1907] (Hereafter P), p. 104.
[44] *Ivi,* p. 92.
[45] MT, pp. 130-131.

not existing independently of all human thinkers. The reason why we postulate these hypersensible realities is that they help us to organise our thinking and ordering our experiences.

According to this view of the role of hypersensible realities, the purpose of science is not the establishment of structures of the external world by scientists. Rather, its aim is to order our experiences. What makes one theory better that another is not how much it depicts the exact structure of the world, but how good it proves at expanding the limits of our experiences and bringing them to order. If the aim of science is to formulate abstract structures of the world, then it is likely that no immediate correspondence can be found between those mental structures and the world itself. James is offering an interpretation of the relation of 'agreement' between ideas and reality that goes beyond the simple correspondence between these two.

The first class of entities, to which James refers in the previous quotation, is the private concepts, which represent the 'sense objects' and as such are subjective experiences. 'Sense objects', which belong to the second class, are characterised as public realities which are independent of the individual and are representatives of the hypersensible realities. These sense objects are both subjective and objective realities. They are subjective because they are sense realities and so belong to the domain of experience. They are also objective realities in the sense of being *public* realities independent of the individual.[46] James later attempts to bridge the gap between subjective realities and objective realities; between the knower, the subjective individual, and the external world of physical objects. But his outright renunciation of the existence of this metaphysical and epistemological gap is put forward in his *Essays in Radical Empiricism,* where he examines the reality that underlies the common-sense objects of the external world and concludes that experience is the sole and ultimate reality.

In conclusion, it can be argued that the foresaid elements are strongly echoed in James's pragmatic method. In fact, James did think of his pragmatic method as an extension of scientific method. He did regard all philosophical claims as hypotheses to which the pragmatic method could be applied. He tells us that "a normal philosophy, like science, must live by hypotheses."[47] Hence, philosophical hypotheses are subjected to acceptance or rejection according to whether they have or lack certain consequences. The application of the pragmatic method assists us in the process of differentiation between

---

[46] *Ivi,* p. 117.

[47] *The Letters of William James Vol. II,* Longmans, Green and Co, New York, 1920, (Hereafter LWJ), p. 184.

alternative philosophical hypotheses according to the consequences, empirical or metaphysical, that they may anticipate. Just as scientific theories are dependent on sensory experience, philosophical hypotheses are dependent on consequences.

According to James, there was an urgent need to overhaul the concept of truth.[48] At the time, the accepted notion was that of copying, a version of correspondence, which is based on a certain way of looking at the mind's relation to reality. According to this view, truth means the mere copying or simple duplication by the human mind of a fixed, independent and absolute reality.[49] Like Kuhn, several decades later, James rejected the existence of a fixed objective world of independent entities. Thus, the aim of truth-seeking cannot be the determination of whether or not theories correspond to an external and mind-independent world.

In his conception of truth, James gave several statements of his conception of truth which reflect the various aspects of his theory. The main features of his account can briefly be outlined as follows. James maintained that there would be no truth had there been no mind (which can only know reality through ideas). This is strongly reminiscent of Kuhn's idea of 'objective reality'. In one interpretation, Kuhn seems to be saying that we see the world through our theories, without which there is nothing to be seen.

Now, according to James, when deciding which beliefs to accept, beliefs of any kind whatsoever (including religious belief), we are justified in applying subjective criteria. Thus, we are justified in accepting beliefs as true according to their being satisfactory, useful and emotionally satisfying. Consistency is another crucial factor in accepting beliefs. A belief is accepted as true if and only if it is consistent with previously held beliefs or causes minimal change in one's stock of old beliefs. Kuhn also talked about consistency as one of the values that a scientific community shares, upon which theory choice is made.

As it has been already mentioned, James held that there are many viewpoints (paradigms) from which the world can be seen or understood. One cannot speak of the unique and truest angle of vision. As for the term 'absolute truth', James understands it as objective in the sense that it transcends *the subjectivity of individual truths held by any individual.* Thus, there is a natural progressive development of truths from the subjective to the objective, from the less perfect to the more perfect. Compare this to the Kuhnian concept of conversion from one paradigm to another through gestalt switching, whereby the adoption of the

---

[48] P, pp. 93-94.
[49] W. James, *Essays, Comments, and Reviews,* Harvard University Press Cambridge (Mass.) 1987, p. 550.

new paradigm does not happen until the entire scientific community has been converted to it. For James, since 'absolute truth' is an ideal limit to which relative truths may in the future converge: it is fixed, independent of person, time and circumstance and can never be replaced by a better set of truths. Also, it can be described entirely in experiential terms and at the same time it is expected to be objective in the sense of being independent of what any individual may think.

James held that religion, like science, can be justified on 'empirical' grounds. Philosophers who viewed the religious question as merely the provision of intellectual evidence ignore the most important aspect of religion which is the subjective experience of the believer. The religious experience of the believer is more significant than the intellectual argumentation, which tends to miss the whole point of what is significant in religion. This is why James seeks to provide empirical justification for religious belief. Thus, his attitude towards religion is marked by his rejection of the attempts at the provision of conclusive rationalist arguments for it and the adoption of the more appropriate task of trying to articulate the way in which subjective experience provides justification for religious belief which is *per se* 'empirical', as we shall now see.

For James, religion can be no less 'objective' than science. We have mentioned earlier that the experiences of the individuals are the starting point in James's account of truth and so it is in the case of religion; it begins with the personal, relative religious experiences of the individuals. Each individual acquires a certain number of experiences of the world that lead one to form beliefs which are regarded by them as true. The degree of truth contained in these beliefs increases with the number of people who hold those same beliefs. One individual converts to the new framework of beliefs through a *gestalt* switch or a religious experience. If we look at James's treatment of religious experience, we observe that conversion is an important phase of religious experience. James discusses different examples of conversion that possess one or more of the following characteristics: It can be "instantaneous"[50] In some cases, it can be sudden,[51] striking,[52] the ecstasy of happiness produced these shiftings of character to higher level.[53] He gave several instances of conversion which have been permanent. Furthermore, he tells us that "the effect of conversion is to bring with it "a changed attitude towards life, which is fairly

---

[50] W. James, *Varieties of Religious Experience: A Study in Human Nature.* (Centenary Edition). Routledge, London, 2002 [1902] (Hereafter VRE), p. 178.
[51] *Ivi*, p. 185.
[52] *Ivi*, p. 188.
[53] *Ivi*, p. 199.

constant and permanent".[54]

The experiences of a single individual, however, because of their limitations, cannot account for the formulation of certain beliefs over a long period of time. The sharing of the experiences of other individuals is crucial and vital for the establishment of a belief over a period of time. This requires some kind of co-operation among individuals which materialises in their sharing of their experiences through the social exchange of ideas and verifications. Hence, the total sum of gestalt switches leads to the establishment of a new paradigm, in this case, a religion.

Kuhn described the way in which the shift between paradigms occurs. This he calls a conversion experience which has its own characteristics. This shift happens after the whole of the scientific community has changed allegiance completely to a different and new paradigm. This is a process that does not happen instantly for the whole scientific community, it would rather take time for that conversion to actually happen-though for the individual scientist, the conversion could happen as a gestalt switch. Kuhn talks about the individual scientist's conversion from one paradigm to another without going through any intermediate positions. When the scientific community as a whole is converted to the winning tradition, this indicates that this specific paradigm has obtained its most possible confirmation.

Religion is one such case that expresses this harmony between the subjective and the objective. As it is the case with truth, *the objectivity of the religious hypothesis is not obtained in one person's experience.* Nor is it founded on a certain theoretical argument. It is based on the long term experiences of those who adopt the religious hypothesis in their lives. For the individual, the religious hypothesis is one which is subject to 'empirical' testing within the believer's own experience. The falsification of the religious hypothesis is not dependent on the individual's own empirical testing of it. For, the personal beliefs that the individual holds are only relative and subject to change over time. However, the accumulation of the experiences of individuals over a long period of time may be the means by which the confirmation of religious hypothesis is produced. Hence, the believers who act upon their religious hypothesis are collectively the ones whose conduct and action are likely to produce the confirmation of religious belief. The objective truth about religion may one day arrive at in this way. The objectivity of religion, as it is the case with truth and science, needs to be analysed in terms of the relative experiences of the individual believers.[55]

---

[54] *Ivi*, p. 202.
[55] WB, p. 86.

We examine next how within the experiences of the individual believers, religious beliefs can be empirically verified. The objective account of religious claims which James gives, is analysed in terms of the religious experiences of the believers. This James discusses in lecture XX, entitled 'Conclusions' and in the 'Postscript' to his monumental work on religious experience. In his *The Will to Believe,* James was mainly concerned with highlighting the wide divide between religion and science on the issue of the justification of beliefs. In the *Varieties of Religious Experience,* we find him occupied with narrowing the gap between science and religion as much as possible.

James argues for the abandonment of the vacuous formulations of theology and the concentration on the 'cash-value' of the religious hypothesis in the actual religious experiences of the individual believers. This can be achieved by realizing that in the matter of religion, we are dealing with a plurality of religions. Each making different claims from the other which are in many cases inconsistent with each other, or even incommensurable. Furthermore, James tells us, some religious theses are often 'absurd or incongruous' from a scientific perspective.[56] Thus we must identify the basic characteristics of religion which involves getting rid of the intellectually problematic aspects of each religion with its local and historical characteristics and concentrating on what is common to all religions. Once we have obtained the essential characteristics of all religions, we can test the religious hypothesis empirically. In order to achieve this, religious claims must have empirical consequences in the physical world.

James holds that a religious hypothesis, such as the hypothesis of God, is subject to empirical verification, just as is a scientific hypothesis. However, what distinguishes scientific hypotheses is that they may already have been verified, while religious hypotheses await verification. This kind of verification in the case of religious hypothesis is characterized by James as follows. He tells us in the *Varieties of Religious Experience,* that the experiences that he surveys are intended to persuade us that we might assume that connections with the divine may actually happen. On this assumption, he goes on to argue that there is a multiplicity of Gods which co-operate with us in a certain way. This hypothesis, he continues, can only be made true, verified in the long run, when enough people have held that view. Complete verification occurs when the consensus is total. So in the end, what establishes the credibility of this hypothesis is empirical evidence, namely, the support that the hypothesis might eventually gain through the believers believing it.

---

[56] VRE, p. 359.

3. Final Remarks

Now, we can highlight the areas of similarity between James's and Kuhn's views. According to James, the conception of a scientific theory or a law that is a literal transcript of reality seems to be somewhat impossible to maintain. Consequently, our conception of scientific truths has become more flexible. We can look at the relation between our propositions and reality in a broader way, in which truth is no longer absolute and non revisable nor is it literally objective, and where reality is not fixed but plastic and malleable to our needs and purposes. In principle, it cannot be said that Kuhn is in disagreement with James on this issue. Kuhn was opposed to the view that successive theories provided successively closer approximations to nature. By the same token he had to dismiss the correspondence theory of truth, emphasizing that truth can only be 'lexicon-dependent'. This dismissal of the relation of correspondence between propositions and reality gives way to the view that we may offer various viewpoints of the world; that the world can be seen and understood in a variety of ways. Thus we cannot speak of the *truest* view of the world or *the* one theory that explains certain physical phenomena. We can now talk about a multiplicity of paradigms which may account for the same physical phenomena.

Both James and Kuhn argue that in such cases we must turn to subjective factors that would assist us in theory choice. James argued that when the choice between rival theories cannot be decided on empirical or logical evidence, we are justified in applying subjective factors like elegance, simplicity and taste. Kuhn argued that the values of accuracy, consistency, scope, simplicity, and fruitfulness provide the shared basis for theory choice among the scientific community as a whole.

Kuhn talked about 'conversion' in two senses: Firstly, the experience of conversion of the individual scientist which could happen as a gestalt switch, by which the scientist 'sees the problem or the anomaly in a new way,' and moves from one way of seeing science and the world to another. Secondly, the conversion of the entire scientific community from one normal science tradition to another.

We have seen Kuhn claiming that a conversion experience cannot be "forced by logic and neutral experience."[57] Also, we find that with respect to "personal and aesthetic considerations. . . Men have been converted by them at times when most of the articulable technical arguments pointed the other way." Accordingly, it can be argued that Kuhn is bringing scientific revolutions closer

---

[57] *The Structure of Scientific Revolutions*, cit., p. 150.

to instantaneous religious conversions, in which 'rational' control is not the dominant factor.

Similarly, James talked about the individual's religious experience of conversion which can happen instantaneously. He also considered the conversion of the entire community of believers to the religious hypothesis through the accumulation of their experiences over a long period of time, by which the religious hypothesis is confirmed. Thus, the scientific experience in Kuhn's sense does not differ much from being a religious experience as James has outlined.

Finally, it is fascinating to observe that Kuhn has expressed views that are in accordance with James's over a half century after the latter's death. As has been said earlier, Kuhn understands the practice of science in terms of the rivalry of alternative paradigms, whose adequacy is measured by their pragmatic success, rather than the extent to which they succeed in depicting a pre-existent reality.[58]

As Kuhn showed how the idea of alternative paradigms is a helpful way to understand competing ideas within science, James showed decades earlier that such a notion is helpful in comparing and assessing the scientific enterprise as a whole with other domains such as religion and philosophy. The persistent influence of Kuhn's proposals, across a wide range of disciplines, grants contemporary support for the attractiveness of James's views.[59]

---

[58] *Ivi*, p. 158.

[59] I would like to thank Professor Timothy Sprigge for his encouragement to write this paper. I also thank Professor Othman Malhas for reading several drafts of this paper and for offering helpful comments.

Is Religious Experience the Experience of Something? 'Truth', Belief and 'Overbelief' in The Varieties of Religious Experience

Sergio Franzese (Phd)[*]

In the final chapter of *The Varieties of Religious Experience*,[1] James tries to identify the common core shared by all the forms of religious creed. Such a common core—James holds—is a composite experience that develops through two stages: first, the experience of some sort of uneasiness or inadequacy in one's own relationship to the world. Second, the experience of *being saved* "making a proper connection with the higher powers", whatever such powers may be.

The individual who attains this second stage of experience enters the religious state or condition, in which one identifies one's own real being with the highest part of oneself and, in turn, feels this latter as connected with a superior power in the universe. James describes such religious a state as follows: *"He becomes conscious that this higher part is conterminous and continuous with a* MORE *of the same quality, which is operative in the universe outside of him, and which he can keep in working touch with, and in fashion get on board of and save himself when all his lower being has gone to pieces in wreck."* (VRE, 400)

Such an account, however,—as James openly recognizes—refers to the psychological state of the individual in a religious condition only and does not state anything about the nature and existence of the higher powers with which the religious individual feels in touch. Briefly, James's account shows universal religiosity *a parte subjecti*. This recognition on James's part puts in tension the objective validity of religious experience which, without an adequate "object", is liable to be reduced to a merely subjective psychological matter or to a pious (self)illusion.

In this context James asks a second, and apparently obvious, question: *What is the objective 'truth' of religious feelings' content?* (VRE, 401)

The question appears, however, quite problematic because of James's use of the word "truth". In a related footnote, James explains that *"'truth' here is*

---

[*] Assistant Professor at the Dept. of Social Sciences and Communication, Università del Salento (Lecce, Italy)
[1] W. James *The Varieties of Religious Experience*. Cambridge: Harvard Univ. Pr., 1985. (Hereafter VRE)

taken to mean something additional to the bare value for life, although the natural propensity of man is to believe that whatever has great value for life is thereby certified as true." (VRE, 402)

By this addition James is apparently introducing another notion of truth, quite different from the account of truth presented in his "pragmatist", epistemological works. This peculiar discrepancy entitled some of his interpreters to argue that it could be more correct to assume the existence of two notions of truth in James.[2]

As a necessary corollary to such a problem, there is the question whether James's doubts about an objective "truth" of religious feeling does not put in question his own theory of belief, according to which, at least as for the metaphysical objects, belief and value for life are sufficient conditions for the *truth* of the believed objects.

The question appears more than legitimate and needs an answer or at least a clarification. As first we can exclude the easiest solution of a mere inattention, since James had already made the same move a few pages above when dealing with the power of prayer from a philosophical point of view.

As James points out, a great energetic power results from prayer, which is the very essence of true religion. The meaning of prayer—which is neither the begging for favors from the divinity, nor a mechanical repetition of empty formulas—is in getting in touch with the very spring of the life of the universe, namely, with the mysterious power at which the religious sentiment points (VRE, 366). Prayer is communication with the divine; it is the access to its inexhaustible energy and a therapy for the sickness of soul. It is a silent and inner prayer that evokes an ineffable and nameless God, whose existence is the first and insuperable enigma of the universe.

Yet, prayer turns out to be another difficult issue for the philosopher, who cannot help wondering whether any entity is there listening to it or *"in cassum missae preces"*[3]: *"The genuineness of religion is thus indissolubly bound up with the question whether the prayerful consciousness be or be not deceitful."*(VRE, 367) Indeed, if there is no certainty about God's existence; if such a certainty is by definition excluded from the horizon of human

---

[2] Hilary Putnam, for example, raised the question at the International Centenary Conference in celebration of the Gifford Lectures that took place in Edinburgh in July 2002. Analogously R.R. Niebuhr in "William James on Religious Experience" (*The Cambridge Companion to William James.* Cambridge Univ. Pr., 1997) writes: "Consequently, in following out his own overbelief to conclusions he holds as appropriate, James ventures again into the realm of 'truth' as distinct from value (401, n. 23)."

[3] See T. Livius *Ab Urbe Condita*, II, §49.

experience, nothing prevents us from assuming that prayer is nothing but inner soliloquy, self-suggestion, self-hypnosis, or simply, indulgent self-deception, or in other terms, that prayer does not attain any source of energy simply because there is no source to attain.

Here, again, James's analysis seems to suggest that belief and the vital benefit of an increasing spiritual energy are not enough to affirm the "truth" of the content of the belief that lays at the basis of the prayer. Indeed, James presents the standard pragmatist argument on behalf of prayer. If the meaning of prayer is in the increasing of spiritual energy that actually follows from praying, and to the extent that such an increasing occurs—we have experienced beyond any doubt that it occurs, and it is the core of every religion that prayer is a source of spiritual energy (VRE, 367+376)—the validity of prayer is perfectly verified. As for the origin of its power, this is a metaphysical question that can be put aside, as an empty and unanswerable question, to the extent it does not affect the effectiveness of prayer.

James, however, does not seem to be fully satisfied with such a pragmatic answer and pushes his inquiry forward, toward the unconscious dimension of the ego studied by the mind-curers and by his friend F.H. Myers, the author of the essay *Subliminal Consciousness*.[4] The subliminal dimension leads to a different interpretation of the spiritual power of religion. In the religious sentiment, through the highest part of oneself, the individual feels the connection with an immense power which operates in the universe and by which his spiritual power is increased. Such surplus of energy is what is called the divine, or God, and it is also the "more" that is felt in the religious state, whose objective 'truth' James is inquiring about. Can God's existence be conceived in terms of objective 'truth'. What is puzzling is that at the very moment the pragmatic method would allow James to get rid of one of the most traditional and uncanny metaphysical question, James seems to put aside the pragmatic method to seek for an unattainable "objective 'truth'" about God's existence. Does this mean that he thinks such a truth exists and is attainable? In fact, this is not the case and we need to reconsider the entire question from a different perspective.

1. The Objective 'Truth' of Religious Experience

It seems important to state two obvious but significant facts. In the final

---

[4] F.H. Myers, "Subliminal Consciousness", *Proceedings of the Society for Psychical Research*, vol. VII, (1892), p. 305

chapter of VRE James's concern is with the general structure of the religious attitude, namely, the "common nucleus" that lies "under all the discrepancies of the creeds" and "to which they bear their testimony unanimously." A substantial part of this inquiry is whether we have "to consider the testimony true." Consequently, he wonders about the "objective 'truth'" of the religious experience on which such testimony is based. The second fact is that the word *truth* is bracketed, meaning that he is using it in a special or differential meaning rather than using it *prima facie,* that is, as if he fully endorsed the existence of an "objective 'truth'". These clues seem to indicate that James is not changing his notion of truth or adopting a second one, but rather that he is taking an external and professional critical standpoint, from which he is considering what others would usually call "truth", that is, the actual existence of a thinkable object independently of its being actually thought by a particular mind.[5] Now, even though belief is for the believer a sufficient condition for the "truth" of the object of his/her belief, it is also evident that the critical philosopher is entitled to wonder whether from an external perspective, that is, beyond the particular creeds, the object of such a belief has a "truth", that is, whether it is a *real* entity.[6] In other words, James is taking advantage of the philosophical privilege to play in between the *ordo essendi* and the *ordo cognoscendi* in order to verify their correspondence. James's methodological attitude is consistent with the main purpose of the essay, which is a psychological and philosophical-anthropological inquiry on human nature and in particular on that peculiar kind of human experience called "religious experience".

In this sense, once James has stated that religious experience, as well as prayer, is a relationship between an individual and a MORE, he cannot but move to the next step and wonder whether the second term of such a relationship exists; what is very much the same as wondering whether what has been

---

[5] See VRE, p. 393. "The world of our experience consists at all times of two parts, an objective and a subjective part, of which the former may be incalculably more extensive than the latter..- The objective part is the sum total of whatsoever at any given time we may be thinking of, the subjective part is the inner 'state' in which the thinking comes to pass."
[6] See W. James, *Essays in Radical Empiricism,* Univ. of Nebraska Pr., 1996 (Hereafter ERE), I, §3, p. 24 nn. 1 and 2. In footnote 1 James stresses "the ambiguity" of the term "truth" which "is taken sometimes objectively and sometimes subjectively." In footnote 2 James through the reference to Perry's view of consciousness, distinguishes between immediate experience taken as "fact" and the same experience that becomes "opinion" or "thought upon reflection, or in retrospection". Once again the hypothesis that for James immediate experience or belief exhaust all the possible meaning and instances of truth seems quite unsound.

accounted for as a relationship is actually such, despite the particular feelings of single individuals. The actual topic of the question, then, is the structure and validity of a certain kind of human experience and not God's existence as such.

Such a professional philosophical inquiry does not seem at odds with the pragmatic account of truth. The pragmatic theory of truth states that "true", as "in agreement with reality", is what is valuable for life to the extent that it is the most expedient way to deal, whether practically or intellectually, with reality. In fact, *true* is what successfully leads the unfolding of our experience in the world of our activity; for they are fit and adequate to such a reality (P, 102). True ideas, then, *"are those that we can assimilate, validate, corroborate and verify."* Subjective value for life is not the single criterion and meaning of truth but only the primary and "common sense" level of truth (P 98). At a further level, the professional scientific or philosophical level, the adoption of a pragmatist account of truth means not only a right to believe in what is a value for life but also a permanent right to challenge the credit that such beliefs enjoys and, consequently, a never-ending process of verification, which needs to cope with "reality". This process includes the question about the existence and nature—the "objective 'truth'"—of the objects we deal with.[7] There is no other possible way in which "true ideas" could perform their leading function in the realm of experience and keep their "value for life". *"The object's advent is the significance's verification. Truth in these cases, meaning nothing but eventual verification, is manifestly incompatible with waywardness on our part. Woe to him whose beliefs play fast and loose with the order which realities follow in his experience: they will lead him nowhere or else make false connections."* (P, 99).

In the case of religious experience, the increasing of spiritual power, together with other possible beneficial, although merely psychological effects,

---

[7] James had already stated in the *Principles* that at a higher intellectual level a theory or an idea need a reference to the reality of the object they refer to, and the emotional value of the theory is only one of the necessary requirements for a theory being believed in. See W. James *Principles of Psychology*. New York: Dover Inc., 1956, (hereafter PP), vol. II p. 312 "The conceived system, to pass for true, must at least include the reality of the sensible objects in it, by explaining them as effects on us, if nothing more. (…) That theory will be most generally believed which, besides offering us objects able to account satisfactorily for our sensible experience, also offer those which are most interesting, those which appeal most urgently to our aesthetic, emotional, and active needs." See also ERE chap VI: "Nothing shall be admitted as a fact…except what can be experienced at some definite time by some experient; and for every feature of fact ever so experienced, a definite place must be found somewhere in the final system of reality. In other words: Everything real must be experienceable somewhere, and every kind of thing experienced must somewhere be real."

would be a complete verification and the whole meaning of the existence of higher powers, were we not able to produce the same effect by self-suggestion. Given such a possible alternative origin of the dynamogenic effects, of which James is well aware, the question about the actual existence of the object of religious experience is not a slip into a metaphysical notion of truth but just a necessary part of the process of verification of the idea of religious experience.[8] The factual character of such a verification makes the question about the "objective 'truth'" of religious experience perfectly consistent with the anti-dogmatic premise of the work and it is pragmatist in character through and through.

As a matter of fact, from the philosophical standpoint, James, while struggling with the question of God's existence, keeps himself deliberately away from any positive (or negative), namely, dogmatic, statement on the subject. This is the only possible sensible attitude, since James's philosophical quest for the "objective 'truth'" of religious experience, with no surprise on his and our part, eventually reaches a negative answer: *"In all sad sincerity I think we must conclude that the attempt to demonstrate by purely intellectual processes the truth of the deliverances of direct religious experience is absolutely hopeless."* (VRE, 359).

2. From the Object of Experience to the Object of Belief

Now, the question is: granted that what has been stated above is valid for all sorts of truths we can run across in our process of experience, does it make any sense to apply it to metaphysical beliefs, or "overbeliefs", the way James seems willing to do? The problem is evident. If the question about "objective 'truth'", here, is but a question on God's existence; and if, as for the metaphysical objects, which are not susceptible of factual evidence, belief is all the "truth" it is possible to have, it is not clear what is the point in looking for further evidence. Or, in other terms, could James ever gain from his inquiry any other result but another belief? Is not, then, such an inquiry a philosophical exercise in futility? Apparently, belief is the key and the only solution for the problem. Things are not easy as they can appear and there is a reason why James, here,

---

[8] In much the same way in ERE I, 3, p. 21 James states the importance of "percepts" as "reductive" of the "world of thought". "Were there no perceptual world...our world of thought would be the only world and would enjoy complete reality in our belief. This actually happens in our dreams, and in our day-dreams so long as percepts do not interrupt them."

has to be at least cautious in talking of "belief".

On several occasions, and for pragmatic reasons, James, from an intellectual standpoint, rejects the scholastic theological definition of God, the natural theology and in general the Judaic-Christian dogmatic account of God.[9] In the VRE in particular James states: "*If, namely, we apply the principle of pragmatism to God's metaphysical attributes, strictly so called, as distinguished from his moral attributes, I think that, even were we forced by a coercive logic to believe them, we still should have to confess them to be destitute of all intelligible significance. (...) candidly speaking, how do such quality as these make any definite connection with our life?*" (VRE, 351)

Apparently James saves the moral attributes of God, because of their genuine value for human life. In fact, "pragmatically they stand on an entirely different footing. They positively determine fear, hope and expectation, and are foundations for the sanctity of life." (VRE, 353). Philosophically speaking, however, James cannot escape the oddity of some moral attributes belonging to something the ontological status of which has just been put in question. Accordingly, James wonders: Is there any being to which such moral attributes belong "objectively", that is, independently from the valuable connection they can make with our life? We face again the ontological limits of our knowledge. James appeals to Kantian and post-Kantian idealism to deny any validity even to the moral attributes argument and to "bid a definitive good-bye to dogmatic theology", thus—he concludes—"our faith must do without that warrant." (VRE, 354)

It seems evident that James's criticism to the scholastic theology is only the signpost of the wider assumption that, generally speaking, we cannot define God through predicative statements, because for any set of predicates we decide to adopt, the concept of God turns out to be either *nonsensical* or in need of a prior metaphysical theory able to grant its meaning. Consequently, we find ourselves not only without a factual experience but also without an intellectual definition of God. At last, it seems that the entire question about the "objective 'truth'" of religious experience, namely, about God's existence, eventually comes down to a matter of belief. *Q.E.D.*

Before we rejoice at such a conclusion, however, we need to focus "in cold blood" on the problematic turn the question of belief has taken in virtue of James's argument. Belief is attribution of reality, namely, of existence to something. In turn, the reality, or real existence, of something is the object of belief. Existence, however, James argues quoting Kant "*is something quite*

---

[9] See "Reflex Action and Theism" and the dismissal of natural theology in "Is Life Worth Living?"

different from all the other predicates which a subject may possess." (PP II, 297) Belief, James repeats in VRE, is a positive intellectual content associated with a faith-state (VRE, 398); thus, the attribution of reality does not enrich the picture of the intellectual positive content of which we claim the existence. Then the problem is: granted that the question of God's existence has to be solved by belief, once we have denied the meaning of God's attributes, we no longer know what would be believed in such a belief.[10] In other words, by belief we are attributing existence to something for which we have no definition. *"…do what we will with our defining, the truth must at last be confronted that we are dealing with a field of experience where there is not a single conception that can be sharply drawn."* (VRE, 38-39) Rigorously speaking, the statement "Is!" should be the whole content of our entire faith and theology. What kind of expectations, hopes and fears, and what kind of definite connection with our life we can draw out of this is something each one has to decide on his/her own.

We cannot believe in God, because of God in itself we cannot speak, since God *qua* God transcends and escapes all our conceptual grids. Of God, — whether God exists or not, and what God's nature might be—actually is impossible to know or say anything.[11] As far as we talk of/about God we cannot but talk of God's meaning and function as conceived by human beings; that is, we can only provide a human, and often expedient, account of God (VRE, 264+266). Therefore, to the extent that we still like to talk of a religious "experience", we need to recognize that this is a *constructive* experience, that is, we are making up the object of the experience more than we are experiencing the object in itself. Such an object is not God but the "divine", as James calls it, that is, the human feeling, perception and/or understanding of "God" (VRE, 39). Thus the divine is the only actual correlate of religious experience and its meaning and existence is entirely included in such

---

[10] See VRE, p. 53. "The sentiment of reality can indeed attach itself so strongly to our object of belief that our whole life is polarized through and through, as it were, by its sense of the existence of the thing believed in, and yet that thing, for the purpose of definite description, can hardly be said to be present to our mind at all."

[11] In this perspective James's quote from Professor Leuba sounds extremely significant: "The truth of the matter can be put in this way: God is not known, he is not understood; he is used—sometimes as meat-purveyor, sometimes as moral support, sometime as friend, sometimes as object of love. If he proves himself useful, the religious consciousness asks for no more than that. Does God really exist? How does he exist? What is he? Are so many irrelevant questions. Not God but life, more life, a larger, richer, more satisfying life, is, in the last analysis, the end of religion. The love of life, at any and every level of development, is the religious impulse." (VRE, p. 399)

experience. The divine is a part of human spiritual experience and exists to the extent that it is experienced and believed, whereas God, whatever might possibly be, stays *ineffable* beyond such experience.

3. The Experience of the Divine

With such premises religion can be an inner subjective fact only, and the most we can say about it, following James's analysis, is that *"apart from ecclesiastical or theological complications, (it) has shown to consist everywhere, and at all its stages, in the consciousness which individual have of an intercourse between themselves and higher powers with which they feel themselves related."* (VRE, 365-366) The nature and definition of such higher powers is an entirely subjective matter that depends on human emotional, moral and aesthetical needs or inclinations. Every creed is the legitimate expression of particular emotional needs and has a right to be respected as such, not because it is *"objectively 'true'"* but because *religions, apart from any other transcendent consideration, even as purely subjective phenomena, "are amongst the most important biological functions of humanity."*

As a matter of fact, James argues, human beings have no need for God, but rather for "believing in God", that is, they need a religion, or a religious feeling, able to makes them feel at home in the world and stimulate their moral energies. The idea of God—James states, quoting Kant again—has no theoretical meaning, but displays a huge practical value (VRE, 52). Such a "practical value" is perfectly embodied in the "divine" and James, on his part, does his best to provide a sensible picture of the divine, consistent with the account of religious experience as a connection with higher powers and source of spiritual power. In fact, James is trying to define God "backwards", that is, from the effects we have from our belief, from the need humans have of it and from the hope such a belief can satisfy. This leads James to seek for the divine in what he and his friend F. H. Myers call the unconscious dimension of the ego, better defined also as a subliminal, or subconscious, dimension.[12]

Now, at first sight, pushing the quest for the divine toward the subconscious

---

[12] The notion of subconscious, or subliminal consciousness, was quite popular in James's times because of the application the "Mind-Cure Movement" was doing of it in the religious field. There is of course no relation between James's notion of the unconscious and the homonymous notion in Freud. On the relations between James and Freud see A.A. Roback, *William James*, Sci-Art Publishers, Cambridge (Mass), 1942, ch. VI, pp 82-83. See also J. Barzun, *A Stroll with William James*, The university of Chicago Press, 1983, pp. 227-239.

dimension could appear as if James had definitively waived any claim to a real object for religious experience and bounded himself into the subjective perspective. It is the case, however, that through Myers's notion of a *subliminal self* James is providing an extremely concrete and powerful account of the "divine", in order to account for the spiritually empowering and dynamogenic effects of faith and prayer and to avoid the self-suggestion and self-deception argument.

The subliminal dimension opens for James the way for a different interpretation of the spiritual power of religion. The "divine" is the profound dimension of the ego, the unfathomable mass of the iceberg of the human psychical life, of which the "I" is but the visible top. Through James's account, Myers's subliminal theory is enlarged beyond the boundaries of the individual organism to attain the view of a spiritual world, which wraps and pervades the visible world, and in which the subliminal self merges and gets in touch with the spiritual energy of the universe. Through the feeling of the divine, by means of asceticism and prayer, human spirit draws from such a reservoir that "surplus" of energy that is the main meaning of religion. The visible and the invisible world are intertwined in a continuous effusion of energy, which makes the boundaries of individuality vanishing and blurred. As James writes in *Human Immortality*: *"We need only suppose the continuity of our consciousness with a mother sea, to allow for exceptional waves occasionally pour over the dam."*[13]

Thus, the religious sentiment that characterizes human spirituality can be explained as the experience of an individual rooted in the sea of energy, wherein he is connected to all the other living beings, and at the same time as the possibility to plunge in such a sea to absorb its energy.

At last, such an account, for James, is pluralistic and "open" enough not to exhaust the entire sphere of the divine. The energetic "pantheism" does not necessarily and definitely rule out the possibility of the existence of God, as a mental, individual entity, who could be the source of the energy that pervades the universe, although we have no idea what such a God would look like.

Such a God, even though it cannot be an object of experience, is, however, still available as the object of an 'over-belief' that can create active connections with an individual's existence and being real and true. (VRE, 406-407). The ambiguity between God taken both as personal entity and as energetic texture of the universe, then, is not solved, and lies at the very core of James's account of the "divine".

---

[13] W. James *Human Imortality. Two Supposed Objections to the Doctrine*. Boston: Houghton Mifflin, 1898; p. 27.

James does not really try to solve the ambiguity. Rather he seems deliberately to swing between one meaning and the other replacing any possible clear-cut definition by a sort of emotional and semantic *nebula*, that is, by an endlessly escaping point in which the faith of the common person, the devotion of the saint and the speculation of the theologian converge. *"But the whole array of our instances leads to a conclusion something like this: It is as if there were in the human consciousness a sense of reality, a feeling of objective presence, a perception of what we may call* 'something there'..." (VRE, 53) As a matter of fact, such a "something" is not in itself a more significant object of belief than the statement "Is!" Yet, it is true that for James the real meaning of religious belief is moral and human rather than theological and transcendent. To believe in God is essentially to believe in the value and tenacity of human enterprise.[14]

Such a view was already exposed in the letter of August 1882 to Thomas Davidson, where James associated the rejection of traditional theology with a view of God as *primus inter pares*, that is, as a helpful power. God is the source of the unlimited trust in the effectiveness of human struggle against pain and for the achievement of a moral order.[15] God, in its essential features must be conceived as "the deepest power of universe" and as a "mental personality", but at the same time God as unknowable personality cannot but remain alien to human experience and existence.[16]

Davidson, as a rigorous agnostic, quite rightfully resisted to such a view of God, for it was merely wishful and could in no possible way stand for a demonstration, or even a simple statement of God's existence. The fact that the belief in God makes much more sense of the world cannot mean that God exists or that the world actually makes sense. It means only we would like that to be the case. The confrontation with Davidson will grow out in time extremely significant and fruitful for the clarification of the relation between the human and the divine. James's humanistic view of religiosity, which from the last

---

[14] See *Pragmatism*, p. 139. See also VRE p. 35-36. The anonymity of the experience of the divine in James can be strictly related to the strong humanistic foothold of his philosophy. See V. Boublik "L'expérience anonyme du sacré" in *Archivio di Filosofia*, 1974, pp 397-406. "L'experience du sacré dans le contexte d'une culture dominée par l'humanisme sans-Dieu peut avoir une dimension religieuse anonyme, si la recherche de la liberté parfaite et d'amour totale est alimentée par l'experience de l'insuffisance radicale et par l'invocation de 'quelque chose', de 'Quelqu'un' qui rend possible la réalisation de l'avenir de la liberté et de l'amour." (p. 400)

[15] Letter 8/1/1882 "W.J. to Thomas Davidson".

[16] See W. James, The *Will to Believe and Other Essays in Popular Philosophy*, Harvard Univ. Pr., Cambridge (Mass), 1979 (Hereafter WB), p. 98

pages of VRE moves on to the last lecture of *Pragmatism*, will reaffirm the anthropological and moral meaning of James's religious "overbelief", which entails James's reinterpretation of Davidson's *apeirotheistic* view of the 'divinity of man'.[17]

From the perspective of James's philosophical anthropology, the divine is not exhausted in the human nor can the human be explained through the divine. Rather, God and human beings are convergent arrays of activity heading toward an infinitely escaping point, which is at the same time a perfect achievement of human spiritual life and an absolute epiphany of the divine in the world. The moral work of humankind is the cooperation of human beings among themselves, but also of human beings with "God", understood as the presence of an "unseen order" toward which the human world should converge.[18] The 'overbelief' in this cooperation is the very content of human spirituality and the highest source of energy and relief for humans. Insofar as the belief in the cooperation with God is alive, and deploys its beneficial effects; insofar as human beings actualise their communion with God in the achievement of world's salvation, God fully exists in such a communion. To the extent God's being is in that 'making itself' that is the activity of human beings as spiritual beings, namely, to the extent that the human is divine and the divine is human, God *is* and *is in the making*.

4. James's "Overbelief"

The analysis of James's discussion of religious experience from a philosophical perspective, with its negative results and ambiguous proposals, leaves open a final question, which apparently is a major question for many of his readers, namely, whether James believed in God.

The most honest, although the most unpopular, answer to this question, however, is that, philosophically speaking, such a question is absolutely irrelevant and for several reasons. Above all, it is irrelevant because James is extremely careful in keeping his philosophical work as far as possible separate from his personal "overbeliefs". In this sense it is noteworthy that every time James refers to his own personal beliefs he is extremely cautious in stressing that a certain idea is just his own personal (over)belief.

---

[17] On James and Davidson, see M.H. DeArmey, "Thomas Davidson Apeirotheism and Its Influence on William James and John Dewey". *Journ. Of Hist. Of Ideas*, n. 8, 1987; pp. 691-707

[18] See VRE, pp. 53 ff.

Such a neat separation between philosophical speculation and personal life is clearly exhibited in his letter of April 9 1907 to C. A. Strong Apr. 9, 1907; "[...] *Your warnings against my superstitious tendencies, for such I suppose they are... touch me, but not in the prophetic way, for they don't weaken my trust in the healthiness of my own attitude... The 'omniscient' and omnipotent' God of theology I regard as a disease of the philosophy-shop. But having thrown away so much of the philosophy-shop, you may ask me, why I don't throw away the whole? That would mean too strong a negative will-to-believe for me. It would mean a dogmatic disbelief in any extant consciousness higher than the 'normal' human mind; and this in the teeth of the extraordinary vivacity of man's psychological commerce with something ideal that feels as if it were also actual (I have no such commerce, I wish I had, but I can't close my eyes to its vitality in others)."*

The quoted passage marks beyond any doubt the clear-cut distinction James established between philosophy and personal religious belief, grazing the threshold of a "double-truth" theory. Philosophy stops where personal religious belief begins and essentially they follow different paths. Such an attitude, by the way, is perfectly consistent with James pluralistic and anti-dogmatic approach not only to religion but also to life in general. In conclusion, if we knew whether James believed in God or not we would not obtain a better insight into his philosophical theory than that which we obtain from the indications he has already explicitly provided by himself.

James's account of God, we said, is extremely ambiguous and at the very moment we try to define James's own notion of God the picture appears blurred. In a few case he refers to "us Christians" but this seems to be intended more easily as an inclusion of himself into western cultural religious tradition, which predefines the range of options and mental habits he and his listeners could consider meaningful, rather than as a statement of personal religious belief. Whatever the case, he never uses, as we have already seen, any Christian belief or category as a philosophical argument. Moreover, more than once he explicitly excludes himself from the group of people who enjoy religious or mystical experience of any sort.

Quite significant in this sense is the opening of the lecture on "Human Immortality" where James speaks of himself as "the man like him who stands before you, certainly not because he is known as an enthusiastic messenger of the future life, burning to publish the good tidings to his fellow-men, but apparently because he is a university official. Thinking in this way, I felt first as if I ought to decline the appointment.(...) And yet, in spite of these reflections... I am here to-night, all uninspired and official as I am." In the preface to the second edition of the same lecture James states not without a certain cunning ambiguity "Now I am myself anything but a pantheist of the monistic pattern." Does it mean that he is not a pantheist at all or rather that he is a pantheist of a pluralistic pattern? Hard to say. At the personal level the most that James allows us to say is his pragmatic and energetic religious "overbelief": "...that the world of our present consciousness is only one out of many worlds of consciousness that exist, and that those other worlds must contain experiences which have a meaning for our life also...the two become continuous at certain point, and higher energies filter in." Yet, James stresses "What the most characteristically divine facts are, apart from the actual inflow of energy...I know not."

This appeal to an infinite of consciousness and energy,[19] leads us to the question of the mystical side of James's temperament. On James's alleged mysticism Richard Gale, in his monograph on James,[20] based a whole reinterpretation of James's character and philosophy. Thus, he stands out as a necessary reference for such a topic. Gale deals with what he considers the oddity between James's claim not to have ever had any mystical experiences (VRE, 301) on one hand, and James's mystical "morbid" self and his sympathetic inclination to others' mystical experiences, as to accept their cognitivity. Gale, however, in explaining the alleged oddity of James's attitude toward mysticism suggests what apparently sounds as the most sensible answer. *"My first response is that even if it were true that James did not have any mystical experiences, at least of the more developed type, it could be the case that he had a deep sensitivity to and appreciation of them and what they seemingly reveal, just as someone who lacks the musical genius to compose an Eroica Symphony can resonate to it aesthetically."* (p. 254) A few lines below, however, Gale adds that in any case James had some sort of mystical experiences thanks to his experiments with nitrous-oxide, mescal and alcohol; what could be an interesting hint, provided that religious mystical experience and "mystical" experiences from intoxication of any sort would share some sort of structural analogy.[21] Whatever the case might be, Gale's point is that one

---

[19] On James's energetic turn and the centrality of the notion of "energy" in his late philosophy see Sergio Franzese *William James and the Ethics of Energy* (PhD dissertation) Vanderbilt Univ. 2002 and "James vs Nietzsche. Energy and Asceticism in James." *Streams of William James*, vol. 5, Issue 2, Summer 2003.

[20] R. Gale, *The Divided Self of William James*. Cambridge: Cambridge Univ. Pr., 1999; pp. 253 ff.

[21] See also W. James "A Suggestion about Mysticism" in *Essays in Philosophy*. Cambridge: Harvard Univ. Pr., 1978. Here, James explains mystical experiences in terms of enlargement of usual field of consciousness with no reference to special objects of mystical

does not need to enjoy mystical experiences to have a mystical inclination in one's own temperament. The argument is sound enough; apparently, then, the only problem is that there is no contradiction involved in James's statement. This leads Gale to develop a second long answer that reaches the following conclusion "*The clash between James's active Promethean self and his passive mystical self, along with the one between the Ontological Relativism favored by his Promethean self and the nonrelativized reality-claims made by his mystical self, are the two deepest aporias that arise from James's quest to have it all.*" (p. 272) Whatever such a statement could possibly mean, it seems evident that the second answer does not solve the contradiction that the first answer had excluded so effectively. What makes the second part of Gale's analysis quite puzzling.

It is legitimate, then, to stop at the first answer in order to define James's mystical attitude as part of his religious "overbelief". James had a mystical tendency although he never had mystical experiences. In other words, although he has never enjoyed visions, lights and voices, he had the aptitude to "see" the universe as an *ineffable* totality. Or, in Wittgenstein's terms, he had the ability to think what cannot be objectively and theoretically spoken about. James's mysticism is that special "awareness of infinity" that Hermann Lotze, one of James's favorite reference, considered as the mark of human transcendence and the very essence of the human being.[22] This attitude allowed James to conceive the statement "Is!" as the meaningful and worthwhile, exclusive content of the genuine religious experience, and at the same time as the most fundamental and permanent enigma in the universe.

5. Final Remarks

In conclusion we return to our original question "What is experienced in religious experience?" Everything and nothing should be the answer.

There is no special object experienced in so-called "religious experience" (see VRE, 31); rather, we could say that religious experience is an entirely transformed experience of the world as a whole, or in other words it is an experience of every thing as completely inhabited by a special mood

---

experience. In this same text James affirms he has personally experienced three cases of such peculiar phenomenon during trivial occurrences of everyday life or while dreaming. No special illumination or vision of transcendent objects, according to James, is attached to such experiences, which stays in the range of human psychological possibilities.

[22] See H. Lotze, *Mikrokosmus*, Leipzig, 1923 [1858], II, v, 5.

(*stimmung*) that makes the religious person's world entirely different from layperson's everyday life world. Such a mood is a complex emotional state filled with solemnity, awe, a sense of infinity, fear, hope, longing for beauty, order and justice, feeling of empowerment, sentiment of human brotherhood and cosmic unity, feeling of connection with some higher power, sense of safety and so on. "The religious person's world" –James says—"is not the usual materialistic world plus a religious feeling" (VRE, 408); it is another world with a different "natural constitution", and another meaning, sense and value. There is no point in trying to attain a "picture" of such a world (a *Weltbild*) —here lies the falling short of any philosophy or science of religion—since such a world is a vision (a *Weltanschauung*). That is what James means by defining religion as a "total reaction" upon the life (VRE, 36-37) and religious sentiment as a "collective name" (VRE, 31). Such a vision possibly does not change the barely physical appearance of the worldly objects; it changes, however, the nature of their mutual relationships and of our relationships to them. Thus religious experience is the experience of a transfigured world in which things speak a peculiar language that follows the grammar of the "unseen order".

Such an experience, however, still depends upon James's general doctrine of experience, that is, 1) subject and object are factually one in it; 2) such an experience is not contemplative, or not merely contemplative, but in its very essence it is mostly and above all a "doing", that is, it is an activity.[23] In this sense it would be far more correct to say "I act religious", rather than "I am religious". The world appears religious to the extent we make it religious in the run of an experience that is an infinite process of reciprocal constitution. It is such an active and constitutive process that grounds religious *belief* as such, that is, as a will to act religiously to a religious world, whatever we mean by the latter. Such a legitimation does not follow from the demonstration of God's existence, and it could never do. It rather follows from the necessary activity, which is the only condition and occurrence of the achievement of the unseen, divine order, namely, the same order with which the believer feels connected in the religious emotion. The divine order "is" somewhere out there exactly

---

[23] See ERE, p. 23 "As 'subjective' we say that experience represents; as 'objective' it is represented. What represents and what is represented is here numerically the same; but we must remember that no dualism of being represented and representing resides in the experience per se. (...) The instant field of the present is at all times what I call the 'pure' experience. It is only virtually or potentially either object or subject as yet. For the time being, it is plain, unqualified actuality, or existence, a simple *that*. In this *naïf* immediacy it is of course *valid*; it is *there*, we *act* upon it..."

because we achieve it here and now in our action, and conversely it can inform our action only because it is somewhere out there waiting and attending to us. Our religious experience of it is its own divine existence.

"However particular questions connected with our individual destinies may be answered it is only by acknowledging them as genuine questions and living in the sphere of thought which they open up that we become profound. But to live thus is to be religious…By being religious we establish ourselves in possession of ultimate reality at the only points at which reality is given us to guard." (VRE, 394-395).

Unamuno's Reading of The Varieties of Religious Experience and its Context

Jaime Nubiola - Izaskun Martínez[*]

> "I am inflamed at the idea of seeing and knowing Spain."
> (Letter of July 10th, 1877 from Henry to William James)

William James sailed on the steamer *Spain* from New York to Europe on 10th October 1873,[1] but he did not visit Spain nor stay for any length of time in any other Spanish-speaking country throughout all his life. James had particularly close ties to the philosophical communities in England, Italy, France and Germany, but his personal links with Spain were much weaker. In those times Spain was not only an isolated and declining country, but also —as everybody knows— there was a war between Spain and the United States in 1898 over the Spanish dominance of Cuba and the Philippines.[2] In spite of that strong sociological and cultural contrast between both countries, James's thought and books were soon received in Spain by prominent scholars such as Miguel de Unamuno (1864-1936), José Ortega y Gasset (1883-1955), and Eugenio d'Ors (1881-1954). In fact, it is possible to assert that, contrary to a superficial impression, there is a deep affinity between the central questions of American pragmatism and the topics and problems addressed by the most relevant Hispanic thinkers of the twentieth century.[3] Amongst them probably the best and the earliest Spanish reader of James was Miguel de Unamuno, one of the foremost intellectuals of the Hispanic cultural world in the past century. Unamuno is most well known for his *Life of Don Quixote and Sancho*.

---

[*] Jaime Nubiola is Professor of Philosophy at the University of Navarra, Spain; Izaskun Martinez is PhD at the University of Navarra
[1] I. Skrupselis and E. M. Berkeley (eds.): *The Correspondence of William James*, Charlottesville, VA, University Press of Virginia, 1995, vol. 4, pp. 446-449.
[2] For William James's position in the Spanish-American war, see L. Simon: *Genuine Reality. A Life of William James*, Harcourt & Brace, Orlando, FL, 1998, pp. 279-282, and his letters in *The Correspondence of William James*, vol. 3, pp. 25-36.
[3] See J. Nubiola: "C. S. Peirce and the Hispanic Philosophy of the Twentieth Century," *Transactions of the Charles S. Peirce Society* 24/1 (1998), pp. 31-49.

Our aim in this article, after providing the general framework of the reception of William James in Spain, is to trace the reception of *Varieties* through Unamuno's reading of this book. With this goal in mind, our article has been divided into the following three sections: 1) the reception of William James in Spain, 2) Unamuno's reading of *Varieties*, highlighting some peculiar aspects of his way of reading that book, and 3) some suggestions about further work to be done in order to explore in greater depth the reception of William James in Spanish-speaking countries.

1. The Reception of William James in Spain

The aim of this section is to describe some of the main facts of James's reception in Spain and the Hispanic world, starting with the translations and following with those readers of James who introduced him to the Spanish speaking audience. A number of names and facts are to be mentioned, because they provide the general framework for understanding this long process that extended throughout all the past century, and which is enjoying a general resurgence.

Without any doubt, a sign of the warm reception of William James in Spain is the early translation of a number of his books. The first translation of James into Spanish appeared as early as 1900. It was a two-volume translation of the *Principles of Psychology* (1890), by Domingo Barnés (1870-1943), published by Editorial Jorro of Madrid. A second edition appeared in 1909. Barnés was a well known Spanish educator of his time, member of the famous *Institución Libre de Enseñanza*, and an expert in psychology and sociology. Besides the *Principles*, Barnés translated a dozen books by contemporary authors such as John Dewey, Henri Bergson and others.[4]

The second James's translation into Spanish was the work *Talks to Teachers on Psychology and to Students on Some of Life's Ideals* (1899), which appeared in 1904. The translator was Carlos M. Soldevila. Three years later, the first translation of *The Varieties of Religious Experience* into Spanish was done by Miguel Domenge Mir. It was published in three volumes under the title *Fases*

---

[4] W. James: *Principios de psicología*. (Translation of Domingo Barnés). Madrid, Editorial Daniel Jorro, 1900, 2 vols.; 2nd edition, 1909. A useful source on Barnés is R. Cardá and H. Carpintero: "Domingo Barnés: Biografía de un educador avanzado," *Boletín de la Institución Libre de Enseñanza*, II época, n. 12 (1991), pp. 63-74.

del sentimiento religioso. Estudio sobre la naturaleza humana.[5] This probably had a very small print run, because very few copies remain in the Spanish libraries today. Roughly eighty years later, in 1986, a new translation circulated widely,which has since been reprinted five times. This edition includes a foreword by the well known Spanish philosopher José Luis L. Aranguren, in which he writes that the year 1901-02 of William James's Gifford Lectures, "was a milestone in the history of psychology, and, therefore, in the history of religious psychology and in the consideration of religion by learned people."[6]

The fourth translation of James into Spanish was The Will to Believe and Other Essays in Popular Philosophy in 1909, under the title of La vida eterna y la fe (Eternal Life and Faith), reprinted in 1922 as La voluntad de creer y otros ensayos de filosofía popular. [7] The translator was Santos Rubiano (1871-1930), an army doctor who was a pioneer in the application of the methods and concepts of modern psychology in the Spanish army. A veteran of the Philippines and North African wars, he was trained as a psychologist at Cornell University in the United States in 1916, funded by the Spanish Ministry of Public Education[8]. In that year Rubiano translated the Psychology. Briefer Course, which had a second edition in 1930. After the opening page there is a photographical reproduction of a hand-written text from William James dated on the 22nd of March of 1908. The text is the following:

22.III. 08
... and am very glad to authorize you as my official translator.
 Believe me, dear Doctor, with sincere and grateful regards,
Yours very truly .
Wm James

---

[5] W. James: *Fases del sentimiento religioso. Estudio sobre la naturaleza humana.* (Translation by Miguel Domenge Mir), Barcelona, Carbonell y Esteva, 1907-08, 3 vols.
[6] W. James: *Las variedades de la experiencia religiosa.* Translation of José Francisco Yvars. Barcelona, Ediciones Península, 1986. There is also a translation into Catalan of M. Mirabent y J. Bachs, *Les varietats de l'experiència religiosa: estudi de la naturalesa humana.* Barcelona, Edicions 62, 1985.
[7] W. James: *La vida eterna y la fe.* (Translation of Santos Rubiano). Barcelona, Heinrich, 1909; reprinted as *La voluntad de creer y otros ensayos de filosofía popular.* Madrid, Editorial Daniel Jorro, 1922.
[8] See J. Bandrés, y R. Llavona: "Santos Rubiano: la introducción de la psicología científica en el ejército español," *Psicothema*, IX/3 (1997), pp. 659-669.

Dr. Santos Rubiano[9]

Rubiano includes a lively "biographical-critical foreword" in his translation of the *Briefer Course*. He writes that in this book "not only speaks the professor alone, but also the genius and the believer," and that James "was able to create from his own personality his own method of teaching, and [that] in his personality it was possible to find not only a philosopher but a good man."[10] Besides these two works, Rubiano translated *Pragmatism* into Spanish in 1923, and in 1924 *The Meaning of Truth* as well as a new translation of *Talks to Teachers.*[11]

In the 1930's the interest in James seems to have faded in the Hispanic world. Nevertheless, publishers in Argentina and Mexico in the following two decades produced reprints of old translations as well as some new translations. Among them there should be mentioned at least the translation of *Some Problems of Philosophy* by Juan Adolfo Vázquez in Tucumán, Argentina, in 1944, and the new translation of *Pragmatism* by Vicente P. Quintero in 1945, which includes a preliminary note by Jorge Luis Borges[12]. In that text Borges described James as an "admirable writer" to the point that he was able to make attractive such a reasonable way of thinking as the pragmatism of the first two decades of our century, with "halfway solutions" and "quiet hypotheses."[13] Years later, for unknown reasons, Borges refused to include that foreword in his compilation of prefaces. For the same period the Spanish translations by Luis Rodríguez Aranda of *Pragmatism* in 1954 and of *The Meaning of Truth* in

---

[9] W. James: *Compendio de psicología*. (Translation of Santos Rubiano). Madrid, Editorial Daniel Jorro, 1916; 2nd edition, 1930.

[10] S. Rubiano, "William James. Bosquejo biográfico. Nota crítica sobre su ideario psicológico," p. xiii. It is still pending to explore in more detail the relations between Rubiano and James.

[11] W. James: *Pragmatismo*. Madrid, Editorial Daniel Jorro, 1923; W. James: El significado de la verdad. Madrid, Editorial Daniel Jorro, 1924; W. James: *Psicología pedagógica (para maestros). Sobre algunos ideales de la vida (para estudiantes)*. Madrid, Editorial Daniel Jorro, 1924.

[12] W. James: *Problemas de la filosofía*. (Translation of Juan Adolfo Vázquez. Tucumán), Argentina, Editorial Yerba Buena, 1944; and *Pragmatismo. Un nombre nuevo para algunos viejos modos de pensar*. Translation of Vicente P. Quintero with a preliminar note of Jorge Luis Borges. Buenos Aires, Emecé Editores, 1945.

[13] J.L. Borges: "Nota preliminar," in W. James, *Pragmatismo*. p. 10; about that connection see also J. Nubiola: "Jorge Luis Borges and William James," *Streams of William James. A Publication of the William James Society* I/3 (1999), p. 7.

1957 should be mentioned.

With the revival of pragmatism in the last decade there has been a new impulse for translating James into Spanish. In 1992 two manuscripts of James on substance and phenomenon that appeared originally in Perry's *The Thought and Character of William James* were translated,[14] and in 1998, on the occasion of the centennial of *The Human Immortality*, a translation of this work by Angel Cagigas was published[15]. The most recent publication of James in Spain has been a new translation of *Pragmatism* by Ramón del Castillo in the year 2000, including a foreword and editorial notes.[16] As a summary of this enumeration we can say that by the end of this century most of William James's books had been translated into Spanish: only *A Pluralistic Universe* (1909) and *Essays in Radical Empiricism* (1912) are awaiting a Spanish translator.

Turning now to the secondary bibliography on William James available in Spanish, it may be arranged in two groups. First, the books and papers in Spanish written by Hispanic authors, and second, the translation into Spanish of books and papers from foreign authors. A thorough study is still required, but we can say in advance that probably this second group is bigger than the first one. This fact may be interpreted as a sign of the interest in James in the Spanish speaking countries and at the same time as a sign of the lack of real scholarship and of original production on American pragmatism.

Amongst the early translations of secondary bibliography it should be mentioned Emile Boutroux' *William James* (A. Colin, Paris, 1911), which was reviewed by Eugenio d'Ors in the journal *Arxius de l'Institut de Ciències*, and translated in 1921 into Spanish in Montevideo and published with a foreword of d'Ors. Also a paper of Emile Boutroux on William James's pedagogical ideas was published in the *Boletín de la Institución Libre de Enseñanza.*[17] Other later

---

[14] R.B. Perry: *The Thought and Character of William James*, I, Little, Brown, Boston, 1935, pp. 525-528 and pp. 578-580. Translation of Sebastián M. Pascual Sastre in "Manuscritos sobre la sustancia y el fenómeno," Taula, 17-18 (1992), pp. 101-109.

[15] W. James: *La inmortalidad humana*. (Translation of Ángel Cagigas). Jaén, Editorial del Lunar, 1998.

[16] W. James: *Pragmatismo. Un nuevo nombre para viejas formas de pensar*. (Traducción, notas y prólogo de Ramón del Castillo). Madrid, Alianza Editorial, 2000. In 1997 Ramon del Castillo published under the title Lecciones de Pragmatismo (Madrid, Santillana) the old translation of Rodríguez Aranda with an introductory study.

[17] E. d'Ors: "Review of Emile Boutroux's William James," *Arxius de l'Institut de Ciències* I, 1, (1911), pp. 150-153; E. Boutroux: William James y su filosofía. Translation of Mario

relevant translations are Ralph Barton Perry's *The Thought and Character of William James* (briefer version) by Eduardo Prieto in 1973,[18] and Jacques Barzun's *A Stroll with William James* in 1986, in which the affinity between William James and the Spanish thinkers Unamuno and Ortega, "both fighting positivism," is already noticed.[19]

Coming now to the original production of the Spanish speaking countries on James, in 1961 Pelayo H. Fernández studied in detail how Miguel de Unamuno read William James, his frequent quotations of James and his marginal notes in the works by James in his library. Fernández's conclusion was that Unamuno's pragmatism was "original with respect to that of the American, from whom he absorbed only complementary features."[20] However, in our opinion, the abundance of facts that Pelayo Fernández lists bears witness to a great influence, and a great similarity between the two thinkers on many issues and problems. In any case, Fernández's doctoral dissertation and the subsequent monograph is the starting point for everybody interested in the reception of James in Spain, especially through Unamuno.

In the case of José Ortega y Gasset, John Graham published a careful study in which, after noting Ortega's hostility to American pragmatism, he reveals "many basic connections, similarities and points of identity, so that concrete influence and dependence seem more plausible than 'coincidence' between Ortega and James."[21] Graham gives evidence that Ortega read James early in his career, and that Ortega was aware of James's radical empiricism as having anticipated the central notion in his own "rational-vitalism."[22] His evidence of James's impact on Ortega by German sources, themselves

---

Falcao Espalter. Montevideo, Editorial Claudio García, 1921; E. Boutroux: "La pedagogía de William James," *Boletín de la Institución Libre de Enseñanza*, n. 617, (1911), pp. 222-231.

[18] R. B. Perry: *El pensamiento y la personalidad de William James*. Translation of Eduardo J. Prieto. Buenos Aires, Editorial Paidós, 1973.

[19] J. Barzun: *Un paseo con William James*. (Translation of Juan José Utrilla). México, Fondo de Cultura Económica, 1986, p. 228.

[20] P. H. Fernández: *Miguel de Unamuno y William James. Un paralelo pragmático*. Salamanca, CIADA, 1961, p. 13.

[21] J. T. Graham: *A Pragmatist Philosophy of Life in Ortega y Gasset*. Columbia, MI, University of Missouri Press, 1994, p. 145.

[22] J. T. Graham: *A Pragmatist Philosophy of Life in Ortega y Gasset*, pp. 147-152.

influenced by James, is specially convincing.[23]

In contrast with Ortega, the aforementioned Eugenio d'Ors is perhaps the Hispanic philosopher most conscious of his personal connection with American pragmatism. By 1907 he had defined himself as a pragmatist, driven by the same desires as moved his American counterparts, whom he hoped to outstrip by recognising an aesthetic dimension of human action that could not be reduced to the merely utilitarian.[24] Forty years later, in 1947, in his *El secreto de la filosofía* which crowned his philosophical career, he generously acknowledges his debt to the American tradition.[25]

In Latin America the connection with American pragmatism can be traced back to the hostile reactions of the philosophers Coriolano Alberini (1886-1960) from Argentina, and Carlos Vaz Ferreira (1871-1958) from Uruguay, against the pragmatism of William James and F. C. S. Schiller: the latter because of the spiritualism of these pragmatists, the former on the grounds of its being a threat to the traditional religious background.[26] The contrast between both readings has made difficult an open reception of William James and in particular of his *Varieties*. These difficulties are also apparent in Enrique Molina's reading of James. This philosopher, defender of positivism in Chile, understands James as a contradictory thinker holding at the same time both skepticism and dogmatic traditionalism.[27]

In recent years, there has been a small revival of books and dissertations on William James. We will only mention here the books of our colleagues Jorge Pérez de Tudela *El pragmatismo americano* (1988) and Angel Faerna *Introducción a la teoría pragmática del conocimiento* (1996).

2. Unamuno's Reading of *The Varieties of Religious Experience*

Miguel de Unamuno y Jugo was born in the Basque city of Bilbao in 1864.

---

[23] A. Donoso: "Review of Graham's A Pragmatist Philosophy of Life in Ortega y Gasset," *Hispania* 78 (1995), p. 499.

[24] E. d'Ors: *Glosari de Xenius*. Barcelona, Tallers Gràfics Montserrat, 1915, vol. II, pp. 373-375.

[25] E. d'Ors: *El secreto de la filosofía*. Barcelona, Iberia, 1947, p. 12.

[26] C. Alberini: *El pragmatismo*. Buenos Aires, Otero Impresores, 1910; Carlos Vaz Ferreira, *Conocimiento y acción*, Montevideo, Imprenta El Siglo Ilustrado, 1920.

[27] E. Molina: *Filosofía americana. Ensayos*. Paris, Garnier, 1914, pp. 212-213.

He studied Philosophy and Arts in Madrid, and lived almost all his life in Salamanca, where he held a chair in Greek Philology. He was twice the rector of the University of Salamanca (1901-14 and 1930-36). Unamuno was a philosopher-poet and an educated mind, "who sought to save Spain with rationalised religiousness."[28] He was deeply religious, but far from Catholic orthodoxy, a faith which he lost in his youth. All his works were characterised by a strong philosophical struggle to reconcile reason with religion. After his son's death in 1897, Unamuno sought to regain his childhood faith, oscillating between retreating to orthodox Catholicism, converting to liberal Protestantism or yielding to scepticism. As a philosopher Unamuno did not create a systematic presentation of his thought. He objected strongly to academic philosophers, and stressed that the deepest of all human desires is the hunger for personal immortality against all our rational knowledge of life. As Orringer writes, "obsessed with mortality, Unamuno achieved philosophical maturity with a blend of liberal Protestant theology and the philosophies of James and Kierkegaard in his conception of 'the tragic sense of life' — the theme of his essays, novels, dramas, poetry and journalism."[29]

Unamuno is one of the most representative writers of the group so called "Generación del 98" (from the year 1898, when Spain was defeated in the war with the United States over Cuba and Philippines), a group deeply concerned with the future of Spain in the contemporary world. Unamuno's option was to "*españolizar Europa*" ["to *hispanize* Europe"] in order to overcome the isolation of Spain. Unamuno's main philosophical works are *Del sentimiento trágico de la vida en los hombres y en los pueblos* (1911-12) [*The Tragic Sense of Life*], *Vida de Don Quijote y Sancho* (1905) [*Life of Don Quixote and Sancho*], and *La agonía del Cristianismo* (1931) [*The Agony of Christianity*]. He died by a stroke in Salamanca the last day of the year 1936.

As we have said, Unamuno had a vast culture, and he also had well-stocked library of literature, philosophy and humanities in all languages, preserved now in the Casa-Museo Miguel de Unamuno in the University of Salamanca.[30] That library contained over 100 volumes of prose, poetry and fiction by Americans, ranging from classic nineteenth-century authors like Emerson and Thoreau to

---

[28] N. A. Orringer: "Unamuno y Jugo, Miguel de (1864-1936)," in E. Craig (ed.): *Routledge Encyclopedia of Philosophy*, London, Routledge, 1998, vol. 9, p. 519.

[29] N. A. Orringer: "Unamuno y Jugo, Miguel de (1864-1936)," p. 519.

[30] Casa Museo Miguel de Unamuno: http://www.acamfe.org/unamuno_s/unamuno_s.htm

contemporary authors such as Pound or Wharton.[31] For our present research there are three relevant works of William James found in that library: *The Will to Believe* (1902), *The Varieties of Religious Experience* (1902) and *Pragmatism* (1907). The copy of the *Varieties* is of the first edition, and in the margins of 32 pages of that volume there are hand-written pencil annotations from Unamuno.[32]

An important fact in relation with these three works is that the copies of *Varieties* and *Pragmatism* that Unamuno owned are first editions, from 1902 and 1907 respectively. In the case of *The Will to Believe* (1897) the copy in Unamuno's library is of the printing of 1902. This shows not only that Unamuno was well aware of the novelties of his times, but also that he was personally involved in the process of reception of pragmatism in Spain and in Europe. Unamuno was well versed in English and read William James very early and in the original sources. Beginning in 1896 Unamuno quoted regularly from William James's books and ideas in his papers and books, and pioneered the spreading of pragmatist ideas in the Spanish-speaking world.

In Unamuno's published works throughout a total span of forty years there are 32 quotations of William James: 19 from *The Will to Believe*, 7 from the *Principles of Psychology*, 5 from *Varieties* and 2 from *Pragmatism*. His first quotation of the *Varieties* —which is a translation of Mrs. Annie Besant's quotation in page 27 of *Varieties*— occurred in 1904. The last quotation, in 1913 in his *The Tragic Sense of Life,* is a remembrance of God as producer of immortality for the great majority of men, Kant, James, and Unamuno himself included.[33] In Unamuno's copy of the *Varieties* the conclusion James draws is marked with six vertical lines and one horizontal: "Religion, in fact, for the great majority of our own race *means* immortality, and nothing else. God is the

---

[31] See M. Thomas Inge: "Unanumo's Correspondence with North Americans: A Checklist," *Hispania* 53 (1970), p. 277. For a catalogue of that library, see M. J. Valdés and M. Elena: *An Unamuno Source Book: A Catalogue of Readings and Acquisitions with an Introductory Essays on Unamuno's Dialectical Enquiry*, Toronto, University of Toronto Press, 1973.

[32] We are grateful to the Casa Museo Miguel de Unamuno for allowing us to photocopy those annotated pages. These volumes were carefully studied by P. H. Fernandez in his *Miguel de Unamuno y William James*, see especially pp. 15-20 and 45-48. According to the catalogue of Unamuno's readings, he also owned Spanish copies of James's *Los ideales de la vida* (Barcelona, Henrich, 1904, 2 vols.) and *La vida eterna y la fe* (Barcelona, Henrich, 1904): M. J. Valdés and M. E. de Valdés, *An Unamuno Source Book*, p. 125.

[33] See M. Unamuno: *Del sentimiento trágico de la vida*, Madrid, Renacimiento, 1911-12, pp. 10-11.

producer of immortality."[34]

Unamuno's reading and references to *Varieties* are strictly connected with one of the deepest of Unamuno's concerns: the problem of human immortality. This issue forms the axis around which all his work turns. One of the main ideas that will lead Unamuno to deal obsessively with human immortality is that death confers fullness of sense to life. Unamuno vacillated between believing in the survival after death of a part of the person, or complete extinction. Unamuno's last quotation from *Varieties* is particularly relevant: in *Varieties* Unamuno finds corroboration for his own idea of God as producer of immortality. If human immortality is warranted by God, we can trust that we shall not die completely, because something from ourselves will survive death. There are two other references from Unamuno to God as producer of human immortality in *The Tragic Sense of Life*: "Another professor, the professor and man William James, has already said somewhere that for the generality of men God is the provider of immortality. Yes: for the generality of men, including the man Kant, the man James, and the man who writes these lines, which you, Reader, are reading."[35] And eighty pages later, Unamuno writes again, "one so ardently desirous of the immortality of the soul as William James, a man whose entire philosophy aims at establishing this essence on rational grounds (...)."[36]

The exploration of Unamuno's library and of his texts reveals him as an avid reader of James. "I know well the professor James, whose works *The Will to Believe and Other Essays* and *The Varieties of the Religious Experience* I own," Unamuno writes in a letter of 1904.[37] Unamuno feels himself to be linked with James, whom he likes to describe as "the pragmatist, another hopeless Christian," and as "such a serious man, of so sincere a spirit and so deeply religious."[38] As we said before, Fernández's conclusion was that Unamuno's pragmatism was "original with respect to that of the American, from whom he absorbed only complementary features." However, in our

[34] W. James: *The Varieties of Religious Experience*. The Works of William James, vol. XIII Cambridge, MA, Harvard University Press, 1985, p. 412.

[35] M. de Unamuno: *The Tragic Sense of Life*. Translation by Anthony Kerrigan, Princeton, NJ, Princeton University Press, 1972, p. 7.

[36] M. de Unamuno: *The Tragic Sense of Life*, p. 91.

[37] M. de Unamuno: *Letter to Alberto Nin Frías*, 15 August 1904; quoted by H. Benítez: *El drama religioso de Unamuno*, Buenos Aires, Instituto de Publicaciones Universidad de Buenos Aires, 1949, p. 124, n. 20.

[38] M. de Unamuno: "¿Qué es verdad?," in B. G. de Cándamo (ed.): *Ensayos*, Madrid, Aguilar, 1951, 3ª ed., vol. I, p. 809.

opinion, it should be said more accurately that there is not only a great similarity between the two thinkers on many issues and problems, but that James had a permanent impact on Unamuno's intellectual development. Recently, Pedro Cerezo has studied more precisely the real scope of James's influence. According to Cerezo, Unamuno's reading of William James in the first decade of the century was a turning point in the evolution of his mind, taking Unamuno away from metaphysical pessimism and turning his attention to practical reason, to that action which is able to provide orientation and sense to life.[39]

Finally, we want to explore another peculiar link between James and Unamuno centered in the figure of Don Quixote. In *The Varieties of Religious Experience* William James wrote:

In these remarks I am leaning only upon mankind's common instinct for reality, which in point of fact has always held the world to be essentially a theatre for heroism. In heroism, we feel, life's supreme mystery is hidden. We tolerate no one who has no capacity whatever for it in any direction. On the other hand, no matter what a man's frailties otherwise may be, if he be willing to risk death, and still more if he suffer it heroically, in the service he has chosen, the fact consecrates him forever. Inferior to ourselves in this or that way, if yet we cling to life, and he is able 'to fling it away like a flower' as caring nothing for it, we account him in the deepest way our born superior. Each of us in his own person feels that a high-hearted indifference to life would expiate all his shortcomings.[40]

With these words, William James defines the heroism of saintliness. For a Spanish reader, these lines strike a very special chord: the hero of William James may be understood as the same hero of Cervantes described by Unamuno in his *Vida de Don Quijote y Sancho.* The "saint" described by James is Cervantes's hero as Unamuno conceives him. Unamuno sees in Don Quixote the Jamesian characteristics of the saint: strength of soul, purity, charity, chastity, poverty and obedience. These virtues are incarnated in Don Quixote, especially the strength of soul which leads him to bear all kinds of bodily and spiritual sufferings in his quest for making the world a place of justice.

---

[39] Pedro Cerezo: *Las máscaras de lo trágico. Filosofía y tragedia en Miguel de Unamuno,* Madrid, Trotta, 1996, pp. 278-289.
[40] W. James: *The Varieties of Religious Experience,* p. 290.

Furthermore, "few things elevate Don Quixote more than his disdain of worldly riches": Don Quixote is an example of poverty and purity of soul, because of "his spiritual childhood and his heroic innocence."[41]

Don Quixote regarded evil from the Jamesian perspective of healthy-mindedness, by which "evil means only a mal-adjustment to things, a wrong correspondence of one's life with the environment."[42] Evil is a maladjustment between his imagined world and the real one. Don Quixote goes out to the real world willing to fulfil divine law. The two kinds of character in which James divides mankind (healthy-minded and sick souls) come together in Don Quixote. Indeed, Don Quixote healthy-minded respecting his conception of evil, but sick in soul, as he is one of those who must be born again to be happy. For this reason Cervantes's hero is reborn in his particular conversion from Alonso Quijano to Don Quixote. In this sense, Don Quixote is the quintessential hero. It can be said —in a Jamesian sense— that we find in Don Quixote all that we look for in a hero. We forgive all his weaknesses because of his courage and his willingness to risk his life, heroically defending the noble cause he has chosen. This is Don Quixote, this is the pragmatist hero.

---

[41] M. de Unamuno: *Vida de Don Quijote y Sancho*, Madrid, Alianza, 1987, p. 57.
[42] W. James: *The Varieties of Religious Experience*, p. 114.

A Chronicle of Pragmatism in France Before 1907. William James in Renouvier's *Critique Philosophique*.

*Mathias Girel**

1. Reception and Distortion

What would be our understanding of Kant's philosophy if his *Critique of Pure Reason* had never been translated? If Spinoza's *Ethics* was still in Latin? There was, and there might still remain fine Kantian and Spinozist scholars; they might be aware of all the minute details of those systems, but the *general* reception of these two thinkers, the way their ideas are used in argumentation, would definitely be quite different. If these two questions must remain pure speculation, in this country at least, the case of James's work provides a concrete example of such a situation. Two major works by James have never been translated into French so far: (1) The *Principles of Psychology* (even if the briefer *Psychology* has been available since 1909),[1] and (2) the *Essays in Radical Empiricism*,[2] even though one of the key chapters, *La notion de conscience*, was written directly into French in 1905. Most of his works were not translated in full before the debate over pragmatism was over. This of course is not enough to explain the many misunderstandings James had to face, since most of the "misunderstanders" referred to in the *Meaning of truth* were English speakers, but this limited "availability" of James's texts played a major role in the *distortion* his pragmatism suffered in the first years of the XXth Century.

Max Fisch, in a fascinating paper entitled "American Pragmatism before and after 1898",[3] described the way in which an average reader, having access to

---

* Équipe EXECO, Université Paris I.

[1] W. James, *Précis De Psychologie*, Paris, M. Rivière, 1909. A new translation has been published recently: William James, *Précis De Psychologie*, Paris, Les empêcheurs de penser en rond, 2003.[Hereafter Pp]

[2] Since the present paper was submitted, a translation of the *Essays*, by the present writer and G. Garreta, was published: *Essais d'empirisme radical*, Agone, Marseille, 2005. [Hereafter ERE]

[3] Max H. Fisch, "American Pragmatism before and after 1898," in Robert W Shahan (Ed.), *American Philosophy from Edwards to Quine*, Univ of Oklahoma, Norman, 1977, pp. 78-110. Retrieved in Max H. Fisch, *Peirce, Semeiotic, and Pragmatism: Essays*, Bloomington,

fine libraries and bookstores, would get a rough idea of pragmatism before James's famous 1898 lecture. One of the results of the first section of this paper was to show how little the 1898 lecture added to James's previous statements. In the present paper, a similar task is taken up but with a different twist: many French readers thought they had sufficient evidence of James's thought, when he published his *Pragmatism,* and they read the later James through this lens. French readers were provided with James's works in a far different chronological order than that of their original publication.[4] I am not claiming that this kind of "cinematic" effect is always decisive to understand James's philosophical insights in general, and I shall not enter here into what are the minimum materials to describe the "center" of one philosopher's vision, nevertheless, I think that this kind of details is crucial if we want to understand the philosophical *debates* and *polemics* which surrounded them. As early as 1908, James had to protect the pragmatic approach from "misunderstanders", and at least some of these misunderstandings have their origin in the kind of details we are investigating here.

A simple instance might help to substantiate this claim and to make clear what I call here a "distortion". It is often forgotten that most people first read what James had to say about pragmatism *not* in the 1898 Lecture, *Philosophical Conceptions and Practical Results*, whose circulation was quite limited, but in *The Varieties of Religious Experience* in 1902[5]. This is a first important point: James's pragmatism seemed, to many readers, deeply connected with his approach to religious experience, *i.e.* with the import of the moral attributes on one's conduct of life, whereas the other methodological aspects of the pragmatic maxim—for example the pragmatic treatment of the "One and the Many"—were less prominent in 1902 than in the original lecture. Readers had to wait for the reprint of the 1898 Lecture in 1904, under the title "The Pragmatic method", and in *Pragmatism* in 1907, to have the complete picture. If one judges James's pragmatism only from the 1902 formulation, one might certainly have interesting things to say about belief and conduct, but I guess it is safe to say that one imposes a *distortion* on James's thought if his

---

Indiana University Press, 1986. My title is of course a reference to another excellent and very famous paper by M. Fisch, "A chronicle of Pragmaticism, 1865-1679," retrieved in the same collection, pp. 114-136.

[4] *La théorie de l'émotion*, Alcan, Paris, 1903; *L'expérience religieuse* [=VRE], Alcan et Jündig, Paris, Genève, 1906; *Philosophie de l'expérience* [=PU], Flammarion, Paris, 1910; *Le pragmatisme* [=P], Flammarion, Paris, 1911; *L'idée de vérité* [=MT], Alcan, Paris, 1913; *Introduction à la philosophie* [=SPP], M. Rivière, Paris, 1914; *Aux étudiants, Causeries* [=TT, part. 2], Payot, Paris, 1914; *La volonté de croire* [=WB], Payot, Paris, 1916.
[5] VRE, 1902, p. 444.

utterances are assessed only with the materials available in the *Varieties*. Thus, it should be remarked that I am using this term without implying that there is an "absolute" meaning or "univocity" to a particular philosophy: it is enough if we can show that some readers project the whole of a philosophy on a particular or minor occasion.

There are reasons to think that this is what happened here, on a larger scale. First, as in many countries, a lot of confusion was involved in all the quarrels over pragmatism. Useful information about this period is provided by the reports of the *Third Congress of Philosophy at Heidelberg* in 1908,[6] where the writer complains that "a wave of pragmatism and humanism, coming from Anglo-Saxon countries, has kept sweeping this Congress."[7] The last lines of this text give a sufficient idea of the general mood: "Instead of confining themselves to a few formulas which cannot even claim for them the faint glory of an antique tradition, the pragmatists should consider that, if war often leads thought to go to sleep, blows have never promoted an idea."[8] The confusion between Schiller's, Papini's, and James's positions certainly did not help. But a decisive element needs to be taken into account, which helps to understand why James's position was generally construed from his early statements: James's *Pragmatism* was translated, with a foreword by Henri Bergson, only in 1911, i.e. after James's death, and also at a time when the debate over pragmatism was a little less vivid. Before 1907, most of James's texts were available in the columns of the *Critique Philosophique*. In 1903, a short collection of James's essays on emotion, including important later views, was published and translated by Georges Dumas, but they belonged to the series of papers on psychology. None of James's *books* (*The Principles of Psychology*, *Psychology Briefer*, *The Will to Believe* and the *Talks to Teachers*) was translated at that time.[9] The first work to be translated was *The Varieties of Religious*

---

[6] See, for an account, the report in *Revue de Métaphysique et de morale*, Paris, 1908, pp. 930 sq.

[7] *Ivi.*, p. 930.

[8] *Ivi.*, p. 950.

[9] In most of the bibliographies, following a note by E. Leroux in the *Journal of Philosophy*, 1927, p. 202, references are made to a 1900 translation of the *Talks to teachers*. The present writer has never had such a volume in hand. The first references I have seen point to the 1907 translation by Pidoux (See: E. Reverdin, *La notion d'expérience d'après William James*, Georg, Geneva, 1913, p. 219; A. Ménard, *Analyse et critique des Principes de la psychologie de W. James*, Alcan, Paris, 1911, p. 2). Such a 1900 translation would severely conflict with items in James's correspondence. See James, William, Elizabeth M. Berkeley, and Ignas K. Skrupskelis, (Ed), *The Correspondence of William James*, University Press of Virginia, Charlottesville, 1994-2004, 12 Volumes [Hereafter CWJ], vol. 10, p. 242 (May

Experience, in 1906, by the Swiss philosopher Frank Abauzit. It was introduced by a preface by Boutroux, who, at that time, also devoted several studies to James's philosophy of religion. So, in 1905-1906, when pragmatism was in every column, readers had to gather what James's brand of pragmatism was all about from these two sources: the earliest papers of the *Will to Believe*, published in the *Critique Philosophique*, and the *Varieties*, translated in 1906. References to James's essays on radical empiricism, most of them published in English in 1905-1906, and to his more considered views, as developed in *Pragmatism*, were quite exceptional. Popular versions of James's philosophy became available, *Psychology briefer* as far as psychology is concerned (in 1909), *Pluralistic universe* as far as James's views on radical empiricism are concerned (in 1910), while the *Principles* and the *Essays* were — and is still, for the first — missing. Even these published materials were a poor starting-point for the reader: Abauzit, the translator for the *Varieties*, has edited, and sometimes rewritten, large portions of the work (Bergson declined to give a preface in reason of the poor opinion he had of that achievement). The French translation of *Pragmatism* is also notoriously unsatisfactory.[10]

We face thus a complex phenomenon and it should be treated piecemeal. As I have already shown elsewhere what happened to James's concept of experience when it fell into Boutroux's hands,[11] and, as some literature on Bergson's role is already extant,[12] I shall focus here on another important occasion: the prominent role Renouvier and his "lieutenants" took in the early reception of James's thought in France. As mentioned above, for a long time, the papers collected in the *Will to Believe*, translated by Renouvier as soon as they were published in English, in the 1880s, have been James's only texts available in French. As a result, the other features of James's work, his pragmatism, his radical empiricism, and in a lesser degree his psychology, have often been read *from this standpoint*, that is to say, as if they were further developments of what James had already said in the *Will to Believe*. From the perspective of the authors of the *Critique philosophique*,[13] the "real" James was

---

1st, 1903), where James writes: "My *Talks* (nor any other of my works) ain't been translated into French". See also CWJ 10, p. 51, 1902.

[10] A commentator wondered, in 1933, how a text, containing only four paragraphs ending with an exclamation mark, could turn, after translation, into one where they were one hundred and twenty two! (See E. Callot, *William James*, Jouve, Paris, 1933, p. 5, n. 2)

[11] See Mathias Girel, "Varieties of Experience in Boutroux and James," *Streams of William James*, 5, no. 2, 2003.

[12] Frédéric Worms, "Bergson et James: Lectures croisées," *Philosophie*, no. 4, 1999.

[13] Pillon first edited *L'Année Philosophique* (*L'Année Philosophique*, Paris, 1868-1869 [Hereafter AP]), then it was replaced by the *Critique Philosophique* (Charles Renouvier

that of the early essays, with a clear emphasis on the moral postulates and the early theory of belief, and accordingly, these authors assessed James's later development against this standard. They repeatedly presented James as a "criticist", *i.e.* as a philosopher close in spirit from the Kantian type of moral philosophy they were advocating, and read what was not in line with this reading as slips or betrayals. Thus, I shall address the general question, the "distortion problem", through a close examination of what Renouvier and the renouvierans *made* of James's philosophy.

2. James's "Renouvierism"

At first sight, James's "Renouvierism" seems an obvious matter, not worthy of any serious dispute. Horace Kallen wrote, just after William James's death, reviewing a French book on him, that "it was from France that William James first received his philosophic inspiration, from France that he received his earliest recognition and his greatest honor."[14] This was a clear reference to Renouvier's complex role in the diffusion of James's ideas, both as an inspirer and as a promoter, and any reader of James's early texts will certainly miss their point if she overlooks this reference.

Renouvier's long shadow can indeed be found both at the beginning and at the end of James's career. One quotes often the page of James's diary for April 30, 1870, where he records the impression made upon him by Renouvier's texts: "I finished the first part of Renouvier's second *Essais* and see no reason why his definition of free will – "the sustaining of a thought *because I choose to* when I might have other thoughts" – need be the definition of an illusion. At any rate, I will assume for the present – until next year—that it is no illusion. My first act of free will shall be to believe in free will."[15] Nearly forty years later, James will record, in the draft of *Some Problems of Philosophy*, another aspect of this influence, but in a way that implies that it was at its strongest in

---

(Ed.), *La Critique Philosophique*, Paris, 1872-1889 [Hereafter CP], and afterwards by a new version of l'*Année Philosophique* (François Pillon (Ed.), *L'année Philosophique*, Paris, 1891-1913). The main difference between these periodicals is the room devoted to the publications of the year (much more important in *L'Année Philosophique*).

[14] H. M. Kallen, Review of Boutroux's *William James*, in *The Journal of Philosophy*, 8, 21, 1911, pp. 583-584.

[15] As quoted in Ralph Barton Perry, *The Thought and Character of William James, Briefer Version*, Cambridge, Harvard Univ Pr, 1948, p. 121. Hereafter we use the full version: *The Thought and Character of William James*, Little, Brown & C°, Boston, 1935, 2 vols. [Hereafter *Thought*]

his very early texts:

"[Charles Renouvier] was one of the greatest philosophic characters, and, but for the decisive impression made on me in the seventies by his masterly advocacy of pluralism, I might never have got free from the monistic superstition under which I had grown up. This is why, feeling endlessly thankful as I do, I dedicate this textbook to the great Renouvier's memory."[16]

This is an important acknowledgment indeed, and it turns into an overwhelming one when one opens the *Principles of Psychology*. They are dedicated to François Pillon, one of Renouvier's lieutenants, editor both for the *Critique Philosophique* and for the *Année Philosophique*, with a clear emphasis on the role this periodical played in the diffusion of James's ideas: "To my dear friend François Pillon, as a token of affection, and an acknowledgment of what I owe to the *Critique Philosophique*."[17] What exactly is the extent of James's debt to Renouvier and in general to the *Critique Philosophique*?

The thesis of the present paper is that this debt, important as it may appear on a first reading, seems, on a second reading, to be confined within a limited number of issues; after the 1870s, important disagreements appear, which will grow more important after 1900 (and also after Renouvier's death in 1903), when James will defend his pragmatism.[18] Again, my point is not the trivial claim that there are some differences between philosophers, but that the *Critique* dogmatically assessed James's views from the standpoint of Renouvier's philosophy, whose main tenets were not to be doubted or even qualified. This is turn contributed to complicate James's reception around 1900. The tone, mild enough concerning the *Varieties*, will clearly turn, from genial

---

[16] W. James, *Some Problems of Philosophy*, Longmans, New York, 1912, pp. 164-165. [Hereafter SPP]

[17] William James, *The Principles of Psychology*, New York, H. Holt, 1890 [Hereafter PP].

[18] Phillippe Devaux, "A propos du 'Renouviérisme' de William James," *Revue Internationale de Philosophie* 32, 1978, pp. 385-406, argued that James's renouvierism had to be qualified. This paper should be used with caution (there is no reference to extant literature on that topic, including Perry 1935!). One important objection comes to mind when reading it: the author makes much of an alleged annotation on Renouvier's weakness as regards the "logic of relations"(*Op.cit.*, p. 399). Knowing that the book was lent to Peirce for some time in 1898 (See CWJ 8, p. 605), it would be important to know if the annotation were his or James's; there is no mention of that possibility in that paper. Perry, *Thought*, vol. 1, Ch. XLI-XLII, is, as always, very useful and still reliable, though quite short on the analysis of this relationship.

to plainly hostile: to the Renouvieran staff of the *Année Philosophique* James did not seem in line with his earlier papers anymore, and he was clearly held to be wrong for that. My purpose being to show how the staff of the *Critique*, while welcoming James's works, gradually refused some of their main tenets, I will try to show now that the main lines of disagreement appear in the 1880s, as witnessed by several kinds of documents: James's reviews of Renouvier's works; Renouvier's translations and remarks on James's works and letters in the *Critique Philosophique*; an important correspondence between the two thinkers, now available in the excellent edition of the *Correspondence of William James*, but already published by R.B. Perry in a famous historical edition;[19] further remarks and interactions with Pillon and Dauriac, two "renouvierites". Even though the whole correspondence ranges from 1872 to 1896, its richest period is between 1878 and 1884. Several threads cover the whole period, but three distinct stages nevertheless clearly stand out. At first, James is a Renouvier reader, and sometimes reviewer; then, in 1877-78, James becomes a contributor of the *Critique*; finally clear lines of divergence appear after 1884.

3. Readings and Reviews of Renouvier

The James-Renouvier correspondence starts in 1872, when James writes to Renouvier to ask him a copy of Lequier's *Recherche d'une première vérité*,[20] and confesses that he found for the first time in Renouvier's *Essais de critique générale* "an intelligible and reasonable conception of freedom": "I accept it almost entirely. On other points of your philosophy, I am beginning to experience a rebirth of moral life; and I assure you, Monsieur, that it is not a small thing."[21] Much has been written on James's crisis in 1870 and on the influence of Renouvier's philosophy of freedom on James, and no further repetition is needed here of a topic that is nicely and widely displayed in the available literature.

James, however, was not satisfied with merely reading Renouvier, and he

---

[19] Ralph Barton Perry (Ed.), "Correspondance de Charles Renouvier et de William James," *Revue de Métaphysique et de Morale*, no. 1, 1929, pp. 1-35; pp. 193-222, and Ralph Barton Perry (Ed.), "Un Échange de lettres entre Renouvier et William James," *Revue de Métaphysique et de Morale*, 1935, pp. 303-318. [Hereafter RMM].

[20] See Donald Wayne Viney, "William James on Free Will: The French Connection," *History of Philosophy Quarterly*, 14, 1, 1997, pp. 29-52.

[21] RMM, 1929, p. 3; Nov 2, 1872.

also devoted considerable energy to make this philosopher popular to American readers. Thanking James for his reviews (in 1873, and again in 1876), Renouvier praised their accurateness, in particular as to his assessment of the differences and common tenets between his own philosophy and the British empiricist, associationist and determinist doctrines;[22] indeed a decisive acknowledgment for the young William James.[23] Renouvier's views seem to refuse any absolutist approach—he is a phenomenist— but his system sounded as an alternative to the determinist views of most of the empiricist writers James was reading at that time. It is however striking that, while Renouvier thanks James for having correctly described the "new criticism"[24]—that is to say the revised form of *Kantism* Renouvier was advocating—James sees in Renouvier the classic representative of the "tendency launched by Hume".[25] The whole ambiguity turns on Renouvier's phenomenism, which can be read from either standpoint. Actually, Renouvier was critical both of the Kantian and of the Humian tradition, as appears in the concise account François Pillon gave for Renouvier's obituary in 1903, an account we shall take here as correct, although insufficient:

"The essentials principles by which the reformed criticism or neo-criticism [Renouvier's philosophy] contrasts with Kant's criticism consist in the triple negation of noumena, of the infinite of quantity, and of the universal determinism of phenomena. On the other hand, due to the room he makes for— and the importance he gives to—the categories and laws of reason, it contrasts with David Hume's empirical phenomenism. It is accurately characterized by the terms *rational phenomenism, finitism* and *libertarism*."[26]

Thus, from the young James's standpoint, several aspects of Renouvier's work sound appealing. First, we should not overlook his craving for alternative "champions". Renouvier's conceptions are a convincing alternative to the extent he appears, in James's eyes, as no minor philosopher at all. He is, for James, *the* French Philosopher, quite a controversial statement for American readers of his time, and his *Essais de Critique Générale* are deemed "the ablest philosophical speculation to which France has given birth during this century",[27] which was a confirmation of his very first opinion of the

---

[22] RMM, 1929, p. 6.

[23] As it would be still later on, see CWJ 5, p. 56 (1879).

[24] RMM, 1929, p. 6, Jul 17, 1876.

[25] RMM, 1929, p. 7, Jul 29, 1876.

[26] AP, 1903, p. 310.

[27] James, *Essays Comments, Reviews*, Harvard, 1988, p. 266 [Hereafter ECR]. See a later description at CWJ 5, p. 503: "A philosopher armed from head to foot with all the implements of his profession".

philosopher:

"A review of the state of philosophy in France for some years back is by one Charles Renouvier of whom I never heard before"[but who is] "so different from the namby pamby diffusiveness of most Frenchmen [*sic*]."[28]

Then, besides this acknowledgment, there are two other evident lines of attraction for William James, which appear in his first review[29] in 1873: Renouvier's *phenomenism*, and his refusal of the doctrine of necessity, the two aspects being tightly connected. Renouvier is not a basic phenomenist, since "possibility" is for him an ultimate factor of the universe, what clearly separate him from the British brand of phenomenism:

"The knowable universe is for him, as for the school of Mill and Bain, a system of phenomena, and metaphysic is an analysis or inventory of their elements. But among these elements he finds the *possibility*, which British empiricism denies, of absolute beginnings, or, in other words, of free will.[30]

Real possibilities, real beginnings and endings are thus not a matter of mere ontological concern: they are crucial for a philosophy where free acts can initiate new beginnings, where novelty is not only an appearance but an indefeasible dimension of action. Interestingly enough, the building of a philosophy itself —a peculiar kind of act— was seen by Renouvier as a major manifestation of freedom. As James well remarks, the first act of free will is thus its own self-affirmation "so that we have an *act* enthroned in the heart of philosophical thought."[31]

These points are further developed a few years later. James's 1876 review[32] deals with both Bain and Renouvier, but the latter is given the prominent part of the review. Two points stand out, with James's later development in mind. First, we find again what James took as Renouvier's main insight—and what

---

[28] WJ to Henry James Sr, CWJ 4, Oct 5, p. 342. Renouvier had indeed made a survey of French philosophy in the first issue of l'*Année Philosophique*, stressing the sundry advantages of the "philosophie critique". *De la Philosophie du XIXe Siècle*, par Ch. Renouvier, AP, 1868, pp. 1-108.
[29] "Renouvier's Contribution to *La Critique Philosophique*" (1873), ECR, pp. 265-67.
[30] ECR, p. 266.
[31] *Ivi.*
[32] "*The Emotions and the Will*, by Alexander Bain and *Essais de Critique générale*, by Charles Renouvier" (1876), ECR, pp. 321-327.

was to become the basic thrust of his own *Will to Believe*—, namely, the idea that philosophical systems are not only theoretical constructions, but also involve the entire human nature: "the entire nature of man, intellectual, affective, and volitional is (whether avowedly or not) exhibited in the theoretical attitude he takes in such a question as [determinism vs. indeterminism]."[33] Secondly, such a philosophy involves an account of belief that James would develop for the next twenty years: in Renouvier "the act of belief and the object of belief coalesce, and the very essential logic of the situation demands that we wait not for any outward sign, but, with the possibility of doubting open to us, voluntarily take the alternative of faith."[34] Many Renouvieran arguments could be detected in the detail of the first essays of the *Will to Believe*, and it is noteworthy that James had made extensive use of most of them before 1880, even if he did not accept all of them.[35]

4. James as a Contributor

James soon becomes a contributor of the *Critique Philosophique*. The end of 1877 is a turning point in James's development: his first piece, "Quelques considérations sur la méthode subjective",[36] written directly in French, a defence of indeterminism in favor of the efficacy of free will, is published and introduced by Renouvier. The gist of this paper, in complete agreement with "the principles of philosophy to which [Renouvier's] review is dedicated",[37] was the question whether "one (can) be justified in rejecting a theory which many objective facts apparently confirm, solely because it does not in any way respond to our inward preferences."[38] James's answer, relying on the "subjective" method, and on the upshot of the subject's efforts, was affirmative and laid a clear emphasis on two essential faculties, that of "setting ourselves a task in virtue of an act of faith which can be accomplished only by our own effort; and that of entering boldly into action in circumstances when success

---

[33] *Ivi.*, p. 325.

[34] *Ivi.*, p. 326.

[35] *WJ to Renouvier*, Jul 29, 1876: "As I stand today, unable wholly to commit myself to your position, to burn my ships behind me, and proclaim the belief in the One and the Many to be the Original Sin of Mind", COWJ 4, p. 541.

[36] CP, 1877, n°2, pp. 407-413; See the remarks by Renouvier, CP, 1878, n°2, pp. 97-106.

[37] James, *Eph*, p. 331.

[38] *Ivi.*

can not be assured in advance."[39] James presented his claim as consistent with Renouvier's views,[40] a diagnosis shared by Renouvier himself.[41] A line of thinking, prominent in Chapters from 2 to 5 of the *Will to Believe*, appears thus for the first time in the late 1870's, in Renouvier's *Critique*. These papers often pay due compliments to Renouvier,[42] and develop the insights we have discerned in the two reviews.

Still, this first paper in French will be the only contribution written solely for the *Critique*, since the next ones will usually be published in the US or in *Mind* first, and then translated or summarized.[43] Typically, Renouvier would ask the consent to translate a paper James had sent him. Then James would accept and warn Renouvier that his time would be better spent developing his own philosophy. Several installments would soon follow, which, in retrospective, may be classed in two groups: some will belong to the *Principles*; but most of them will be included or used in *The Will to Believe*. James, then, is by no means a minor contributor of the *Critique*: his contributions are frequent between 1878 and 1884, and he is the only non-French regular author for this journal. In addition to Renouvier's short introductions to his own translations,[44]

---

[39] *Ivi.*, p. 338.
[40] "To talk of freedom in the *Critique Philosophique* is to carry gold to California", Eph, p. 338 (=CP, 1877, n°2, p. 412).
[41] James's thoughts are deemed "conform to the criticist method and we would be glad to sign them (*nous nous estimerions heureux de pouvoir les signer*)", quoted in Eph, p. 31 (=CP, 1877, n°2, p. 413).
[42] For example, the *Dilemma of Determinism*: "It is my duty to say that my reasonings are almost entirely that of Renouvier; they can be found in the *Psychologie rationnelle*, and in the periodical *La Critique Philosophique* as well", Le dilemme du déterminisme, CP, n°2, 1884, pp. 273-280, 305-312, 353-362; the quote is p. 273.
[43] *De la caractéristique intellectuelle de l'homme, d'après William James* (partial translation and commentary upon *Brute and Human Intellect*; CP, 1879, n°1, pp. 369-376, 394-397; n°2, pp. 17-26, 41-48); *Le Sentiment de la rationalité* (tr. of The Sentiment of Rationality), CP, 1879, 8, 2, pp. 72-80, 81-89, 113-118, 129-136 (See the note p. 136 where Renouvier reports that James is lecturing on his *Essais* at Harvard); *Le Sentiment de l'effort* (tr. of "The Feeling of Effort"), CP, 1880, 2, pp. 123-128, 129-135, 145-148, 200-208, 220-224, 225-231, 289-291.; *Les Grands Hommes, les grandes pensées, et le milieu* (tr. of Great Men, Great Thoughts, and their Environment), CP, 1880, n°2, 396-400, 407-415, CP, 1881, n°1, pp. 1-14; *Action réflexe et théisme* (tr. of Reflex Action and Theism), CP, 1881, 2, pp., 385-391, 401-410; CP 1882, 1, p. 5-13. *Rationalité, activité, foi* (tr. of Rationality, Activity and faith), CP 1882, n°2, pp. 129-140, 145-154, 161-166; *Le Dilemme du déterminisme* (tr. of The Dilemma of Determinism), CP 1884, n°2, pp. 273-80, 305-316, 353-362; *Ce que fait la volonté* (What the will effects), 1888, n°1, p. 401.
[44] Charles Renouvier: "La question de la certitude. IX. Le pari de Pascal et le pari de M. W. James", CP, 1878, n°2, pp. 97-106. "De la caractéristique intellectuelle de l'homme d'après

some of his views are discussed in detail in Renouvier's books. For example, Renouvier gave in his *Esquisse d'une Classification*[45] a lengthy account of the way James understood the triadic nature of action, the teleological nature of mind, and faith;[46] James is also mentioned in the late *Nouvelle Monadologie* (1899),[47] but the most obvious mark of consideration given by Renouvier is certainly the time he spent translating James, and introducing him to the French audience.[48]

My first claim was that these publications gave James's philosophy a definite shape to French readers, and one should not overlook the influence of these translations. To take just one instance, Joseph Delboeuf devoted some fifteen pages in the widely read *Revue Philosophique*[49] to James's paper on "the Feeling of Effort", just published in the *Critique*. As early as 1882, in a book on "Human personality", James is referred to as a "noted" writer, and his account of effort offered as one of the "most interesting" views extant.[50]

M. W. James", CP, 1879, n°1, pp. 369-376, 394-97; n°2, 1879, pp. 17-26, 41-48; "Quelques remarques sur la théorie de la volonté de M. W. James", CP, 1888, n°2, pp. 117-126, reply by WJ, *Ivi.*, p. 401-404, "Quelques mots sur la lettre qui précède", pp. 404-406.

[45] In Charles Renouvier, *Esquisse d'une classification systématique des doctrines philosophiques*, Bureau de la critique philosophique, Paris, 1885-1886, vol. 2, pp. 176 *sq.*

[46] See in particular Renouvier, *Esquisse*, pp. 176-185; pp. 280-283; pp. 320-324. For an excellent introduction to Renouvier, see Laurent Fedi, *Le Problème de la connaissance dans la philosophie de Charles Renouvier*, L'Harmattan, Paris, 1998.

[47] Charles Renouvier, *La Nouvelle Monadologie*, Armand colin, Paris, 1899, p. 164, p. 213.

[48] Renouvier's attempts are not the only ones. One should not overlook the numerous reviews of WJ's papers in the *Revue Philosophique*. In particular, as regards the early papers: "Définition de l'esprit par Spencer", vol. VI, p. 433; "La fonction de la connaissance", XIX, p. 348; "La Perception de l'espace" XXIV, p. 207, p. 670; "La Qualité propre de l'espace", VII, p. 590; "La perception du temps", XXIV, p. 670; "L'Association des idées", X, p. 229; "Le Sentiment du rationnel", VIII, p. 442; "L'Intelligence chez la brute et chez l'homme", VII, p. 102; "Quelques omissions dans la psychologie d'observation intérieure", XVII : 235; "Qu'est-ce qu'une émotion?" XVIII, p. 482; "Sommes-nous des automates?", VII, p. 585; "Sur quelques maximes hégéliennes", XIV, p. 458; "Psychologie de la croyance", 1889, II, p. 447; "La psychologie comme science naturelle", 1892, II, 108. "L'immortalité de l'homme", 1899, 1, p. 198; "La volonté de croire", 1899, 1, p. 223; "Humanisme et vérité", 1904, II, p. 667; "La conscience existe-t-elle?" 1905, II, p. 224; "Un monde d'expérience pure", 1905, II, p. 224.

[49] J. Delboeuf, "Le sentiment de l'effort", *Revue Philosophique*, 1881, pp. 513-527.

[50] See Charles Jeanmaire, *L'idée de la personnalité humaine dans la psychologie moderne*, Douladoure-Privat, Toulouse, 1882. WJ had browsed that volume at Pillon's (CWJ 5, p. 427). Jeanmaire, in the few pages he devoted to James, had seen – a point still overlooked by the majority of James's commentators – that it was not relevant to make a crude distinction between will and belief in James's texts: "si la volition, considérée en elle-

Moreover, Bergson, in his *Essais sur les données immédiates de la conscience* (Paris, Alcan, 1889), quotes the same paper on effort in the opening pages of the book.[51] It is no accident if James's papers in the *Critique* have given his philosophy a particular shape in France: when the debate over pragmatism started, French readers were already acquainted with James's early ideas since twenty years. Not only had they been available, but they had also been discussed with a thoughtfulness and a patience, that the later papers on pragmatism and radical empiricism will not receive.

At this time, Renouvier still reads James as an ally,[52] and praises him for his resistance to Hegelianism at Harvard. James had expressed his struggle in vivid terms: "It is a strange thing, this resurrection of Hegel in England and here, after his burial in Germany. I think his philosophy will probably have an important influence on the development of our liberal form of Christianity. It gives a quasi-metaphysical backbone, which this theology has always been in need of, but it is too fundamentally rotten and charlatanish to last long. As a reaction against materialistic evolutionism it has its use, only this evolutionism is fertile, while Hegelianism is absolutely sterile."[53] James made no secret that in this "war" his best weapons were Renouvier's "pluralism and empiricism".[54] Renouvier's encouragements are thus no wonder, but they contain the first acknowledgment we know of James as the possible "founder" of an "American philosophy": "Your originality, your direct view of that which is really *to be seen*, will lose rather than gain by much reading, and especially by the reading of German philosophical books. It seems to me when I read you that you are called to found an *American philosophy*. So it would not do for you to make sacrifices to alien gods (*dieux étrangers*)."[55]

---

même, ne consiste qu'à agir sur les idées, pour les maintenir, les suspendre, les écarter, en quoi diffère-t-elle de la croyance, qui est aussi un acte par lequel nous acceptons ou repoussons les idées? M. James, à l'exemple encore de M. Renouvier, pense que la différence n'est pas grande."(*cit.*, 315) Jeanmaire quotes Renouvier and James's account nearly in the same breath. WJ, reading the book, remarks that "such glory and fame come from Renouvier's translating my feeling of effort" (CWJ 5, p. 427, to AHGJ).
[51] H. Bergson, *Essais sur les données immédiates de la conscience*, Alcan, Paris, 1889; reprint P.U.F., Paris, 1993, pp. 16-17
[52] CR to WJ, Aug 21, 1879: "your version of *criticisme* is presented with a startling originality, or happiness of expression, with an accent of your own", RMM, 1929, p. 12. Translation in Perry, *Thought*, 1935, vol. 1, p. 669.
[53] Dec 27, 1880, RMM, 1929, p. 17, Perry, *Thought*, 1935, vol. 1, p. 675.
[54] May 8, 1882, RMM, 1929, p. 21.
[55] CR to WJ, Sept 5, 1882, RMM, 1929, p. 24; tr. Perry, *Thought*, vol. 1, p. 679, slightly edited. Italics are Renouvier's.

Still, when James and Renouvier met in August 1880,[56] one might wonder whether James's admiration had not already tarnished, at least in part. Three points should be considered.

(1) The year before they met, James had lectured on Renouvier at Harvard (1879-1880), and this experience is likely to have led him to reassess their relationship. In that occasion he realized that Renouvier's "exposition offer(ed) too many difficulties",[57] as he phrases it to Royce, a diagnosis confirmed by a letter to Renouvier where James confesses that this course had left him "more unsettled that (he had been) for years".[58] One of the main reasons for this statement was his difficulty to explain his students Renouvier's denial of the infinite, as is witnessed by an eighteen points letter to Renouvier on that topic.[59] James did not object directly to Renouvier's "principle of number" (*le principe du nombre*), that is, to the assumption that an infinite number is self-contradictory—that would have been Peirce's way to approach the question. He instead questioned Renouvier's way of constructing a dilemma between the finiteness or the infinity of Space. He already suspected that to hold space (and time) as "either finite, or infinite" was not relevant at all and pointed then to the "boundlessness" and "continuity"[60] of these forms, as eluding Renouvier's dilemma. The questions were soon followed by a lengthy answer,[61] which, according to James's confession, "fail(ed) to awaken conviction".[62] The broader question, whether the "*principe du nombre*" was sound at all, remained an interrogation mark, in James's thought, and for a long time indeed. Later on, James will seem to entertain serious doubts over Renouvier's account of the infinite, especially after he had become aware of the new mathematical theories on that topic.[63]

(2) Despite James's later efforts to point up the parts of Renouvier's system

---

[56] CWJ 5, p. 135.

[57] *Ivi.*, p. 84.

[58] *Ivi.*, p. 98.

[59] *Ivi.*, pp. 75-79.

[60] *Ivi.*, p. 76

[61] RMM, 1935, pp. 310-318.

[62] CWJ 5, p. 98.

[63] "The new infinitists have disproved the contention of Renouvier *et al.* that the realization of a cardinal infinite is *impossible*. They may have proved it possible. They haven't yet proved it actual" ("Fragment on the Infinite", 1902-1910), James, *Manuscript Essays and Notes*, Works, Harvard, H.U.P., p. 217. [Hereafter MEN]

which would agree with Darwin's ideas about evolution,[64] Renouvier was extremely dubious, to say the least, about the very idea of evolution. Also this could be the source of later disagreements, since, in 1878, while James was trying to find the real Darwinian insights behind Spencer's oversimplifications of them, Renouvier wrote to him:

"Evolution is a craze (*une toquade*). It will last fifteen or twenty years, and then we shall again speak of it as one spoke of the system of Lamarck at the time of Cuvier. So the world goes. It will be found strange to have, on behalf of gratuitous inductions and in the name of experimental method, denied such a fact as the existence of species, which *crève les yeux* (stares you in the face), as we say in French."[65]

(3) Another important dissent involved the importance of *conceptual categories*. In my view, but I can just broach it here, much light will be cast on the development of James's thought through a careful reading of his assessments of Renouvier and Hodgson around 1880. An important episode during this period is the debate between Hodgson and Renouvier. In 1881, Hodgson submitted Renouvier's *Essais de critique générale* to close-reading in the pages of *Mind*,[66] the result of which is quite an interesting document, since the two men were both phenomenists, with strong commitments in the field of practical philosophy,[67] but they were at odds on some issues: on free will, on the role of conceptual categories, defended by Renouvier against Hodgson, on universal determinism and the Infinite, defended by Hodgson against Renouvier. Hodgson's reading was translated in the *Critique* and commented at length,[68] soon followed by Renouvier's analysis of Hodgson's *Philosophy of Reflection*,[69] followed in turn by a long reply by Hodgson.[70] Having in mind James's enthusiasm with Renouvier, and knowing the consideration he also paid to Hodgson, it is interesting to see what remained unshaken by Hodgson's

---

[64] James, ECR, p. 444.

[65] CR to WJ, May 14, 1878. RMM, 1929, p. 10. Perry gives only part of the letter in *Thought*, vol. 1, p. 667.

[66] S. Hodgson, "Mr Renouvier's Philosophy," *Mind*, 1881, pp. 31-61, pp. 173-211.

[67] See CWJ 5, pp. 43-44. Hodgson, contrariwise to Renouvier, did not admit that the denial of free-will involved the denial of moral distinctions between right or wrong.

[68] CP, 1881, n°2, pp. 188-192, 209-216 (reply by CR, 216-221), 225-234, 305-312, 342-351, 353-364, 369-374.

[69] CP, 1882, n°1, pp. 17-27, 55-63, 170-176; CP, 1882, n°2, 209-219, 241-246; CP, 1883, n°1, 36-48, 65-75, 97-104, 113-123, 134-143.

[70] *Ivi.*, pp. 241-253, 373-379, 391-400.

attacks. In several letters, James is very clear that Hodgson's criticisms of Renouvier did not seriously diminish his confidence in this latter's philosophy, and even confirmed the hopes he had put in him, since only an important philosopher could deserve such a careful, although critical, reading, as the following letter to makes plain: "Despite the fact that he rejects Renouvier's two most important tenets, the finiteness of the world, and free will, he says enough to make Renouvier the most important philosopher of our time—You can think how it pleased me to have this evidence that I have not been a fool in sticking so to Renouvier."[71] He further seemed to side with Renouvier against Hodgson on free-will.[72] Still, Renouvier's Kantism as regards categories, the focus of many attacks by Hodgson, in *Mind* as well as in his "Replies" in the *Critique*, was something that James could not miss, and it is tempting to think that Hodgson's criticisms—on that very point—found their way into James's thought. Granted what he was undertaking against Kantian approaches to perception,[73] from the "Spatial Quale" on, James could not but agree with Hodgson on that matter. Interestingly, Hodgson assumed that Renouvier had retained the worst part of Kant's philosophy:

"He makes just the same mistake that Kant made, namely, to assume a spiritual agent working in certain indispensable forms of thought … I class him with the German Cognition-theorists."[74]

This was precisely the position James was trying to undermine in the field of psychology. Assuming as he did that there was no need of any "Kantian machine-shop" in order to explain the articulation of experience, Hodgson's remarks about Renouvier "who starts with a list of conceptual categories as his ultimates and basis of experience"[75] certainly did not meet much dissent.

It is thus tempting to claim that, around 1880, James had taken all he needed from Renouvier: the core of the *Will to Believe*. If James—although lesser and lesser—still read Renouvier's works, most of what he could use of Renouvier's insights had already been taken. It is no accident if, mentioning a possible stay with Renouvier and the Pillons, as early as 1883, he was ready to affirm his

---

[71] CWJ 5, p. 109, to AHGJ.

[72] *Ivi.*, p. 396. See an interesting letter by Hodgson, *Ibid*, p. 200.

[73] See Mathias Girel, "The Metaphysics and Logic of Psychology: Peirce's Reading of James's Principles," *Transactions of the Charles S. Peirce Society* 34, no. 2, 2003, pp. 163-203; esp. §1.

[74] Shadworth Hodgson to WJ, Oct 17, 1882, CWJ 5, p. 276.

[75] SH to WJ, March 6, 1886, CWJ 6, p. 120.

own philosophical independence:

"Philosophers must part, as soon as they have extracted each other's juice; that is, if they are each working on his own line there inevitably comes a day when they have gone as far together as they can ever go, & after that it is nothing but the accentuation & rubbing in differences, without change."[76]

On the other hand, the *Critique* had been a platform for James's early texts, and gave the keynote of James's reception for a long time, even when the development of his thought led him in a different direction.

5. Dissents

Not every paper from James, however, did raise the same enthusiasm in Renouvier. After the reception of "What is an emotion" and of "Some omissions of introspective psychology", as new trends emerged in James's psychology, the tone of their correspondence will never be the same again, although in his very last letter to Renouvier, James still insisted that he was one of his disciples.[77] Renouvier objected to several major tenets of James's psychology, and this sentence about James's papers on space, in a letter of 1887, possibly summarizes accurately his general attitude during the last years of their correspondence: "My Kantian habits of mind make this reading and the understanding of your processes of thought and your language more difficult than I should like."[78] Renouvier also frowned at James's interest in the new "psychic research".[79] Explicit dissents started to develop. Actually, it might be argued that two asymmetric processes started: in James's eyes, the differences between Renouvier and the narrow rationalism he was allegedly fighting were becoming less and less evident; as for Renouvier (and his staff), James seemed to reach conclusions which were in tension with his earlier commitments.

---

[76] WJ to AHG James, Jan 29, 1883, CWJ 5, p. 410.

[77] WJ to Renouvier, Aug 4, 1896: "… an article […] called "the Will to Believe" in which (if you took the trouble to look at it) you probably recognized how completely I am still your disciple. In this point more than any other; and this point is central."(CWJ 8, p. 179) See also James's attempts, in 1900, to have Renouvier elected as a foreign correspondent for the Berlin Academy of Science, CWJ 9, p. 224.

[78] CR to WJ, March 27, 1887, RMM, 1929, pp. 211-212; tr. Perry, *Thought*, 1935, vol. 1, p. 701.

[79] CR to WJ, Feb 5, 1886, RMM, 1929, p. 208.

As my point, here, is to focus on Renouvier's dissents from James, rather than the other way round, I shall consider briefly James's reactions. James's late review of Renouvier's *Principes de la nature*,[80] certainly did not add much to his early insights. All the salient aspects of the doctrine are those which had attracted his interest in the 1870s—the points specifically developed in the *Principles of nature* are just browsed, and James can complain this time about the "strenuous abstractness of Renouvier's terms".[81] Of course, signs of consideration, and some dramatization, are still present. Renouvier is now put forth as the major opponent to the "through and through" vision of the universe advocated by the different brands of Hegelianism, but as we saw, this was no news to James.[82] The terms, however, are more striking: "As Bonaparte said that the Europe of the future would have to be either Republican or Cossack, so, to put the matter ultra-simply, the present reviewer feels like saying that the philosophy of the future will have to be that either of Renouvier or of Hegel."[83] In the same way, his formulation of Renouvier's main insights is perhaps a little closer of his ideas about belief and doubt: "For philosophies are acts. Whether men admit or deny the fact, passion always plays some part in making them reject or hold to systems, and volition, whether predestinate or unpredestinate, always will play a part in deciding when to encourage and when to suppress one's doubts."[84] But a new element appeared more clearly, which is not consonant with James's ideas at that time, Renouvier's finitist *monadology*. This involved a tychist and pluralist worldview, which is certainly the distinctive mark of Renouvier's late philosophy: "the world, so far as real, is like an immense pulsation composed of a number (unassignable though at all times determinate) of concerted elementary pulsations of different grades."[85]

Interesting as this worldview may seem, there is no doubt about James's view of it: "Renouvier cannot be true – his world is so much dust."[86] Several matters were at stake: the relevance of *monadology* in general, which seems at

---

[80] "*Les Principes de la nature*, 2nd ed., by Charles Renouvier" (1893), *Essays, Comments and Reviews*, H.U.P., Harvard, 1987 [Hereafter ECR], pp. 440-446. See also "*L'Année Philosophique*, 2e année, ed. by François Pillon" (1892), in James, ECR, pp. 426-432.
[81] James, ECR, p. 440.
[82] See CWJ 5, p. 48, 1879: "The (Hegelian) school and that of Renouvier are the only serious alternatives today."
[83] James, ECR, p. 441.
[84] *Ivi.*, p. 442.
[85] *Ivi.*, p. 443.
[86] WJ to J. Royce, Dec 18, 1892, CWJ 7, p. 351.

odds with James's own brand of *pluralism*, the discontinuity in Renouvier's worldview as opposed to the continuous connections of experience,[87] and finally, the form in which Renouvier's arguments were clad. Slowly, Renouvier entered the list of philosophers whose insights are important, but whose "form" is defective: "[Renouvier's] form is atrocious, but I am thankful to him for a number of points of view rather vital to me. The whole of my essay "The Will to Believe" is cribbed from him."[88] In a letter to Flournoy, James depicted Renouvier as a "classical" philosopher: "I entirely agree that Renouvier's system fails to satisfy, but it seems to me the classical and consistent expression of *one* of the great attitudes, that of insisting on logically intelligible formulas. If one goes beyond, one must abandon the hope of formulas altogether."[89] The whole question revolved on the necessity of going "beyond" Renouvier.

More important for our purpose is a short survey of the three topics on which Renouvier started raising explicit objections, further re-activated by his "lieutenants" Dauriac and Pillon: Emotions, Will, and Stream of thought.

– *Emotion*. Renouvier – and we shall see that the same argument holds for Pillon and Dauriac – did not accept James's theory of emotion. The physiological strain adopted in that field became thus the first important bone to pick with James. Renouvier, starting in 1884 with "What is emotion?", repeatedly read these texts as attempts to *reduce* consciousness and to give too much credit to reflex action. He first objected to James's theory in the correspondence,[90] and expressed further doubts in his *Nouvelle Monadologie*.[91] According to Renouvier, (1) either James said something that sounded quite Cartesian in its spirit, namely, that all our emotions are caused or *accompanied* by bodily motions (what left open the question of specific cerebral emotions); (2) or he held a more radical thesis, that is, our emotions are the perception of bodily movements, what sounds uncanny: "When I try to grasp what this means I am forced back to the principle of former theories such as Cartesian occasionalism, for I cannot rationally think that *fear*, for example, *is* the perception of a certain molecular vibration."[92] This will become more obvious when we pay attention to the reactions of Pillon and Dauriac; Renouvier

---

[87] For these two first points, see Perry, *Thought*, vol. 1, pp. 660-661.
[88] WJ to C.S. Peirce, 1897, CWJ 8, p. 324.
[89] CWJ 7, pp. 317-318, 1892.
[90] See CR to WJ, Sept 11, 1884, RMM, 1929, p. 204; Perry, *Thought*, 1935, vol. 1, p. 696.
[91] *Op. cit.*, p. 213.
[92] Perry, *Thought*, 1935, vol. 1, p. 697.

himself, however, did not welcome that part of James's thinking. It is noteworthy that in response to Renouvier James reformulated his account in a shape much more open to Renouvier's criticism: "I don't mean that the emotion is the *perception* of bodily changes *as such*, but only that the bodily changes give us a feeling, which is the emotion (...) Now all I say is that the nerve process is the incoming currents, produced by reflex movements which the perception of the exciting cause engenders".[93] Even though there are elements in James's works to make sense of this concession, in Renouvier's eyes, it meant a choice in favor of the "Cartesian" reading of the theory. Finally, despite this concession, Renouvier never could subscribe to James's views on this point.

- *The Will.* The most interesting documents are provided by the papers on the Will. In 1888, Renouvier translated James's paper on "What the Will Effects",[94] and added some remarks, which were soon followed by a reply from James.[95] These remarks expressed both admiration for James – insofar as his views converge with Renouvier's own utterances, thirty years before, in the Second Essay of the *Critique générale* (1859)[96] – and criticisms. Renouvier, as James after him, started with the observation of involuntary movements and concluded that, since the Will was separable from (was not responsible for) them and that nearly all animal movements could be explained with them, the Will could not be necessary to account for them: ideas or sensations were enough for that. The Will is not, in Renouvier, a mysterious and "mythological" entity, but the *power to sustain an idea*, the idea itself giving

---

[93] James, Eps, pp. 362-63.

[94] *Ivi.*, pp. 216-234.

[95] "Quelques remarques sur le théorie de la volonté de M. W. James", CP, 1888, n°2, p. 117.

[96] As early as "The feeling of Effort"(1880), translated in the *Critique Philosophique* the same year "Le Sentiment de l'effort," (See full references above), James claimed that Renouvier's "account of the psychology of volition was the firmest, and in (his) opinion, the truest connected treatment yet given to the subject" (Eps, p. 109). James argued in this paper against traditional conceptions of volition, i.e. against the assumption that any act of the will had to be preceded by a decision. The will was only another name for the domination of an idea on others: "Attention, belief, affirmation and motor volition are thus four names for an identical process, incidental to the conflict of ideas alone, the survival of one in spite of the opposition of others" (*Feeling of Effort*, Eps, p. 124). This was the basic thrust of Renouvier's texts on that subject and James did not claim any originality on that issue, no more than he did in 1888 in "What the Will Effects", translated the same year in the *Critique*, and described by WJ as "little more than what you said long ago in your *Psychologie Rationnelle*"(Eps, p. 407, WJ to CR, March 12, 1888).

rise to movements and actions. There is no need of an intermediary act between the representation and the movement, as the classical account of the will would have it: Representations themselves are followed by movements, whether voluntary or not. For Renouvier, this helps to explain that the action of the will is psychical through and through: it is only a name for a certain relationship our attention has with a representation. James illustrated his theory with the example of the person in his bed, thinking of waking up, and then waking up, without any intermediary representation or act,[97] this, however, was merely an echo of Renouvier.[98] If the two men agreed on mythological nature of most representations of the Will, what Renouvier could then object to James? His fault, in Renouvier's eyes, was to give too much credit to the "new psychology" and to the psycho-physiological scheme, blurring the distinction between mere reactive movements and "acts" of consciousness. He suspected that, once the reflex act scheme is applied to all acts, whether they are psychical or not, James could be read as denying consciousness a real power of initiative. The second important dissent, here, involved concerns on the nature of the ideas reinforced by the attention: for Renouvier, they are the perception of *changes in the environment*; whereas in his reading, James would only be considering the *sensations* we are to expect if we undertake such and such a move. Yet, in most cases, we don't know exactly what sensations we are to expect. In his interesting reply,[99] James made a concession on this second point, but resisted on the first: the Will is only regulative of actual nervous tracts, equipossible and leading to different results. This called for a new account of consciousness, still less likely to be shared by Renouvier:

"We only have to admit that the consciousness which accompanies material processes can react in such a way that it adds at leisure to the intensity or the duration of some particular processes; a field of *selection* opens at once, which leads us far away from mere mechanical determination."[100]

James will maintain such a reading in later texts on radical empiricism, in

---

[97] PP, vol. 2, p. 524.
[98] Renouvier's *Psychologie Rationnelle*, 1859, quoted by himself, in CP, 1888, n°2, p. 121: "Au moment, par exemple, où je me demande si je lèverai le doigt, ou si je ne le lèverai pas, que puis-je saisir dans ma conscience? Ou ceci: le doigt représenté comme levé, sans opposition de fin contraire, ni intervention d'aucune autre idée; et alors le doigt se lève, comme dans le phénomène du vertige, dont j'ai rendu compte; ou cela, la représentation du même acte comme suspendu, et alors le doigt ne se lève pas."
[99] James, *Essays in Psychology*, Harvard Univ. Pr., Cambridge (Mass), 1983, pp. 235-238.
[100] *Ivi.*, p. 238.

connection with the problem of *novelty*. "Will" is not a substance, not a force, and Free-Will is not a supernatural power, but *consists* in the novelty contained in an activity-situation, as the following text makes explicit:

"I have found myself more than once accused in print of being the assertor of a metaphysical principle of activity. Since literary misunderstandings retard the settlement of problems, I should like to say that such an interpretation of the pages I have published on Effort and on Will is absolutely foreign to what I meant to express. I owe all my doctrines on this subject to Renouvier; and Renouvier, as I understand him, is (or at any rate then was) an out and out phenomenist, a denier of 'forces' in the most strenuous sense. [...]. The misinterpretation probably arose at first from my defending (after Renouvier) the indeterminism of our efforts. 'Free will' was supposed by my critics to involve a supernatural agent. As a matter of plain history the only 'free will' I have ever thought of defending is the character of novelty in fresh activity-situations."[101]

Renouvier was no more there to comment, but his reservations, in 1888, are enough to get an idea of what he would have objected.

- *The stream of thought*. Another major difference concerns the *continuity of consciousness*. It is an important thesis of the *Principles* that the stream of thought is continuous. This is topical for James's account of mind as well as for the methods of psychology, since the confusion between the different clear-cut concepts of the analyst and the "vague" of most of our mental states is what James names the "Psychologist's Fallacy"[102]. Renouvier, commenting on *Some Omissions of Introspective Psychology* (a 1884 paper containing the substance of Ch. IX of the *Principles*, "The Stream of thought"), objected to James's statements on the "stream" and on the continuity of that latter: Renouvier's objection was Kantian at heart, for James's claim in his view would prevent in advance any attempt to speak rationally of our intellectual powers:

"The human, psychical function, is rational only by virtue of groupings of phenomena under different categorical functions, which bring order and classification into the manifold of these impressions and ideas—forming, as they do, an apparent infinity. There, it seems to me, are the file-leaders which guide the sensible phenomena, as they are the stakes and surveyor's marks for

---

[101] ERE, 1912, p. 184, p. 93, n.
[102] See PP, vol. 1, Ch. 9.

the understanding. How can we classify and create science in psychology, without recognizing an intellectual basis for such general terms as *where, who, when, what, for what, by what, etc.*?"[103]

This time, the very foundation of James's approach to consciousness was at stake, and the reply was sharp and firm:

"You accuse me of bringing *To apeiron* into the mind, whose functions are essentially discrete. The categoric concepts you speak of are concepts of objects. [...] But before it is reflected on, consciousness is *felt*, and as such is continuous, that is, potentially allows us to make sections anywhere in it, and treat the included portion as a unit. [...] But as we divide *them* arbitrarily, so I say our divisions of consciousness are arbitrary results of conceptual handling of it on our part. The ordinary psychology, on the contrary, insists that it is naturally discrete and that the divisions *belong* in certain places. This seems to me like saying that space exists in cubes or pyramids, apart from our construction."[104]

What was then the image of James's works by that time, from a Renouvieran standpoint? The will-to-believe papers would be retained, and some parts of the papers on the will, but crucial arguments, involving the physiological processes in psychology—James's views on consciousness, on emotion, his methodological recommendations—would have to be dismissed. This interpretive standpoint will be reinforced by other contributors: it would not be possible to give an account of the way James was presented in the *Critique* without mentioning briefly two other minor authors: François Pillon and Lionel Dauriac. The *Critique Philosophique* was a collective undertaking, and the picture would not be complete enough with Renouvier as its only protagonist. More importantly, when the debate over pragmatism was at its highest, Renouvier had already died. Although Renouvier is the source of most of the objections Pillon and Dauriac will raise, they were those who expressed a clear opposition to this aspect of James's philosophy, on behalf of Renouvier's immaterialism. In the light of our main argument, their reviews of James's works were instrumental in presenting his early writings as the core of his philosophy, and his later psychological and pragmatist writings as some misguided views, a reading which proved to be unfortunately influential. I shall thus be concerned, in this last section, with the way Pillon and Dauriac tried to

---

[103] CR to WJ, RMM, 1929, p. 204; Perry, *Thought*, vol.1, p. 697.
[104] WJ to CR, Sept 30, 1884, RMM, 1929, p. 206; transl. *Eps*, p. 403.

dismiss James's arguments.

6. Pillon and Dauriac

François Pillon, to whom the *Principles* are dedicated, is more a friend of James than a major philosophical interlocutor, and indeed James's correspondence sometimes point to Pillon as James's "only friend" in France.[105] As time went by, James, who made picturesque descriptions of him[106], was fascinated by Pillon's "domesticity", by his reluctance to leave his quarters. For example, he warned Hodgson, who considered Pillon as a possible lecturer: "you write of inviting Pillon, he is the best of men, but of that cat-like French domesticity that I doubt whether he would dare to enter a foreign land."[107] James stayed several times with the Pillons; first in 1883,[108] and again in 1893, but at this time the tone had grown more distant. He describes them, after his stay, as "the best of human beings both of them, but with that curious French timidity about the outer world which made me think of two mice living in a hollow cheese",[109] or, in another letter: "These little French bourgeois live like mice in a cheese—all right as they don't move outside."[110] In 1905, James met them again, but the distance now seemed even wider: "I called on the poor Pillons yesterday P.M. & kissed them, but I am almost sorry I went—we have grown so far apart that the combination no longer existed. Their life is too narrow, though they are *coeurs d'or*"[111]. James reviews Pillon's essays in l'*Année Philosophique* in 1892 and 1893,[112] and expresses only a mild appraisal: Pillon's essay on idealism "is well written and instructive", and his sixty notices for the books published are "full of pith and vigor", but at the same time, James remarks, Pillon holds "a language which might come from the mouth of a doctor of the Catholic church".[113] In 1892, his long essay on Atomism was deemed an unsurpassable "short *vue d'ensemble* for students'

---

[105] CWJ 7, p. 540.
[106] "He is the most unpretending and genial of men, poor and shabby, with a plain looking & excellent wife, reads English but doesn't speak a word …", CWJ 5, p. 501, 1884.
[107] CWJ 7, p. 254.
[108] CWJ 5, p. 422, Feb 1883.
[109] CWJ 7, p. 458.
[110] CWJ 2, p. 272, Jul 24, 1893.
[111] CWJ 11, p. 49, May 28, 1905.
[112] ECR, pp. 423-36 (1892) and ECR, pp. 455-457 (1893).
[113] *Ivi.*, p. 457.

use"[114]... In most of the cases, he is mainly a disciple, his attitude "is the pluralistic and phenomenistic one of M. Renouvier".[115] Still, it is to Pillon that James wrote interesting descriptions of his own philosophical development, insisting each time on what made him part his way from Renouvier on important matters. His own philosophy was more "gothic" than "classic":

"I expect, on returning to the country, to begin the writing of a somewhat systematic book on philosophy—my humble view of the world —pluralistic, tychistic, empiricist, pragmatic, and ultra-gothic, i.e, non-classic in form. Renouvier, to whom I owe so much, still remains to me too classic in the general rationalism of his procedure."[116]

In the same way, James gave Pillon a vivid picture of his "tychism" in the making, claiming that his own picture assumed a finite universe, without making of it the most salient point of this *Weltanschauung*, as Renouvier had done:

"My philosophy is what I call a radical empiricism, a pluralism, a "tychism," which represents order as being gradually won and always in the making. It is theistic, but not *essentially so.* It rejects all doctrines of the Absolute. It is finitist; but it does not attribute to the question of the Infinite the great methodological importance which you and Renouvier attribute to it."[117]

Against James's treatment of emotions Pillon urged nearly the same argument as Renouvier.[118] In his eyes, James's account of emotions was either untenable or it was a platitude. In the strong form, it is untenable: it is not possible to state that moral pain and pleasure are *direct* awarenesses of changes in brain cells: we are not "conscious" of these changes. If the thesis means that emotional states and brain states might be *correlated*, this is nothing but the weak traditional Cartesian thesis, and anybody would agree with that. Pillon expressed further doubts concerning the possible division of moral emotions into "cerebral" and "peripheral", so that "if it must be allowed that M. James's theory does not apply to every affective state, it cannot be argued that he has

---

[114] *Ivi.*, p. 435.
[115] *Ivi.*, p. 432.
[116] CWJ, 10, p. 279.
[117] CWJ, 10, p. 410.
[118] AP, 1902, "Review of G. Dumas (Ed), *W. James, La théorie de l'émotion*, Paris, 1903", pp. 156-158.

won the day".[119] The same line of thinking was adopted in later papers,[120] and Pillon urged the same criticisms as Renouvier against the continuity of consciousness, in nearly the same words.[121] Pillon implied that James's development, after 1900, was opposed to the spirit of Renouvier's criticism. The most telling statement can be found in a review of Th. Flournoy's *La philosophie de William James* (1912)[122]: referring to the letter from James to Flournoy we quoted above, where James said that Renouvier was a representative of one of the great philosophical attitudes, "that of insisting on logically intelligible formulas",[123] Pillon added: "These are curious remarks indeed. They explain why the American philosopher, not being content with Renouvier's philosophical attitude, which aimed at explaining things in an intelligible manner for our thought, was naturally lead to abandon any hope of logical understanding, and, as a result, to conclude to anti-intellectualism, pragmatism and radical empiricism."[124]

Although he had praised the *Varieties of Religious Experience* in private correspondence,[125] Pillon made a critical review of the French translation of the *Varieties* in *L'Année Philosophique* for 1905,[126] where he expressed clear doubts, and even an "opposition", concerning James's overall pragmatic

---

[119] AP, 1902, p. 158

[120] AP, 1906, pp. 90-96; see also AP, 1909, p. 196.

[121] "On ne saurait mieux saisir ni mieux faire comprendre l'importance qu'il faut accorder, dans l'ouvrage, au chapitre XI intitulé *Le courant de conscience*. Ce chapitre rapproche la psychologie de M. James de celle de M. Bergson. Il est inutile de dire que nous aurions des réserves à faire sur cette idée-image d'une continuité qui serait un caractère essentiel de la conscience, et qui réduirait à des abstractions formées par une sorte de morcelage les éléments psychiques que les premières analyses du sens commun y ont distingués." AP, 1909, pp. 195-196 (Review of the 1909 French translation of James's briefer *Psychology*).

[122] "Review of Flournoy, *La philosophie de William James*, Saint Blaise, 1912," AP, 1912, p. 275.

[123] CWJ, 7, p. 318.

[124] AP, 1912, p. 275. See also AP, 1900, pp. 111-116, on James's alleged confusion between "substance" and "person". AP, 1912, "La quatrième antinomie de Kant et l'idée de premier commencement", pp. 63-120; esp. pp. 116-120, on some differences between James and Renouvier over "first beginnings" and "substance". AP, 1913, pp. 202-203, in the review of *L'idée de vérité* (French title for *The Meaning of Truth*), Pillon mentions only a part of "The pragmatist account of truth and its misunderstanders", where James allows that the term "pragmatism" might have been ill chosen, inasmuch as it seems to overlook theoretical concerns.

[125] CWJ 10, pp. 106-108. The appraisal of VRE concerns esp. Ch. XVIII and XX. Pillon introduces Abauzit as a possible translator.

[126] AP, 1905, pp. 214-219.

orientation. He focused on Chapter XI ("Spéculation", in the French translation, and "Philosophy" in the original) where James had applied for the first time the pragmatic method to the traditional proofs for the attributes of God.[127] James's pragmatism is equated, here, with the general utilitarian standpoint: "We would have serious reservations to make concerning this critique and the systematically empiricist and utilitarian philosophy from which it proceeds."[128] Even where the two men seemed to agree, on the impersonality of science as opposed to the personalism which is central to the religious standpoint (and to Renouvier's final philosophy), Pillon's approach was at odds with James's:

"(This conclusion) can be drawn, we believe, more clearly and with more necessity from neo-criticist idealism than from radical empiricism. What philosophical value can be assigned to the impersonalism of Science, when one realizes, through the critique of matter and space, that the work of science only applies to the order of appearances resulting from the constitution of our sensibility; that it cannot claim to have reached, even partially, the actual bottom of things; and that its tendency to depersonalize beings must precisely lead it to misunderstand and deny the true principles of nature?"[129]

What is not clear is whether this immaterialist approach was an alternative to James's view or whether it was implied by some points of his philosophy. This is confirmed by the review of *Pragmatism*. Pillon was much dubious about James's account of truth in *Pragmatism*, and thought that, in every field of knowledge, "looking-forward" truths had to be balanced by "looking-backwards" truths; in other terms, that there were categorical truths and truths of observation which were not explained in James's account. The only positive point was in the "Third Lecture" where, "the present reviewer finds with pleasure the spirit of phenomenist neo-criticism in the pages devoted to the

---

[127] James's 1898 lecture, where he first introduced the term, had only limited circulation.
[128] AP, 1905, p. 217.
[129] *Ivi.*, p. 219. See also, AP, 1908, "Review of *Science et religion*, by Emile Boutroux", and some developments about James, pp. 120-138 (and p. 193 n.). More general statements on pragmatism can be found in AP, 1909, pp. 209-211. Pillon opposes the truth of science and the truth of philosophy. The latter is "absolute" while the former can be said, "pragmatic": "la vérité de la science proprement dite est relative et symbolique: elle représente le réel sous un aspect, en une forme qui vient de notre sensibilité. Conforme aux conditions, aux fins, aux besoins, de l'action dans la vie présente, elle peut très bien être dite *pragmatique*."(AP, 1909, p. 211)

problem of *Substance*".[130] So much so that the common character of Pillon's criticisms is that: there are some insights in James, but the latter was prevented to make proper use of them because of his prejudices in favor of empiricism. For Pillon, most of James's claims would be better secured on the foundations Renouvier had helped to lay.

This opposition, explicitly founded on the commitment to a special school of philosophy, is even clearer in Dauriac. Even though James read his essays with interest, he does not seem to hold Dauriac in high esteem. Dauriac's "style lacks the clearness of that of Pillon and the weight of that of Renouvier."[131] An important "lieutenant" of Renouvier, Dauriac makes frequent references to James, but their overall tone is far more critical than that of Renouvier and Pillon. I will not get into the particulars of his reading of James, for it is much less influent than that of Renouvier, but there are two distinct ranges of criticisms: against James's psychology, against pragmatism in general (and thus against James as a leading character in that movement). Two clear examples can be provided. For example, reviewing, in 1891, *The Principles of Psychology*,[132] he devoted a large part of the—long—paper to the criticism of James's physiological stance, whose implications he was not ready to accept.

"Would it be to betray the cause we were just advocating if we went so far as to say that consciousness has to be identified not just with a secretion, but with a sort (*horresco referens*) of excrement of the brain? When one is not terrified at such a term anymore, the very *idea* of physiological psychology will have reached its culmination."[133]

According to Dauriac, such a standpoint had to be dismissed, if James wished to remain consistent with his early views, in particular those published in the *Critique*: "M. James has too much written in the columns of the former *Critique*, not to be considered, at least, as a half-criticist."[134] In the same way, Dauriac objected to James's theory of emotions, not by finding faults within it,

---

[130] AP, 1911, p. 214.

[131] ECR, p. 435. Dauriac is mentioned by WJ, CWJ 10, pp. 409-10 (To Pillon, 12 June 1904); CWJ 10, p. 619. Dauriac is mentioned by Papini, CWJ 11, p. 599, 1906.

[132] AP, 1891, paper by Lionel Dauriac, "Du positivisme en psychologie : A propos des *Principes de Psychologie* de M. William James," pp. 209-252.

[133] *Ivi.*, p. 229.

[134] *Ivi.*, p. 209.

but by rejecting at once James's philosophical presuppositions.[135] He criticized the physiological account of emotions provided by James, and tried to prove that what James took to be the main content of emotions—some organic movements following directly some perceptions—was in fact the physiological echo of a psychological phenomenon. This was obviously begging the question, but it was explicitly so, since Dauriac thought that James's account needed to be "demolished", "on behalf of the immaterialist phenomenism and, by way of consequence, of the philosophy in the name of which we have kept fighting, and which postulates the psychological side of emotion as an essential character."[136]

After 1900, as James develops his own radical empiricism, and as controversies about pragmatism become a prominent element in philosophical journals, the general line of Dauriac's remarks grows more critical. To make room for practice among the main truths of philosophy, for Dauriac, meant to give up the philosophical task.[137] Accordingly, he often described pragmatism as a form of coarse irrationalism.[138] In a long paper on Bergson's philosophy,[139] he quoted Bergson's claim that intelligence was connected to the necessities of action, which prompted incisive criticisms of pragmatism: "the author develops with rare skill this definitely new thesis of one of the newest and of the boldest types of contemporary philosophy, where pragmatism is in germ and not only pragmatism. Taken at its face value, pragmatism is connected to the necessities of action and does not try to know whether these necessities are, or are not, constant. It does not care. Pragmatism covers every truth, which comes back to the claim that it is not only the opponent of some philosophies, but also of *any* philosophy."[140] This interpretation of pragmatism as "irrationalism" was urged

---

[135] AP, 1892, pp. 63-76

[136] *Ivi.*, p. 76.

[137] Lionel Dauriac, "Questions préliminaires : L'objet de la philosophie; le commencement de la philosophie", AP, 1910, pp. 159-186, esp. 184-186.

[138] A point can be made that it was already the case in his reading of James's very first texts. See L. Dauriac, *Croyance et réalité*, Alcan, Paris, 1889, p. 274.

[139] AP, 1911, La Philosophie de M. Henri Bergson, p. 69.

[140] AP, 1911, p. 69. See also his Review of William James, *The Meaning of Truth. Revue Philosophique*, 1910, pp. 643-649. I am here concerned with *CP* and *AP*, but the reader should be aware that Dauriac also developed critical views in the *Revue philosophique*: Positivisme et pragmatisme, criticisme et pragmatisme, 1911, pp. 584-605; Le Pragmatisme et le réalisme du sens commun, 1911, pp. 337-367; Review of A. W. Moore, *Pragmatism and Its Critics*, 1911, pp. 546-552; Review of F.C.S. Schiller, *Riddles of the Sphinx*, 3rd ed.,

again in one of the last issues of l'*Année Philosophique*.[141] This time, James's tychism was guilty of removing any possibility of refutation from his system: "What is "tychism"? I shall offer this definition: "it is the philosophy of the *as such* (*philosophie du* sic!)." Do you not understand? I shall say, then: "it is the philosophy of the fact, meaning behind which there is nothing, except perhaps other facts likely to contradict it, and in that case the contradiction is just registered [...]." I am aware that I am here exaggerating William James's theses, but I am following their own direction."[142]

7. Conclusion

At the end of this survey, I hope that I made clearer the "distortion" I was hinting at the beginning. James's first texts are published by a philosopher whose views are already settled and to whose philosophy his collaborators are already committed. Typically, James's early texts, which in their spirit are very close to Renouvier's views, are welcome and much use is made of them. Then, a strange situation develops: the *Critique*, which is James's "tribune" in France, as it were, is, because of its philosophical commitments, at odds with several of the main trends in James's thought. This is particularly clear as regards the psychology, whose cornerstones are dismissed by Renouvier first, and then by Pillon and Dauriac. Some themes in the *Varieties*, in particular the criticism of the im-personalism of science, were congenial to the personalist spirit of the *Critique*, but the way in which James reached his own conclusions was not acceptable to Pillon and Dauriac: the pragmatist philosophical background seemed ill-chosen to them. Thus, the journal where most of James's texts were available had turned critical of James's pragmatism. The last remarks by Dauriac we have quoted are just making more explicit the general problem involved by James: the mystery of a philosopher who had started in the same atmosphere as them but who had gradually developed in different, if not opposite, directions.

If we add these remarks to other insights gained by the examination of what Boutroux and Bergson did with James's works, a common aspect emerges: James was introduced to French readers by "settled" philosophers. The "first

---

1911, pp. 541-546; Review of William James, *Introduction á la philosophie*(= SPP), 1915, pp. 557-561 (See in particular pp. 557-58 on Renouvier's legacy).
[141] In a review of Henri Reverdin, *La notion d'expérience d'après William James*, AP, 1913, pp. 216-218.
[142] *Ivi.*, p. 218.

198

wave" generated interesting philosophical moves —they made a genuine philosophical use of James's texts—but they certainly did not allow a comprehensive view of James's thought; his works were mainly instrumental for purposes which were independent of his own development. The first full scale survey of James's thought, a survey which took into account James's radical empiricism, made by a philosopher who "started with" James was certainly Jean Wahl's thesis, *Les Philosophies pluralistes d'Angleterre et d'Amérique*[143], but this was in 1920, when the whole debate concerning pragmatism was in a large measure over.◆

---

[143] Alcan, Paris, 1920; new edition with an introduction: Les empêcheurs de penser en rond, Paris, 2005. For a little sketch of Jean Wahl's works and life, see my foreword to Jean Wahl, *Vers le concret*, Vrin, Paris, new revised edition, 2004.

◆ I am very grateful to Felicitas Kraemer for exchanges about a previous version of the present text, and to Sergio Franzese for his very helpful comments and suggestions.

The Early Bulgarian Reception of William James. A Brief Survey

Nataliya Nikolowa[*]

In many of the eastern European countries, only now, after about a century since its first appearance, readers have the chance to appreciate William James's *The Varieties of Religious Experience,* to enjoy its topicality and richness, and to take advantage of the bearings of the pragmatic theory of experience. Yet, canvassing the considerable number of critical readings and reviews this book received in eastern Europe, and in particular in the ex-Soviet Union and Bulgaria, even when the approach to this text was strongly discouraged for ideological reasons, it appears that, against all odds, whereas James's original views on religion had a tremendous reception in ex-Soviet Union, they went almost unnoticed in Bulgaria.

From the historical standpoint, the steps of Bulgarian reception of William James are marked by a slow and scarce array of translations [1]whose rare occurrence witness the difficulty of the reception: *Talks To Teachers On Psychology* in 1902, *What is Pragmatism?* in 1930, and then, with a gap of about sixty years, *Pragmatism* in 1994, *The Stream of Consciousness* in 2000, and finally *The Varieties of Religious Experience* translated in 2003. A complete Bulgarian edition of the *Principles of Psychology* is still lacking and this prevents a broader knowledge of James's major work.

In fact, despite the translations of some his works at the beginning of the 20th century, James's religious views reached Bulgaria much later than other countries. James's psychology in turn enjoyed no better reception. So that it is fair to say that today in Bulgaria, even more than in the other European countries James is a forgotten author.

Such a difficult or even hostile reception can be easily tracked back to the Bulgarian political situation in the years between the two World Wars and in the five decades after World War II, for James's thought was extremely hard to include in the ideological frame which characterized eastern European countries during the most of 20th century.

In Bulgaria, in particular, William James could not count on a favorable

---

[*] MA in *Social Science and Psychology* at University of Veliko Tarnovo; MA in *Southeast European Studies* at the National and Kapodistrian University of Athens.

attitude on Bulgarian authorities' part, since he was considered as an apologist of religion. Accordingly, it is no wonder that most of the debates on James's pragmatism and theory of religion took place in Bulgaria between the '20's and the '30's. Thus, in order to account for Bulgarian reception of James we need to refer to this period in which it is possible to find the major Bulgarian James scholars and critics such as, Ivan Sarauiliev, Tseko Torbov, Dimitar Mihalchev, Atanas Iliev and Asen Kiselinchev

1. Ivan Sarauilev and the Pragmatic Theory of Truth

The first Bulgarian reception of James in the early '30's was quite friendly and James philosophy found a good audience thanks to Ivan Sarauilev, who can still be considered as the most prominent representatives of pragmatism in Bulgaria.

Three popular articles of James were published in 1930 by the publishing house "Naturphilosophical Reading", collected in a single book entitled *"What is Pragmatism?"*[2]. The publication of this book was immediately followed by a set of critical essays by Ivan Saruiliev: *"Studies on Pragmatism. Charles S. Peirce and his 'principle"*,[3] printed in the official Journal of the Ministry of Education, "School Review," Vol. 6 (1933)," *"The Pragmatism of William James"*(1934)[4] and an important monograph *"Pragmatism. A Contribution to the History of Contemporary Philosophy."* (1938)[5] whish is still the broadest composition on pragmatism in the Bulgarian language so far.

In time, however, Saruiliev's attitude toward James and his thought turns out quite ambivalent. He is extremely critical of James's "new psychology" but at the same time he claims that "Pragmatism is one of the most important philosophical movements at the beginning of the twentieth century" and particularly differentiates its role as a criterion of finding the truth. It is noteworthy, however, how despite the full acceptance of James's philosophy, Saruiliev cannot help stressing some weaknesses of James's definitions and other inconsistencies in the development of his theory of truth.

---

[2] W. James, *Sto e pragmatizum?*, Naturphilosophical Reading, Sofia, 1930.
[3] I. Saruiliev, "Studii varhu pragmatizma. Charles S.Peirce i negoviyat princip", *Spisanie Uchilisten Pregled*, 6, (1933), pp. 725-736.

[4] I. Saruiliev, *Etudi varhy Pragmatizma. Pragmatizmut na Uilyam Dzheims*, Godishnik na Sofiiskiya Universitet, Sofiya, 1934.
[5] I. Saruiliev, *Pragmatizmut. Prinos kam istoriyata na modernata filosofiya*, Sofia, 1938.

In his first article on pragmatism in 1933, Saruiliev starts with an account of this new movement presenting himself as a defender of pragmatic ideas, and articulating clearly and precisely his support. He even provides biographical notes on William James's personality, calling him not only a philosopher, but also an educator. James, Saruiliev says, "is helping mankind and wanted, with his philosophical problems and discussions, as the beliefs, related to them, lead to many different ways of acting" (p.5). In this context, Saruiliev hints to the relation between pragmatism and futurism and labels pragmatism as "futurism in philosophy": "both the intellectual and social life of our time is saturated with futurism, as far as pragmatism is a certainly the expression of an important trend of our age." (p.12)

At the end of the article an emphasis is put on James' personality as leading in the establishment of the very ideas of the pragmatic movement, which "has distinguished itself as one of the most characteristic philosophical movements from the first quarter of the twentieth century."

As a continuation of the ideas presented in the above mentioned article of 1933, a whole volume of Sofia University series comes out, entitled "Etudes on Pragmatism. In *The pragmatism of William James* (1934),[6] Saruiliev provides short clarifications, explanations and apologies of the pragmatic ideas.

Later on, in 1938, Saruiliev publishes the volume *Pragmatism,* coming out of a first-hand study of James texts, in which a special focus is on the question of truth seen as the central issue of James' pragmatic philosophy, or, in James's words, "the core" of the whole pragmatic teaching. The book still displays complete support and sharing of James's doctrine, yet Saruiliev is also challenging some relevant aspects of James's theory of truth.

Saruiliev's "critical" examination of pragmatism applies "the very pragmatic method", which evaluates a theory, (in this case pragmatism), through its useful consequences. Through this method, Saruiliev realizes that the pragmatic theory of truth cannot explain absolutely all cases and facts, but is applicable only to a limited number of instances and facts.[7]

In the final chapter of "*Pragmatism*", Saruiliev takes a critical stand to pragmatism as a theory of truth, and states three main objections. The first one is against the pragmatic understanding of the criterion for truth and can be resumed by the statement that not all truths are useful and not all useful ideas are truthful." The second objection concerns the relativism of pragmatism and the denial of absolute truth. The third one puts in question the humanist

---

[6] I. Saruiliev, *Etudi varhu pragmatizma.Pragmatizmut na Uilyam Dzheims*, Godishnik na Sofiiskiya Universitet, Sofiya, 1934.

[7] I. Saruiliev, *Pragmatizmut,* cit., p.212.

standpoint and the possibility of human verification of truth. Accordingly, Saruiliev cannot but conclude to the unsoundness of the pragmatic theory of truth, what appears pretty odd in such a self-declared supporter of pragmatism. Thus Saruiliev's position appears at least eclectic and shows his own limits in reaching a consistent theoretical view of pragmatism. At last, Saruiliev's wishful conclusion claims that no single theory can explain satisfactory all problems of truth, and that is why it is necessary to create a broader all-inclusive theory of truth, in which the basic stipulations of pragmatism would be included.

2. Truth, Science and Religion: Further Criticisms

A stern rejection of the pragmatist theory of truth had already been formulated by the NeoKantian philosopher Tseko Torbov in his article "*Usefulness as a criterion of truth*".[8] Here, Torbov, while remarking the connection between Bergsonism and pragmatism, objects the concept of usefulness as a criterion of truth, and also the very possibility of creating another theory of knowledge whatsoever.

The most influential critique of pragmatism, however, is given by the famous Bulgarian psychologist and philosopher Dimitar Mihalchev. Mihalchev reveals the unsoundness of pragmatism as a method for disclosing truthfulness on the basis of its consequences. In "Pragmatism as a New Study for Truth," (*Philosophical Review*, V, 1939).[9] Mihalchev, who had studied in Germany, makes a thorough analysis of Jamesian pragmatism, and questions Saruiliev's account of the pragmatic theory of truth. Mihalchev looks attentively at "the seriousness and sincerity" in William James's words and personality, nonetheless the pragmatic method appears to him quite flawed, and limited by the fact that everything comes down to practical life.

It is also noteworthy that Mihalchev analyzes "the new psychology" of William James, which he considers as a reaction to atomistic psychology and gnoseology. An emphasis is put on his agreement with James's account of human experience as a synthesis of the whole and the parts. Mihalchev admits that there is something "original" in it, and that is the original starting point of pragmatism, namely, "the selective, detailed and interested activity of

---

[8] T. Torbov, "Polzata kato kriterii na istinata". *Spisanie Filosofski Pregled*, 5, (1929); pp. 501-505.
[9] D. Mihalchev , D. "Pragmatizmut kato novo uchenie za istinata", *Spisanie Filosofski Pregled*, 5, (1930), pp. 474-531.

consciousness." On the other hand, in the run of his article and critiques, Milalchev criticizes the theory of the *stream of consciousness*, James's major contribution to the history of psychology, which he refuses arguing that "in consciousness not only the states but also the relations between them enter separately." James, Mihalchev's criticism goes, mixes two completely different things: grammatical forms and lyrical contents. Thus James's definition of consciousness as a "stream", in which all states mutually penetrate and continue one in another, is to be rejected as more poetic than scientific. In conclusion, Milalchev rejects James's so called "new psychology" stating that "psychology is not his specialty," and adding some criticisms to Saruiliev: his appreciation of pragmatism comes from his being scarcely familiar with the history of philosophy.

Milalchev's analysis, then, moves onto the religious question and at the end of the article, Mihalchev analyzes James's work *The Varieties of Religious Experience: a study in human nature*, which, by the way, is the first and, so far, the only Bulgarian commentary of such a fundamental James's work work. Here, Mihalchev defines James's essay as "a psychologistic attempt to catch the substance of religious life and justify religion in the light of pragmatism, in order to prove its truthfulness by the use it has for the believer." Such a perspective had already been adopted also by Saruiliev, in a special chapter of his book of 1938. The two authors, however, reach different conclusions in this case too. In fact, whereas Saruiliev emphasized, all along with James, the relevance of religious belief for practical life, namely, that religious faith makes people morally better, more vivid and more hopeful, so that—As Saruiliev argues— "This religious belief is truthful. Its practical value comprises its truthfulness";[10] according to Mihalchev, not only James's assumption of a "sublime Me", through which man enters in communion with God, is unacceptable, but religion in general has no useful consequence, and James's point is mistaken. In fact, following James, the only alleged helpful consequences that can be found in religion, such as a "serene soul", "feeling of trust", "endurance", "peacefulness" and "compliance", far from being a real support of human life are exactly the basis on which people can "fall socially asleep and accept their own economical exploitation."

Moreover, in general, Mihalcev sees a problematic side also in the epistemological use James suggest for "belief" that Mihalcev understands essentially as religious belief. In fact, in his view James mingles too much religion and science, with no consideration for the harm such an overlapping could bring to science; for, as Mihalchev argues, "to put science under the

---

[10] I. Saruiliev, cit. p. 99.

auspices of religious faith, leads only to a surreptitious elimination of science."[11]

A different perspective on the value of religion is held by Atanas Iliev. In his *Soul and Religious Consciousness* (1928),[12] Iliev deals with James's idea of religion, Bergson's dynamic principle concerning spiritual development, and the Freudian concept of removal. Exposing James's view of religion, however, Iliev does not take a position on the issue of God's existence and whether the usefulness of religion can prove the truthfulness of God's existence. In fact, according to Iliev, who by that goes possibly closer to James's original attitude, religious psychology is not supposed to deal with unfathomable metaphysical problems but "only register the understanding of transcendental reality and define their value for the life of individuals and the society."[13]

The problem with James, for Iliev, is rather that the principle of pragmatism is unable to explain religious consciousness, and that is why he tries to enhance James's analysis of religious consciousness with the Freudian concept of reaction to suppressed desires. Later on, Iliev acknowledges that James made a good point in assessing religion as a "progressive factor" in the development and building of personality. In a later work entitled "Contemporary philosophy and history of philosophy" (1936),[14] Iliev raises a criticism to the pragmatic conception of usefulness as a criterion of truth. Such a criticism, however, turns out "quite unsuccessful and unconvincing", as Buchvarov will remark in "Concise history of Bulgarian philosophical thought"(1973).[15]

3. Asen Kiselinchev: Materialist *vs* Spiritualist Psychology

The actual rejection of James's psychology, however, came in the '40's, within a radically changed cultural and political frame. In order to understand the peculiar situation of the Bulgarian reception of James's psychology, the "ambiguous" status of James's psychology should be considered. In fact, whereas James frequently inclines to sheer physiological explanations, what was indeed acceptable for Bulgarian representatives of "psychological materialism", it is also the case that, paradoxically enough, James shows at the

---

[11] D. Mihalchev, cit., p. 524.

[12] A. Iliev, *Ducha i religiozno saznanie*, Sofia, 1928.

[13] Ivi, p. 118.

[14] A. Iliev, *Savremenna filosofiya. Istoriya na filosofiyata*, 1936.

[15] M. Buchvarov, *Kratka istoriya na bulgarskata filosofska misul*. Sofiya, 1973.

same time a spiritualist viewpoint of psychic life, which comes as a necessary consequence of his introspective psychology. Spiritualism appears as a major tenet in pragmatic psychology that assumes consciousness as an original and independent activity. Apparently James pays very little or no attention to whether such an activity is named "soul", "I", or "spirit", and this is his downfall in his materialist critics' eyes. Accordingly, James is criticized for his mingling together empirical psychology, spiritualism, and intuitive insight. Such a criticism is raised in particular by Asen Kiselinchev, the major Bulgarian critic of James's psychology, who in evaluating James in the context of contemporary American and Western psychology, reaches the conclusion that James's views are in "a complete decay and impasse".[16] A severe judgment indeed, which was possibly determined also by the current Bulgarian political situation at the time. It is however true that on this point Kiselinchev goes along with Saruiliev. Both of them, despite their different critical perspectives, agreed in labelling James's psychology as completely spiritualistic and idealistic, and stressed the point that pragmatism at last necessarily leads to the need for God and religious faith, what for Kiselinchev meant a complete dismissal of James and his work as unacceptable.

4. Conclusion

William James's pragmatism and psychology are reflected, though concisely, in books, articles and scientific journals and notes in the Bulgarian periodical press at the beginning of the twentieth century and in particular around the 30's

From this short survey, however, it appears evident that for ideological and cultural reasons, Jamesian, and in general pragmatist, philosophical, psychological, and pedagogic views had a limited and difficult reception in Bulgarian cultural environment. In particular James's psychology found a strong resistance. As a matter of fact, in Bulgaria, James is known less as a psychologist than as a pedagogue and a philosopher, and even too often his presence in Bulgarian literature comes down to several trivial and sometimes odd statements such as that which defines him as both a pragmatist and an idealist.

Much of the difficulty with James's reception is due to the fact that the

---

[16] A. Kiselinchev, "Pragmatichnata filosofiya i savremennata reaktsiya", *Godishnik na Sofiiskiya Universitet- Istoriko Filologicheski fakultet*,1. (1948).

greater part of Bulgarian "intelligentsia" received its education predominantly in Germany, Austria, and Switzerland, and very seldom in Anglo-Saxon areas, what made Bulgarian intellectuals and scholars more keen on German than of British or American philosophy. Moreover, a generally poor knowledge of the English language turns out a major hindrance to a broader penetration of James's ideas and that is the reason why pragmatism has always been approached mostly through the few available translation in Bulgarian or Russian, rather than through a direct approach to the original works, what explains also the misunderstanding and the coarse misinterpretation of its bearings. It is also the case that a more widespread diffusion of other competing philosophical and psychological doctrines such as Bergsonism, and Freudism barred the way to a broader and deeper reception of pragmatism and its representatives.

Last but not least ideological reasons during the second half of the XX century urged toward a removal of James and pragmatist theories from the Bulgarian cultural horizon, for they were considered politically "erroneous" and "uncomfortable" to explore.

INDEX